and minimize others. Serious stuff, but one of Gershow's many gifts is writing funny, making us love the relatable characters in *Closer* even when they flip-flop between perceptive and clued-out, and barrel toward tragedy."

—Mary Rechner, author of *Marrying Friends* and *Nine Simple Patterns for Complicated Women*

"Miriam Gershow has her finger on the pulse of high school angst and the forever adolescent who resides in every one of us. Her characters are so tender, flawed, and deeply real, we can't help but root for them as they chase the alluring spell of true love. At the same time, we feel the mounting dread of all that this spell endangers. Like Tom Perotta's *Little Children* without the satire, *Closer* dismantles illusions of parental ability to protect their offspring's inner lives—or their own. Children of all ages will fall prey to love's illusions in this multigenerational tragedy."

—Aimee Liu, author of *Glorious Boy* and *Gaining*

"Miriam Gershow has written a work of extraordinary breadth and depth, filled with delicious scenes of carefree teenage infatuation and middleage lust. I'm awed by Gershow's funny and detailed rendering of the twined lives of these likable dupes, none of whom see the dark future coming until it's too late."

—Susanna Daniel, author of *Stiltsville* and *Sea Creatures*

"With warmth and humor, Gershow deftly navigates a tangled web of crisscrossing landmines—family, friendship, class, race, adolescence, and love. It is a combustible stew that a lesser writer might shy from, but Gershow attacks these thorny topics head on. With multidimensional, nuanced characters and gorgeous, propulsive prose, this is a story that will stay with readers long after the shocking, heart-stopping end"

—Jennifer Oko, author of *Just Emilia*, *Lying Together*, and *Gloss*

CLOSER

Miriam Gershow

Regal House Publishing

 Published by
Regal House Publishing, LLC
Raleigh, NC 27605
All rights reserved

ISBN -13 (paperback): 9781646035892
ISBN -13 (epub): 9781646035915
Library of Congress Control Number: 2024944697

Cover images and design by © C. B. Royal

Printed in the United States of America

Regal House Publishing, LLC
https://regalhousepublishing.com

To Eli,
joy of joys

WINTER SEMESTER 2016

WOODY

What Woody would remember later was Doug Epstein, vice principal and jogging fanatic, appearing in his doorway, looking like he'd just finished a sprint, middle-aged man with the skinny body of a boy, interrupting Woody in the middle of a meeting with a student. Which student? It hardly mattered. *The chaff,* Woody had once joked at a holiday party back when they still served beer at the holiday parties.

Doug's face was screwed up like a knot, the kind of knot Woody recognized, presaging the worst of times (Lucy Binet, freshman, cystic fibrosis in the early aughts; Roy Eccleston, drunk driver the fall before last).

Woody had been up most of the night—phone calls, churning gut—fearing something like Doug in his doorway, though not Doug in the doorway. Doug in the doorway was too specific. At 2 a.m., he'd been crouched on the toilet. 3:30, again. Once more at 4:15. "Sorry," he'd whispered each time he got back in bed, though unnecessarily. Alison slept and slept, Alison, a champion sleeper.

"What?" Woody said to Doug, but what he was thinking was: *Livvy.*

"Olivia Albrecht," Doug said. And here, memory skipped. How had Doug told him? Had he searched Woody's face as he spoke? Had he paused with intent? Had he clapped Woody on the shoulder?

What Woody remembered was being alone in his office after and with the oddest feeling of not being able to feel his cheeks. Also, his insides were vibrating, like when he'd been very, very cold as a child, leaving a lake after the sun dipped below the tree line, needing a towel and his mother's hands rubbing the lengths of his arms up and down, up and down to make him human again. He almost called Baz Fenning out of class. Instead, he called for Lark Stevenson, Lark not even one of his (Woody always and only *A–H*).

When the girl arrived and sat in the fake leatherette chair—same fake leatherette chair where more students than he could count had sat the last decade and a half—he saw how small she was for her age, perched forward as if not to disturb the chair. Lark Stevenson was a kid like so many kids, who Woody knew mostly from across expanses (cafeteria, hallways, classrooms), which was to say not at all. Calling her in had been a terrible idea. Had he thought he'd find communion? Her face was as plain and unknowing as a field.

"I wanted you to hear it from me," Woody said. Lark was trying to disappear into her own shoulder. Had he called her in here to find someone smaller and more scared than he? "Livvy," he said, and Woody would misremember what came next as eloquence, he kind and wise in unthinkable circumstance. He would forget his broken stammer: "She died from killing herself."

PART I

WINTER SEMESTER 2015

LARK

So, what is it about?" Baz said, holding Lark's civics paper. He'd read it and now he was asking her, and Lark had no idea what to say. She'd never had a conversation with Baz Fenning before, and this was a terrible way to meet someone, in the library, all of Woody's Woodpeckers paired up with all the stupid kids at the round tables in back. Students existed in strata at West, though most of the time the striations weren't so apparent. Normally, they had the sense to quietly self-segregate.

Lark knew most of the other stupid kids; those were her classmates, her comrades in academic probation and repeat courses. They slouched in their chairs, chewing on pen caps, picking at their own eyebrows. Roger Bass rocked so far back in his chair, it looked like he would fall onto his skull. He and Miles Cobain burped and barked back and forth like they did in class, Penny the librarian all the way up at the front desk, too far to hear.

Miles Cobain was writing something on the back of his left arm with his pen; Lark couldn't see. His tutor was a big girl with her hair in a headband that showed off her broad forehead. She even *looked* big-brained. "Come on," the forehead girl kept saying to Miles. "Please." Once in civics, Lark watched Miles Cobain write F-U-C-K and S-U-C-K across the knuckles of both hands. Most kids weren't so loud about being stupid.

Heather Onigan sat a few tables away, covering most of her mouth with one hand like she always did when she talked; Angela Dulles stuttered, red-faced, taking her usual interminable time saying whatever needed saying; Joey Bertram laid his head against his crossed arms on the tabletop, eyes closed, and Lark wished she had the guts to do the same. Joey's tutor tapped his finger on the tabletop like a metronome, right beside Joey's nose, *tap, tap, tap,* Lark impressed with Joey's non-responsiveness; maybe he really was asleep.

Lark didn't know the Woodpeckers, juniors and seniors, straight-backed in their glasses and button-downs, fingers braided, nodding and saying *um hmmm*, play-acting adulthood. She knew Baz by sight, only because everyone knew the Black kids.

"A quick summary," he said.

Lark rested her chin in her shoulder now, burying it into the curve of her shoulder bone, her clavicle-bone maybe. Whichever the bone was. Peer support was supposed to be *non-threatening* and *feedback from someone who's been there*. This was what Mr. Langston had explained when he'd had her stay after in language arts fundamentals to hand back her paper, the paper Baz Fenning was now holding, Mr. Langston's big red question mark at the top. *Try again?* he'd written instead of a grade, which was worse than just giving her the F. Mr. Langston had pulled some strings with Mr. Hanover to get her into peer tutoring this far into the semester, he'd told her.

"Thanks?" she'd told Mr. Langston.

"I don't want to see you fail," Mr. Langston told her at the front of the empty room, and Lark had to bite the inside of her mouth to keep from crying. It wasn't the question mark; she was used to red question marks. A question mark was a question mark. It wasn't even the failing. It was the way Mr. Langston looked at her, straight on and earnest, like it mattered, looking at her like how Baz Fenning was looking at her right now. She hated all the looking.

"I don't know," Lark said. "Can I see it?" She pretended to be reading but could feel her head going foggy like it did when she had to write a paper or think about writing a paper. Or read. Whenever she tried to explain the feeling in her brain—like saran wrap inside her skull? something clouding behind her eyes? too much tired but an awake tired, *too* awake, like worn out, but in her head, not her body?—she couldn't. Trying to explain it also made her foggy, so she'd stopped trying to explain it a long time ago. She had an IEP, so whatever. Everything was supposed to be good now. Extra time to take tests.

"Health care?" she said.

"Okay," Baz said. "And what about healthcare?"

Here was everything Lark knew about Baz Fenning: he was a junior, and he mostly hung with Shocky the Arab. Shocky's name wasn't Shocky but everyone pronounced his name wrong for so long, he turned the mispronunciation into a nickname. There was only like one Black kid per grade, and Lark wasn't friends with any of them. She knew some of the Asians from elementary school, but she didn't really consider them Asian, just smart. She only had them in things like music and PE because they were in AP for math and language arts, except freshman year, when Louie Saeu had been with her in speech, speech the class for kids who wanted language arts credit without all the reading, but Lark was pretty sure Louie was Hawaiian or something.

She pulled out the *Time* magazine with the $160,000 heart surgery on the cover. "We were supposed to read an article and write our opinion. Everybody's writing about how we'll have a woman president, so I wanted to do something different."

"Lurk!" Roger Bass called out. He loved to call this out. Miles Cobain laughed the way Miles loved to laugh at Roger calling this out. If the stupid kids weren't so stupid, maybe they'd try to stick together. Except no one wanted to be a member of the club they were in. Easier to call out *Lurk* than punch yourself in your own dumb face.

Lark pretended to be looking at the *Time* article now, really studying it, trying not to let *Lurk* get stuck in the warm insides of her mouth.

"Shut up, Roger," Baz said without looking.

"Shut up, Roger," Miles Cobain repeated in a falsetto.

"Ignore them," Baz said quietly, which was her first sense that Baz might be nice, not a kiss ass like the Woodpeckers were supposed to be, all of them back here so they had one more thing to put on their college applications.

"Can I see it?" he said of the magazine, and Lark was glad for him to have it, glad to be sitting there while he was reading something she didn't write. He skimmed fast and then talked to her about single payer versus private insurance versus Obamacare. He talked for a while.

"How do you know all this?" Lark asked.

He shrugged, looking her in the face. Most boys couldn't look a girl in the face without saying something shitty or laughing or looking quickly away. "My mom works at the hospital," he said.

"Nurse?"

"Pharmacist."

"What's a pharmacist do at the hospital?" Lark said.

"Run the pharmacy."

She kind of laughed. "My mom's *not* a pharmacist," she said to keep them from talking about her paper.

"That's okay," Baz said, which she thought was funny too.

"What does your dad do?" she said. She was stalling.

"Professor."

"Of what?"

"Boring stuff mostly." He shrugged. "Poor people."

He had a way of talking. Everything he said was funny and not.

"He's a professor of poor people?"

"Economics," Baz said.

"Lurk," Roger Bass called out. "Your girlfriend's here."

Miles let out a wolf whistle, long and low. His big-forehead tutor shushed him and slapped a hand on his arm, and Miles called out, "You're not allowed to hit me!" real loud, clutching his arm like he was seriously injured.

Livvy was at the front of the library, holding Stoner's big hall-pass paddle, talking to Penny the librarian, who hardly ever did anything, librarian-wise. She had aides who rolled the groaning carts, re-shelving books. You checked out your books yourself, using the computer. Penny mostly sat at the desk and made sure kids minded. Sometimes school—no, the whole world—seemed to Lark like a whole bunch of adults with nothing better to do. Livvy was leaning over Penny's desk with Stoner's paddle, talking with her hands, her face serious. Soon, she was hiking back toward their table.

She kissed Lark on the top of the head, ran her hand over Lark's hair, Lark liking the feel of Livvy's chunky rings over her scalp. "So, what's the deal here?" Livvy asked, squinting at Baz. Lark had complained and complained last night over having to start peer tutoring, having to explain herself to a new person.

"We're in a lesson," Baz said before Lark could answer. It was funny: lesson. Like he was 100 years old.

Livvy ignored him. "Going okay?" she said to Lark, and Lark told her so. She liked the smell on Livvy today, lemony. Livvy had a bunch of oils lined up on her windowsill in her bedroom, choosing different ones on different days. Lavender. Lemon. Lark liked the one called frangipani.

"Listen," Livvy said to Baz. "Don't fuck with her. People try to fuck with her."

"I'm not fucking with her," Baz said like he was testing out the word for the first time. "We gonna do this?" he said to Lark. "We need to do this."

Miles coughed *dyke* into his fist.

"Fuck off, Miles," Livvy said, plunking down next to Lark. Beneath the lemon, a chemical tang of fake butter, which meant Livvy hadn't showered after her shift at the movies the night before, Lark so happy Livvy was here now. She was always happy for Livvy, and especially now when it was Livvy instead of her paper.

"Know how I got in?" Livvy said, motioning toward Penny up front. "Dying Dad."

Livvy's dad had been dead since before Lark knew her. Lark used to ask what she remembered about him, because dead dad seemed infinitely more interesting than no dad at all, and Livvy said things like, "purple scarf" and "bedtime song about Casper the Friendly Ghost" and "mustache that swirled up at the ends" and "missing a thumb on one hand" before Lark realized she was making it all up.

"Your dad's dying?" Baz said.

"He died in childbirth," Livvy said.

Baz squinted at her and made a *pfft* noise. "That's cold," he said and asked her name, and she told him, and she didn't have to ask his name because she knew, like Lark knew, like they all knew without ever talking to them: Monique (freshman, basketball), Devin (sophomore, tuba), Jerry (senior, football).

"Excuse me, Miss Albrecht," Roger Bass said, he the one with the falsetto now. "You're not supposed to be back here." Livvy stuck her arm up in the air and flipped him off without even looking.

Baz told Lark that from what he could tell, her paper was repeating what the article said already. She needed to come up with an opinion and then have an organized way of supporting it. "Free write," he said, flipping her paper over to the blank back of it—*Free write* one of Mr. Langston's favorite things to say too. "Write your opinion on healthcare."

Lark let the pen loll over the paper. She had no opinion on healthcare. She wrote down some of the words Baz had said about single payer and private, she doodled a spiral.

"What kind of a name is Baz?" Livvy said.

"What kind of a name is Livvy?"

"Olivia," Livvy said. "It's Jewish." Lark had never once heard Livvy say that her name was Jewish. She wondered if Livvy was trying to show off or something because Baz was Black. Like *see? I'm something too.*

"Brian," Baz said, and Lark wrote out the word *frangipani* in block letters and colored it in.

"How you get Baz from Brian?" Livvy said, and Baz told a story of his brother who'd said, "Baz is in the chicken coop. Baz is in the chicken coop," after he was born. His brother repeated sentences, sometimes for months or more (Lark not understanding what he was talking about, but also not caring that she didn't understand) and this was his sentence the year Baz was born, even though they were in Chicago and didn't have chickens or a chicken coop, and his mom decided at some point his brother was talking about him, Brian, the new baby. So, Baz.

It was the most he had said to that point, and if Lark didn't care about the story, she did think about how nice it was to have two people talking past her. There was a strange and simple comfort in it, so much of her life she and her mom, or she and a teacher, so much of her life spent trying not to get called on, trying not to get seen, and even with Livvy, it was always just the two of them, and sometimes Lark was tired-awake even with Livvy, so it was nice to be able to sit back and let words wash past her, unafraid, which came to her as sensation—not really a thought—and the sensation was of the muscles of her shoulders softening from a tenseness she didn't even realize was her all-the-time clenching, and even that only lasted a few seconds because it was all so quick, and unfolding so naturally, before Roger Bass called out, or maybe Miles Cobain:

"Barack! You real busy over there, Barry!"

And then the other: "Yeah, Barack! Barack and the ladies!"

And then one of them made a noise, loud and obnoxious, and the other started making it too, over and over and over, the same noise, and it was Livvy up from her seat, Livvy yelling at the boys, and Lark thought of the very first time she'd ever seen Livvy, summer between first and second grade, a summer Lark had spent mostly inside after the neighbor's dog got her, charging as Lark played alone in the front yard, the dog going for Lark's face, her jaw in his jaw (no memory of any of this), dragging her halfway down the block before a neighbor heard her screaming, Lark with seventy-two stitches, one skin graft, and three sweltering summer weeks indoors until (here, memory began) the first tentative steps back onto the front porch, blinking into the late summer heat, legs gummy beneath her, gauze finally gone from her chin, a jagged pink worm in its place that would burn first in the sun and go cold before the rest of her in wintertime, and a new kid on a bike, doing figure eights in the streets, ribbons riffling in the air from the ends of her handlebars, the rider's gaze alert, her eyes everywhere, but not desperately, a gaze that roamed the street and sidewalks, taking it all in unhurriedly, her hair as long as anyone's hair Lark had ever seen, and as black too, bringing to mind Rapunzel, even though Lark had never gone for fairy tales, blanched by all the betrayal and killing, a kid taking up the whole street in broad loop de loops, damn the cars or the delivery trucks or the mopeds. The world was hers, and Lark had never seen anything so beautiful and powerful as a girl.

Later, when they asked her the noise the boys had been making, what were the noises, she couldn't really explain, and not being able to explain caused Vice Principal Epstein to ask more urgently and then she called it hooting, and when he asked her what kind of hooting, she was so tired-awake, bone-tired awake, her head fuzzed and thick with something she could not name, something no one even asked her to name anymore, because they were all so used to looking at her instead like, *Who is this stupid creature?*

"What kind of hooting?" Vice Principal Epstein repeated.

"Monkeys," she said.

"Monkeys?" Vice Principal Epstein asked.

"Monkeys," she repeated, until he was nodding, and she knew at least that he would stop asking.

STEFANIE

Stefanie was on her second day in a row home since Nathan's PSW quit. It'd been a while since she'd spent whole days with Nathan, Derek the one with the flexible campus schedule, though Stefanie hoarded her sick days for just such an occasion.

"Nacho," Nathan said to her on the couch, same as he had after breakfast, and after *Octonauts*, and before whatever the next thing would be. A snow day feeling, a day home with Nathan.

"Nacho," she repeated, the punchline to a terrible joke Derek had told months before. She saw how Nathan was looking at her, trying to be sly about it from the corner of his eye, his mama so close to him on the couch, sidling up in a way Baz would never let her, even though Baz was her baby. It made her laugh, Nathan's side eye, and he let out a good echo, her laugh like a bark out his mouth. He put the heel of one hand up to his right eye. He pressed. Always Nathan loved to press his eyes.

"What should we do?" Stefanie said. Carlos had been Nathan's personal support worker for nearly a year, adept at the rhythms of Nathan and their household, and Stefanie tried not to be bereft about losing him. PSW was a shit job, combination of orderly, home health aide, schoolteacher, and monk, lots of repetition, lots of patience, occasional ass wiping. The position was inglorious enough, it served as a catchment for the Hispanic men, even the few Black men in town, for which Stefanie was grateful. Carlos had talked to Nathan in English and Spanish when he talked at all, a man of few words, gruff and no-nonsense, but ever consistent, unflappable, even when he got a nasty bruise from Nathan falling into him in the bathroom. Carlos had made Nathan laugh by throwing him the whiffle ball in all sorts of goofy trick shots— behind his back and over the shoulder, between his legs.

Nathan listed toward her a little, either on purpose or simply moving his body. It was snow day and also an itching at the back of her throat. She was not good at being bored, never had been, terrible at just sitting here or the pretend play Baz used to beg for. "Do a scene with me, Mama!" He would hand her a police action figure, or a robot turned into a truck, and she would think of how her mama never once got down on the floor with her, how it would never have occurred to her to hand her mama a doll and ask her to make believe, her mama incapable of such nonsense, just as it turned out Stefanie was too.

"Hold on!" Nathan called out from beside her, his voice pitched high and happy. "This could get bumpy!"

She hated the unknown of the in-between. The county never moved quickly, Nathan either. Stefanie's restlessness was the outlier, though it was nice, at least, to be next to her boy, unmediated, no other noises in the house, no other bodies. Always so many bodies. It felt like living inside a secret, being close to Nathan, a feeling that was easy to forget when she was at the hospital, and Nathan's days were Derek, then Carlos, then one of their regular, rotating sitters, then Derek again, then back to Stefanie. She'd start to see Nathan in parts, distracted by a flapping hand or "Buncha muncha crunchy carrots!" But Nathan was not skimmable. You could not know him in passing.

"Should we bake something?" she said. She was no good at baking, but neither was Nathan. He put hands all over the flour, kneading and kneading the dough until she said, "Enough," and, "Okay enough." After, she ran his hands underneath the faucet, which he sometimes loved, sometimes did not. Stefanie would run her fingers between his, getting the sticky dough out from under his fingernails, his hands a marvel, broad palms, knuckles swollen with wrinkles. Hands alone, they could have been Derek's. A man's hands.

"Let's at least get up," she said, doing jumping jacks while Nathan bellowed at her. "Already on it, Captain! Already on it!" until she told him fine, fine, maybe a little yoga, yoga the sort of thing Stefanie used to make fun of back in Chicago. Yoga was for white ladies, but the hospital offered it in their free wellness program, and she didn't hate it. Good to stretch herself out, good to breathe. Whenever Derek saw her leaving for work, yoga mat sticking out the back of her bag, he called her *West Coast*. "Have a good day at work with your chakras, West Coast." "Don't forget your spirit animal, West Coast."

She baby-posed Nathan on the living room rug, *sss sss*'ing him down to the floor and telling him to get his knees up under him, lay his arms down at his side. She was surprised sometimes by his litheness. He was a big guy, bigger than Derek by now, and needing more exercise. He had the gut of a middle-aged man; start losing hair and he'd look forty-two not twenty-two.

Stef pushed it, trying to get him up and into tree pose, handling his arms, twisting his torso. When his breath started coming through his teeth, she kept trying to hold his hips straight, because once she got something in her head. Of course he started bellowing, and she backed off and gave him his CD player, and he listened so loud from the corner of the couch, she could hear the terrible lite-rock saxophonist out the headphones, Nathan's eyes screwed shut.

Truth was, he could tolerate her far less than she him. She could go a couple days without getting worn down by Nathan. He was the one who didn't need her right up on him. He wanted her only as long as he wanted her, then she had to go away. She recognized this in him maybe the most she recognized anything. Derek could take Stefanie and take Stefanie and never start chafing, which was maybe what drove her most crazy about him. *Get tired of me like I get tired of you.*

Phone rang while she was readying the flour, the salt, and the rolling pan in the kitchen. A day could be broken into parts with minimal effort. It was her brother, Calvin, two hours later back home, three in the afternoon. Cal never worked regular hours.

"She's losing it," he said, not bothering to wonder why Stefanie was answering her phone midday at a time it would normally go straight to voicemail. Cal was the baby and a boy, which gifted him the ability not to mind past his own nose. He only ever called to ask for something or complain.

"Losing it how?" Stefanie could hear the noise of television in the background, their mother settled in for the day with her beloved *Food Network, TLC, Animal Planet,* same mother who'd never let them turn on the television weekdays, who'd stand by the couch on weekends, hand on hip, harrumphing, "What's this?" to their music videos or Nickelodeon shows. Stefanie and Cal never had had an answer because the question was rhetorical, a reminder of their mother's broad umbrella of *trash,* which included but was not limited to: girls in bikinis twerking in videos, hip hop artists with gold grills, curse words (didn't matter if they were bleeped), sitcoms that centered on sarcastic white children who talked back to feckless adults, cartoons with white babies who sassed and sassed.

Calvin told a story: last night Mama got up again, put a rain slicker and sandals over her nightgown, went into the kitchen where Angie found her, who knows how long later, all the windows steamed up, nearly four a.m. and Mama boiling and boiling six chicken thighs still wrapped in their deli case packaging. "Baby, I got your favorite," Mama told Angie, and then: "When did you cut all your hair off? Why'd you go do something like that?"

"She thinks my favorite is boiled chicken? She *is* losing it." Their mother for years now had mistaken Cal's second wife for Stefanie. Stefanie sometimes wondered what that meant for Angie. Was she subject to the full gauntlet of Mama's suspicions and accusations? Did Angie come through the door and get sniffed for signs of cigarette smoke or weed? Did she have to answer if she was lying down with boys?

"I'm not joking," Calvin said, and Stef could hear the real grievance in his voice. It was the voice of all her childhood. She loved her baby brother but couldn't deal with him today.

"I'm home with Nathan," she said at the same time Calvin said: "She could've burnt down the house."

Another call came in; it was Hidaya, Stefanie's one mom friend, Stefanie happy for the excuse. "Have to take this," she said as Cal was on about live-in help, Stefanie acting like she didn't hear. Every conversation was the same conversation, Cal looking for someone to come save him.

"You heard about the boys?" Hidaya said.

"The boys?" Stefanie said, assuming Hidaya meant their kids, Shekib and Baz, friends since Baz was the new kid in middle school.

"The boys in the library," Hidaya said, and later—much later—when Stefanie tried to catalog backward to when the sense of being behind and needing to play catch up began, she would return to this conversation. She would return to here:

"The library? I don't—" Stefanie's least favorite feeling was being caught unawares. She prided herself on being someone who didn't get caught, unawares or otherwise.

Hidaya talked about boys messing with Baz, calling him names. Acting foolish. Obama something. Shekib wasn't there but heard about it from Baz after. Shekib had told them about it at dinner. "It was a *thing*," Hidaya said, and then with less certainty: "I guess."

Stefanie pictured Baz at dinner the night before, Derek ribbing him for eating around his peas, Baz never having grown into eating peas. What else had they talked about?

"When?" Stefanie asked as a stellar jay flew past the kitchen window. They lived high on a hillside, a pebbled and rocky street without sidewalks, forested with firs, the houses architectural beauties, no two the same, though each one with views out onto the city, which gave the feeling of being in the middle of nowhere and perched at the very pinnacle. Theirs was an upside-down house, built into the hillside. You came in on the ground floor and walked down to the boys' rooms, down again to the master suite. Three stories of windows. It was the improbability and impossibility of the street and the house that had so enchanted Stefanie on their trip out, after Derek had accepted the job—his dream job, R1 university, flagship state school, on a coast instead of a tech college in the cornfields of a rectangular state or a commuter school in the gator marshes down south, both of which he had said no to in his first year on the job market.

Yesterday, Hidaya thought, maybe the day before. "I don't know all the details, dear," she said. "But I can find out."

"No, no, no need," Stefanie said, scanning back to Baz's face the night before. She couldn't call up anything but his orthodontia-straight teeth and his fade needing freshening; Baz, seventeen and a blur.

She put the bread into a basket in the middle of the dinner table, calling it bread biscuits. Everything they baked came out hard from Nathan overworking the dough. Stef always called it biscuits. Bread biscuits. Muffin biscuits. Cookie biscuits.

Baz leaned bodily over his plate, gnawing on corn, trying to bite into biscuit, giving it up for potatoes.

"Boys messing around with you at school." Stefanie didn't ask. She said. Baz looked up from the potatoes on his plate, and if nothing else, she liked the little bit of wonder in his eyebrows. She could see him thinking: *How you know?* It felt good to know. "Obama? Some boys messing with you about Obama?"

Baz's cheeks were fattened with the potatoes, making him look like the younger version of himself. He was a tall and skinny kid, his body grown, but not yet filled, the outline waiting for the rest of him. He nodded, then made a noise and shook his head.

"Naw," he said. "It was stupid. They were just being stupid."

"That's not what Shekib said."

"Shocky wasn't even there," Baz said, still shoveling in the potatoes.

Skinny like a scarecrow, but could pack it in. "Seriously, Ma, it wasn't anything."

"Don't talk with your mouth full," she said. It came out hard.

"What your mom means," Derek said, a quick squeeze under the table. "Is what happened? Will you tell us?"

Baz picked up the piece of chicken by the bone, not looking up, like his dinner plate was the most interesting thing to happen to him today. He shrugged. He wasn't going to tell them, and fine, she wouldn't make him; Stef had a mama who made her tell everything, and Stef wasn't trying to be that mama. Her heart, though, beat hard in her throat, almost painfully, unsoothed by having her boys both right across from her, close enough to touch.

"Listen," she said. "You know to keep out of trouble, right?" People were *nice* in Horace, the Starlingers next door asking if the Fennings could cat sit, the Clark-Mintons to the other side bringing the occasional sour dough loaf, talking too long about their starter. The Fennings didn't have much trouble here, except for the kind of trouble when the middle school PE teacher insisted Baz should be better at basketball, and a girl in freshman history said it was really upsetting discussing slavery with Baz in the room, and the patients at the hospital every day mistook Stef for an orderly.

"No trouble, Ma," he said to his plate.

"You keep your head down," Stefanie said, "and you do your work, and you don't stoop to their nonsense. There are kids who are stupid or ignorant or who knows what. You don't need to know what. It's not your job to know what. You mind yourself. Look at me. You keep your focus, and you don't let them pull you down. Are you listening to me?"

"Look at your mother," Derek said.

"Nacho!" Nathan called out, and Baz put a quick hand on Nathan's shoulder the way Nathan needed when anyone sounded like a fight.

"Okay, Ma," Baz said, looking at her, plainly, no sass. "I got it," still with his hand on Nathan's shoulder. God, he was a good kid. Stefanie wanted Baz to be huge and proud in the world and take up all the space he deserved, but also sent up a silent godless prayer to the universe for making him such a good kid, kind and quiet and did his work and always had one or two good friends. He hadn't inherited her impatience or Derek's need for approval, ending up with both of their drives and determination. He was made up, it seemed, of the best of them, which, reasonable or not, she felt they'd earned by number two.

She put Nathan to bed later, Nathan oniony and in need of a shower she was too tired to give. He didn't want her handling his blankets, didn't want her help tucking him in. He could tuck himself in.

"Okay, okay, okay," she told him, watching as he burrowed deep beneath the blankets, covering all of himself. In sleep, he would smoke himself out with the hot air of his breath. Hours later she would look in on him before she went to bed, and his head would be out from the blankets, and she would be able to take his face gently in her hands and kiss him on his eyelids, the tip of his nose. Such indulgences she took with only Nathan, even though she could kiss Baz's sleeping face too, but her secret was this: it was easier with Nathan, easier for the reasons everyone thought it was harder, his life bounded, circumscribed, all of him right here and all she had to do was protect.

WOODY

Doug wanted Woody to meet with the boy, Doug at Woody's office first thing in the morning, asking for "a quick check in" to see how the boy was doing. Doug kept calling him "the boy," and Woody wondered if it was because he couldn't remember Baz's name or if it was just Doug in the morning: couldn't stand still, bouncy, mind ticking to the next thing and the next. He and Doug had tried for several seasons to be buddies, Woody even joining Doug's basketball team, though all the knee braces and protective glasses over regular glasses depressed him, and he got tired of being elbowed in the face.

"Since it happened during peer tutoring," Doug explained, though there was no need to.

"Of course," Woody said. "Sure," already pulling up Baz's schedule, though Doug said, "Sinclair for home room." Doug had met with the boys. The other boys. The previous afternoon. Detention and an essay on diversity.

"Got it," Woody said, though Doug did not move from his spot. Doug got like this under particular sets of circumstances. Last year, a group of girls started calling Lucy Tan—not one of Woody's, one of Sandy O'Hare's (S-Z)—Affirmative Action, as in "Hey, Affirmative Action, how's it going?" Lucy Tan's mother was on the school's fundraising committee, her father a research-something on the faculty senate at the university. A particular set of anxieties and fears arose in such circumstances. Last thing Doug wanted, last thing Georgina Vonn wanted, last any of them wanted, was a brouhaha. It was all hands on deck to quash the brou before it escalated into haha.

Woody was happy to help. That was his genuine feeling: happy. He liked having Doug at his door first thing, not because of Doug, but for how Doug being here stiffened the spine of Woody's day. Woody had been at this job for sixteen years. He was the guy who sat to the side at faculty meetings, announcing PSAT dates, reminding teachers to remind students of his drop-in hours for help with college admission essays, permanently in the school's peripheral vision. But not today.

Today, Doug was inviting Woody (A-I) into the thick of it. Roger Bass and Miles Cobain, too, B and C, they were his guys too, if Doug needed any following up. Any anything. All of them were his guys. He could take meetings with these kids all day.

Baz sat like a person. So many kids in his office drooped all the way down so that it was their back occupying the part of the chair meant for their butt, their head at a painful-looking right angle, Woody left to stare at their knees.

Baz sat upright. "It wasn't anything," he said, one hand fidgeting a little, his thumb scratching at the side of his pointer finger. "Just stupid." He was looking and not looking at Woody.

"Well sure," Woody said. "Stupid." They'd all had diversity training the year before, and a few years before that. Last year, the focus was intersectionality, everyone having to draw themselves as intersecting circles of identity on big pieces of butcher paper posted along the walls of the cafeteria, Woody feeling stupid about his circles—white, man, father, husband—and a little jealous of Penny Lester, the librarian. Never knew she was a lesbian. Or left-handed. "How are you doing, generally?"

"Fine," Baz said. "Good. My mom was freaking out last night."

Woody didn't know Baz's parents. He only knew the parents of the kids who risked not graduating, the kids who'd taken algebra two and a half times.

"Sorry to hear that," Woody said, waiting for Baz to say something more. Kids could be sorted into two categories: ones who blabbed to fill the silences, ones who did not. He drank some of his half-warm coffee, his mug a Father's Day gift, a picture of him, Alison, and Francie sitting on a log at the coast, the camera having been perched on a tripod, Woody running from the auto-timer so that the picture looked as if Alison and the preschooler in her lap were posed against a department store backdrop, while Woody had been blown in wild-eyed by a recent tsunami. "What was she freaking out about, specifically?"

"Like, stay out of trouble, that kind of stuff."

"I don't really think she has to worry about you causing trouble." He chuckled into his hand. Baz Fenning, like the rest of the peer tutors, were the smart kids who volunteered for things like blood drive, not popular enough for student government, but could be counted on to show up in non-provocative costumes for spirit week, girls in pigtails for pajama day, the boys in ill-fitting fedoras for silly hat day.

Baz shrugged, and Woody asked him where he was thinking about for colleges, never too early to be thinking about colleges, Baz saying Penn, maybe U Illinois as a backup, when Livvy Albrecht popped her head in the doorway.

"Hey, you losers!" she said, and Woody laughed, feeling an outsized feeling he wouldn't identify until later, after both kids had cleared out, and Woody was alone again in his office. The feeling was a warm pride for the way his office must have seemed to Baz like the sort of place where students popped their heads in with sarcastically familiar greetings. Deirdre Benson (J-S) next door was the counselor who regularly had students lingering in her doorway all day, Deirdre Benson nearly fifteen years younger than Woody and looking like she stepped out of one of those overly serious nighttime television series about teenagers. Deirdre dressed in a slim raffia cowboy hat for spirit week, the kind you might wear to a music festival, hardly silly at all.

Livvy Albrecht was, in truth, one of the only students who ever stopped by to see him, unbidden. The others, Dexter Hyron (debate team president) and Van Belfour (junior class secretary) were easily recognizable for their brown-nosing. Livvy was of a different ilk, one that Woody never knew how to categorize. She came down here to bitch about Stoner's boring lectures or shoot random shit about daylight savings making her tired so, of course, she was his favorite.

"You guys talking about those assholes?" she said.

"Language," Woody said, hardly meaning it. "We were."

"Fuck those fuckers," Livvy said.

"Language," Woody repeated, meaning it more this time, and it took them all a few backs and forth for Woody to understand that Livvy had been there in the library too, his warm pride at that point spreading outward, toward the fact that she was stumbling in on him debriefing with Baz Fenning, Woody the lynchpin, really, Woody on the leading edge of this troubling incident.

"Come in," he told her. "Sit," looking to Baz to make sure this was all right, Baz doing a combination of nodding and shrugging and the slightest of smiles, the most teenaged he'd looked since coming into Woody's office.

"No seriously," Livvy said. "They're such fucks. Sorry. Roger was complaining in Hammerle's and I was like, *shut up*." She had a habit

of crossing one leg over the other, then slipping the heel of her shoe
on and off as she talked, today's not a shoe so much as a slipper, the
sparkly silver rubbed bare from the toes. They were the same type of
shoe favored by Francine, though Francine's were red, and they were
lined up next to the front door alongside her tiny gym shoes and tiny
cowboy boots and tiny ballet slippers. Alison loved to take Francine
shopping, Francine's mouth often sweet still at the end of the day from
the hot chocolate in the Starbucks inside the Target. Francine was four
and wore play-earrings clipped to her lobes, strings of plastic jewel
necklaces, tutus over pants.

"They just want to be important," Baz said, shrugging, and Woody
thought this was either very profound or nothing. He wasn't sure what
Baz meant and didn't ask.

"Thanks for being nice to Lark," Livvy said to Baz. Woody was
aware of Livvy and Lark, always alone together in the hallways and
the cafeteria, leaning into each other as they walked, pressed against
the cafeteria table over their tin-foiled sandwiches, theirs the particular
intensity of pairs of girls this age. You never saw boys like that, boys
were all shoulder shoves and shouting, moving in packs or alone.

Baz shrugged. "She's nice."

"She's not stupid," Livvy said.

"I never thought she was," said Baz. "I don't even really know her
yet."

Livvy laughed a strange laugh.

Baz laughed a strange laugh back. The strange laughing sent a prickle
up the back of Woody's neck and into his hairline, a prickle of jealousy.
It wasn't a lascivious jealousy. He didn't want to sleep with Olivia Albrecht, or any of the many young girls who walked the halls, even in
their tight skirts and too-short shirts that exposed their lithe bellies. He
appreciated the gleam of their youth, was sometimes even intimidated
by the outrageously plumped lips and plucked brows, but he was not a
pervert. The jealousy was something rawer and more inchoate. Olivia
was one of the only kids who sought him out, took an interest in him,
an interest, in truth, that he did not even have in himself. Her strange
laugh suggested attention, diverted. It would not be so different from
the prickle he would have a few years later when Francine's first grade
teacher sent home a note reporting a pattern of her mistakenly calling
him *Daddy*. Mr. Han would end the note with a smiley face and *FYI*.

"You work at the Cinemark?" Baz said. "I've seen you there."

"I know you have," Livvy said. "I've seen you there seeing movies."

More laughter. Still strange.

"I can sneak you in sometime," Livvy said.

"Eh, eh, eh," Woody said. "Don't talk about lawbreaking in front of me."

"I don't think that's a law," Livvy said.

Woody knew Olivia's mother, Susan. They'd gone to high school together in this same building, several iterations ago. He knew about Susan's life in the way locals knew about each other—glancingly, half-interested. She'd married young, had a kid, had another kid, and then Len Albrecht had up and died of some virulent form of blastoma. There had been fundraisers for his treatment. Woody hadn't gone, but he'd stuffed a few dollars in the collection jar at the credit union.

Susan and Woody had had a season of flirting as kids—or, more accurately, a kiss in a closet in a long-ago party while their classmates cackled on the other side of the door. Neither Susan nor Woody had been the type to look at the other, once emerged, so that the only memory of her was mingled with red rat poison pellets sprinkled in the far corner, and then darkness and a mouth he'd thought would be open but was not. Dry, tight lips at the time seemed the very opposite of a mouth, the farthest thing from a mouth, though he'd been very young and knew very little.

That this girl would come from Susan was amusing and inexplicable, the same way Francine was amusing and inexplicable in her pretend high heels, backless and plastic, his daughter tromping then sliding around the hardwood, bending one ankle, then the other, pinwheeling her arms, steadying herself.

"Mr. Hanover," Baz said. "We done?" and it wasn't really a question because the boy was already up from his chair, leaving Woody no choice but to tell him of course, of course, thanks for stopping by, Livvy up from hers too, so that Woody stood from his chair on reflex, though it was silly as soon as he was up; they weren't at a formal dinner party, and it was pointless, being on his feet as the kids filed quickly out, he then she, and he could have sat right back down, they were already gone. But he felt like once up, he had to commit, so he walked out from behind his desk and headed to the copier, pretending like he had somewhere to go.

Excerpt: "Diversity is NOT a joke"

by Miles Cobain

Everybody is different. Some people get their feelings hurt real easily. They are like, "That joke hurt me! And I'm going to tell on you to teacher! You made monkey noises!" and you're like, "No, I didn't. All I said was O! O! O! for Obama. Who is our president." And they're like, "Boo! Hoo! Hoo! I'm still so sad." But then there are people who can take a joke, like, for example, Shocky. You go "Alloo Akbar" to Shocky, and Shocky laughs. Shocky thinks it's hilarious. You go, "You're from ISIS" and he doesn't get upset. He's like, "Yeah, I'm going to blow you up." The most upset Shocky ever gets is when he goes, "I'm not Arab, I'm Persian," and he's not even that upset, he's just telling us. That is why people love Shocky and people think Baz Fenning is…I can't say what Baz Fenning is because then I'll end up having to write another essay.

What should we do when people are different from us? We should go: "Hello. My names is Miles. First of all, can you take a joke?" If they go, "No," then you go, "Okay, Person Who Is Different, it was nice meeting you," and then you walk away fast and never speak to them again, except to go, "Oh, please." "Oh, thank you." "You are so great." But if they go, "Haha! I love jokes!" then you can be friends with them and act like a normal person and even say stupid things and not end up in detention for something that was not even an insult…

FACEBOOK POST, 6:09PM, 4/24/15

SHAINA ABRAMOVITZ

Listen #WestHS students, I dont know if your aware, but VP Epstein put Miles Cobain and Roger Bass in detention for complimenting another student about being Black which I guess your not allowed to do. If you believe in #freespeech, please LIKE and FORWARD this to everyone u know. This is not ok. How are we supposed to get along if we cant even compliment each other? Click on this link to sign my change.org petition to get #justiceformiles and #justiceforroger.

LARK

Lark and Livvy took the city bus to school together, four stops away from each other, Lark always against the window, Livvy always at the aisle because Livvy's stop was four stops after Lark in the morning (four before Lark in the afternoons, if they were taking the bus home in the afternoon, which they weren't because Baz drove them home now), making fun of the hobo up at the very front whose fingernails were thick and yellow ("Your boyfriend is so hot this morning") and the fat, dykey bus driver ("Didn't know your mama got a job driving the bus"), Livvy telling Lark everything that happened the night before in the hours between Baz dropping Lark off at her house and Livvy having to go to the Cinemark or Baz having to go home before Livvy's mom caught them at Livvy's apartment. It's not like Livvy's mom would have been mad, or maybe she would've been, but that was beside the point. All of life was kept from their mothers, their mothers beside the point.

Lark and Livvy had been two; now they were three. Lark did not envy Livvy the attention from Baz, nor Baz the attention from Livvy, not really, because she felt a part of it, Baz in the hallway with them during passing time, Baz and Shocky with them at lunch, even though the boys were juniors and could leave campus. Baz driving them home. Had she a different kind of mind, she would have conceptualized the three of them as an ever-shifting triangle, obtuse, oblique, isosceles, Lark most often at the furthest point; but instead, she thought of them as a line, Livvy the center-point.

"Third," Livvy said, *third* as in base and like it wasn't a big deal, except it was. Baz was Livvy's first real boyfriend, first boyfriend of either of them.

"Him or you?" Lark asked.

"Him."

"Him doing it to you or you doing it to him?"

"Him doing it to me." Livvy's face was nuzzled up to Lark's shoulder, saying the words to Lark from an inch away from her face, Livvy the only human being Lark would let that close to her face. Lark had a feeling like *she* had made this happen between Livvy and Baz, because Baz had been her peer tutor first, even though she had only known him for twenty minutes before Livvy. Still, Lark liked the her-ness of it, as if those twenty minutes gave her a rightful place. He was nice, quiet, but easy to laugh; didn't start most conversations, but he didn't let them drift off into silence either. He ran his hand over and over his hair, which Lark would have liked to too but did not ask to because once when Lark was in eighth grade and Monique Deveraux was in seventh, Monique showed up one day with an honest to goodness afro, buoyant and expansive, and Lark had never seen anything like it, and she'd reached out a hand from the desk behind Monique's in pre-algebra, and Monique had whipped around. "Don't touch my hair, girl!" and Lark had been so surprised, she'd nearly cried.

Lark especially liked the mornings now, the way it was guaranteed to be only the two of them. "Tell me," she said to Livvy.

"Tell you what?"

Lark didn't know. Everything. How it worked, what it felt, how'd they, where'd they, what during, what after, what. Tell her everything without making Lark ask, Lark ashamed of her want, which sat in her neck like she had a neckbone that went crosswise and bisected her throat.

"Whatever," Livvy said, and the hobo farted from the front of the bus, a loud fart that woke him up, blinking and confused, his scraggly beard with something fleshy caught in it, Lark and Livvy laughing at the fart and then the stink, the four or five people nearby giggling or looking at each other like *did that happen?* and Lark liked when the world folded in on itself like this and people came together out of nowhere, the strangers on the front of the bus suddenly linked, everyone a *thing*, everyone but the hobo.

A crowd of kids stood outside the school on the front steps. Normally, the bus pulled up a couple minutes shy of the 8:15 bell, and Lark and Livvy had to run, no one else out front but the last-minute stragglers. But this morning, a bunch of people milled around the stairs and the fat shrubs, teachers and administrators, too, Principal Vonn telling kids to get going, head inside, nothing to see out here. Lark wondered if Joey Bertram had had another seizure, because that's what teachers were always like when he had a seizure, "Nothing to see here," when obviously, there was something to see. Freaked Lark out, watching Joey have his seizures, his body trying to beat him up from the inside out.

The 8:15 bell rang, and everyone started to shuffle slowly inside. All it was was some spray paint on the stone entryway. The front of the building got tagged regularly, Lark not getting what the deal was, why Mr. Hanover was out there with one of the janitors, trying to stick a big sheet of paper over the spray paint using blue painter's tape, not getting why Principal Vonn was swinging her arms like a flight attendant, announcing, "Let's go, you're officially all late, you don't want another tardy on your transcript. I don't know about you, but I can't afford one more tardy on my transcript."

The paper Mr. Hanover and the janitor were trying to tape kept flopping down, the blue painter's tape not working, so Lark saw *Fennig* before being ushered past, which didn't help her understand, this her least favorite feeling, that of not getting it, of missing out. But of course she hadn't missed out, since myriad kids had arrived before Lark and Livvy, and those kids had had their phones, and on their phones, their cameras, and the nimblest among them had already posted online, Lark stuck only with an embarrassing emergency phone from her mom, paid for by the minute, not good for anything except texting Livvy. But a spirit of generosity moved among the students this morning, like the generosity that came after Joey's seizures when girls who barely knew each other grasped arms to look at each other with concern and say, "So scary." This morning, people held their phones up in the hallways and the classrooms. People said: "Look."

Emergency Faculty Meeting Notes (excerpt)

5/10/2015, 4:10 p.m.

…*VP Epstein*: bring everyone up to speed on the troublesome graffiti found this morning. Custodial already repainted, but the issues to discuss are if and how to communicate to the student body about this.

Ed Pfeiffer: Troublesome how?

VP Epstein: An inflammatory word and image targeted at one of our students.

Ed Pfeiffer: *The* inflammatory word?

VP Epstein: No.

Principal Vonn: Specifics are not as important as our zero-tolerance policy toward discriminatory language or actions against any persons in underrepresented groups.

Navid Langston: Is there a reason we're not sharing specifics?

[cross talk]

Danita Leininger: All the kids already saw it. It was a picture of a monkey with Baz Fenning's name above it.

Chuck Kloster: No. It only said Fennig, not Fenning, and there was some scribbling and the word *Monkey* below the scribbling. You wouldn't even have known it was a monkey without the word.

Danita Leininger: What's your point, Chuck?

Chuck Kloster: My point is, let's not go off half-cocked. Maybe it wasn't even about the Fenning boy. Maybe Fennig is a gang tag.

Navid Langston: Christ, Chuck.

Penny Lester: So, this is related to the library incident from a few weeks ago?

Principal Vonn: It's too early to draw such conclusions.

Chuck Kloster: How do we even know it was a student? It happened outside of the school when the school was closed. Could have been any community member.

Navid Langston: That's asinine.

Annette Midlarsky: It's 4:32 and we have been talking about this for nearly twenty minutes.

Danita Leininger: This is not who we are as a community. Can I make a motion that we, the faculty, condemn unequivocally any action or language that is racist or discriminatory?

VP Epstein reminds *Danita Leininger* that faculty meetings are no longer governed by Robert's rules of order.

Dan Stoner seconds.

VP Epstein reminds the faculty that there is no motion to second since meetings are now run by Consensus Building Approach (see: Faculty Meeting Notes: Jan 20, 2015).

Navid Langston: What are we building consensus around exactly? Is there an agenda for this meeting?

Kathy Sinclair: I second. Joking. About the seconding, but I have the same question about the agenda.

Stuart Hammerle: We should be thankful it wasn't swastikas. If it was swastikas, there would have been news vans parked out front when we got here this morning.

Principal Vonn: The agenda is what is the appropriate response to the student body.

Kathy Sinclair: Did the poor student see the graffiti? What are we actually doing for the student?

VP Epstein: Woody has been working with the student already. He'll continue that work.

Navid Langston: Might want to reach out to the family. Probably a good time to check in and make sure the student is getting everything he needs.

VP Epstein: Yes, yes, sure. Woody, put that on your list?

Woody Hanover: Of course. On my list. I'm on it. Come to me, anyone come to me, make an appointment to get on my calendar via Jennifer if you want to come talk about this further with me. The student in question is a peer tutor in my peer tutoring program, and the first incident happened during his peer tutoring duties, and I was out front this morning, so I saw the graffiti up close. He and I have talked about it. We've checked in. Not about today. But about the first incident, the preceding incident. On it. I'm on it.

Chuck Kloster: But wait, Woody, are you on it?

VP Epstein. Zip it, Chuck. Maybe the diversity committee can advise us on how to best communicate to the larger student body.

Navid Langston and *Danita Leininger* ask for a recess to convene as the two Diversity Committee members.

[5-minute recess. Meeting reconvenes at 4:50]

Navid Langston and *Danita Leininger* ask for volunteers for an emergency ad hoc committee to work with administration to program a diversity assembly.

Chuck Kloster: The solution to every problem can't be another committee.

Danita Leininger. You can't call for input from the diversity committee only to denigrate the diversity committee.

Chuck Kloster. How is disagreeing denigrating?

Navid Langston: Chuck, if you are so offended by the work of the diversity committee perhaps you should join it to make it better.

Chuck Kloster. I'm not offended. If I were easily offended, I would work on the diversity committee with all the other folks who are easily offended...

WOODY

You can put the backpack on him, the backpack, see the backpack over there. It's weighted. Go grab that. Please."

"Hello? Mrs. Fenning?"

"Hello? Yes, right there, green one, on the hooks. Yes. Hello? Who is this?"

"Mrs. Fenning, this is Woody Hanover from West High School. Baz's guidance counselor. Catch you at a bad time?"

"No. Yes. It's fine. How can I help you? We're planning to come for financial aid info night. I think my husband RSVP'd."

"No, I'm not calling about financial aid night, but I'm glad you'll be there."

"Hang on a second please— Nathan, shhh, shhh, sit, sit for a second. Why don't you give him a minute? Take a break, give us some space. Okay, Mr. Hoover, sorry what did you say you were calling about?"

"Hanover. You can call me Woody. I'm happy to call back at a better time."

"No, it's fine, I'm home with my son, my other son. How can I help you, Woody?"

"Really, it's about how I can help you and help Baz. I don't know if you're up to speed on the recent events here with Baz and the peer tutoring, I oversee the peer tutors, there have been a few incidents."

"Incidents?"

"There was an unfortunate joke between a few boys and Baz several weeks ago, where it sounds like some boys, boys receiving the peer tutoring services, got carried away, I think, with some Obama jokes directed at Baz."

"Jokes? I heard about that incident. It didn't sound like a joke."

"Sorry, not a joke. Poor choice of words, and I can assure you, the school did not treat it as a joke. The school took quick disciplinary action."

"I'm glad to hear that. Can you tell me what the disciplinary action was?"

"Well, no. Another student's disciplinary record is confidential."

"—Cheerios? Shhh. Shhh. I'll get you more Cheerios. Sit. She went outside. She'll be back. She's coming right back. I know."

"Mrs. Fenning?"

"Yes, I'm here. You said incidents, plural."

"Well, this is really what I'm calling about. It looks like there may have been an incident of targeted graffiti."

"Targeted graffiti?"

"Someone wrote a picture, of what was supposed to be a marsupial, and Baz's name. It was really a scribble and *Fennig*."

"Fennig?"

"We think it was a misspelling."

. . .

"Mrs. Fenning?"

"By marsupial, you mean a kangaroo?"

"Not a marsupial. Sorry. I meant primate."

. . .

"Mrs. Fenning?"

"A monkey?"

"Yes, there was Fennig, and a scribble, and beneath the scribble, the word *Monkey*. You couldn't really tell it was a monkey."

"Jesus Christ."

"I know, I'm sorry. I'm sorry to be the one to tell you. I want you to know that we're taking this matter very seriously and we've already called the Horace PD to see if they can help us track down the perpetrator or perpetrators."

"The Horace PD."

"That's right. And also, our diversity committee is already hard at work on an assembly to address this, and students have really catalyzed in Baz's corner too. There are vocal students in his corner, I don't want to give the impression that he's being targeted at school."

"Well, clearly he's being targeted at school."

"Well, sure, of course, I can see how you feel that way, and we feel that way too. Baz has the administration on his side, and the PD, and other students, and me, and really, I was calling to see what we could do or what supports you need or if Baz needs any more support at home."

"At home? Nobody is calling Baz a monkey at home. Baz has plenty of support at home. What kind of support is he getting from West is what I want to know."

"Sure, sure. Like I said, there's going to be an assembly and the PD. An investigation, which I'm not really involved in. We painted it over right away. I should have said that to begin with. The graffiti is gone, if that's what's worrying you."

"If that's what's worrying me?"

"If that's what's worrying you."

"—No, I think he's in the living room. I don't know but I bet you could find him if you looked. Wait, Naomi, did you leave any butts on the lawn? I'll give you a glass, we don't like butts out front."

"Mrs. Fenning?"

"Sorry, I need to go, Mr....Woody. I'm sure we'll be back in touch with the school. I don't think this conversation is over."

"No, no, nor do I. That's why I was reaching out, to open the channel, to begin the conversation, I see this as a beginning...Mrs. Fenning?"

STEFANIE

It was near impossible to keep training the new PSW after the call. It'd already been hard, the new PSW small and unreadable, Nathan unhappy the way he was always unhappy in the early days of a new personal support worker, Stefanie unhappy in the same way, except with words. Whatever Stefanie said to the new girl—"There are some ringtones he can't tolerate"; "He'll point to the apple if he's hungry"; "Give him Mat if he is having a hard time settling his body down in a new room";—the girl looked at Stefanie or looked at Nathan without any indication of listening. Stefanie started to add, "You got me?" "You with me?" and even, "Naomi, did you hear what I just said?"

Naomi had thin blond hair clipped to one side with a plastic barrette better suited for someone much younger, though the girl looked pretty young, her face pale and lineless. "How old are you?" was one of the questions Stefanie was not allowed to ask. Naomi smelled like an ashtray.

Marjorie from county had called the day before. "Naomi's one of our best," she'd told Stefanie. "Particularly good with non-verbal adults. We've seen some nice outcomes when she's dealt with aggressiveness. She has a way."

"Nathan's not aggressive," Stefanie had said.

"You know Carlos reported an uptick."

"It was not an *uptick*," Stefanie said. "Nathan slipped in the bathroom. It was an accident. He's not aggressive."

"Let's save this conversation for in person. I called to tell you to give the girl a chance."

Nathan slapped and slapped his hand on the table now, his agitation from any of a number of things: Stefanie wound up from the guidance counselor, the existence of the girl in their kitchen, their daily schedule not yet settled into normal. Naomi tried to hand Mat to Nathan, though Nathan was already past Mat and flung the stuffed bear aside.

Baz was socked away down in his room, barely a hello when he'd gotten home an hour earlier. It was Derek's evening seminar; he'd be home after dark, buzzing with excitement over a great crop of PhD candidates. Stefanie had followed up with Baz about the library boys once, but Baz *Ma*-ed her and said it was nothing. It'd never been anything, *Ma*, he told her. Her and Derek's attention was soon diverted to the cagey way Baz was holding his cell phone, the extra stutter each time he got the ding of a text, and the goofy smile while reading messages. One night at dinner, a purpling bruise peeked out of his collar.

"You see that?" she'd asked Derek later, and the way he'd said, "Your boy has a hickey" was with a disturbing amount of pride.

In the following days, Derek employed the same unassuming curiosity he used to charm students, his *aw shucks* play at humility, and sussed out: yes, there was a girl; yes, Baz liked her; no, they weren't sexually active; no, he didn't need to go buy condoms; yes, he knew how to get them for free in the health office at school.

"Our baby boy," he'd goofed in bed. "Is all gwown up." He'd run his finger up the side of Stefanie's neck where she always laughed and squirmed, though this squirming was maybe with a sliver of envy. Derek and Baz had a whole ecosystem between them now in the hours Derek was home from campus, Stefanie still at the hospital. Whatever had grown taut and attenuated between Baz and Stefanie in his teen years—that shrug, that dismissive *don't know*—stayed soft with Derek, at least in the unseen hours they spent together, Stefanie imagining it as an updated version of the rolling around they used to do on the carpet together, static electrifying the ends of their fingertips, a zap to the cheek, to the lip, laughing and playing at hurt and *Uncle! Stop it! Uncle!* their tangle of arms and ankles, their yelps and grunting, their laughing. Stefanie didn't know from roughhousing; it'd been her, Calvin, her mama.

Point now was she'd let herself get distracted, the phone call from the stumbling counselor the worst kind of pyrrhic victory: she'd known the library boys weren't nothing. Something like that was never nothing.

"It's getting bumpy!" Nathan yelled now. "It's getting bumpy!"

Naomi got the weighted backpack off the hook where Stefanie had shown her, but Nathan wouldn't let her put it on him, making his arms stiff, yelling, "Hold on! Hold on!"

"Stop," Stefanie finally said. "Don't." It was impossible to explain when to intervene and when to leave him be. The most maddening thing about training PSWs was Stefanie couldn't train them into knowing Nathan. What they needed was familiarity. Nathan wasn't going to let Naomi do anything today.

When Stefanie saw the girl's chin crumple, she softened. "Let's call it good," she said. "Everyone's tired."

Baz sat curled at his desk, all the lights off except for his computer screen and his desk lamp, bent over his book, the nape of his neck exposed, dark fuzz, haircut growing out.

"Jesus, Ma. Scare the crap outta me."

She hadn't meant to come up on him. She knew she should wait until Derek was home. They were better together.

Baz's face was stern, then something else, then serious again, though she'd seen the bobble, the quake at the corner of his lip he was now trying to bite back, reminding her of times he was little, running all the way home from a brutal game of tag or stick ball, blood running down his calf, trying so hard not to lose it.

"School called," she said.

"Don't," he said. "Don't, Ma."

"Don't *don't* me," she said. "Don't you don't me." He wasn't even looking at her, fiddling with the stack of university catalogs piled in one corner of his desk; they kept coming and coming, a tsunami of Black and brown and white faces sitting in grassy quads, peering through microscopes, U Penn on top; Baz had wanted Penn forever, since he was a boy in Chicago and a parent had come in for career day in a shiny gray suit, a businessman, something to do with railroad switches. "Penn," the man had said, and Baz had decided it so, with all the whimsy of childhood, like the summer he said he was a vegetarian and the time he began a lawn-mowing business. Except this one stuck. That they couldn't afford the seventy-five grand a year, not by a longshot, the open secret of their household. Everybody knew; no one said.

"What do you want to tell me?" Stefanie said.

The low light from his desk lamp cast him in shadows, bringing out his cheekbones, his hands flying around his face in the strangest, helpless flutter. God, he was still so young. She kissed him on the top of his head, and he let her, even let her wrap her arms around him, his head in her belly. He smelled of Baz—shea butter, coconut oil, perspiration. She hadn't been prepared for the love affair that was boyhood; it had been different with Nathan. Years and years, Baz wanting nothing so much as to tangle his body into hers, his little hand hot at her back, his fingers twiddling the lobe of her ear.

"They spray painted some shit," he said when he let go. "Sorry. Some stuff. Can we not make it into a big deal?"

"It *is* a big deal. Having to find things out from Hidaya, the school. Why don't you tell us?"

He made a noise then, one she hadn't heard from him before, the sound of sucking something out from between his teeth, and it surprised her. It was the noise of the boys on the corners of her childhood. A noise that might have meant: *Lookit that ass* or *Keep it moving*.

"You think you're grown," she said. "You got a car. You got college. But you're not grown. You're a kid. You tell us and we'll help. We're your parents. Don't tough guy me. Your father and I are going to work with the school because this is not okay, and it needs to stop. You hear me?"

"I hear you," he said, not looking, his laptop gone to screensaver, a slideshow of birds in formation, giraffes on savannah, a default screensaver; they'd never seen giraffes on savannah.

His phone chimed on his desk, the screen lighting up, Stefanie glimpsing columns of text bubbles; there, the emoji with hearts for eyes, there, three red hearts in a row. He grabbed up the phone so quick, she didn't even see the name. It chimed from his pocket, and the way he was trying to look some way—blasé, unconcerned—almost made Stefanie laugh.

"I know," she said, trying to affect Derek's devil-may-care voice, his nothing-to-see-here. "Daddy filled me in."

Baz made a half-laugh, shrugged his shrug. She could see the way he was trying very hard not to give anything up.

"She a friend of Shekib's?" Stefanie asked, not helping herself. Once she started not helping herself, it came so easy.

He shook his head. "No one calls him that," he told her, not for the first time.

She could have said to him about his tone. About don't give me sass. But she didn't, thinking herself magnanimous for it. She wasn't one of those mothers who needed her son to be a suckling. But Baz didn't yet have the sense of what to secret away and what to share. "She have a name?"

The slightest of pauses. "Livvy," Baz said with another shrug, head half-cocked, staring at his knees like a tiny version of the girl was there in his lap.

LARK

It was loud at Increasing Our Strengths Through Togetherness, and not only from the *I Have a Dream Speech* Mr. Langston was playing though the PA; loud in the way that only Lark seemed to notice, the hum of restlessness from all of the students in the gym bleachers, the edge of panic or hysteria or danger that she could not define but could very much feel, the general shifting, barking, coughing, the hooting boys nearby, all of it combined into a force of attention on her—or at least very, very close to her, attention on Livvy at her side and Baz at Livvy's side, attention that had a feeling attached to it and that feeling was a *scream*.

Ms. Leininger had passed out copies of the transcript of the speech. "Enough for everyone to share," she'd announced, with emphasis. "Find a partner, buddy up with the two or three people nearest to you." Livvy held the speech as Lark and Baz and Shocky to the other side of Baz looked on, and it was hard for Lark to bring the words into focus, the black letters swimming, making their own kind of noise, a skritching inside her head, a blurring fuzz.

Dr. King's voice crackled on the recording. "…until the Negro is granted his citizenship rights," he called out, and someone nearby—a boy—repeated *Negro* and chuckled. When Lark's grandmother was alive, she used that word, as in, "Not the Negro's" when they were choosing checkout lines at the Safeway. Her grandmother had the same wide hips as her mother, the same drooping breasts, the same scored lines across her forehead, the same thinning hair, the same angry whisper and tight grip on Lark's wrist. Lark had spent so many days in front of a mirror staring at her own wisp of a body, no breasts yet even at fifteen, her shoulders curling her into the front half of a parenthesis, a secret even from herself, wondering when the change would come, wanting it desperately and not at all, trying to imagine the bulges of fat and sag that lay beneath. Sometimes she felt it in her bed at night, when she could not sleep, her future trapped inside, trying to out. She felt it right now at the assembly as Livvy pressed her thigh to Lark's thigh. Livvy's future had already broken through, and it was curvy and soft smelling. Livvy's future was a more beautiful version of Livvy's past, her lips plumped as her breasts, her face thinned, her hips curved, but not too much, and Lark was full of admiration and envy for the way Livvy did not have to wonder anymore.

Livvy sat very, very still beside her now, and it could seem that she was oblivious to the force of attention were it not for her defiant chin. Lark saw how it jutted more pointedly than usual, the twitch at the hinge of her jaw where she was clamping her teeth. Baz, too, held his face tightly, his eyes staring exactly in front of him. Livvy whispered something to Baz, Baz drawing his head toward her, Livvy cupping her hand over his ear. Shocky looked at Lark and quickly looked away. During lunches, he said things to her like, "Weren't we in Hammerle together last year?" but they were not. She was still gutting out algebra. Lark and Livvy had things to say to each other, and Livvy and Baz did, but she and Shocky didn't need to have things to say to each other.

Mr. Langston talked now into a squelching microphone. "…makes America America…" There was a map of the United States projected behind him, though he stood in the way of the projector, squinting into its light, a shadow of his head over western states. People had made *I Have a Dream* into accordion fans, airplanes. A crumpled ball hit Lark in the head. She turned around—she couldn't help it—but the ripple of laughing people was too wide a swath. She heard someone call *Frankenstein*. Mr. Langston talked and talked. Baz had two tiny wads of paper stuck to the back of his hair. Lark wanted to pick them off, but she was afraid to draw more attention. She wished Livvy would see and pick them off. It was always like this, the universe of teachers and the universe of students orbiting on their own axes, sometimes the gravitational pull of one affecting the other, mostly not.

Soon kids were standing, row after row streaming to the bleacher aisles. The microphone sat back in the stand, a new picture on the projector screen: a collage of a bunch of different kids, some reading, some playing baseball, though Lark didn't recognize any. It was kids from the internet, all posed with their white teeth and sunshine, Black and Asian and Hispanic and white strangers.

In the aisleway, the thunder of footsteps on wood, the buzzing and the hum, it was loud enough for Lark to want to put her hands to her ears. She tried to think of the noise as tidal, the mass of bodies a wave, though the sweaty heat of laughing barks and barking shouts and shoulders and footsteps filled her so thunderously that walking felt like falling, so much so that for one confused second, she thought it was her fault when Livvy lurched forward, toppling into the bodies in front of them. Lark turned in time to see two palms shoving Baz from behind, so that he too lurched, and then everyone was falling and screaming, and Lark got caught up in it. Before she hit her temple on the corner of a bleacher and got her fingers crushed under a boot heel, when she was very briefly airborne, she had the feeling that they *were* a tidal wave, no one in control and no one knowing, everyone moving together as one, and what that felt like for the fleeting moment before the moment became something else entirely was: love.

'FREAK ACCIDENT' INJURES SCORES OF STUDENTS AT WEST HS

Don Delouth, *TheDailyRegister.* May 21, 2015.

In what Principal Georgina Vonn refers to as a "freak accident," over twenty West High School students were injured when an exit from a school-wide assembly turned into a stampede. "There was some sort of confusion on the stairs during exit," Vonn explained, "which resulted in students falling, which led to further injury when other students panicked and began to run." Emergency medical responders were dispatched to West High School. Most students were treated for contusions on the spot. Six were seen at Riverside hospital and later released.

"There were, like, seven people who fell over me," sophomore Steven Henries said. "It was crazy." Henries suffered a contusion on his forehead. "I have a concussion," he reported.

Marsha Lessig, secretary of the PTO, was not satisfied with the school's explanations. "Parents are angry," Lessig said. "Parents are concerned. You drop off your child and you expect they will be safe. You don't think they're going to get trampled. The administration needs to get their priorities straight."

When asked why a Martin Luther King Jr. assembly was held five months after MLK Day, teacher Danita Leininger, responded, "Inclusivity is never out of date."

However, several unnamed sources confirmed that the assembly was in response to recent incidents of racial harassment at West, including verbal harassment and racist graffiti. Superintendent of schools, Marcus Jay-Johnson, said, "Be assured, the district has zero tolerance for discrimination…"

WOODY

Thank you for joining us," Georgina said, her voice already reedy with strain, 8:45 in the morning. Susan Albrecht shook Georgina's outstretched hand. Susan's hair was short; in Woody's mind, he thought of it as *shorter*, though he couldn't remember the last time he had seen Susan, so he wasn't sure of his point of comparison. Now it was cut like so many ladies his age, bluntly along her jawline, making her chin more prominent, her lips, the lipstick already faded from the top lip.

Livvy sank into one of Georgina's leatherette chairs, her left eye blackened, a cut across her left cheek, already clotted and beginning to scab. A children's Band-Aid, blue and patterned with Smurfs, covered one small bit of it. He recognized it as a teenager's idea of irony.

The hallways had been so strange in the days after assembly, Baz with a sprained wrist, Matt Briar (senior, debate) on crutches; Lecie Delapeña (sophomore, flag team) with a bandage on her forehead, a deep gash beneath stapled with gruesome metal teeth, anyone's for the looking; more kids than he could count, kids up the alphabet and out of his purview, bruised or scraped. Woody had never been in the service, but he imagined this was what it was like after battle, the coterie of injured on display, the air thick with both hysteria and solemnity, which at West unfortunately coincided with the usual end of year hysteria (it was 72 and sunny outside!) to combine into something ill-considered and combustible. "What about graduation?" Georgina had shrieked at the latest emergency faculty meeting, and her face was so red, the collar of her blouse so embarrassingly tangled upon itself, no one could bear to look, let alone answer.

"This is Mr. Hanover," Georgina said now, today's blouse much less complicated, her collar sitting straight and stiff. Susan turned to Woody and nodded, not letting on that she knew him, not offering *Woody* as a familiar. Instead, she stuck out her hand.

"I know Susan," Woody offered, and though he was talking to Georgina, he was looking at Susan in her pale blue skirt suit, so he was shaking her hand while talking about her in third person, and that led him on a strange trip down a rabbit hole, which Susan did not appear to accompany him on. She barely looked at him, her lips pursed, mouth downturned, committing neither to knowing him or not, a perfunctory shake of his hand. It was clear all she wanted was to get down to business. Her eyes were green, a fact that Woody had not known, or had known as a boy and forgotten, so that when they did not meet in Georgina's office, he was struck by their greenness as if she were a stranger, which, for all intents and practical purposes, she was.

"So," Georgina announced as she sat, "we've wanted to talk to each family affected by the accident." She clapped one hand on her desk blotter. This was how she'd opened all of these meetings, with a speech about the assembly, the safety of students, the concerns that this has raised for all involved. The board attorney had fed her the language. "We wanted to touch base with you and Olivia," she closed, "since Olivia has been at the fulcrum."

This was the point when the Albrechts were to speak, though Livvy was hunched down low in her leatherette chair, chewing on a pinkie nail. The black eye gave her a pirate-like appearance. Kids with their parents were different animals than kids without. Parents hemmed them in, making them small. The air around Livvy seemed to shimmer with her discomfort. When Woody tried making sly, silent eye contact, she wasn't having it. Kids, when put in a room with their parents, generally hated all adults. Woody felt disappointed by how quotidian this was of Livvy. Her eyes were not green. Hers, brown. Did she look like her father? Woody strained to recall Len Albrecht, though that was years ago, when they all ranged free, back home after college, or never having left, nothing tying them together but a shared past, which didn't mean then what it meant now with Facebook and Instagram and whatnot tying people to their past ever after. Back then, that Susan Hoffman had married someone already and had a kid was as strange as Woody going back to work at the very place they'd all struggled to free themselves from for four years.

"Fulcrum?" Susan said now, her face unreadable. Nobody was saying anything. It was normally Doug Epstein who had meetings with families, Doug capable of channeling his frenetic energy into eager listening. Georgina only stepped in for PR purposes, when the import and statesmanship of principal was necessary.

"I think," Woody said, "what Principal Vonn means is that Livvy is closely linked to Baz Fenning, who has been the target of the recent racial harassment."

Livvy made a noise then, one that Woody furiously hoped Francine never would make in his direction, one that he knew she inevitably would, parenthood a straight dive into one's own humiliation.

"Closely linked?" Susan said to Livvy, and it was embarrassing, the way she was echoing words. The whole school knew about Livvy and Baz, even those who had known neither Livvy nor Baz weeks before. Susan bounced one knee, and it reminded Woody of the way Livvy bounced her shoe on and off her heel. Susan's skirt suit was of the type one might find at a discount shop at the mall, the material too shiny, and he knew she was a secretary to something important: bankers? Lawyers? Business titans? and this fact depressed him, and he wanted to say to her, *Remember when we were the kids of all this?*

"It wasn't an accident," Livvy said, looking at Woody. "Why's everyone calling it an accident?"

"We are still sorting through what happened," Georgina said. "No one has reached a definitive conclusion."

"Some racist asshole pushed us," Livvy said.

"Livvy!" Susan said, taking hold of the girl's arm, a strange grab from one leatherette to the other. Once she had hold, perched forward, still sitting but barely, it was clear she wasn't sure what to do with the forearm. "Honey," she said more quietly, looking at her daughter as if blinking away a dream. Livvy made the noise again. Kids were never as uninteresting as they were with their own parents.

"Why don't we," Woody said, "all take a step back." The board's attorney had counseled Georgina: only say accident, say they're looking into it, admit no culpability. The purpose of these meetings was to get in there and establish a caring relationship and lay a solid foundation before an ambulance chaser got a hold of their cell phone numbers and entreated them to sue. "First, Livvy, how are you feeling?"

Susan let go of her arm. "I have a headache," Livvy said.

"Sure," Woody said. "That makes sense. Susan." Saying the name gave him an odd thrill. She was wearing a Star of David necklace, this as surprising to Woody as the green eyes. Livvy was not one of the klatch of kids in the Jewish Student Union. "What questions do you have for us?"

Susan looked at him, her mouth opening then closing again. Woody thought of those long-ago sealed lips, the rat-poison closet, the dark. The dark had been obliterating, save for the tiny strip of light beneath the door, out to the rest of the party, a place he did and did not want to return to. It had felt to him at the time, and well afterward, that if he had gotten this moment right, a trajectory could have unfolded. Susan had a look to her now, a wide-eyed question. He had imagined her differently as an adult—blithe, matter of fact, suffering nothing. Susan looked to Livvy, but Livvy was refusing to look back, intent on the pinkie nail she was picking at, flecked with old, dark nail polish.

"You don't," he said, "need to ask us anything right now. If you have questions, you can call. Email."

She nodded, though not in a way that signified understanding, and when Woody looked to Georgina, she looked mostly relieved that she was not the one talking anymore.

"I think," Woody offered, half-statement, half-question, "we're good, otherwise. I mean, not good. But I think we wanted to touch base to see how we could help, what help we could offer—"

"Mrs. Albrecht," Georgina said. "We want you to know that Olivia's safety, every student's safety, is paramount. We ask that you give us a chance to earn back your confidence."

When no one offered a rejoinder, Georgina stood from her desk chair. Susan stood as well, and so Woody did too. It reminded him of the Simon Says game Francine loved so dearly, the way Woody would eventually take the fall so she could laugh and clap and remind him, in her high-pitched imperiousness: "I didn't say Simon says!"

People shook people's hands. "It's okay," he said to Susan because he felt compelled to say something. Livvy remained in her chair.

"Olivia," Georgina asked. "Do you need help getting back to your third period?"

"Help?" she said, as if she were unfamiliar with the word.

"Where are you headed?" Georgina tried again.

"Hammerle's," Livvy said.

"I'll walk you out," Georgina said, and the girl slowly stood.

Susan put her hand on the back of her daughter's neck, Livvy letting her, even listing a little toward her mom, and Woody was startled by this easy intimacy after the discord. He was so distracted by their tableau— did he understand kids at all?—he was the last to see the Fennings in the waiting chairs, Baz between his parents and with an ace bandage around his right wrist, Mr. Fenning a striking figure, tall and handsome in his chair, button-down and khakis, Mrs. Fenning all cheekbone, a boldly colorful scarf holding her braids back, whose word Woody felt he should know: A keffiyeh? Kente cloth? Something with a *k*.

There was a moment when Baz looked at the passing parade and perked in his chair, his face blooming into a grin, and Livvy simultaneously listed away from her mother and toward his chair, but then something imperceptible changed. Was it the way Mrs. Fenning cleared her throat into her fist? Was it Susan's gaze, turned to the chairs? Was it Mr. Fenning's reflexive hand on the boy's shoulder?

Baz smalled himself. Woody knew that smalled was not a word, but it was the only one that came to mind as Baz flattened his expression and receded into his chair, drawing himself flush with his parents. He looked—in one quick second—away from Livvy, then back again, then to his father's khaki pant leg. Livvy, coincidentally or not, stumbled, and Woody watched as Susan's fingers pressed into the girl's neck, five indents into the pale skin as Susan tried to head off the fall.

STEFANIE

The principal was a type Stefanie was familiar with, whole layers of hospital administrators of exactly the same ilk, full of declarations that sounded like something until you actually listened. The principal kept repeating that *safety* was *tantamount* but did not specify what it was tantamount to. The guidance counselor was eager like a puppy. "Baz is a very respected member of the West student body," he said. "Everyone really likes Baz," as if that was what troubled Stefanie.

Baz sat ramrod straight, hands on his lap. Stefanie asked about tangible safety planning. "What is written down in policy?" she asked. She asked about resources specific to the well-being of Black students. The principal said diversity committee. She said policies were "in progress." Derek nodded and nodded. Ever since the second call from the school, the trip to urgent care, the ace bandage on Baz's wrist (*Just a sprain,* the doctor had said, almost cheerily, looking young enough to be a paperboy), Stefanie had the feeling like nobody was alarmed enough or worse, everyone expected Stefanie to be alarmed enough for all of them.

Her phone kept vibrating from her purse.

Call me.

Can you call me?

Call plz.

It was Cal.

Busy, Stefanie texted back.

"You and Livvy," the counselor said more than once to Baz, as in: "You and Livvy are under a lot of scrutiny right now." "You and Livvy are handling this with real aplomb."

The fact that it was all seemingly of a piece—the "incidents," as the principal kept bloodlessly referring to them, and the girl—made Stefanie feel like she was losing the thread or hadn't had the thread to begin with.

She'd almost missed the girl and her mother as they'd walked past, mistaking them for any pair of bodies. She and Derek had spent so little time inside the school during its working hours. They were used to it being culled and curated for parents: orientation, conferences. In the daytime, it was full of bodies and noise and stink. When the girl walked past, her face bruised, her T-shirt tight against her breasts, long skinny legs in ratty denim shorts, Stefanie had barely given notice, until she saw how the girl and Baz looked at each other. She'd felt all at once a stutter of relief that she was not one of those stunning blond girls intimidating in their perfection, and also a surprise at how—well, what was the word?—how *cheap* she looked. Strange Band-Aid across her face, dime store flip-flops slurring against the floor, janky toenails with chipped black polish, a fat silver ring around a big toe. The mother followed too close at the girl's heels, worrying a purse strap at her shoulders, letting out a little noise when the girl nearly tripped.

"Do you need to get that?" the principal said of the sustained vibration from Stefanie's phone—Cal was calling now—and Stefanie felt unexpectedly chastened, even though the woman's tone was neutral. Everything the principal said was neutral, betraying nothing. Stefanie needed a little betraying.

"No. No, no." She turned off her phone.

Baz refused to linger with them in the waiting area afterward, telling them bye while trying to get out from under Derek squeezing his shoulder. "Chin up," Derek told him, and Baz made a dismissive noise. "Don't *ffft* me," Derek said, though lightly, before Baz disappeared into the hallway.

In the parking lot, afternoon sun glinted off the windshields as they stood next to Derek's Subaru, Stefanie saying the meeting was a whole lot of nothing, why had they taken off work, Derek saying give them time, they're scrambling.

"That was her before the meeting," Stefanie said. "That was Livvy."

"Seems so," Derek said, and casually, "That's how they met. First time those boys were being fools in the library. She got up in their faces. She yelled at them." Derek put her fist to his mouth and laughed.

"I don't see how that's—" Funny. She was going to say funny, but Derek's phone rang and when he fished it from his back pocket and said, "Calvin! Hey, man!" Stefanie watched his face change from congenial to intent to alarmed in seconds. She was already late back to work. The pharmacy would be scrambling without her, scripts piling up, charge nurses calling, then calling back after twenty minutes, then calling back again after another ten. The pharmacy was singular in its ability to bring the hospital to its knees. She'd taken off so much time in the past few weeks. She heard her brother's tone—a mile a minute, his voice pitched and high. "Okay, okay, man," Derek tried to interject. "She's right here. We got you." And then he held his hand over the phone as if he were telling Stefanie a secret. "Your mom. She left the house. She's missing."

Calvin went to bring their mother her lunch, and she wasn't in her room. The front door was open. Mr. Arias, their next-door neighbor, saw her in her slippers and robe about an hour before.

"He didn't think to come tell you?" Stefanie said. And: "You didn't notice she was gone for an hour?"

"Don't," Cal said.

Their mother had moved in with Calvin three years before, after ending up confused in the middle of the night in a neighbor's attached garage, trying and trying with the door to their house. The neighbors—a young couple with a toddler—called 911, thinking her a burglar. Cal drove an hour to end up at an unfamiliar police station at four a.m., their mother half dressed with a silver emergency blanket around her legs. It wasn't the first time she'd gotten confused, but it was the most public.

"You try Walt's?" Stefanie asked of their mother's favorite grocery store in Cal's suburb. "You try her physical therapist?" Their mother was fixated on her young, buff physical therapist, Philip, who she was sure was flirting with her. "My Mr. Philip," she called him. *My Mr. Philip put his hands all around my knee.*

"She doesn't know how to get to Philip's," Cal said. "That's five miles away."

Stefanie was 2000 miles away. The thought of her mother wandering through the streets in her slippers and robe; and why wasn't their mother dressed more than halfway through the day? "You called the police?"

"I don't want the police all up in this."

"All up in what?" She imagined Cal in his room, getting stoned all morning while his mother went on her way. "Your mother is missing."

"She needs memory care," he said.

"I thought she needed live-in help," Stefanie said. They'd had this conversation a hundred times. A hundred and one.

Derek and the Subaru were gone—nothing for him to do here—Stefanie sitting in her car, driver's door open so she wouldn't get baked by the sun. What was she supposed to do here? She'd been there to help with the move, her mama going from combative (toward Stefanie, who Mama mistook for her long-dead sister Abilene) to tearfully remorseful (toward Cal, who she never mistook for anyone). They had moved Mama into Kiki's old room, Angie's grown daughter from her first marriage. Half of Kiki's things were still there, a closet full of girl clothes, old posters of Ghostface Killah and Snoop Dogg. Stefanie had only been back once since; travel was expensive, getting Nathan on a plane.

"Get in the car," she told Cal. "Go look for her. How far could she get?"

"I can't leave," Cal said. "What if she comes back?"

"Can you ask," Stefanie said, trying to make her voice the voice Cal wanted, the assured older sister who judged nothing and felt only debt to Calvin even if he was the one who collected Mama's social security, along with a healthy check from Stefanie every month, "Mr. Arias to come over for a little while? Can you go and ask him that?"

She was useless at work. Texts back and forth to Cal. Derek checking in. A Facebook post asking #chicagoareafriends to keep an eye out with two recent pictures of Mama downloaded from Angie's Facebook page: grinning behind a turkey at Thanksgiving, all dressed up in purple for church. Angie called about if Stef thought they should call the police. Yes, she thought they should call the police! She was about to do it herself. Okay, Angie would. Nothing on Facebook except likes and shares and all her old friends saying *oh no* and how worried they were about Eileen and how they were praying for her. Adrenaline was making her pit out her blouse. She smelled ripe and her hip ached from stress, and they were woefully behind on scripts, the ICU charge nurse about to grab her by the throat.

When Cal called, nearly four hours after he'd first texted her, he was laughing: "Look who came back home," he shouted, and Stefanie could tell she was on speaker. "You want to say anything to your daughter, Queen for a Day?"

She could hear her mama saying something about *this fuss*, Stefanie calling out, "You okay, Mama? You okay?" no one listening, all kinds of noise, more than Cal and Angie and Mama. "Are the police there? Mr. Arias?" But no one was listening, Stefanie imagining Cal waving around the phone like a prize. She yelled at him to take her off speaker, she wanted to know how Mama was doing, she wanted to know about her feet, all those hours out in slippers. What about her feet?

❧

At dinner, there was Baz with his phone and his grin and his texting in his lap. She'd brought the day home with her—all of it, the trailing adrenaline, the sweat, the stink, the unease in her gut—and even having showered, even Derek having picked up Thai, she couldn't shake it. The day had cost her something.

"Enough," she said, "with the phones at the table. When did we start with the phones at the table?"

Baz and Derek passed a look between them. It was the look between them that really got her. Who were the adults here? Baz gave her an okay and put his phone away, but too late, the specter of the girl raised here at their table.

"Daddy tells me you met this girl during the library incident." Seeing her had catalyzed something in Stefanie. The girl, the school, the terrible turns of events were married in her mind now.

"Don't say it like that," Baz said.

"Like what?"

"The library incident." He said it in a baritone.

Nathan screwed his eyes up and laughed. Nathan was in a great mood at dinners lately, grinning anytime anyone said *Naomi* or called him *Nay* the way Naomi did, laughing at everything.

"She spoke up," Stefanie said. "Got in those boys' faces." It wasn't a question.

Baz nodded.

"I can see why you liked that," Stefanie said, picturing the girl's black eye, her Band-Aid. "I know you like this girl, and she likes you, but it's possible you're finding trouble and bringing it to you."

"She's not trouble," Baz said.

"Sure," Stefanie said. "But you can slow down too. You don't have to rush into something." Derek pressed his leg into hers. She knew that meant *honey*. She knew that meant *come on*. "You have a future to focus on. You have a summer internship. You have college. You have one more year. That's it. You have things that are more important than a girl."

Nathan was still laughing, Baz staring hard at her, and all she wanted was a feeling like everything was copacetic with everyone she loved all at the same time, everyone safe and accounted for. Had that feeling ever even once existed in her? She felt like she had once known that feeling but she could not be sure.

"You've always been so good," she said. "I know that, your father knows that, we know that. Right?"

"Right," Derek said, though not with enough feeling to mistake this for his fight.

"You have all sorts of options," Stefanie said. The way no one was really listening to her made her dig in. "It doesn't have to be this one girl."

❧

In bed, she and Derek talked about her mom, imagining where Eileen was for those four hours, how she found her way back, Derek's voice growing heavy with sleep. Derek was always so good at falling asleep, never one to count sheep, never one to stare up at the ceiling listening to the breaths coming slow and even from the other side of the bed.

"Maybe ease up," he said, and she'd been waiting for this. "It's his first girlfriend," and "It's not easy being a boy."

"It's easy being a *girl*?" Stefanie was nowhere near sleep even with her body exhausted. Her left hip throbbed such a deep throb.

He leaned over and bit her shoulder lightly. She swatted his face away, but not hard. They were playing or playing at playing. "Take it easy, lion-*ess*," Derek told her. "You're in charge. You're always in charge. Nobody here's messing with your pride."

At breakfast, it was only she and Baz in the kitchen, Derek in the shower before campus, Nathan out at the dining room table with Naomi, paper and scissors spread across the tabletop, Naomi with her typical low murmuring that made everything between her and Nathan seem a secret, Nathan slapping his hand against the side of his chair, happily. Stefanie was glad to be wrong about Naomi.

Baz stood at the toaster, his face tired, bags under his eyes. She asked him if he slept all right. Sure, he told her. She'd slept terribly, awake in the middle of the night. She went right up close to him as his toast popped up, and he spread on the butter.

She took his chin very gently in her hand, ignoring the way he tried to pull away. "Don't let some girl with a savior complex swoop in," she said quietly. This was between them. She was his mother, and she had spent the middle of the night staring at the dark ceiling, trying to make out shapes. "When she sticks her neck out, whose gets chopped?"

LARK

She stood outside the ticket booth. Usually, she could make faces through the glass or press her hands like she was trapped out here or go up to the spot with the microphone and go: "Two adults for *Naked Lola Discos in the Basement*," which was stupid but at least made Livvy say, "Shut up" and smile. When Gabe was working inside, Livvy would let Lark through without a ticket to sit for free in one of the theaters and Lark would sink into the fat recliner chair and nurse the free water from concessions and watch the boxing movie or the Disney cartoon about the warring emotions inside the girl's brain.

But Gabe wasn't working today. And Livvy barely looked at Lark from behind the glass in her red golf shirt, the *Olivia* tag pinned cock-eyed to her chest.

"One for *Disco Girls Locked in the Attic*," Lark said in a funny voice.

"I got to work," Livvy said, even though there was no line. All she had to do was sit. Her black eye had faded to red, the cut on her cheek scabbed. All Lark came away with was a sore knot beneath her hair.

Lark put her lips up to the glass, making them into a kissing fish. "Quit it," Livvy said. "Imma have to clean that off."

"No, you won't," Lark said, though Livvy probably would. Baz had broken up with her six days ago and nothing was helping. He'd broken up with her on Sunday and now it was Friday and Lark had nothing to do. It wasn't that different from most Fridays except that Livvy didn't think anything was funny.

"You guys were only together like a month," Lark had said on Wednesday when Livvy slumped through another lunch, not eating anything, picking up her egg salad sandwich and squinting at it before setting it back down. "Like you know," Livvy had said, and it was not the words, but the way the words had come out, a way Livvy never spoke to her. Lots of people talked to her that way, but never Livvy. Lark had waited for the apology, waited for Livvy to pet Lark's arm. But Livvy sat there, and it didn't occur to Lark that she could hiss something back or stand and walk away.

"One for *Peter Takes a Tugboat in His Underpants*. In 3D."

Livvy stared at her.

Lark wandered into the mouth of the mall, past the pretzel stand and the cell phone booth, going into the bright accessory store, with its walls of mirrors and spinning rack after spinning rack of sparkling headbands, earrings, phone cases, rings. Lark tried on headband after headband, all of them looking stupid. Her hair was too thin for headbands. "Help you?" a salesgirl said with aggressive niceness. She looked Lark's age, maybe older, her face perfectly done, dark swooshes of eyeliner, glittery lids, lips glossy and pink.

"I don't know," Lark said, wearing a headband of pink plastic flowers, its fat tag flopping over her ear.

"That's really *cuh-yoot*," the salesgirl said, touching the back of Lark's wrist lightly. "It looks good on you."

Lark had seven dollars in her pocket, two of which were for the bus back home, the 11:48, mostly drunks and vagrants, Livvy tired beside her at the end of her shift, head on Lark's shoulder, hair smelling of salty chemical tang.

"Try this one," the girl said, handing her a fat zebra-striped one. It looked stupid, but she let the girl say it was adorable. She let the girl clip a rhinestone barrette into her hair. She let the girl slide several clanking metal bangles onto her wrist. The girl's breath smelled like mint. Lark waved her arm around, watching the clanking. "You are so cute," the girl said, a girl who never normally would've talked to Lark, but Lark didn't care.

"I like your eyeliner," Lark said, and the girl laughed.

"You know what would be super cute?" she asked.

"What?"

"You need to get your ears pierced. It would look so good with your hair." She took Lark's hand—her hand!—and led Lark over to the counter, with spinning racks of stud earrings. Hearts. Smiley faces. Rhinestone flowers. "Piercing's free when you buy a starter pair." The girl talked about white gold or stainless-steel posts, aftercare solution, three weeks' maintenance. In the mirror, Lark's barrette sparkled at her, her hair pulled back in a way her hair was never pulled back. It made her forehead new. When she was little, she'd desperately wanted her ears pierced, but her mother had dismissed it. Waste of money. Earrings don't make a girl pretty. Her want had eventually burned off, which was the best thing, in Lark's estimation, that could happen to want.

It doesn't hurt like at all, the girl told her. Candace, she said her name was and she asked Lark's name. Lark! she called out. I love that! It hurt less than a shot, seriously. Babies get their ears pierced all the time. I pierced a little Black girl's ears this morning, Candace told her. She was like three months old, still in her car seat, pacifier in her mouth.

Lark loved Candace even while knowing better. It didn't matter. Love was love.

Each pair of studs she turned over said: $59.99 or $39.99 or $19.99. The rhinestone flower: $45.99.

"Aftercare is only an additional twelve dollars!" Candace said. Lark could see the end of this already, and it filled her with something beyond sadness: a flat nothing. "But you don't," Candace said, maybe seeing something in Lark's face, "have to do the aftercare." Salt water was fine. "They like us to push the aftercare solution."

Lark didn't know who *they* were, and she tried to sound like her new forehead when she asked, "What's the least expensive pair?" Was that disappointment in Candace's eyes, the quick flash of something?

Candace twirled one of the far racks slowly, showing Lark the half-off studs: stainless steel hearts and stars: $10.99. Stainless steel balls: $9.99. Already something was fading in Candace, especially when Lark took off the barrette and the bracelets and asked Candace to hang on. She'd be right back.

"K'I borrow five dollars?" she asked Livvy after the line was finished.

"No." Livvy squinted at her. "Why you need five dollars?"

"It's a surprise!" Lark said, and the hardness of Livvy's face made Lark think she'd keep saying no, but Livvy shook her head and reached under the ticket window for her purse, handing Lark four ones and four quarters, with a look like *don't do anything stupid.*

"Thanks, Mom!" Lark said as a joke.

Candace was with another girl who was getting a tiger-spotted purse and trying to decide on a phone case. She and Candace leaned close over the display, Candace handing her a sequined case. The girl squealed, and Candace squealed back. The girl had rings on most of her fingers and one thumb, three cool strands of silver necklaces. Lark didn't even have a wallet, the money all stuffed in her front pocket. She wasn't sure where to stand. She went back to the earring stand and picked up the stainless-steel balls. A girl who was not Candace—severely parted brown hair, too much mascara—asked if she could help Lark. Lark told her she was waiting for Candace. She watched the mascara girl go say something to Candace, now behind the register, and Candace looked Lark's way and nodded. "Hi," Lark called, then wished she hadn't.

"Hey," Candace said, finally coming over from the register. "Sorry about the wait."

"Nothing," Lark said from nervousness. "No problem."

"D'you pick one?" Candace asked and Lark held up the stainless-steel balls, Candace unclasping them from their velvety square, taking out what looked like a huge stapler, loading an earring into it, and swabbing Lark's left earlobe, front and back. She moved quickly now, a new, wordless efficiency. She held the stapler to Lark's ear.

"Okay, one—"

The flash of pain in Lark's ear was so hot, she gasped, pain radiating quickly into the side of her head as Candace pinched the backing on and moved to the other side, Lark wanting to stop her, wanting to call out, "Liar!" but Candace was so quick—so wordlessly quick—with loading the gun, with swabbing, with "Okay, one—"

Lark felt tears springing to her eyes, both ears pulsing with painful heartbeat.

Candace took out a hand mirror and said, "Look!" and "Look at you!" with a trace of her earlier warmth, though all Lark could see was the bright red of her lobes, fat around the tiny balls. And her chin. Lark could forget about her chin for a long, long time—even in the mirror—before she saw the thick worm of it again. The earrings brought her chin into relief. There was a reason she never did things like this.

Already Candace was marching up to the register, repeating about the salt water. But sea salt. Not table salt. Keep the starter earrings in for six weeks. Twist them but don't take them out. Sleep on your back. Candace went on and on—no rubbing alcohol, try not to touch your ears, always wash your hands—and now she was talking like everyone talked to Lark. She handed Lark a thin pamphlet, *Taking Care of Your Pierced Ears.* Lark didn't even get a pink bag. Candace rang her up, and Lark lay all her dollars and quarters on the counter. She tried to iron out the crumpled bills with her hand.

"It's fine," Candace said. "Do you want your penny?" It seemed shitty to make her say so. Lark shook her head.

She sat on a bench in the mall trying not to touch her ears, her jaw angry from the pain. Soon enough, everything would be closed except the entrance closest to the movie theaters and the circle of benches within spitting distance of the ticket booths. There used to be a Maserati sedan that was being auctioned off for charity, parked outside the theater behind velvety ropes. After the mall closed, while Lark waited for Livvy, she would slip under the ropes and sit in the driver's seat until the mall security told her to get out. One time she crawled into the back and fell asleep for the last while of Livvy's shift.

She sat on the circle of benches until the sides of her face were no longer on fire and the final rush of the nine p.m. shows had thinned. When she walked up to the ticket window, she saw how tired Livvy was, her face drawn. She was picking at a zit at her chin, making a scab.

"Hi," Lark said.

"What's your surprise?" Livvy said, and when Lark turned her head to the side, it took Livvy a minute. "What?" she said, not hiding her irritation. But then: "Holy fuck! That's so crazy! Look at you!" and that quick, Candace was obliterated. Livvy was clapping her hands and yelping, far in excess of the thing itself. It was a stupid pair of earrings, but Livvy's face bloomed into a huge grin, the first Lark had seen in days, and it wouldn't occur to Lark that perhaps it was not the earrings, but the unexpectedness of Lark doing something without Livvy that pleased Livvy. It wouldn't occur to Lark that she herself had a weight, a heft, which was momentarily lifted from Livvy by Lark going and doing something for herself, something as silly and stupid as punching holes into her own tender lobes.

She only cared about how Livvy took her hand at the end of the shift, braiding her fingers into Lark's through the dark mall parking lot; how Livvy tried to twiddle Lark's earlobe on the bus, Lark pulling away because they still ached and throbbed and you weren't supposed to touch; how they climbed the stairs to Livvy's apartment two by two, Lark sleeping over, telling Livvy all the rules Candace told her and Livvy saying, "Jesus, it's not like you got open heart," but so that the joke was on Candace, not on Lark, and Lark saying, "It is very important that I sleep on my back," in a funny voice so Livvy would laugh, but Livvy had made it up the stairs first, and when Lark got to the landing, Livvy's hand was up at her mouth, both hands, in fact, a crisscross over her lips, and Lark would think later about how ripped off she felt, their good time only lasting as long as the ride home; her ears hadn't even stopped pulsing. The earrings, in fact, would never come up between them again, even with a fiery infection the following week, the starter pair forced out by pus, the left hole sealing up on itself, then the right.

The paint on Livvy's door was still tacky, the word so huge and messy and dripping, it didn't even register as a word, but a snaking mess, Livvy standing there, so Lark stood there too, her least favorite feeling rising, until she understood it as a vertical message, five letters strung together in a strange cursive, but still, what does *lotch* mean? After Livvy woke her mom, and Susan came out, sleepy-headed and blinking, and tears sprang from Livvy's eyes, and the apartment manager came over in his robe, and the police showed up, Lark felt grateful for having pretended to know all along.

Police Log excerpt

6/1/2015-6/2/2015

...11:23 p.m. POLICE RESPONDED TO HIT AND RUN, CAR VERSUS BICYCLE. Officers dispatched to scene. Ambulance services dispatched to scene. Bicyclist suffered possible broken leg. Car identified as gray sedan, partial plates: CL9xxx

11:48 p.m. MULTIPLE MIPs CITED. Officers responded to noise disturbance in northwest neighborhood. Many minors found in home without parental supervision. Party dispersed, numerous minor in position citations.

12:08 a.m. CITIZEN REPORTS TARGETED VANDALISM. Officers dispatched to southeast apartment complex. Vandalism found on apartment door (profanity: "bitch"), with alleged target a minor. No security footage, no witnesses. No action taken...

WOODY

Doug sat straighter than usual, reading quickly off the end-of-year high-touch list, those students most in need of administrative contact in the final week of the semester. Roger, for all of his recent celebrity, was staring down two Ds and one F. Beau Cooper got caught cheating in algebra and was going to have to sit out this week's track meet. Olivia Albrecht was on her fourth absence in a row, the robocalls to the home and to mom's cell unreturned.

Woody had heard about the vandalism to Livvy's apartment—everyone had. It hadn't taken long on Monday morning for word to spread, though it did take some sorting to determine which story was true: a brick through her window, *dumb cunt* on her door, keyed side panels of the family car. In the end, *bitch* seemed comparatively tame, though Woody spent most of first period trying to flag her to his office before she was confirmed absent. The rest of the week had rolled by as weeks were wont to: finalizing next year's student schedules, quadruple checking senior transcripts against graduation requirements, and now it was Thursday, Livvy still gone.

"Anyone talk to the boy?" Woody asked, and he knew full well Baz's name, though he had a mild contempt for teachers like Danita Leininger and counselors like Deirdre Benson (J-S) who traded in closeness with the kids, taking up their battles as their own, cawing at their indignities, proudly bearing the hyphen: teacher-friend, counselor-friend.

"It's finished with the Fenning boy. That's what I heard, at least. Broken up." Doug held his hands up in the air, a strange shrug that meant possibly: *what do I know?* Or *win some lose some*. Or simply, *kids*.

"Sure," Woody said, "sure sure," though he felt surprisingly stung. If there was anyone who eschewed the hyphenate, it was Doug Epstein. The kids made fun of his occasional bolo tie and called him Taz for the devil who dervished around the desert. Kids never told Doug anything. Doug was always the last to know.

"I can follow up, see what's up," Woody said.

"Who's on first," Doug said. "What's on second. All that jazz."

When Woody called the Albrecht residence, Susan's voice on the answering machine told him to leave a message, and he did: Woody, Woody Hanover, from the high school, concerned, wanting to check in, attendance policy. When he tried Susan's cell, it was the computerized voice announcing that the user's voicemail had not been activated.

End of day, no return call.

Home visits normally came after a full week of non-excused absences and in coordination with one of the district's school-home liaisons, but Woody could fuzz the line with barely a week left of the school year. When he called home, Alison and Francie were still at the open rec hours of the gymnastics gym where Francie took her pre-K tumbling class and "jazz dance." For jazz dance recital, the nine girls wore silver-sequined berets and manipulated pink fluffy boas behind their necks while they step-step-kicked across the tumbling mats toward their parents, a discomfiting row of loosely synchronized, tiny, pot-bellied showgirls.

There was a din from Alison's end, different in pitch from the din of the high school, though a close cousin: many children, colliding. "You should see her on the trampoline! She learned seat drop. Yeah, seat drop! You go, girl! I'll get a video. Do it again in a second for Daddy. No, let this little boy have a turn and then you can go again, and I'll video. Come off, Francie. Do you want to go home right now? Let this little boy, let this little boy. I'm talking to Daddy. Honey—Woody, you still there?"

Coming home later was fine. Al would pick up something on their way back, a McSomething. Hour? Hour and a half? That was fine.

Woody pulled the Albrecht residence from the student database and drove east and then south a bit, past the neighborhoods of well-tended Craftsmans into one of the outer spokes of the district. District lines had been redrawn repeatedly during Woody's tenure, often to retract the bounds of West, West the best high school in town, the district accused of its own version of gerrymandering to keep the middle class safely in-bounds and the rest of the town, out. The district defended itself by pointing to the neighborhoods of rental properties like the one Woody drove through now. The Albrecht's complex was small, two identical buildings, each with pale siding, a blue rooftop that matched blue railings of the back patios. Woody could see how the recessed stairwells to the second-floor units would make for the perfect shadowy cover for a Roger Bass and a Miles Cobain or any of their many compatriots with spray paint cans and endless appetite toward ill-gotten injury. The new paint was bright on their door, the repair sloppy, only covering the offending word, the original, dingy color still visible around the edges.

"Oh," Susan said when she answered the door (he'd had to ring twice), the front of her hair clipped in a barrette, her face damp, a face towel in her hands. She was in a skirt and blouse, though her stocking feet were bare. She looked like she wasn't used to her doorbell ringing.

"Sorry," Woody said. "Woody. Woody Hanover from West. I left a message... I tried to call..."

Susan patted the towel to her chin. "I know who you are, Woody," she said, though not unkindly. "How can I—? What are you—?"

"We've been leaving messages about Livvy, Olivia's absences, but we haven't heard back."

"Absences?"

"She hasn't been to school this week. She here?"

"Fuck."

The word from her mouth so surprised Woody—she was among the last people he would guess let loose with a spontaneous *Fuck*—he may have uttered an inappropriate *guh* or *gah*, and he most certainly (and inappropriately) smiled, which was why the school-home liaisons were always to accompany, because you never knew what you were going to get with people on their home turf.

"Come," Susan told him, stepping backward in her stockinged feet. "Come in."

It was nice inside, nicer than he expected from the outside, minimal without being spare, and with surprising touches—a butcher-block dining room table with four molded plastic chairs, three white, one a bright red. Beside the living room loveseat was a chaise—or at least he assumed it a chaise—that looked like nothing so much as a large gray stuffed cube topped with pillows. He'd never seen anything quite like it. Was it for sitting? Day sleeping? A low bookshelf was taken up by cookbooks and travel guides, half a shelf devoted to *Gates of Shabbat, Choosing a Jewish Life: Revised and Updated*, and several maroon Bibles side by side by side, but not Bibles; he knew they weren't Bibles, but couldn't think of the word, the spines unhelpful. *Tanakh*, said one. *Kol Haneshamah*, another.

Where he expected a television atop the sideboard were instead two stone sculptures. No, not stone. Susan had excused herself to the back of the apartment, leaving Woody alone out here. Livvy wasn't home. Susan hadn't seen her since before work, when the girl was up, dressed, convincingly ready to catch the bus with her backpack on.

Close up, Woody could see the sculptures were clay, a deep, browned clay, and one of them possibly a figure: a person-type thing lifting one leg in the air. The other, he wasn't sure. Smaller sculptures—a few an earthy red, one a stark white—dotted end tables and the kitchen counter, all with the same strange, leggy appendages.

When Susan came back, she'd changed into a gray track suit, her hair unclipped. The track suit surprised Woody like the *fuck* had, and the strange furniture, and the sculptures. I mean, what had he expected? Something more workaday or maybe tragic or maybe close-lipped. More prudish, less weird.

"Can I get you a drink?" she said on her way to the fridge.

"No, no, thanks. This a person?" he said of the sculpture.

"Shore bird."

"Shore bird?"

"A whimbrel. Do you mind if I have one?" She was holding up a beer bottle.

"Not at all."

He met her at the table. She chose a white chair, so he did too. "Livvy's?" he said of the bright red one, and she made a noncommittal noise.

"Okay," she said. "I'm ready. As ready as I will be. Tell me."

He told her—the absences, the messages, the unreturned calls. Four days and counting.

"God," she said, hands over her mouth. "I had no idea. I mean, really, I had no idea. She leaves in the morning. She comes back around, I don't know, now-ish." Susan looked to the door, as if mentioning might make it so. "I'm not keeping exact tabs. She's home after me sometimes. That's not usual. Afternoons with Lark…" She trailed off.

"The school has been robocalling this number and your cell every day."

"No," she said, shaking her head, drinking her beer. "Nothing."

Easy enough to deduce what was happening to the answering machine messages. Kids did worse than erase robocalls, that's for sure. He told her about her cell phone not accepting voicemails.

She held her hands out to either side of her head and shook them as if zapped with electricity, and made a loud, growling "arrr-aggggh" noise. It was strange to know someone like Woody knew Susan Albrecht, which was to say for half his life and not at all. "I hate my phone. I mean, I hate the existence of cell phones generally and I hate mine in specific. I mostly ignore it, which is why I'm the least popular mom in the soccer mom set." She half-laughed and then looked entirely serious and then swigged a long swig from her beer.

"The jazz dance set," Woody said, a throwaway line Susan ignored. She was fishing her phone out of her purse—it was an old flip phone— and pressing at the keys. Woody had forgotten how long it took to tap out messages on those things, 3-3-3 #-#-#-# 9-9. Maybe he would take a beer. A big gray cat loped into the room, making a strange noise, as it came right to Woody, pressed the top of its head to Woody's pant leg.

"Wall-E," Susan said. "He likes everybody. He thinks he's a dog."

Woody did not mention his cat allergy. *Morp morp,* said the cat. "What's that noise?"

Susan laughed, the sound of it ragged, the sort of laugh that could be mistaken for crying. "He's meowing," and then: "Do you know what they wrote on our door?"

He did.

"Does this have to do with that?" she asked.

"I really don't know."

"Obviously she's being bullied. I mean, is she being bullied? I know she stood up for the Bass kid, and I'm really proud of that…" She trailed off. She was barefaced, not a lick of makeup, her green eyes almost like a child's, so full of question.

"I wouldn't say bullied." He wasn't trying to be obtuse. It was complicated, and there was so much he could say. Livvy was a minor, and theirs was a guidance, not a therapeutic relationship, so he wasn't bound by confidentiality. He was well within his rights to tell Susan anything Livvy had told him, anything he'd observed or even heard secondhand. He could disclose about the relationship to Baz, the escalation from there, the apparent breakup. It would be a kindness, in so many ways, to tell Susan about her daughter. But he liked Livvy, and he was protective of their relationship.

"Is she being slut-shamed?" Susan blurted, and then she put her hand over her mouth. "Oh god, I don't even know if she's a virgin. She doesn't talk to me, but she was really upset about the graffiti. So was I. I kept asking her who she thought did it and why, and she kept telling me she had no idea."

"She's a good kid, Susan." It was strange saying a person's name the first few times. It made a new shape in the mouth. "Ask her what's up. It's been intense at West lately."

"Yes, sir," she said. And then: "Thanks."

He would take a drink if that was still okay.

Yeah, of course it's okay.

"Sorry," she said, walking back from the fridge with an IPA. "You want a glass?" she asked, after setting the bottle on the table. No, he was fine. She flipped open her flip phone, looked, flipped it back closed. "You know the worst thing about being a single parent?"

"The guidance counselor showing up at your door unannounced."

She laughed a little. "Not having anyone to talk about your kid with. Is she out doing meth right now? Is she on angel dust?"

"I don't think angel dust is a thing anymore," he said, trying to be funny, but also, he was pretty sure it wasn't a thing.

She gave the same half-laugh. "Now it's molly and special k. What happened to uppers? Or downers? Where did that stuff go?"

"Medicare?" He was trying to be funny again, less successfully, and she rolled her eyes as she held the beer bottle to her lips. There, that disapproval, that was the Susan Hoffman he remembered from high school.

They drank their beer. She checked the flip phone a few more times. "The one person I'd like to communicate with via this damn thing…"

"She'll call," Woody said, not believing himself. The molded plastic chair was surprisingly comfortable. It curved to Woody's back, holding him straight and pressing at his lumbar.

"That one's funny," he said of the red chair.

"I don't think I skipped a single day of high school," Susan said.

His phone made a noise from his pocket. Alison. **We're home! Food is warm!** By his watch, Woody had been here twenty-five minutes.

"Life is always one text away, isn't it?" Susan said. He couldn't discern her tone. Did she have a tone? "A whimbrel," she said, pointing to the person-like sculpture. "Has these long legs and this crazy beak. The beak discombobulates you. You can't make sense of it. We'd see them all the time up in Alaska when we visited Len's parents. I was a little obsessed."

"Len was from Alaska?" It occurred to him from the drift in the conversation and from the way Susan kept an ear cocked to the noises outside, she was trying to keep him here until Livvy returned.

Yes, Len was from Alaska. Most of his family was still up there. Lea, her oldest, had moved there to work after a couple years of college. "It didn't take," Susan said.

"College?"

"Yeah, and staying close to me, I guess too."

"She work in one of those big processing plants? Or on a boat?" Woody couldn't picture Alaska aside from snow, icebergs, that kid who died in his van.

"Car insurance." Susan and Len had gone up to Alaska every summer with the kids when the kids were little, before Len got sick. "I think it got in Lea's blood. Olivia was barely a preschooler. She hates when we visit in the summers now. She can't stand all the daylight. She says it makes her queasy."

"Maybe she's a vampire," Woody said stupidly. Susan was kind enough to ignore him.

"Harlequin duck," she said, pointing to another sculpture. "Black-legged kittiwakes," another.

"I'm not seeing—" he said, squinting, trying to understand how the sculptures were birds. "I don't quite—"

"Don't worry. They're figurative," she said. "Not literal. I was never good enough to try literal."

"You made these?"

"I made these."

"You're a sculptor?"

"I'm a legal secretary," she said with a certain pitch. "And a mom. Mother of the year." She smiled a wry—or maybe tired, end of day, daughter nowhere to be found—smile.

"You're doing fine," he said. "When did you make these?"

"A long time ago. A looooooong time ago. I keep them out to embarrass Olivia." She took the final swig from her beer. "It's so funny that you're a guidance counselor now because you used to be such a shitty listener."

"When did we even have a conversation?"

"Exactly. You don't remember me telling you I wanted to be an artist, do you? You were one of the very first people I told, and you never talked to me again." She was smiling.

"Seriously, I think you're mistaking me for someone else."

"No, I am not, Woody Hanover. I told you I was going to be an artist when we were locked in Steve Malcolm's closet."

Woody coughed a little on his beer.

"I remember Steve Malcolm's closet," he said, finding it more than a little surreal that here they were talking about Steve Malcolm's closet at her butcher-block table in strange plastic chairs, waiting for her teen-aged daughter to arrive home. "But there was no talking."

"*You* didn't want any talking, but it was dark in there and I barely knew you and so I said it. It was the first time I said it aloud to anyone but my sister. And then you lunged at me." Still, a laugh to her voice.

"I was fourteen! And I swear to you, you said nothing to me."

"I said it all to you." She was looking at him straight on, serious for a second, and then, a smile. She checked her watch. "I need to get the licht."

Woody didn't know what the licht meant. Susan disappeared into the kitchen, and he listened to her in and out of drawers. "If I'd known I'd have company, I would've made a challah."

"You make challah?" Woody said. She was back with two silver candle holders, two thick white candles. She set up the candles and candle sticks with quick efficiency, lighting the bottoms of the candles, soldering their wax to the candle holders. He felt—what was her word?—discombobulated. "How did I not know you're Jewish?" he said.

"That's not your shitty memory," she said. "I converted when I got married."

"Len was a Jew from Alaska?"

"It's all very weird."

Woody laughed so hard at this—it was the truest thing she'd said all night—it came out like a bark. There was the Jew from Alaska, and whimbrels, and Steve Malcolm's closet, and one red chair, and his family at home. Susan asked if he would like to light the candles with her. She said, "I never thought I would take to it like I have, but I have loved it so much." He wasn't sure of the meaning of *it* but did not ask. He wanted to ask, but his family at home. He knew he should go.

"I should," he said, up from the plastic chair, his beer nearly empty. "Dinner," he said, waving his phone.

"Of course, of course," she said but quickly blanched—he saw it—her eyes wide, lips in a small *o*, before her face went back to normal, or what he assumed was normal for someone he had not been in a room with for twenty years and now had seen twice in one week. "Go," she said, patting him on the arm, still holding the lighter. "You should go. I really appreciate you stopping by. It's above and beyond."

He got his coat, his keys, foresaw the sitcom moment in which he opened the door only for Livvy to be on the other side of it. "She's a good kid," he repeated, opening the door only into nighttime. "I like her a lot, and I don't say that about most kids."

"The guidance counselor who dislikes children." She was smiling.

"Ask her what's been going on. Come right out and ask her."

Susan breathed a deep breath. "Yes, sir," she said, and it wasn't sarcasm, it was the same tone she'd had the whole time, a joking/not joking that he realized the girl had too. Livvy looked nothing like her mother, but she was quick and clever with him too, jabs that weren't jabs, pokes that weren't pokes, all of it code for *help me, Woody. Fucking help.*

"Goodnight," Susan called behind him. "Thanks."

"Happy Shabbat," he called out, then felt silly for it, and after he went through the door, he turned around one last time as he started down the stairs. Why had he turned? To see if she was still standing there? It was only the closed door, the new paint looking even worse under the glare of the porch light, the shadow of most of the letters clear beneath, as if the painter had started out with vigor and quickly lost steam: ITCH.

He climbed the stairs quickly, pulling a card from his wallet, knocking. "My number's on there," he said, as soon as she opened the door, answering the question she did not yet ask. He could have added on so many conditionals—*if you need anything, if there's trouble, if Livvy doesn't come home*—conditionals what he traded in all day long: *if you need one more set of eyes on your essay, if you don't get your grades up, if you find an online geometry course this summer.* But it was late, and his family was at home, and the names of strange birds filled his head, and at any moment, Livvy could round the corner and bound up this very staircase, and all of this made it seem he should hurry, demanding a declarative: "Call."

SUMMER

LARK

It was delicious, the way days weren't days, they were just time, and time was shapeless, elongated, forming around nothing. Afternoons spread and spread. If Livvy was working matinees, Lark might not get out of bed until noon, her mom closed away in her room, and as long as Lark was quiet, her mom wouldn't come out for hours. Lark would put the TV on low, flip through old comics on the couch, let ice chips melt on her tongue.

Days when Livvy was off, they would lie around Livvy's apartment, eating Otter Pops, their lips turning blue, purple, red. When they were little, they used to pretend like they were ladies with red lipstick, prancing around on tippy toes, invisible high heels. "Oh, I'm going to a meeting," they sang. "Oh, I have to go get little Bobby from the sitter." Days when Baz didn't have his internship (downtown software firm, friend of his dad's), he was at Livvy's too, spread out on the gray cube-couch with Livvy.

They were back together. They'd stayed broken up a week, and then there was another week that Livvy ditched school, during which Baz drove off-campus at lunch to meet at her place. He picked her up after school and they drove and drove for hours. Nobody knew, nobody except for Lark. After Livvy's mom busted her for skipping, Livvy and Baz passed each other dead-eyed in the hall during the final week of school, back to sitting at their separate lunch tables, Baz with Shocky and Monique in the cafeteria, Livvy with Lark. Lark marveled at their self-control, no stolen glances, no smirking half-smiles. Lark alone knew of their near-constant text messaging, the way Baz snuck each afternoon to Livvy's apartment where Livvy was supposed to be grounded, Livvy's mom calling on the landline to check.

That the three of them held a secret together was electric to Lark, exhilarating, marking her place in their lives as indelible. There was her relationship to Livvy, then her relationship to Baz and Livvy, then her relationship to the secret, which was perhaps the meatiest of all. She often felt like life held an undercurrent that everyone else had better access to than she. What a joy, to be in that undercurrent, existing inside the answer to a question other people didn't even know to ask!

Today the three of them flipped through TV channels on the tiny television that Livvy's mom kept hidden behind bureau doors, Lark lying across the loveseat, her knees hooked over one arm, Baz and Livvy on the pillow-couch, the apartment swollen with humidity. When Baz was over, there was none of Livvy and Lark's usual summertime wanderings—the city pool, the 7-Eleven for Slurpees, the Goodwill for cheap tank tops or new (used) shorts. She would think back on this brief period with great fondness, the three of them closed off together from anything but what was right here: Wall-E curled on Lark's belly, purring; the noise from the TV; Baz's lips even redder than theirs from his Otter Pop. For long stretches, Lark sometimes stared at Baz's Blackness, which in fact was not black but dark, dark brown, the backs of his hands grayed around each fingernail. *It's not polite to stare*, her mother always told her.

He and Livvy lay propped up on the nest of pillows, their legs intertwined across the gray cushion. Livvy was half watching TV, half looking at her phone. Each time Lark tried to shift out from under Wall-E, Wall-E stood, arched his back, pawed Lark's belly, and settled back down. She couldn't bring herself to shove him off. The heat and the secret and the TV made Lark far away and blinky. Blink, blink. The slick of her eyeballs, the sweat of her lids, her body hers and not, which was how she normally felt but now more pleasantly.

Dr. Phil yelled at women about their alcoholic husbands, their crying children. Ladies used paper towels to clean up perfectly spilled messes. Girls talked about tampons while wearing white shorts that gave them wedgies up the butt.

"What do you think it's like to be the girl in that commercial?" Baz said. "Is she embarrassed at her school or is she showing off like she's a famous actress now?"

Livvy laughed and pretzeled herself deeper into Baz, Baz skinny though something about his Adam's apple suggesting *man*. Lark was impressed and embarrassed that he could reference the tampon commercial, since Lark had waited for the thirty seconds to quietly pass. Livvy and Lark could spend entire afternoons in silence together; it was Baz who turned out to be the talker. "Like, can you see her strutting around being like *I'm the shit*." His girl voice was a lot like their ladies with lipstick voices. Livvy laughed, harder than necessary, holding her belly.

Sometimes it seemed like Livvy was performing for Lark: *this is what it's like to be in love.* The way Livvy's thigh was wedged between Baz's legs now, the way he wriggled and squirmed, it seemed Livvy's thigh was probably pressed against his penis. It reminded Lark of the safer sex assembly when Belfry had said the words "dry humping" in front of the whole ninth grade, and people shrieked and hooted.

"She's like, *bow down to me, bitches,*" Livvy said. "*I'm the tampon queen!*"

Tampon, Lark said inside her mouth, tampon something she wanted and dreaded and found unfathomable. She'd taken tampons out of the box in Livvy's bathroom and scrunched the wrappers off, picking at the cotton batting. Always, all the time she had a feeling like she was missing something, an emptiness needing filled, but with *this*?

"Jesus Christ," Livvy said. "Shaina Abramovitz posted a picture of her and Lindsay Nichols at the pool. Check out their stomachs." She stretched to hand the phone to Baz, who screwed his face up as he looked and then clucked a noise.

"Put that away," he said. "Stop paying attention to those fools."

"What?" Lark said.

"They're total idiots," Livvy said. "I'm gonna comment."

"Don't," Baz said, his voice serious for the first time. "You'll only feed them."

"Everyone's telling them how great they are. It has 207 likes. Who's *briarpatch*? They wrote: 'I like my girls hot and smart like you too' and he spelled 'two' wrong." Livvy laughed at this, but it wasn't her regular laugh, something pokey to it.

"Don't," Baz said. "Pretend they're nothing."

"They *are* nothing," Livvy said.

"Ignorant fools," Baz said. They'd untangled a little, backed against their pillows.

"What?" Lark said.

"Lindsay wrote *Bass* and Diane wrote *Cobain* in sunscreen on their stomachs. Now they have sun tattoos," Livvy said. "Don't they have anything better to do with their summer?"

"Like us," Lark said, raising her Otter Pop. She was serious and not serious and serious. Wall-E had one too-long nail that poked through Lark's tank top. She tried to shift him, a bear of a cat.

"Why you even friends with Shaina on there?" Baz asked.

"We were in Hebrew school together. She didn't used to be such an idiot."

Lark had always been jealous of the Hebrew school era, even if she'd never want to go to school on a Sunday. But it was a whole vein of Livvy's life that had nothing to do with her, a whole *language*. Lark and her mom weren't anything; never went to church, had Christmas like everyone else (except Livvy). She'd been here for shabbat a million times (when they were little they screamed a dinosaur song and got to tear the challah with their hands) and years of seders, but even so, she'd been stunned by Livvy's bat mitzvah: Livvy up on the stage, in a tasseled shawl, singing in Hebrew to a tune that made no sense to Lark but also kind of did. It all seemed impossible to Lark, Livvy chanting, and the backward prayerbook, and Livvy carrying around the Torah while singing through the aisles. Lark was supposed to kiss the backward prayerbook and press it to the Torah as Livvy passed, but she had felt unworthy and afraid. After, she'd talked and talked and talked to Livvy about that day, how none of it made any sense but also, it was amazing. Livvy got tired of it; she kept telling Lark to stop making such a big deal. Livvy didn't even know what the words meant, and the best part was that she got a treadmill for her room and $1,200 in checks. The other best part was she didn't have to go to Hebrew school anymore.

Dr. Phil came back on now with a new lady whose pale roots grew like straw from the part in her hair. Box fans blew the hot air from outside to in.

"It's so stupid here," Livvy said, the kind of thing Livvy said only when Baz was here. They could do what they wanted at Livvy's. They didn't have to be careful. Lark's mom was home all day on disability ("for nerves," she used to say before she stopped saying) and they had to make sandwiches from saltines and margarine, eat Raisin Bran dry, sucking the raisins for their sugar.

But when Baz was over, Livvy was sorry all the time. Sorry the TV was so small and no pay channels. Sorry they had to walk through her mom's room to get to the one bathroom with the unclogged sink. Sorry her mom's sculptures were stupid and everywhere. Lark hated Livvy a little during the sorrys, without realizing. Mostly she just felt ashamed.

"When do we get to go to *your* house?" Livvy asked Baz. She asked this regularly. Lark was never sure the meaning of *we*.

"My dad's home. I don't want my parents all up in my—" He waved a hand, then brought it down to rest on Livvy's hair, tucking it behind her ear.

"He teaches a class, you said." This was the closest thing they had to a fight. "You said he goes to campus."

"Like two hours a day."

"Let's go during those two hours."

Lark recognized this Livvy, the one who wanted and drilled straight down into that want. Lark, not that anyone asked her, didn't much want to go to Baz's. She knew where professors' kids lived, either in the neighborhood where kids from all over the city trick-or-treated for the full-sized Snickers bars or on the fancy streets near campus, but not too near so as to mingle with the frat houses and cheap undergrad apartments.

"Fine," he said. "My mom's out of town next week. She has to go back home. My gammy keeps running away."

"You call your grandma Gammy?" Livvy poked him in his side, and he laughed and told her to shut up. "Your mom isn't even home during the day."

"I know," he said. "But you never know with her."

"Dun! Dun! Dun!" Livvy said, making horror movie noise, poking him again. There was a lot of poking.

Baz tried to grab her hand. "And my brother's there with his aide. You got to be okay with that."

"Of course I'm okay with that." She bit his ear. "I want to meet your brother."

"He's cool," Baz said in answer to a question no one asked. There was something in the brevity of this declaration, and in the air of non-chalance that was effort toward nonchalance that made Lark love Baz, the way he was escaping something too. "It's not like they're gonna narc us out," he said, as if he were convincing himself. "He'll be fine. We don't really have people over too much. It's hard meeting new people," he said. "It's hard."

"Oh, I know it is," Livvy said. "It sure is," a joke in her voice, rolling over onto him in such a way that Lark stopped looking, both of them laughing and rustling and making general couch noises as the camera panned to Dr. Phil's wife, who had to sit there every day, upright and smiling in the front row.

Livvy and Baz made nipping murmurs and half laughs until Livvy stood, though slowly, her body languid with heat, shimmers of sweat across her collarbone, in the crooks of her arms. She held a hand to

Baz, and he took it, letting out a long groan as she pulled him off the couch. They were blocking the TV, though Lark hardly cared. Dr. Phil kind of scared her or grossed her out, so she didn't say, "Move it." They were going to move it soon enough. That's what happened when Baz and Livvy got up from the couch like this, Livvy taking him by the hand to Livvy's mom's room with its window air conditioner, the only room they weren't allowed in. They didn't even say anything to Lark anymore like *see you soon* or *be right back*, this a part of their day-less days, their timeless time, the secret within the secret, Livvy handing Lark the remote control as they passed.

Baz's eyes glistened with the heat too, both of their stares far-off as if they were already imagining what they would do to each other in that dark, cool room, things Lark and Wall-E would hear through the wall, the noise of bodies and mouths and bed frames that made no sense and all the sense, noises she didn't particularly like or enjoy but could cover with the television as she changed from channel to channel. She always landed on the same bright cartoons of the kids' station they'd long outgrown, the explorer girl and the sea sponge. She listened for when Baz and Livvy were nearly done in the other room, so she could change the channel quick to the housewives or the tattoo shop so that Baz and Livvy wouldn't make fun of her even though they never had. But she couldn't be too careful, because the moment of return, their eyes no longer glistening, their cheeks newly pink, it was the moment she was most different from them, and they from her. If she knew it, they did too, and it felt dangerous, all the knowing without saying, Livvy and Baz big as the world, Lark a tiny slip, dwarfed by even a cat, and she had to be someone be something be anything they still wanted around.

WOODY

He was building a playhouse out back. It was less a playhouse and more a shed. Less a shed and more a rectangular pod, absent one long wall. As Woody sawed the 2x4s and ran the drill, he came to liken it to Francine's dollhouse, fourth wall similarly removed, though in this case Francine was the doll. It was for Francie and her friend Tamara and their friend Vincent so they could all play at the little wooden table and chairs he'd gotten off Craigslist, the plastic tea set, the tempera paints, the easel. Currently the three kids ran in and out of the actual house in their bathing suits, in and out of the baby pool, long wet trails behind them as they screamed and chalked pictures on the back patio's cement, yelled about ants spotted in the cracks, fought over the tire swing. Inside, Alison and the two other mothers, Allison #2—how quickly preschool mothers bonded, the two Al(l)isons seeming to need little more than that—and Deborah (pronounced de-BORE-ahh) sat inside the sliding doors at the kitchen table.

Last time Woody had gone inside to refill his water, his Alison was recounting their IVF treatments without a hint of embarrassment. "Deborah," Alison announced to Woody, "is trying to get pregnant."

He'd nodded from the sink.

"We tried everything, right, honey?" she said. Alison reeled off the list: Clomid, then Bravelle, then Fertinex, then insemination, he and Alison with different notions of what was private.

Depending on the angle of the sun, Woody could see their faces from out here, the coffee cups, the way Deborah opened her mouth preposterously wide when she laughed. Mostly they were silhouettes.

Regularly, Alison—his Alison—came out to tend to the children with trays of fresh orange slices, fresh towels, fresh chalk. She refilled the pool when it got too grassy. She reapplied sunscreen with army-like efficiency, the kids lined up in a row while she ordered them to close their eyes, spraying them from tip to toe. Alison was gifted at curating Francie's days. Woody often had the sense that his daughter's experience of childhood was so different from his own, the word *childhood* no longer held, this no more evident than in the fact of spray sunscreen.

Woody could still feel the unpleasant plying of his skin as grown-ups rubbed in the lotion. Childhood without suffering was—?

Eventually, Alison brought him an iced tea.

"I'm the envy of the neighborhood with you out here," she said. "The ladies are impressed."

"It must be my strapping manliness," Woody said, making a Popeye muscle-armed pose. He'd sweated through his T-shirt, and it stuck now to his less-than-lean chest.

Alison threw her head back and laughed. It looked like Deborah's laugh. Every school year, home slipped more and more from Woody, especially since Francie. He'd watch the height chart on her door tick up, same as he noticed the rug in the living room change—start of year, Indian-patterned elephants; winter, bright stripes; spring, interlocking geometric squares. One month, they were giving up processed foods, the next dairy, first due to Francie's constipation, then because of a documentary. He spent nine months nodding, saying, "Okay, okay, okay."

Summer was the time to ease back, to come up with projects in close proximity to his family, to work with his hands, to watch how Francie's belly still popped out beneath a polka-dotted swimsuit, though her left cheek dimple seemed to have disappeared. It was the time to drink iced tea, so refreshing with mint leaves floating at the top. Alison was really good with the fresh mint leaves. She kissed him, even though he was disgusting. Woody appreciated the way Alison still bothered with lipstick and eye makeup when the other moms went barefaced, sitting around the table in their flip-flops and saggy shirts, as if guarding against someone mistaking them for a person. He looked to see if the other women were watching now, his hand on Alison's waist, but he couldn't tell; silhouettes.

Susan had called.

He'd been waiting without realizing he'd been waiting. The Tuesday after his visit, Livvy back in school for three days, he picked up a voicemail. *Hi, Woody. Wondering how it's going there. How she's doing. Nothing specific. General is okay, you know? An update.* She sounded nervous—or like she was bad at leaving messages. For a beat and then another, Woody listened to the sound of someone not hanging up, and then a final *Okay.*

He'd only seen Livvy once before school's end, when he'd pulled her out of Midlarsky's on her first day back. "I'm okay," she'd said, declining his invitation to come chat in his office. They stood in the hallway,

Livvy chewing on the side of her lip, looking at her feet. "I'm fine," she repeated, and Woody couldn't help but feel deflated, having imagined a renewed intimacy from her, expecting that the night before in her apartment had cemented something between them, even if such a thought was nonsensical, even if there was a good chance Livvy had no idea he'd even been there. He wanted, simply, parity in their consciousnesses; if the Albrechts were foremost in his mind, Woody should be lodged too in theirs.

He called Susan back that first time, late for an administrative staff meeting. She seems good, he told her. Making it to all of her classes, catching up on work. He didn't know the last part to be officially true, but he hadn't heard otherwise. She's not talking, Susan told him. Her normal withdrawal now seemed downright expansive. It's like she's challenged herself in a contest to not speak a single word.

"Why does she hate me?" Susan said, and the question was so plaintive and bare, so without shame, it was not self-deprecating or rhetorical. She really wanted an answer.

"It's developmental," he said. Deirdre (J-S) walked past his office door. *Coming?* she mouthed of the ad staff meeting. He held up a finger. "It's not you. This is how kids are supposed to be at this age. You know the ones I worry about? The ones who still cuddle with their mommies. The ones who still say *Daddy*."

Susan laughed. "There are ones who still say Daddy?"

"You wouldn't believe what those parent conferences are like," he said, and he heard Susan say something not to him: *In a minute. As soon as the copier is fixed. The repair guy's been called.* She too was at work, between obligations.

"Is there lap sitting?" she asked, not missing a beat.

"Practically."

The next call: Monday, back from the weekend.

"My therapist," she said plainly, "says all of my codependence with Olivia is misplaced guilt over Len's death."

Woody thought of how Alison talked and talked to girlfriends on the phone, her mother, her sister in St. Louis. In the earliest days of Francie, when the breastfeeding wasn't working and Alison's nipples sprouted brutal blisters, and Francie screamed in her arms, Alison's most doleful middle-of-the-night cry came when she said, "How am I supposed to talk on the *phone*?"

Woody's phone calls were normally transactional. He called the high school two counties over for transcripts. He called the bank because there was a duplicate charge on his debit card.

"You killed Len?" he joked, wishing immediately he hadn't. "Why do you feel guilty?"

"Isn't that what motherhood is?" she said with the same plainness. If she was offended by the joke, she didn't let on. "Guilt and more guilt."

"I don't know."

"Fatherhood is to motherhood like fish is to solar system."

The next call was Tuesday, the very next day. He'd been waiting for it while realizing he'd been waiting.

"I'm hiding in the bathroom," she said. "My boss is on a rampage."

"Against you?"

"Me insofar as I'm someone with a heartbeat in his general proximity."

"Crouch on top of the toilet seat. That's what kids do during bathroom sweeps."

"You sound like you work in a prison."

"If it walks like a prison, and talks like a prison…"

Susan laughed.

"Quiet," Woody said. "You'll give yourself away."

He wasn't normally good at banter. Al was good at banter. Deirdre (J-S) made an entire career out of banter.

It had been his last week on the clock, the students gone, the expansive quiet so delightful, he suspected that keeping faculty in the building one week past students was the district's way of tricking them into coming back the following fall.

"I'm not going to be in my office this summer," he told her.

"Oh," she said, and then: "Of course. All right."

They sat with a silence and in that silence, Woody said something to himself. He said: *We're friends. This is my new friend, Susan.* He said it to himself as if from a script, he reading the part of: Self.

"I mean, though, if anything comes up with Livvy, you have my email, right? My school email?"

She did not. He gave it to her. "I don't check it every day, but I do check it."

He, it turned out, checked it every day. Susan was a good writer, funny, very much herself. He was done being surprised at what herself was, couldn't remember what he thought herself should be or what herself was in the long-ago dark closet, Susan herself having replaced all previous ideas of Susan.

Nine words my daughter has said to me in the past ten days: <eye-roll> (not technically a word); guh; dunno; bye <accompanied by door slam>, pshht (the sound of her answer to any question); we're out of ketchup.

He tried to be funny back to his new friend, Susan. He couldn't remember the last time he had a new friend. That wasn't part of adulthood. He had a wife, a child, a job. He had Alison's friends, and couple friends (Alison's friends plus their husbands). There were two guys he'd known since high school, Raymond Cowley and Dan Sheridan, who he watched football with sometimes, went out for an occasional beer, listened to Dan complain about palimony and his second wife's champagne tastes, ribbed Raymond about his novelty facial hair: muttonchops or a long and trailing soul patch. Woody had forgotten how friendship happened: first you didn't know someone, and then bit by little bit, you did, which was as exhilarating as it was unexpected.

Often, he responded while he and Alison were side by side in bed, watching late-night television, tablets in their laps. Alison loved all the games of matching jewels or candies or fruits. *Plink. Plink. Kazoom. Plink. Plink.* She did not like the South African comedy news host who'd replaced the American comedy news host, but they still watched the show. Or half-watched.

My four-year-old has a pretend cell phone on which she pretend texts. She asked me if I was on Facebook, and when I told her no, she said, "Why not? Facebook makes everyone famous." This is a sign of the apocalypse, no?

In writing, he was clever, quick, lithe. This story wasn't true. It had been Vincent who'd said this to Deborah about Facebook, as relayed to him by Alison. There were times he was so pleased with his emails to his new friend, Susan, he turned to Alison and pawed her in the way he used to paw her, nibbling on a shoulder, sucking softly on her ear. The business with the ear used to make her go crazy, used to make her moan, already wet when he put his hand between her legs. Now the *Plink. Plink. Kazoom* persisted long past when he thought it reasonable, but he could be steadfast, squeezing her nipple while he suckled her lobe, until finally she put down her tablet and eased her back from their headboard, sliding next to him. If she wasn't as enthusiastic as she used to be, more workmanlike and efficient, hand on his cock, kisses fast and hard, no arching of her back, no moaning, no giving over like she used to give over, she was never not willing.

Are you very religious? he threw in at the end of one email. He'd been wanting to ask this since the candles.

I am not very religious, his new friend replied. **I am not huge on G-d. But I do love to go to services. I love the songs and it is very much like a meditation practice to me. And I like helping the sisterhood bake hamantaschen. And I love my tallis (embroidered it myself)! And I love the idea of repairing the world.**

His new friend was never not surprising him. He was getting used to being surprised by her, which was not the same as not being surprised.

Now, Alison stood with Allison #2 and Deborah on their back deck, Alison, his Al, the tallest of the three women, the only one with a shirt that didn't blouse loosely over leggings.

"Vincent," Deborah called, Vincent prancing around in the grass in Francie's pink princess heels. "Those shoes are for girls!"

Tamara was sitting in the grass, wet, complaining about her foot. Something was in her foot. Allison #2 walked over, though reluctantly, it seemed. "Is it a splinter?"

Francie lay splayed across the tire swing, her body barely long enough to extend crosswise, her wet bathing suit bottom poking through the hole, the tire swaying more and more slowly. "Push me!" she yelled without even lifting her head from the rubber, a shout to the universe.

Deborah was holding forth on the detestable Republican candidate for president, newly announced. Everything from Deborah was a shout. Alison, his Al, was nodding to Deborah, who said: "Not that I'd vote for Hillary. She's a crook, and she should've left Bill as soon as he stuck his bleep bleep in that intern."

"Or should have cut off his bleep bleep," Number Two said from the grass. "No offense, Woody."

Woody chuckled, sweat stinging his eyes.

"What's a bleep bleep?" Vincent said.

"Take off those shoes," Deborah shouted.

"Push me!" Francie called.

"A bleep bleep is what gets men impeached," Number Two said, and all three women laughed.

"Push me!"

Woody made his way to the tire swing, Francie blinking up at him when his shadow covered her face.

"Daddy," she said, and the word, both an exhale and a sigh, made him happy for summertime. Susan had written, **Meet for coffee?** at the end of her last email. **I can sneak out of work at 10:30 most mornings. What are your days like?** Francie's hair was drying in thick cords, and she would cry later as Alison tried to get a comb through, but now, it looked so wild against the black rubber, so snake-like and free. To be a kid in the summertime was to be anything.

"Francie," he said back, pushing the swing, and she squealed with delight. The first question was easier to answer than the second, though he had not yet replied. Alison didn't know about Susan, though she also had not asked. What was there to tell? He would have told her if she'd asked. A parent, he would have said, I'm emailing a parent of one of my students. An at-risk student, he might've added, depending on her face. She could see the emails if she wanted. He had nothing to hide. Alison, his Al, made friends all the time. Her friends were plain-faced and opinionated and had no patience for cross dressing or bleep bleeps, and they were welcome to yell across his yard as much as they wanted.

What were his days like? Long and strange and hot and sweet. Sweaty and loud. Sawdust and splinters. *Plink. Plink. Kazoom.* Ear lobe.

What were his days like? It was hard to say, like trying to describe the sound of his own voice, the quality of his face.

He pushed the hot tire, Francie laughing. "Dadddddy," she trilled, and the women on the deck laughed, and he didn't know at what and he didn't much care.

Yes, he would type. **Of course. Coffee.**

NAOMI

Nathan's breath stank sweetly of syrup. "Nay, Nay, Nay," Naomi murmured to him as she wiped his fingers. "All ten fingers," she murmured. Up till this week, he'd not let her touch his hands. Face, she left alone. Face he could not tolerate, and what did she care, dirty face? Hands, she'd tried warming up the wet rag, she tried cooling it down, she'd tried paper towel, she'd tried cloth napkin. Lukewarm baby wipe, it turned out. He gargled his *this-is-good* gargle when she swiped the pancake syrup off his hands now.

Everybody, no matter what, enjoyed being attended to. Some people required more puzzling through was all, more piecing together, bit by bit. When she finished wiping, Nathan held up both hands, fingers splayed apart so that Naomi would do more. It reminded Naomi of her cousin Michael and his very gay jazz hands that he liked to pull out in the midst of Thanksgiving dinner. *Jazz hands*, he'd call out as the gravy boat was being passed around, his way of shouting, *Don't forget! I'm the gay one!* Michael was a disrupter; he loved to unbalance everyone. Naomi was the opposite of a disrupter, though she didn't know the word for it. She was a smoother? A wiper?

"Got to grab some lunch." Mr. Fenning came through the kitchen in his shorts and polo shirt. Struck Naomi as kind of cool that professors got to go to work in shorts. "Pup, Pup," he said to Nathan, kissing the boy lightly on his head. "You don't give this one a hard time." He pointed an elbow to Naomi, and Nathan said, not unhappily: "Hold on, this could get bumpy."

"Don't I know it, Captain Barnacles," Mr. Fenning said.

There was definitely a Mr. Mom thing going on in this household, which was fine with Naomi, she didn't really care, but Mr. Fenning was the warm and friendly one, the one who came up with new, dumb nicknames all the time, who told stupid jokes. "What do you call cheese that's not yours?"

She always liked it best when Mr. Fenning left. He was okay, but there was a way she had to be with family members, and it was the reason she'd been so bad at all her other jobs. She'd been a stocker at the Safeway, which she was good at until someone stopped her in the canned vegetable aisle to ask where the Benadryl was, or someone stopped her in the Benadryl aisle to find the ice cream. No, not the regular ice cream; the on-sale ice cream from the weekend paper. Same for data entry at the downtown tech firm: she could type fast, but there were all sorts of "team building" and mandatory in-services and she and Singh, the other data entry clerk, had to tell each other how their "families of origins" dealt with conflict. *A belt, mostly*, Singh had told her, smiling.

She'd applied for her first group home job because it was walking distance from her apartment and all you needed was a high school diploma or GED. To her surprise, *here* she was good with people, not necessarily her coworkers, who were lazy and small-minded, quick to make fun of Rhonda in her adult diapers and Belle's tendency to stick her hand up her own shirt and play with herself, but with the residents, who seemed to like how direct she was and focused with a low tolerance for BS or chitchat, which none of them were capable of anyway, and instead of distracting her from her job, they *were* her job, and she particularly enjoyed figuring each one out: Ruby did not do well with eye contact; Elizabeth liked to be real close, so close you had to tell her to back off, and if you said it loudly and clearly but not aggressively, she would; Zazzy, who was Bernice on her case file and loved to help in the kitchen but was horrible at it, once putting a booger in the cupcakes. It was nearly a year at that group home, and then fifteen months at another, which made her the senior employee at both, and the best at her job out of anyone, which felt good and strange, like winning a race when no one else was bothering to run. Eventually, with her CPR training and her first-aid certification and her upper body strength from a childhood of chopping wood and hauling junk to the dump, she became a personal support worker with the county, and it was, at that point, she guessed, her career.

"Things are good?" Mr. Fenning said to her. "You got everything? What do you guys have planned today?"

He peppered her with questions whenever they were in the same room. To Naomi's relief, she often didn't have to answer. Mr. Fenning would naturally fill silences with his own narration: "Lunch, then off to campus, then a couple office hours' appointments, then back here. Where's the mayo? You seen the mayo?"

"No," she said simply, as she wiped between Nathan's fingers. His hands were clean, but she'd let him decide when he was finished. She knew her quiet made Mr. Fenning uncomfortable, and she wasn't trying to be rude. But she was focused on Nathan, and Nathan knew it. This is what made her good at her job. At her career. The part of her brain that came up with small talk, that tried to set people at ease in their own home, that was a very different part than the one that watched Nathan's face, catalogued his responses into an ever-expanding map in her mind, so she could anticipate his upset and steer him instead toward calm, a little control.

This is what made Marjorie at the county send her out to clients others would refuse—ones who didn't talk, might not toilet, who intimidated less experienced PSWs. Nathan was big, and he was Black, and she knew people were scared of that even if they didn't say so. Naomi had been born a half hour away in a tiny town made tinier from the lumber bust, her father not able to work in the mill that his father had worked in and his father's father, instead trading in wood products and Jesus, cursing the liberals and the gays and the Blacks with equal vigor. If Naomi had felt any surprise that first day when she'd driven up and up the hilly switchbacks, and Mrs. Fenning answered the front door, if she had felt even a twinge of betrayal—*Marjorie didn't warn me*—she swallowed it down so quickly and reflexively, it blunted her very awareness of it. Through force of will alone, sheer daily stubbornness, she would not become her father.

"Nice view out there," Mr. Fenning said as he came to the table. The first time Naomi had pulled into the Fenning driveway, she'd thought it a modest ranch, only one story visible from the road. "You like that view?"

Naomi was inured to the view. Here it was from every room, and the same each day: trees and rooftops. Electrical lines. Cars. Birds. Sky. Clouds. The thing that struck her the most was Nathan's fingerprints dotting the glass. He loved to press against the window. It was a strange house to live in with a kid like Nathan. The cleaning lady spent hours on the windows each week; by the time she was done with one floor, Nathan had already smudged another.

They were in the bathroom, working with the electric toothbrush, practicing holding it and moving it in circles, tooth over tooth, no toothpaste yet, the switch still set to off. Naomi stood in the doorway and called softly, "Nay," whenever he started biting on the bristles, grinning or snarling at himself in the mirror. The main-floor bathroom was not her favorite room, cramped, wallpapered in a bright pastoral scene. Nathan smelled ripe. Some days were long and slow like this one, a headache building up in the back of her neck.

"One tooth then the next," she said quietly. Since her group home days, she'd curated a tone that was not a chide but also unmistakably firm and even. He appeared to be sucking on the bristles, and she was about to redirect when the front door opened into bright noise. Mail arrived through the slot in the front door between one and two, the cleaning lady on Thursdays and always with a hard candy wrapped in crinkling foil for Nathan.

Voices now. Laughter.

Nathan dropped the toothbrush into the sink and let out a slurry growl.

"Front door," Naomi said, calm and low. More laughter, a girl's voice.

Nathan rocked on his heels. Naomi always never forgot how big Nathan was; she tried to brook no fear. Back when she was green, Tracy from the group home jammed her shoulder into Naomi's face, blood running from Naomi's nose, hot and shameless. That time, she'd been afraid something would happen, and it did. She'd watched all sorts of colleagues since, fearful or power-tripping, get their fingers bent back into sprains, take an elbow to their chin, a fist to the mouth. The meanest sonovabitch she'd ever worked with got his two front teeth jammed up into his gums from a girl he was trying to restrain, half his size but with nothing to lose. Calm and even was Naomi's trip. You're predictable, they're predictable. You're good, they're good. You're human, they're human.

The brother: "Hello? Where you guys at?" He sounded funny.

"Already on it, Captain," Nathan said, sounding alarmed, hanging onto the sides of the sink.

"Hey," Naomi said, firmly but not too firmly, close but not too close. "It's okay." To the brother: "Bathroom."

The boy appeared, holding hands with a girl in short shorts and a stringy tank top. She looked entirely too young and too old at once: the lineless face and matted hair of a little girl, yet bold nipples bulleting though the tank top's fabric. The triangular tips of her bra's cups came well up over her shirt's neckline, no attempt to conceal them, the pink straps competing with the tank top's blue.

Nathan said, "Hold on, this could get bumpy," and the girl laughed, the noise a burst, and Naomi immediately hated her.

The brother—his name was Baz, she remembered—said, "It's one of his sentences," while Nathan slapped and slapped the sink, and barked three *Nacho*s in a row, and Naomi tried to hum quietly in time to his slapping, so he'd remember he was all right.

Baz was saying, "It's okay, bud, it's okay, these are my friends," and the laughing girl wasn't laughing anymore, nodding, saying, "hi," holding up an uncertain hand, and it made Naomi grateful not to be a teenager anymore, having to pretend all the time to be something braver and better. A second girl had long bangs in her eyes, one finger up in her mouth, a smaller version of the first, this one in a limp sundress.

"Hey," Baz was saying quietly to Nathan. "We're good." The only other time he brought someone home, it was an Arab boy who'd only rated a little clucking from the couch. "We're good," Baz repeated, his face so like his brother's and yet not, absent the ruddy cheeks and chapped lips, a little less chin, a little less brow, and the ineffable difference too, an awareness. From a certain angle, the contrast of the two boys could break Naomi's heart, but she would not let it. She thought of how Nathan savored frozen grapes. How last Monday he tried to tame his eyebrows with his toothbrush. Every picture he drew was slashes of yellow crayon, then orange, sunset after sunset, endlessly.

"So like," Baz said, looking directly at Naomi in such a way that she realized how rarely he addressed her; Naomi was background, like the chair for Nathan to sit on in the shower or the picture calendar. "We're going to hang out. But my parents don't—" he said and then shrugged, and it took Naomi a minute to understand he was asking her to keep a secret.

She said, "Sure," a reflexive and unaccountable desire to please the boy. "No problem," she said, and he nodded to her with less gratitude than she would've liked.

Noise trailed Naomi and Nathan, every room connected to every room on the main floor. Naomi had gotten Nathan his backpack, weighted with books, and slowly gotten him back into his body, easing him out of the bathroom, into the much more reasonable den. Even here, he was distracted by the chirping from the kitchen—Naomi was, too—the rises in laughter, the occasional *shit* and *what the hell*. "I cannot believe these views," one of the girls said. "And who has two fridges? How is that even a thing? Does the butler make your dinner for you?" and Baz's laugh was unlike any Naomi had heard from him, loose and unbridled. "Shut up," he said, but not meanly. The girl: "You're like, *Jeeves, tuck in my bib for the lobster.*" More laughter.

Naomi and Nathan could do some recreation, lower stakes, less pressure. She got the paper and scissors. When the threesome moved onto the great room couches, Naomi had a view of the back of Baz and the one girl's head on the couch, the other girl dwarfed on the chaise. The den had French doors she'd never seen closed.

Nathan held the mouth of the scissors over the green construction paper in such a way that that it creased instead of sliced the paper. "Already on it, Captain, already on it," he slurred. Naomi tried to angle his wrist, coaxing the position of the scissors, but Nathan was intransigent, putting up a fight at every touch, their normal rhythm lost. The girl on the chaise ate from a pudding cup balanced on her belly. The girl on the couch had her head on Baz's shoulder. From what Naomi could deduce, they were watching a video over and over on his phone, laughing and laughing.

"Come look," the girl on the couch called out to the girl on the chaise. "This dog. Is insane." The other girl did not move from the chaise.

Baz kissed the girl on her hair as she laughed. Naomi struggled to not look. Nathan imitated the girl's laughter, though lowly, crouched full body over the scissors, and Naomi knew she should close the French doors; this was too much for him. It wasn't fair. Baz was laughing too, but it was muffled now by his mouth on the girl's ear. Something about seeing the boy kissing the girl like that surprised Naomi. She realized then that she didn't think of the brother as a teenaged boy with teenaged boy needs; he'd always seemed so neutered with his seriousness, his well-mannered movements through these rooms, an endless patience with his brother. She had wondered when he'd swear or roll his eyes or sass back. When Naomi had been his age, she was six months past having left home, so intolerable the smother of Protestant rules and judgments. She'd only dated the boys who skipped classes, who kept warm beers in the trunks of their beat-up cars, the ones who refused to hold hands in public. They did not kiss her on the side of her neck. They fucked her, and skilllessly, though she'd had no way of knowing that at the time, thinking she was the one bad at it.

She'd felt sorry for Baz, and his mom too, for how closed off they seemed, how dead to themselves, as if they'd let Nathan hold all the wildness of the family, all the abandon, which was perhaps the biggest reason of all that Naomi felt an affinity for Nathan. She was Nathan. Everyone she knew—her roommate waitressing to save for a car after she wrecked the last one in a DUI, her ex-boyfriend who borrowed friends' phones to call her since she'd blocked his number, their across the hall neighbor who smoked out the window and then got in screaming fights with their landlord about the non-smoking clause in the lease—was Nathan, Nathan who'd given up on the scissors beside her, and instead ripped the paper in long strips. He made a yipping noise, a short, sharp bark, which was new and unpleasant.

"Show you my room," Baz announced, up off the couch, not turning around even once to look at Nathan, who persisted with the terrible yipping. "Scis-sors, scis-sors." Naomi tried to match his rhythm, even tried "Octonauts, to the launch bay!" which had surprised him so much the first time (she'd had to Google it), he'd stopped in the middle of his spiraling, looked at her, and laughed, flapping his left arm happily. This time, as footfalls rang down the stairway, and a door closed below, the voices and the laughter began anew, though muted by distance. Nathan stood from his chair, swinging the scissors, yelping, and Naomi tried "Nay, Nay, Nay," which had worked till now.

"Have a seat, have a seat," she sang softly, but he was past listening, his yipping pitched and more pitched, well past Mat, well past backpack, his arms swinging, and surely they heard him from downstairs. Naomi wondered what the boy in his bedroom would do—turn the music up, apologize, make a joke at his brother's expense. "Sit, sit, sit," she tried until finally, she stopped with the pleas and decided instead to step back and give him this for a minute or two—she would give herself this too—the loneliness of proximity, the goddamn grief of it.

STEFANIE

Mama's room smelled like body and dirty clothing, not all that different from the boys' rooms at home, except Mama's laced with disconcerting urine. The whole house stank of cigarettes too, lingering pot smoke. "Medical," Calvin always reminded her. "I have a license."

Mama was propped up in bed against a whole stack of pillows, same place she'd been when Stefanie showed up the night before. Two box fans blew warm air at each other, the television turned up past the noise of their whirring. People shouted about their paternity on Maury Povich's stage. The one window—view to the neighbor's pale siding—was stuck shut. Stefanie tried and tried, sweat getting in her eyes. She hadn't stopped sweating since she walked through the sliding doors of O'Hare.

In the day to day, she often felt like she was visiting Oregon, but still *lived* here, though her body suggested otherwise, no longer acclimated to the viscous summer air. As she'd waited for her rental car, her shirt stuck to her back, sweat collecting beneath her breasts, dripping down her belly. She had the A/C on high all the way to the hotel and then to Calvin's house, though the rental smelled ashy of other people, so she also cracked the window, a jet stream of hot highway air. Calvin lived nearly an hour south of where they grew up in Chicago, so these visits were never visits home. They were visits to her brother's house.

"You get any fresh air in here, Mama?" she asked.

"Get plenty of fresh air," she said. "How many times I have to tell you leave me be?"

"You're stuck with me," Stefanie said. "For ten days. Nine now. Not that I'm counting." Her mama looked a lot thinner in person, her face gaunt, the skin of her elbows hanging loose. Her nightgown sloughed off one shoulder. "You would've whooped us for watching that crap."

Her mother told her hush. "Watch your mouth."

"Tell them to watch their mouths." Stefanie nodded to the television. Her mama was less scary now that she was demented. Mean and demented was better than mean and not. "You done with this?" There was half-eaten toast on the TV tray next to the bed, a cooled bowl of instant oatmeal.

Her mama clasped her arms tightly around her chest, the end of the answering. Stefanie picked up big plastic cups, the kind Calvin and Angie got with their extra-large drink orders at Burger King and Jack in the Box and Arby's. They were everywhere: atop Kiki's old pressboard dresser, two on the TV tray, one on the sill, their bottoms crusted with the dark brown of Mama's favorite Diet Pepsi. Stefanie found one on its side under the foot of the bed, the brown crusted along the side, a sticky spot in the carpet. "How much Diet Pepsi they giving you?"

"Put those down," her mama said. "Stop messing with my things, Abilene."

"It's me. It's Stefanie." By tomorrow—or maybe tonight—she would quit correcting or at least care less when she did.

When Calvin came in—every few hours he got up from the couch or his bed—Mama held her arms out like a child on Christmas morning. "Baby boy! Lookit you. You do your mustache different?" Calvin went to her, and she pulled him in for a hug. Rationally, Stefanie understood this to be its own punishing loop.

"How much Diet Pepsi you giving her?" Stefanie held up the cups. And, "When's the last time you took her to get her hair done?" Her mama's hair was matted down and nappy. It made her look small.

"Awww," Calvin said, grabbing Stefanie up in a side hug. He was big, bigger than last time she saw him, the same steady progression since he hurt his back years ago (grown men, tackle football). As a child, he'd been wiry and athletic. Stefanie always had to get used to how big he was. He and Mama brought to mind Jack Sprat and his wife, in reverse. "Look who's here and giving me the third degree," he said, teasing. He kissed her on the top of her head. "I love you, sis." Her brother had always been corny—it was easy to forget that over the phone—and he still had his thick boyhood eyelashes, his big round eyes. Sometimes she thought Cal got away with everything he got away with because of his gorgeous eyes, red now, pupils so huge, they'd disappeared into his irises.

Angie brought home KFC after work. The window A/C labored from the living room. "Look at you, Mom! Looking good!" Angie cheered as Mama came to the table, which was how you could tell Angie was not blood; she believed Mama could be encouraged out of the squint that took up her whole face. Mama walked with a hobble now, barefoot, her same nightgown hanging loose, her diaper making a plastic sound when she sat. When had the diapers started?

Angie was the fastest moving person in the household, grabbing plates and silverware, impervious to the heat and her stoned husband and her scowling mother-in-law. She let Calvin grab her, asking him how was his day, baby? as she rubbed her hand round and round his back.

Stefanie had known Angie since Angie was fourteen. She'd been one of those gum-cracking girls, all ass and braids and dark, wet lipstick. She'd mellowed out considerably over the years, motherhood settling into her face, her hips, all that former attitude poured now into fierce loyalty and elaborate nail sets.

They sat at the kitchen table, the box fans blowing warm air at their legs. "You two have a good day together?" Angie asked Stefanie as she passed paper towel for napkins. Her nails were made to look like black and white marble, crystals in the pinkies.

"Sure," Stefanie said.

"She was so excited for you to get here," Angie said, the sort of lie best left unchallenged between them.

The next morning, Stefanie took her time at the hotel—continental breakfast, twenty minutes of a movie about inky aliens on HBO, a long shower with the grassy-smelling hotel body wash—pretending herself a vacation. Even at 10:30 a.m. Cal was still sleeping, slow to the door in his Cubs shirt and boxers, waving her off when Stefanie said, "How you going to stop her from wandering off if you're sleeping?"

He had a million reasons: He'd been up in the night, Mama in the kitchen again, emptying all their tea bags in the sink, filling the basin for "sweet tea." His back was killing him, he told Stefanie. He had a license. It was better than painkillers. He was exhausted, he told her. When they weren't taking care of Mama, they were worrying about Mama. "I told you," he said, as if winning a point.

She spent her days cleaning—first Mama's room, then the kitchen, then the carpeting—and trying to coax Mama out of bed ("Get off me,"), walk with her to the corner and back ("Don't need a chaperone."), feed her some vegetables ("Bring me my Diet Pepsi"), and get her to turn down the television ("Can't hear a thing!").

She felt like this was a lot worse than the last time she'd visited, though the details of her last visit blurred in her mind. The details of this house always blurred. She tended to forget the particulars once she was 2000 miles away again, focusing instead on the fact that Cal and Angie were good people, they'd raised a good kid after Kiki's dad took off, they rented the same good house in the same good neighborhood while Angie held down the same good job in accounts receivable at the Chevy dealer for years. This was how Stefanie got herself to knowing they were good to Mama, even if Stefanie would do it all differently, even if Stefanie would never do it in a thousand goddamn years.

She brought Mama into the bathroom one morning—Mama let her—and she wrapped a towel around her mama's shoulders and sectioned her hair in clips. She sprayed each section with warm water, working coconut oil through the tangles, first with her fingers, then a brush. Mama complained that Stefanie was hurting her, and Stefanie watched her angry face in the mirror. The lines of Mama's eyes were etched deep now, her brow. Stefanie watched her own eyes, beady like her mama's and with that same glint of suspicion. Stefanie tried to hold them soft to ease her crow's feet.

She drank a gin and tonic at the hotel bar, a bodily relief for there to be Black people everywhere: the bartender, most of the businessmen at a nearby table, the two gals behind the front desk across the lobby. She could breathe different here, even in a suburb that meant nearly nothing to her in overly aggressive hotel A/C.

She called home.

"You holding up?" Derek said, and the sound of his voice was when Stefanie realized how buzzed she was. She wasn't a big drinker, and she'd barely eaten today, leaving before Angie brought dinner.

"Hardly," she said. "You?"

"We're doing great. I mean, we're barely holding it together without you, but we're managing. Isn't that right, big man?" Nathan made a loud gargle, and Stefanie pictured the way Derek had tugged on his shirtsleeve to get this reaction. She knew exactly how they were sitting, Derek spread out in the middle of the couch, Nathan leaving a person-sized space between them, but leaning toward Derek, so Derek could reach and tickle the back of his neck. Nathan loved for his dad to tickle the back of his neck. It was like a bird in her throat, how bad she wanted to be there. "How was Miss Eileen today?" Derek asked.

"I don't—I can't—" She wanted to talk to the boys. Derek passed the phone to Nathan, and Stefanie listened to the way he moved the phone around his ear, not keeping it still, letting it slide all over his hair. She knew he liked the feel of the glass on his cheek. She told him she loved him and said she'd see him at the end of the week. Derek took the phone to Baz downstairs.

"Not that much," Baz told her when she asked what he'd been doing. "Hanging out with Shocky. Playing Xbox. Dumb stuff. I spent three hours alphabetizing files at Zotech yesterday. I started to forget if *g* comes before *h*."

He'd been like this, warm and chatty, since breaking up with Livvy. There'd been a week or so of sulking—wouldn't look up from his dinner, would barely give her a hello—which she'd expected. He was a teenager; a first girlfriend is a first girlfriend. The surprise was what came next: a sudden openness, a kid again. He made conversation, was easy with her at dinner. Stefanie took this to mean he agreed with her about the girl. He'd understood she'd been looking out for him and was maybe even grateful. Or relieved. She'd never expect him to admit that. Maybe he didn't even consciously realize it. No matter. She didn't need him to know. She had her boy. She had her family. She had a whole and real grown-up life, which was easy to forget here.

She gave in to the indolence of Cal's. Mama refused to get out of bed. Mama kept turning up the TV. Mama yelled for her Diet Pepsi. It was easy for Stefanie to loll on the sectional and position the fans to blow on her face. Even with the A/C and the fans, she was never not sticky. All the living room lights were out in the daytime, the blinds drawn to guard against yet more heat. They were inside a loud, thrumming cave.

Stefanie made lunch from shredded cheese on flour tortillas in the microwave. She opened canned corn and canned green beans and called it salad. Mama yelled at her for bringing her out to the recliner. Mama told Stefanie her face got ugly whenever she thought she was right about something. Mama said Stefanie used to be pretty but no more.

"You know who I am, Mama?"

"Don't you give me that," her mama said.

When Cal came out of his room, his belly slouching out of his T-shirt, Mama called out, "I see you there!" holding out her arms, and Stefanie tried to remember what she was doing here—what was she doing here?—though it was easier to flip through the television stations on the giant television, to let the ice cube she'd fished from her Lipton's melt on her clavicle and drip down the sides of her chest and into a pair of little dark pools on the couch. It was stifling in here, and why not surrender? This, she always forgot but then remembered again, was the lesson of her childhood.

Angie was there when Stefanie arrived one morning, Angie home from work, she and Cal waiting for Stefanie at the kitchen table. Cal slid a padlock kit, still in its clamshell packaging, to Stefanie: padlock, door clasp, two keys on a metal ring. The television blared from behind Mama's closed door. The floor fan blew air at their legs.

"I'm putting this up," Cal said. He pointed to the top of Mama's door.

"No, you're not," Stefanie said.

They'd had a bad night, Angie catching Mama trying to go outside close to one a.m. Mama had been combative on the front porch, yelling and trying to hit Angie, shouting about going to see Delroy. "Let me get to Delroy!" Mr. Arias woke up from the noise on their porch and came over to help get Mama back inside. Cal ended up sleeping outside her door, pointing to his pillow and a dribble of sheets still crumpled on the carpet. Angie showed Stefanie the inside of her arm, a track of three parallel scratches. Stefanie had seen worse from a cat. The most surprising part was the mention of Delroy, Cal and Stefanie's father, the most forbidden word of their childhood, worse than *goddamn*. "You cannot lock her in her room. That's elder abuse."

"She needs memory care," he said.

"She does," Angie echoed.

"Maybe what she needs is for you not to stay in bed all day." Stefanie held up her hand at Calvin's quick, yipping objection. "Maybe what she needs is for you to lay off the weed, clean up her room, get her up and active, not sit her in her room all day in her diaper."

"You're not even here," Calvin said. Every conversation was this conversation. All their life, the other one got off easy. "You haven't been here in a year and a half. You don't get to come in and say."

"I do too get to say. My check's the one you're cashing each month. Who's paying for memory care, Calvin?"

"Medicaid pays for my uncle Nate's nursing home," Angie said. You could tell they had prepared. They were ready.

"He moved into a Medicaid bed, or he had to spend down?" She was ready too. Angie shrugged, and it reminded Stefanie of Baz, that shrug. "Memory care is expensive. You're not going to find a Medicaid bed in a good facility. Get a job," she said to Calvin, "and we'll talk about memory care."

"You don't get to come in and say," Calvin repeated, and Stefanie thought Angie had probably given him talking points. *Tell your sister she doesn't get to come in and say.* "What are you gonna do?"

"What am I gonna do? This isn't on me to do, Calvin."

"Exactly," Angie said, nodding so hard, it looked like her head could bobble off. All these years later and here was fourteen-year-old Angie, all attitude and righteous indignation. Used to be a rumor that Mr. Broganski, the handsy biology teacher, had tried to grab Angie's ass, but she'd kicked him in the balls. Stefanie never asked her about it; Calvin and Angie were four years younger. What had Stefanie cared? But she'd always believed.

Every nursing home with an available Medicaid bed called itself something different—retirement village, rehabilitation center, senior living community—but they were all the same: dank rooms, low gypsum ceilings, hospital beds separated by curtains, abandoned wheelchairs in hallways, garbage cans needing emptying, overly solicitous tour guides gliding past the cloudy-eyed or hobbling or bedbound residents yelling from the nurse's station or the hallway or room. They were like the hospital, but dirtier and more crowded.

Mama began the day with "Would you look at that?" of the cheap Fourth of July pinwheels decorating a wall and "See there," of a cross hanging above a bed. "Who we seeing?" she kept asking, and Cal and Stefanie kept not answering. "Who we seeing?" But the day was long and hot, and they went from Munster to Lansing to Olympia Fields, so much traffic, so much bright sun off the blacktop, and by afternoon, Mama was wilted. They started depositing her in lobby chairs.

"Would she like a wheelchair?" the woman (cheap business suit, leopard print nails Angie would've admired) in Hazel Crest asked. Mama didn't need a wheelchair. Stefanie waited for Mama to yell at the woman, but Mama sat, glassy-eyed and blinking. Cal yelled, "Mama, you want a wheelchair?" as if her problem was deafness, and then he pushed her like a queen. An alarm blared in one of the long hallways, but the woman shouted, "Don't worry! It's the system." Mama held her hands over her ears. The 'model' room (narrow vertical window, bare mattresses) smelled like an allergy of Lysol.

"Would someone," the woman asked when they'd circled back to the lobby, an overhead light beginning to flicker, "like to use the restroom?" and Stefanie realized the shit smell was her mother. In the handicapped stall, Stefanie helped her mother out of the wheelchair. Her mother didn't make easy work of it, heavy against Stefanie, even though there wasn't much of her mother to her mother anymore. Stefanie could feel her bony shoulder, the ridges of her spine. "Mama," she was saying quietly into her mama's ear while she was trying to tug her mama's pants down so she could get at the diaper and sit her on the toilet.

The times she had to do this with Nathan—few and far between now, only on his worst days—she was no match for him. He had to be willing: leaning forward when she pressed a heel of a hand to his back, coming off the seat when she put a hand on his wrist, shimmying his hips back into the pants she pulled up. It was nearly balletic, the closeness of their bodies. There was nothing enviable about the task, though all her energy was focused on making it appear quotidian, keeping her voice bright or at least neutral. She always, always hoped he didn't feel ashamed. She never wanted him ashamed.

"Mama," Stefanie said, she and her mama in a crouching bear hug, Stefanie getting the diaper off, easing Mama down onto the seat, Stefanie so sad for the dirtiness of the diaper, the dirtiness of her mama's skin, her bottom shriveled and the skin gathered in folds. This, the closest she and her mama had been in proximity without fighting. It made Stefanie want to only speak in whispers. It made her want to not make any sudden movements.

The toilet paper was cheap and did not come easily off the roll. She kept ending up with frayed square after frayed square. "Sorry," she whispered to her mama, who sat waiting, still glassy-eyed, her mouth in a funny sag, like her lips had deflated on the left side. Is this what her mama looked like up close? "Sorry," Stefanie said on behalf of the toilet paper, with a terrible feeling that her mama's quiet wasn't exhaustion, but something waking inside of her, something cogent and alert and knowing why she was here.

WOODY

They met at a downtown Starbucks, walking distance from her law office, a twenty-minute drive from his place across town. There'd been much talk about where to meet—the restaurant by the train station, the tea shop, the bank of food carts. Starbucks seemed sufficiently generic and crowded, the tables taken up by grown men with laptops, snarls of homeless folks, college students. Alison loved Starbucks, made regular jokes about wanting to make T-shirts saying CORPORATE COFFEE WHORE. She wouldn't come to the downtown Starbucks, though. She went to the one at the Pottery Barn mall, where women in yoga pants substituted for the unwashed unhoused.

He felt strangely shy in line next to Susan. He'd greeted her at the table where she'd been waiting, paging through the free newsweekly. When she'd stood, he'd had a moment when he thought she was going to hug him, and he stuck out his hand instead, which she looked at, brow knit. "Good to meet you," she said mock-woodenly as she shook. She was, he soon figured out, just standing up to get in line.

Side by side, he stared at the shelves of travel mugs. Susan perused the plastic-wrapped sandwiches and protein boxes in the display case. Was this a comfortable silence?

"I hate eggs," he said.

"Huh," Susan said. "That's a weird thing to hate." She'd chosen one of the protein boxes with a hardboiled egg, cubed turkey, peanut butter, and bread.

"Not really," he said. He didn't actually *hate* them, more of a mild aversion if he had too much at once, but something in him wanted to take his nervous energy and needle her with it. They'd last emailed three days ago, when they'd decided on Starbucks. The absence of communication since made Woody realize what a thin sliver of a thing this was between them. Was there a *thing* between them or had he trumped something up in his mind? The days of silence made him double back and realize how he'd spun a tale in his head. He'd hung something on Susan already, something unnamable and not easily categorized, and yet:

some *thing*. He felt like a fool for this now, beside her in line, her face unreadable, her blouse buttoned to the second to top button, only the slightest swath of skin revealed. He said: "A guy in my college dorm called them chicken periods."

"Jesus, Woody," Susan said, looking at him straight on for the first time since they got in line. Her tone was some combination of irritated and amused. "One more reason I'm glad I didn't go to college." She chuckled and shook her head, and it was the first time her face looked like what Woody had thought it would.

They ordered, Susan a venti something, half sweet, extra foam, Woody a tall iced coffee and a muffin. He didn't want the muffin, but nothing seemed right—cake pops, oatmeal, mini-quiches. When the barista called out their names, it felt very public. He'd told Alison he was meeting a parent. Back at the table, he asked about Livvy. Susan had taken the lid off her drink and was dipping her finger into her foam.

"My favorite part," she said. "I'd order a cup of foam if I could." And then: "Fine. Normal. Whatever." A bit of foam remained on her lower lip and Woody pointed to the spot on his own lip. Susan swept her tongue over the spot, and Woody watched, wondering—no, confirming—that this was a thing, wasn't it? There was something here, yes? He was not simply inventing. "I like to think of myself as running a boarding house. She's my tenant. A tenant is not going to talk about their day. A tenant is going to slip into her room and try not to make too much noise, eat a meal without complaining too loudly about the food."

"I don't think boarding houses provide meals."

"Sure they do. They're only renting out rooms. How are the tenants supposed to eat?"

"Hot plates. Mini fridges."

"You are either an authority on boarding houses or a ridiculous bull-shitter." Her head was cocked in such a way that the insult wasn't an insult. She popped open her protein box, held the egg up like a prize. "To chicken periods." Woody held up his muffin. They toasted. "You have a toddler, yeah?"

"Preschooler. Four and a half."

"Jesus, those days were exhausting."

"I guess," he said. "Sure. But it's mostly Alison."

"Of course it is." Her tone was surprisingly arch. She wasn't being careful with him, which he guessed was a good thing?

"I work, and she's at home."

"Except for summer. When you're at Starbucks." She was nibbling at her egg, chewing a circumference around its middle. "I saw you guys once at the farmer's market. She's young, yeah? Your wife."

"When was this?"

She shrugged. "Couple years ago. She was pushing your baby in the stroller, and I was like, *Damn, Woody Hanover has a hot wife. She's sixteen-years-old.*"

He couldn't read her tone now. She'd bisected the egg right down to its yolk. "Are you...mad at me?" he asked.

"No, no. Sorry. I'm being an ass. When I'm nervous, I'm an ass."

"You're nervous?" he said, and he felt like a braver version of himself.

"I don't know. Shut up, okay?" She laughed, and he laughed, and he said: "That is the strangest way I've ever seen anyone eat an egg," and then: "She's thirty-three." This was nine years younger than he and Susan, and it felt shitty to speak of Alison, but shittier not to. Suddenly, he was his teenage self, as if time were a map, folded in on himself. He was all elbows and knees, his big, dumb hand picking at the crumbs atop his muffin. "I'm nervous too," he said, a statement that bifurcated him into the Woody sitting here and the Woody watching himself sitting here.

Susan finished off the egg in four big bites, chewing and chewing, looking right at him. The Woody sitting here held her gaze until it felt well past when he should be holding her gaze. The Woody watching Woody thought, *Jesus, man. What the fuck are you doing?* and cajoled the Woody sitting here to move his gaze to the clutch of homeless men and girls spread between three tables by the door. The Woody watching himself thought, *Focus on gross income inequality, opioid addiction. Focus on—*

"Are you ever like—" Susan said, and then shook her head, and balled her hands into fists and let out a "Gah!"

The Woody who was sitting here had no idea what Susan was saying or trying to say, and yet, he was utterly charmed. He didn't know anyone so willing to be foolish or strange. The Woody who was watching found this all to be a stupendously bad and stupid idea, thinking of Alison at the trampoline park with Francie, the mother and child bouncing and bouncing. *That* was what was utterly charming, their no-skid socks and their endless leaping and bounding, Alison's attentiveness and Francie's enthusiasms. Sometimes they were at the pool all together, Francie and Alison playing tea party, calling out *one two three* and then ducking underwater, clasping hands, and they felt so far away, even though they were right there beside him, and he would watch as their hair swam up to the surface like beasts from the deep. "Daddy, tea party!" Francie would scream when they surfaced, and each of his girls would reach out a hand for him, and all three would submerge, and they looked at each other underwater, their faces so funny, clenched and smiling and wavy with water, their hair floating around and above them.

Susan asked who he kept in touch with from high school, and he mentioned Ray and Dan, and she shrugged, and he asked her the same, and she said Vanessa someone and Lilah someone, and Woody remembered neither. Were his parents still in town, she wanted to know, and this felt safely like the kind of conversation any two people who were catching up could have. Retired to Palm Springs, he told her. Her dad had early dementia, but he and her mom were still living independently in a small town on the east side of the state. "Sorry to hear that," Woody said, and she looked at him as she ate her cubed turkey. Soon she pulled out her pen and wrote on her brown napkin, an arm hooked round the ways kids did when they didn't want someone cheating off them. She was bent down low over the table.

"What are you doing?" asked both the Woody who was sitting and the Woody who was watching, though their intended recipients, different.

Susan giggled a little but did not look up. The giggle sounded good on her. When she was finished, she held up the napkin beside her head. "Ta-da!" It was a rough sketch and a profile, but Woody recognized the curl of hair over his ears, the thin curve of his glasses frame.

"Portrait," Woody said, not "My portrait" or "A portrait" or "A portrait?" The Woody sitting here couldn't remember the last time he felt this way, this off-kilter, this double-you tee eff, as the kids liked to say. He and Alison had met through an online site, and their courtship had been steady, systematic, a series of check boxes: A volley of clever emails. First date. A nip on the cheek outside a car door. Second date. Kissing and petting. The Woody watching him admonished the Woody sitting here to stop calling Alison up for a convenient stab of pathos or, worse, comparison. If the Woody sitting here didn't have the decency to get up and leave, at least he could have the decency to leave Alison be.

Susan pushed the napkin across the table. "For you," she said, and though her voice held only warmth and playfulness, there was a challenge here, whether she knew it or not. To take the napkin was to make real this thing, to bring evidence of it back with him, even if such evidence lived crumpled in his pants pocket. To refuse it was to cordon off his life with Alison and Francie, save for this small space of a Starbucks table, no larger than three feet by three, soon to be occupied by random strangers, wiped clean of his half-eaten muffin, her plastic box. To refuse it was to make this thing—this some*thing*—calculable. Finite. Subtractable. As in, she drew a portrait of me on a Starbucks napkin, and the next time I saw her was the for spring-term evening program on Applying for Financial Aid for Your Child's College.

The face on the napkin had a line for a mouth, not exactly smiling but not not smiling. He was the *Mona Lisa* of Starbucks napkins. The drawing was silly, but not. Even the Woody watching could see himself in it. She'd gotten something right about his brow. No one had ever drawn a portrait of him.

"Thank you," he said as he picked it up, not wanting to fold it, but also not being able to sit here any longer, so he stood, told her, "thank you," one more time and "good to see you," holding the napkin strangely in his palm, face down as he left the coffee shop (not turning around to see if she was still sitting there, not turning to see if she was watching him walk away), walking the three blocks back to his car in the city lot with the napkin in his loosely closed fist, delicately, like a caught butterfly, finally opening his car door and his glove compartment, not looking to see if the sweat had smeared his face, not looking to see if he'd ruined it, simply opening his palm and letting it fall on the license and registration, the Toyota manual, the host of other collected napkins—McDonald's, KFC—this one not making a sound as he dropped it. Napkins didn't make sounds. They were nothing.

LARK

There was a knock on the door. There was never a knock on Livvy's door. Neighbor? Livvy's mom (but why would she be *knocking*)? Baz's parents (but how would they *know*)? She was alone in the living room, and as with any such crossroads, Lark decided doing nothing was the safest bet. The knocking continued; three loud pounds.

"Can you get that?" Livvy called from the bedroom, her voice strangled, and Lark was embarrassed by it and chastened, her face hot when she opened the door.

"S'up?" It was Shocky, standing on the landing in shorts and a baseball cap. His T-shirt read: *My Spirit Animal* with a picture of a sloth. Lark didn't know how to answer. The explorer girl and her monkey were on in the background.

"Hello," Lark said when she couldn't think of anything else. And: "What are you doing here?"

Shocky laughed, the sound sharp and quick. "Your girlfriend invited me."

She still didn't know what to say. Livvy hadn't mentioned anything about Shocky. Lark didn't know Shocky even knew about Livvy and Baz. She'd thought she was the only one.

"Ask her," he said, as if reading her mind. And: "What, you're the bouncer?" He peered around her into the empty living room. "You gonna let me in?" he said, and: "Where is everybody?"

She moved aside and didn't know how to explain where they were. She tipped her head in the direction of the bedroom, clicked the clicker for the TV. Shocky was squinting at her, standing a couple steps inside the front door. "You kidding me?" he said, and she couldn't tell if he was talking about the TV show or the bedroom or both.

"Is that a joke?" she said of his T-shirt.

He looked down like he had to remind himself. "No," he said. "Dead serious."

She was back on the loveseat, clicking and clicking. "Do you want to watch something?"

"This is what you do?" he said. It sounded like he was picking a fight. "I mean," he said, a little more nicely, "it's kind of messed up."

Lark shrugged. They were being quieter from the other room, though she could still hear the creak of Mrs. Albrecht's bed, some other sounds. "I didn't know you were coming," she said.

He didn't respond, walking to the fridge instead. "Got anything to drink here?" but he was looking inside the fridge, as if asking *it* the question. "At least there's this," he said, holding up a beer bottle to Lark. "Want one?"

"I don't," she said. "I don't think we're supposed to—"

He laughed again. Had she ever heard him laugh before? "And like they're supposed to—" He nodded to the bedroom. He opened and closed kitchen drawers till he found the bottle opener, popped the cap, slugged a long drink. Lark clicked until she found a baseball game. She figured he might like a baseball game. He sat in the red chair at the table. No one ever sat in the red chair. The brim of his cap cast a shadow over his eyes. The room felt big with Shocky at the other end of it, sitting sideways on the red chair. The baseball game was numbing to watch, though she did so intently, not sure which team was which.

The bedroom door opened, and Baz came out, blinking into the light, tucking his shirt back into his pants. "Hey, man," he said to Shocky, ambling over to the table.

"Dude," Shocky said, up from the red chair, the two of them doing a weird boy-hug, chests together, claps on backs. "That's sick that you leave her out here."

Livvy came out, her hair messed up in the back, a modest tangle. She smiled at Lark and spread out on the big gray cube couch. "Shocky," she said across the room, matter of fact, and to Lark, "Why we watching this?" and Lark had expected an apology or something, something more than the way Livvy was spread out now, not caring about Shocky or the beer or he taking the chair no one ever sat in. She handed Livvy the clicker, and Livvy sped through the channels while Baz got a beer out of the fridge too. Livvy's mom would know the beer was missing, she could count, but still Livvy didn't say anything, and Lark had the feeling now like the boys were rolling right over them.

By the time Baz came over to the gray cube, Livvy had settled on a real-life lady wrestlers show, all the ladies monstrously beautiful. She said to Baz, "Gimme a sip," and took a long drink, though Lark could see the way her chin curdled, even if she was trying to act cool. After she handed Baz back the bottle, she turned to Lark and said, "Make room," by which she meant *don't lie across the whole loveseat.*

She made room because what else was she going to do? There was a part of her growing numb, which was not all that unusual, except for the fact of being at Livvy's. She never felt this way at Livvy's.

"Don't be shy!" Livvy called to Shocky, loose and playful, almost flirty. It was her sex voice, her not-yet-back-to-herself voice, and for the first time, Lark was disgusted by the fact of what happened in the other room.

Shocky shrugged over to the loveseat, a big grin on his face, though he was looking at Baz, not Lark, and when he sat down, it was with enough force that she bounced a little on her cushion and she tried to make more room for him, since they were thigh to thigh now, dark, wiry hair covering his. His leg gave off heat. She could feel it through his shorts and hers. She kept trying to scoot. "Don't worry." He leaned toward her face and whispered a loud whisper everyone could hear, his breath hoppy with beer and way too close. "I don't bite."

After a little while, he announced: "This is what you guys do?" and "Hot as shit in here."

"What you want to do?" asked Baz.

"I don't know. Go to the skate park."

"I don't know how to skateboard," whined Livvy.

"We can teach you," said Shocky.

"Too hot," said Livvy. "Lark doesn't know how to either."

Shocky made a noise that suggested he was not surprised by this fact.

"Go to the movies," said Shocky.

"Uch," growled Livvy. "So sick of the movies."

"Let's go play Xbox at your place," Shocky said to Baz. "At least it's air conditioned."

Baz was half-lying on Livvy's shoulder. "Not gonna leave my girl here," he said.

"Bring them!" Shocky announced, and Lark was uncomfortable with the way he talked about them like she and Livvy were one thing, which historically, was how Lark thought of them too, but here, like this, she did not like it. "The girls can keep watching this"—Shocky waved to the show of the ladies trying on wedding dresses and the families making them cry from too many mean opinions—"on one of your other TVs."

Baz looked at his watch. His mom was still out of town, he said. His dad would be teaching in forty-five minutes. That seemed to settle it because after a half hour, Baz and Livvy got up, and so did Shocky. No one asked Lark. She didn't want to go back to Baz's house. Baz's brother creeped her out, and she didn't even like Xbox.

It was the middle of the day, and in the back of Baz's car, music thumped loud from his MP3 player, Shocky and Baz and Livvy rapping along to words Lark didn't know, the noise banging around in her head. They drove up and up the switchbacks of the hillside, the town receding below, and something tight and clenching was happening in her belly. Swerving around a turn, Shocky rocked in his seat beside her, calling out, "Whoa," and placing a hand on her thigh. She remembered how she used to always get carsick in summer from the smell of her mom's air conditioner vents, the way they spewed a burnt, dusty smell at the start of the season. "You're imagining it," her mother would say. "Breathe through your mouth." Shocky's hand was gone, as quick as it had come. She breathed through her mouth.

His brother was in the kitchen with the aide, grunting, lips cracked, his T-shirt long as a nightgown, his afro bigger and scragglier than Baz's.

"Nathan," Shocky said, and the boy, or man, or whatever Lark was supposed to think of him, didn't respond in any way. "How you doing, guy?"

He didn't seem twenty-two, though he didn't seem younger than Baz either. He seemed uncategorizable, his face not like the retarded kids. Lark knew there was a word she was supposed to use, especially with Baz's brother right here, starting to make the screeching sound he made last time, the aide going "nay, nay, nay" from a few feet away.

"'Member my friends," Baz said quickly and already the four of them were scuttling down to his room. Lark heard the boy-man screeching, and the aide saying and saying things, but soon they were in Baz's room, and Baz and Shocky were on the floor at the foot of his bed, Xbox controls in hand. The game was loud, shooting alien robots on a spaceship, lots of yelling and gunfire and explosions, and Lark fiddled with the Star Wars Legos on Baz's bookshelves, and shook up a snow globe of a Ferris wheel (*Navy Pier*, Baz told her last time) and looked out the window—this whole house, windows—and she thought this was the biggest difference between someone like Baz and someone like her, how he could see the whole city from up here, how it was a *whole thing* he could view from bed—or from his dinner table, or from the living room couch, whereas Lark, she was in it all the time, it was her mom, her room, her apartment, her bus, her school. It was a bunch of different parts that didn't make a whole anything except her life.

"Hey," Livvy said, leaning her chin into Lark's shoulder. "You like him?"

"No!" Lark said, so loud that both boys looked up from the game.

Livvy *tsk*ed, braiding her fingers into Lark's. "He's a really nice guy," she whispered into Lark's ear.

Lark whispered back: "He's not really nice, and he doesn't even like me."

"Does too," Livvy said, and Lark found herself, in spite of herself, wanting to believe this. She stayed quiet so that Livvy would say more, but she didn't.

"What do you think," Lark whispered still, liking the whispering, the two of them here together while the soldiers in the game shouted at each other. "Of this view?"

"It's nice," Livvy said.

That wasn't what Lark meant. "What do you think it makes Baz into?"

"Makes Baz into? Don't go all into trippy Lark-land," she said, and she was saying it with a smile in her throat, but it hit Lark hard, right in her windpipe. Livvy didn't say things like this. She'd never had a view of Lark before; she'd always just been in it with Lark. What was *trippy Lark-land* supposed to mean? Livvy was still nuzzling up, still saying things, and Lark was saying things back, but hardly. This moment became a demarcation: before Baz and after, the after starting not when Livvy met the boy, but here, now, in his room.

Livvy's fingers were twined in Lark's, and she led them to the bed, the only place to sit other than the floor, and Baz's pillows and blankets had a boy smell that Lark didn't notice on Baz himself: feet, sweat. Lark couldn't get comfortable, her belly tight and clenching again, not car sick anymore but something. They fell into watching the video game, the screen both bright and dark, the action mired and indistinguishable, an almost soothing oblivion, were it not for the shooting and the screams. Lark tried to shift position to unknot her belly, but nothing helped, and she rolled onto her side and tried to fall asleep. She didn't know how long she was like that—did she? Fall asleep?—when she felt something clammy between her legs, a moistness in her underpants that made her worry that she peed herself, but it didn't feel like pee, and it was with rising horror that she was up, off Baz's bed, growing clammier and clammier, knowing she should excuse herself to the bathroom, but somehow frozen into this pose, legs crossed, thighs clamped together, as if standing here like this would undo what her body was doing. She watched the other three bodies in the room being bodies. Livvy was crawling down the bed, her face next to Baz's, nibbling on his ear, trying to kiss his face.

"Get off! No, get off me!" he said, flicking his shoulder, his tone joking, and he turned to kiss Livvy back, and Shocky yelled at Baz to pay attention, and Baz's space soldier died, and Shocky's did too, and Shocky berated Baz, and Baz stopped kissing Livvy long enough to say, "Priorities, man," and Livvy pulled Baz up onto the bed, and Shocky said, "Damn, don't mind us. Guess we'll go get food or something. You coming?" Shocky said this last bit to Lark, not even pausing to hear her answer before he galloped up the stairs two by two, pulling himself up by the banister, Lark right behind.

The brother and the aide were at the kitchen table, Baz's brother holding a spoon funny, in a backward fist, scooping out cereal from a bowl, eating and saying a slur of words. Milk was on his chin, and Lark didn't like looking at him, finding herself behind Shocky, letting him block her.

"That's some Corn Flakes you got there, bud," Shocky said, and Baz's brother slapped his spoon into the milk. "I don't think I ever saw you with Corn Flakes before. You're a Cheerios guy usually. Right?" The aide wasn't even looking at Shocky, humming her own slur of words, and it was like watching an old married couple who had their own everything between them, and Lark was sick of people having their own everything between them.

"Bathroom?" she said to the back of Shocky's head, and he pointed to a door.

On the toilet, her underpants were a bad dream, the blood thick and brownish. Why had no one told her it would be brown? She had waited so long for this, only to be revolted. She didn't need one more reason to hate herself. She found bar soap, disposable razors, air freshener spray. There were no pads. "Fuck you," she said to the air freshener rolling loudly in the drawer, and she couldn't remember the last time she'd said that to anyone or anything, and it felt good. Maybe the brown blood would make her into a *fuck you* girl.

She was left to clot up a fist of toilet paper and stuff it into her underpants. *Please, please, please,* she was saying in her own head, though she didn't even know what she was pleading for. In the mirror, as she washed her hands, she stared at her same old face, an idiot for thinking it would make her different.

"What you got for us?" Shocky was saying in the kitchen, peering inside the open door of the fridge. The brother was back on the shrill yipping, and Lark tried to focus only on Shocky, the back of his neck, wiry hair coming up out his shirt collar.

Shocky grabbed a bag of grapes from the crisper and a beer from the door. "You want?" he said to her. The brother's noise grew louder, and Lark saw only a shadow in her peripheral vision. Then: the sound of a chair falling over, the aide saying, "Nay-than," no more cooing, no more murmurs. "Nay-than. Nay- Nay- Nay," the sound of things going bad, not just in Lark's head but outside of it too, "Nay- Nay," the sound of trying not to be afraid. And it was only a second, but it felt like much longer, the brother and the aide up from the table, the aide reaching a hand out and the brother shaking, and for a fraction of that second, he looked at the aide, and it seemed like everything was going to calm down. But then the brother did something hard to describe, coiling himself up and hunching himself down, so his body was big but small, still the whole time with *yipyipyip.* He sprang at the aide.

In the final moment before his body hit hers—his weird head and his broad shoulder catching her in the chest, pinning her to the window like a bug, until it sounded like the glass would crack, but it held, the aide letting out a cry that brought Baz up from his room, Livvy right behind him—came a sliver of time when things had not yet fallen apart, but were about to, and spectacularly. And from beneath Lark's fear and surprise came a feeling she later tried to forget, tried to undo from herself because she was nice too, nicer than Shocky, nicer than all of them, but a slur of *yesthisgoodnowgoodthis* rose in her, and what it was was satisfaction of other people trapped in a big, ugly mess too.

Derek

Naomi's beater Corolla wasn't in the driveway. That was the first thing wrong. Second, Derek came inside and there was nobody around. "Hello," he called out. A bag of grapes on the counter, but otherwise no sign of life. "Hello?"

He never came home to an empty house, and for a second, he allowed himself the fantasy that Naomi had planned an outing he'd forgotten; independent living skills trip to the grocery store? To the downtown bus station? But there was a distinctly hoppy smell coming from the sink, and Derek, not predisposed to either suspicion or forensic investigation (he was more a live and let live guy), made a quick perusal of the recycling and garbage, and sure enough there was, stuffed beneath several wads of paper towels, one of his IPA bottles. *What,* he wondered roughly, *the fuck?*

"Hello?" he called down the stairs.

"Dad!" Baz called, though from Nathan's room. Baz was never in Nathan's room. Both of them were in Nathan's bed, side by side, Nathan with his headphones in, connected to his iPad, Baz with his Switch, neither looking up when Derek came in. The last time he'd seen them like this, shoulder to shoulder in one of their beds, elementary school maybe.

"What the heck is going on?" He held up the beer bottle. He'd been solo parenting for nine days. Stefanie would be back in less than twenty-four hours. "Where's Naomi?"

Baz looked up, his mouth partway open, brows trying to furrow, but his eyes gave him away: wide and worried. It was his in trouble face. He'd inherited it from Derek.

Baz unspooled a tangle, whispering in the hallway between the boys' rooms: Nathan attacked Naomi, and Naomi left. ("Attacked?") Pushed or something, he hadn't seen. He was downstairs in his room. Shocky was the one who saw. He was upstairs. With the beer that Baz hadn't given him. Shocky just took it, and Baz made him pour it out before everyone left, which was right after Naomi left. ("Who's everyone?")

Shocky, Lark, Livvy. ("Livvy?") Livvy. ("Who's Lark?") Livvy's best friend. She was upstairs with Shocky. ("So, you were downstairs with Livvy while your friends were upstairs drinking beer. And sometime during this, Nathan pushed Naomi.")

"Fuck," Derek said, pressing both palms into his eyes.

"Dad," Baz said, and Derek could hear in his voice: still young enough to be shocked by the swearing. "Sorry. Dad?"

Derek was normally the unflappable parent. "Give me a minute," he said.

"Sorry, Dad," Baz said again. He wasn't a kid used to reproach, sensitive beneath his posturing, and there was never all that much posturing to begin with. He needed reassuring, Derek could see that. But goddamnit, Derek needed a minute. Give him a minute.

"Hey," he said from the foot of Nathan's bed, shaking an ankle. "You okay?"

Nathan let out one of his groaning yawns. He took a closed fist and rubbed it in circles against his hair, nothing distressing or distressed about him. His face was his normal face. Derek pantomimed taking out an earphone, but Nathan ignored him. When Derek leaned over and plucked it out, Nathan made a squealing gargle, though he was playing.

"What happened today?" he asked, knowing there'd be no answer. He always talked to Nathan. The alternative was not talking to his kid. Nathan tried to put his headphones back in, but Derek stopped him. His biggest fear for Nathan—a fear that had Derek by the throat right now, even with Nathan all in one piece and close enough to touch—was that Nathan didn't know to manage his body and by not knowing, he would get himself in deep, irredeemable shit.

Derek's parents had drilled into him from a very young age how to stand, how to *sir*, how to walk, how to hands out of pockets, how to make eye contact but not too much…and everything he'd achieved felt like a variation on those lessons. He'd made it through college and his PhD by not being too big (or too small, though that turned out to matter less). Through the job market, every class he taught, every dissertation he advised. He knew how to talk, how to shake, how to stand, how to sit, how to be to make the people who needed to be comfortable, comfortable. Baz was good at this too, Baz upright and polite same way Derek was, good with friends, with school, with adults, friendly without being gregarious, a thinker. Baz knew how to keep a little something to himself for the world not to get him by the throat. But Nathan. It was impossible to teach Nathan.

"Things were hard with Naomi," Derek said, and only then did Nathan try to bury his chin in his chest. "We'll get it sorted out," Derek said, knowing no such thing to be true, parenting mostly about making wishful promises and trying to live them out. He grabbed onto Nathan's sock—it was what was closest—Nathan's toes squirming beneath.

When he called Naomi, it went straight to voicemail. He left a message saying he wasn't sure what happened, but he was sorry, and could she call and touch base? He wanted to support her however he could. They all did. Nathan really loved her.

Next, he told Baz to help with dinner and then said as Baz grated cheese: "Your friends are not allowed alcohol when they are here. You understand me?" Baz did. "I could call Hidaya and Abdi to let them know what went down. Do you want me to do that?" Baz did not. "Your friends are your responsibility when you're in this household."

Derek was starting to feel better. This was what he was good at: taking complex problems and breaking them down. This was his *job*. A family was a system just like an economy was a system. The big hit of his 300-person Intro to Microeconomics lectures was always when he explained the concept of the production possibilities frontier using baby pictures of Nathan and Baz. He graphed the quantity of dirty diapers they could produce in a day on the x axis with quantity of crying they could produce on the y axis. The girls *oooh*ed at the baby pictures. The boys cackled at the mention of poop. This *aw shucks* version of professor was always popular among the sea of undergrads in his lecture halls. **He's funny,** they wrote on their student evals. **Prof Fenning is cool and makes stuff interesting with stories.**

At dinner, Nathan slapped the table happily. He was fine. *He's fine,* Derek kept saying to himself.

"Livvy?" Derek finally said. He'd been waiting for Baz to say, but Baz wasn't saying. The dinner table was one of the few times he and Baz were face to face. Normally their conversations happened when they were side by side on the couch or in Derek's car, Derek letting the quiet happen between them while Baz took things at his own speed. "I feel like high school is kind of a joke," he might say. Or "Jazz is too like jangly and discordant. You should listen to some pop."

When Baz didn't say anything, Derek said, "What's going on with that?"

"You know," Baz said, a goofy grin trying to escape his mouth.

"I mean, I can assume," Derek said. "But tell me."

He looked and looked at his fork in his macaroni, spearing and spearing noodles. "I like her," he said.

"Okay," Derek said. "How long have you two been—?"

Baz shrugged. "You're going to tell Mom."

"Of course I'm going to tell Mom. Or you're going to tell Mom. Someone's going to tell Mom."

"She gets all—" He moved his hand through the air. Nathan imitated the motion.

"Knock it off," Derek said. Whatever differences in their parenting, he and Stef were a united front. Derek had learned this from his parents. (*Don't you disrespect the love of my life,* his father was known to say when Derek gave his mom lip.) "She's doing her job."

She called when it was only he and Baz still awake, Derek cleaning up, Baz flipping through TV stations. Baz was normally up in his room by now; Derek found it kind of sweet how he was sticking close. The day had taken something out of Baz.

"Oh my god," Stefanie said. "One more sleep." Her voice sounded the same it had the whole trip: frayed around the edges, nearly girlish. Eileen rode her hard, always had, the one person Stefanie couldn't stare down.

He asked about her day, and she told him *same shit* and asked how his day was. "Tell me everything," she said, and the way she said it was laced with desperation. He wasn't used to the sound of her missing him. He liked it. He missed her too. One more sleep. "We're good. My students *woke up* this afternoon." He told her how they were analyzing markets for the small group project, fighting over which group would get the local cannabis market. Derek had to run an epic rock-paper-scissors playoff. "They're a sharp group."

"The boys?" she said, which he knew meant both *how are they* and *can I talk to them?*

"Good," he said, and it was a split-second decision. What Derek told himself was he didn't want to give her one more thing. He didn't want her stewing for a day, powerless to do anything, suspended on an airplane across most of the country. He could see the way her mouth would be set from all those hours in the air. He could see the lines in her brow, the force of her walk: a clomp. He and Stef existed at different RPMs. If she were a seventy-eight, he was a thirty-three. Stef, and he loved her for it, never let things slide.

He was waiting to hear back from Naomi. Give him a few more hours to set things right, he was thinking. It felt possible, he was thinking, that he could take care of everything. He could have a story to tell the next day, barely a story. A rough day they all got through. *Welcome home! And also, guess who was back in the picture? A certain teenaged girl. Ha. Right? Boys. That's boys for you. Ha!*

"Good, good," he said, and it hardly felt like lying. It felt like taking care of his family. "Nathan's sleeping. Baz is..." He let it trail off to see if she would press. She did not press. "They're excited to see you."

Subject: Coffee
Date: July 26 6:11 p.m.
To: Woody Hanover <woody_h@wesths>
From: Susan Albrecht <salbrecht@lernergable>

Was that weird?

Subject: RE: Coffee
Date: July 26 9:42 p.m.
To: Susan Albrecht <salbrecht@lernergable>
From: Woody Hanover <woody_h@wesths>

Yes?

Subject: RE: RE: Coffee
Date: July 26 9:45 p.m.
To: Woody Hanover <woody_h@wesths>
From: Susan Albrecht <salbrecht@lernergable>

You're not sure?

Subject: RE: RE: RE: Coffee
Date: July 26 9:52 p.m.
To: Susan Albrecht <salbrecht@lernergable>
From: Woody Hanover <woody_h@wesths>

No, I'm sure it was weird. But is that a bad thing?

Subject: RE: RE: RE: RE: Coffee
Date: July 26 9:55 p.m.
To: Woody Hanover <woody_h@wesths>
From: Susan Albrecht <salbrecht@lernergable>

What are we doing?

Subject: RE: RE: RE: RE: RE: Coffee
Date: July 26 9:57 p.m.
To: Susan Albrecht <salbrecht@lernergable>
From: Woody Hanover <woody_h@wesths>

I don't know. I was hoping you'd tell me.

Subject: RE: RE: RE: RE: RE: RE: Coffee
Date: July 26 10:02 p.m.
To: Woody Hanover <woody_h@wesths>
From: Susan Albrecht <salbrecht@lernergable>

You're the one with the wife.

Subject: RE: RE: RE: RE: RE: RE: RE: Coffee
Date: July 26 10:07 p.m.
To: Susan Albrecht <salbrecht@lernergable>
From: Woody Hanover <woody_h@wesths>

Indeed.

Subject: RE: RE: RE: RE: RE: RE: RE: RE: Coffee
Date: July 26 10:11 p.m.
To: Woody Hanover <woody_h@wesths>
From: Susan Albrecht <salbrecht@lernergable>

Indeed? That's all you got?

Subject: RE: RE: RE: RE: RE: RE: RE: RE: RE: Coffee
Date: July 26 10:14 p.m.
To: Susan Albrecht <salbrecht@lernergable>
From: Woody Hanover <woody_h@wesths>

I like that napkin portrait.

Subject: RE: RE: RE: RE: RE: RE: RE: RE: RE: RE: Coffee
Date: July 26 10:19 p.m.
To: Woody Hanover <woody_h@wesths>
From: Susan Albrecht <salbrecht@lernergable>

That napkin portrait likes you too. Is the napkin portrait fucking crazy to like you back?

Subject: RE: RE: RE: RE: RE: RE: RE: RE: RE: RE: RE: Coffee
Date: July 26 10:22 p.m.
To: Susan Albrecht <salbrecht@lernergable>
From: Woody Hanover <woody_h@wesths>

I keep hitting the refresh button, waiting for your replies, ergo (is this the correct use of ergo?) the napkin portrait is not fucking crazy.

Subject: RE: RE: RE: RE: RE: RE: RE: RE: RE: RE: RE: RE: Coffee
Date: July 26 10:31 p.m.
To: Woody Hanover <woody_h@wesths>
From: Susan Albrecht <salbrecht@lernergable>

Google tells me your usage is correct, unless you meant the brand of baby carrier that turns you into a human kangaroo. One time I was pushing Olivia in a stroller while she was drinking from a bottle and a lady passed me on the sidewalk and said without provocation, "If you carried your baby on your body, she could drink breast milk while you walked." Talk about fucking crazy.

The napkin portrait is tired. It needs to go to sleep. Goodnight, Woody Hanover.

Subject: RE: RE: RE: RE: RE: RE: RE: RE: RE: RE: RE: RE: RE: Coffee
Date: July 26 10:36 p.m.
To: Susan Albrecht <salbrecht@lernergable>
From: Woody Hanover <woody_h@wesths>

No wonder your kid is so messed up. (KIDDING! Your kid is great. Even if you neglected her so blatantly. KIDDING!!!)

Good night, napkin portrait. Sweet dreams.

STEFANIE

B az sat on the couch, Derek on the end of the chaise, Stefanie on a dining room chair she'd dragged over, the set up all wrong, everyone too far from each other.

"It is your job," she said. "It is all our jobs to take care of your brother."

"I wasn't even there," Baz said, and it was the feeling of conspiracy that got Stefanie, she arriving home clueless hours before, Derek and Nathan coming for her at the airport when Nathan should've been home with Naomi, Derek with his entertainer smile broad across his face.

"What's up?" she'd asked Derek after they'd waited for her two bags to come off the conveyor belt. Derek had her carry-on slung over his shoulder, insisted on rolling both rolling bags. She felt it generous to have waited this long, giving him the update on her flight (Will Smith movie; he was a thief with a beautiful blond), nuzzling into his neck, side hugging Nathan. It was generous to herself mostly, allowing herself those several minutes of standing between them, an arm slung around each of their hips, taking in their smell of musk and hair cream.

"We'll get to that in a second," she said now to Baz, holding up a hand. "I know where you were. And I know with who." Stefanie had an image of the girl, fixed now from outside the principal's office, her bruised face, her lazy flip-flops, her childish Band-Aid.

Baz made a noise, and Stefanie couldn't even. Her body had been coiled tight for ten days. She felt it in her hip, her lower back, the base of her skull. It wasn't anywhere close to evening yet—3:45 in the after-noon—which belied the fact that she'd been traveling for a whole day. West Coast time, even now, fucked her up. It felt like pretend time. She looked to Derek.

"Don't disrespect your mother," he said, though Stefanie found it hard to shake the feeling like she was the one with her back against the wall. When Derek had showed her the string of text messages with Naomi (the latest from an hour ago: **I won't be coming back. I talked to Marjorie at County. Sorry. Tell Nathan I'll miss him**), the first one had been sent yesterday at 3:17 p.m.

Derek made Baz explain everything again. "We heard a noise, and we came up. Nathan had Naomi like he was hugging her, but he wasn't. I think I yelled at him. I ran up and grabbed him. She was freaked out, and he was yelling, and then she left."

"We take care of Nathan. All of us," Stefanie said. "We are responsible for him. Hard to imagine this would have happened without you and your friends in and out your room, running around like a bunch of—" She didn't know how to finish and didn't trust the sound of her own voice. All of her was tender like bruise. She hadn't expected to feel outside the current of this family too.

"I'm allowed to have friends over," Baz said.

"You're allowed to have friends over," Derek said.

"Except you *lied*," Stefanie said. "You told us you'd broken up with Livvy." The set of Baz's face made it feel like she was coming at him with a butter knife and expecting him to be scared.

"Knew you'd freak out," he said.

A line had been crossed—Baz had crossed a line—into disregard. She had never considered disregard, stupid as that seemed now. When she'd said goodbye to her mama this morning, she'd tried to get up on the bed beside her. *Whatchu doing?* Mama wanted to know. They'd been back to the Hazel Crest rehab, Century Center its bloodless moniker. Stefanie had spent all of yesterday figuring out Century Center's admissions paperwork, calling the Medicaid office and trying to figure out how a spend-down of her mother's assets would work. *Trying to hug you goodbye, Mama.* Her mother had patted her on the arm, told her her nails looked raggedy, she should get Stefanie to do her nails fancy. Stefanie always had fancy nails done up right.

"This is serious," Derek said.

"I know it is," Baz said.

"We don't have a personal support worker anymore," Stefanie said.

"I know," he said, shaking his head. "That's not on me."

"That most certainly is on you," Stefanie said.

"Okay," Derek said. "Can we take a step back? No one willfully did anything to harm anyone. No one tried to harm Nathan or Naomi." Stefanie knew this tone. It was Derek holding forth, like he did in front of 300 freshman.

Baz made a noise of assent, if begrudging.

"You shouldn't have kept it a secret," Derek said. "That's not okay.

You hear me? Your mother and I will talk about those consequences."

"I hear you," Baz mumbled into his hand. "S'ry."

"What was that?" Stefanie said. "I couldn't hear you."

"Sorry, Ma."

"No more sneaking around," Derek said.

Baz nodded to his lap again.

"It's time," Derek said, still orating. "We meet her. Bring her over when we're here."

He looked at Baz, and then he looked at Stefanie, Derek with a thin smile, one that suggested, *You're welcome.*

The consequences were thus: a week of grounding, though they had to define the term. He could leave the house for his internship, for errands or exercise, but there would be no friends over and no social plans. They'd never grounded Baz before, seventeen years and never once trouble, this proof of Stefanie's point about the girl, but she could tell she was losing Derek, Derek half-hearted in his agreement that the girl was trouble; less, maybe quarter-hearted. "Sure, sure sure," he told her, in the way Derek always did, but also, "I think we're past that point."

"Do I," Baz asked, halfway through the week, "like bring her by or what?"

Derek told him Livvy needed to come to dinner, meet his family for real, Derek the one to hold this line, Stefanie glad for him at least to be the one making a line and then holding it, though realizing too late that setting the table for the girl, setting out the water glasses and the place mats, gave the sense that they were consecrating something. "All this is is meeting her," she said to Derek.

"Well, it's not an engagement party," Derek said. He was wearing his apron with all the chili peppers, the apron looking like a dress, coming down past his shorts. It was one week plus one day past the start of the consequences, and Baz had been gone all day, no internship on Thursdays.

"Gone where?" Stefanie asked now. "With who?" But Derek had kissed her on her temple and told her, "Stop," which stung more than Stefanie let on. Since being home, she hadn't shaken the sense of being out of step with her family. She felt the girl was responsible for this too.

They came in hand in hand, Livvy peering at them through her bangs.

"What should I call you guys?" she asked, which Stefanie hadn't thought would be the first question. She had legs that went on and on, a tiny nothing-ass in her shorts.

"Derek and Stefanie," Derek offered before Stefanie could say, "Mr. and Mrs."

"You know," Baz said, pointing to Nathan on the couch.

"Hi, Nathan," the girl called, and it seemed to Stefanie she was showing off that she knew him.

"Nacho," he shouted from the couch, hitting his arm.

It didn't occur to the girl that she had something to make up for. She just stood there at Baz's side, their fingers laced, then later sat at the table beside him, Nathan around to the head of the table, where no one usually sat, Nathan not happy about that, and who could blame him? He banged his palm and then his spoon on the table in ways that Stefanie appreciated, Stefanie wishing she could bang too.

When Livvy caught Stefanie staring at her, she said, "This pasta is good. I like to make it al dente too. My mom always says it's chewy."

Stefanie asked Livvy what her parents did for a living, what her plans were for college. Do you have siblings, Stefanie wanted to know. She saw the way Baz looked at Livvy when she answered Stefanie's questions (just her mom—legal secretary; I don't know; an older sister in Alaska).

"In Alaska," Derek said. "How interesting."

Livvy shrugged. "Not really. Cold. Too light out. Or too dark."

"That's a funny thing to say about Alaska," Stefanie said.

"I mean—" the girl said, but didn't finish.

"Baz tells us you're Jewish," Stefanie said.

"Sure," the girl said, oddly. The girl was odd.

"You're—" Stefanie wasn't sure the appropriate follow up. "You had a bar mitzvah?"

"Bat," Livvy said.

"Bat?"

"Bat mitzvah is for girls. Bar mitzvah is boys."

"Well, isn't that good to know," Stefanie said, and the way Baz looked at Livvy, it was the same way he'd looked at the stray dog he'd brought home in fifth grade, fur matted and covered in burs, its one eye seeping. It had cowered in the corner of their old living room, Nathan screaming at the sight of him, covering his eyes and calling out *shboom shboom shboom*. For months, it had been only *shboom*.

"Please, please, please, please," Baz had said to them all night, and they'd not been used to this from Baz. He slept closed in the den on towels with the stray, feeding it bread and bologna and milk out of the fridge. In the morning, Nathan screamed from the other side of the closed den door, from the sound of the dog's whimpering. It didn't even bark. The towels were soaked in piss. They ended up having to throw out the Persian rug beneath.

When Derek scooped up the dog for the pound, Baz grabbed at Derek's arms and wouldn't let go. Stefanie had to pull Baz off, alarmed and impressed by his strength, by the sound of his howl. The way he watched that mongrel as Derek loaded it in the backseat, it was the same look with the girl: a desperate fury to protect it from them beneath watery regret that he could not.

WOODY

It was the ease of it that stunned him the most. Woody was a stand-up guy; whatever anyone else said or did not say about him, no one would take issue with the fact that he was a stand-up guy. Woody was slow to argue, quick to volunteer, polite to the point of solicitousness. He was the neighbor who volunteered to get on a ladder and clean out Gert Horowitz's gutters, Gert eighty if a day. He jump-started strangers' batteries (black on black, red on red). He gave to Goodwill *and* St. Vinny's.

And yet. There he sat at Starbucks for meetup number two, the tips of their shoes meeting beneath the table in a way that may have been accidental, but then it was their knees and definitely not accidental. Right here in Starbucks! Underneath the table! And he felt both in a dream and not at all in a dream, more like a realer version of reality—reality plus!—and anyone might come in at any moment and see them here like this, and how could he be doing this, yet he was doing this. It was easy to do this. And then before dinner—*honey, I'm going for a jog*—early evening on a park bench, a public park bench, no space between them, a blur of gnats nearby, the sky orange and everything looking beautiful to Woody and the two of them talking straight ahead while their thighs touched, talking about stupid nothings, Susan's boss's halitosis, the blue paint under his nails from the play house-cum-wall-less pod, the feel of her pinky on the hem of his jogging shorts, realer than real, and he wondered why people did this in secret, it was so pure and so good and so expansive, sitting beside another person on a park bench. And then a morning, an honest to goodness morning back in her apartment, Susan having called in sick, having scared away Livvy ("she beat a path as soon as she found out I was sticking around"), Woody telling Alison that his old pal Dan Sheridan wanted help picking out a new car, of all things, Alison not questioning why Woody would be any good at such a task, instead saying, "Good. You never see your friends! Go!" in the way a lovely and decent wife would, and the two of them, Woody and Susan, lying together on her sheets after, the sex having been quick and artless but neither of them seeming to have noticed or much cared, lying side by side, trailing fingertips over each other's sweaty and unfit bodies, Woody surprised and then disappointed and then grateful for the roll in her belly, the sag of her butt cheeks, given his gut and the pimples he knew sprouted on his upper back, Susan's nipples so huge yet inverted at the very tip, Woody saying, "God, you have weird nipples," and Susan laughing, her fingers circling and circling one cheek of his ass, Woody getting hard again and saying, "And your pillows are like really, really dense cake," and Susan saying, "Any other complaints?" while still laughing and Woody told her no, and the second time was better, slower, looking at each other instead of burying their foreheads into shoulders, and when he got back home, Alison gave him a quick kiss on the chin—she'd been aiming for his lips but was busy trying to get the popsicles she and Francie made to come out of the plastic molds.

Francie was swinging on the tire swing. Alison asked after Dan. How's Marsha? Marsha was good, Woody told her, the second wife on a new diet, maybe, he wasn't sure, and this too was easy, the lying, it rolled right off him, even he convinced by his own tone, casual, unpracticed. Alison was only half paying attention anyway, their love for each other careless after nearly a decade. There was no sniffing at collars, no questioning his flushed cheeks, what looked like a new rash of razor burn.

"Will you?" she said, handing him the tray of popsicles as she went to grab clothes from the dryer. His house, abuzz! So many tasks and chores! The popsicle molds were shaped like rocket ships, a layer of orange juice at the tip, apple in the middle, grape at the base. They were artful, and Woody ran them under cold water, pulling each one free. His wife had made gorgeous popsicles while he'd made love to Susan Albrecht in her bed on her yellow striped sheets, her air conditioner making a labored sound of *VRRRR-vrrrr-VRRRR-vrrr*, and he tried to feel bad and sad and a cad, but instead he popped one popsicle free, and the next, and knocked on the glass of the window box over the sink, and Francie looked up from her swinging, and he held up a popsicle, which was already starting to drip onto his fingers, fingers that had been inside Susan Albrecht. Where there should have been guilt, instead there was joy, and it was unclear if Francie could see him or a silhouette, so he knocked more and louder, until she leapt off the swing like Supergirl and came running through the lawn and up the deck barefoot and dappled in summertime, and god he loved his daughter, no he was *in* love with her. Why didn't he feel that way more, swept off in the love of all things beautiful, in love with the gorgeous popsicle, in love with the sore dick in his pants, in love with the raw, chafing tip of it against his underpants, in love with his wife, in love with the secret he kept from her, in love with Susan Albrecht, in love with being really, really good at this, a goddamned natural, in love with love.

PART II

FALL SEMESTER 2015

LARK

All anyone could talk about was leaving campus for lunch now that they were juniors. The whole first week back and into the second, she heard Dana Oxblood yelling down the hall about who's going in her car, Bren Dzikian scampering around trying to find other girls from cross country to go running with her, like the ability to exit the building for fifty minutes had turned them into a new breed of people, which they kind of were with the PSAT coming up in a month, and then the SAT six months after. They were upperclassmen now, supposed to be training their gaze past this building, spying their bright future. Lark couldn't even find someone to have lunch with.

Things had changed after Livvy and Baz weren't a secret anymore. Livvy's mom still didn't know, but that didn't make it a secret. Baz's family knowing was enough to break whatever spell they'd been under for the first half of the summer. Baz and Livvy came and went as they pleased, and Lark wasn't allowed over at Baz's anymore. Shocky either. "There's a new guy with Nathan," Livvy said, as if that were an explanation.

Livvy had asked what happened with her and Shocky and Nathan and the aide, and Lark didn't know what to say but "Shocky got some grapes and a beer." She didn't admit the bathroom or the toilet paper. It felt too much like being guilty of something. When Livvy asked again, Lark added, "I wanted a yogurt, but I didn't take one," and Livvy said, "Stop dicking around, I'm serious," and after that, she wasn't really invited over to Livvy's when Livvy and Baz were there either. She wasn't *not* invited, but she had to ask now—"What are you guys doing today?" and "Can I come?"—which was okay a couple times but then humiliating.

She'd spent the dwindling days of summer in the house with her mom, her mom drifting in and out of her bedroom, Lark making them a cottage cheese parfait one day, which was cottage cheese with cut-up grapes on top and then walnuts on top of the grapes, but she called it a parfait and her mom was so happy, she vowed to do more nice things for her mom, vowed to spend more time together. They sat at the table spooning their parfaits silently into their mouths until Lark said, "So what's going on?" because it had been a long time since they'd tried to actually make conversation, and this seemed like one way to do it, but her mother sighed into her parfait and said, "Oh, honey," as if no one had asked her such a sad question, and then her mom left the dirty dish and the spoon with white trails of cottage cheese on the table for Lark to clean.

She ended up taking a bus downtown, weaving through the fists of homeless kids on corners, who mumbled things at her that were requests, maybe demands, and then walking through the library, through the stacks of books on the second floor and the third, not reading the titles, letting the different sized and colored spines swim over her, twiddling her fingers along them, listening to the murmurs of the library patrons, feeling in the middle of something, even if it was only a bunch of books, a bunch of strangers, and she thought of how Mr. Langston had made them underline verbs as they read, and then call them out to him after, and he wrote them in lists on the board, and the blur of library did not <u>cure</u> or <u>solve</u> or <u>prevent</u> anything, but it <u>eased</u> or <u>lessened</u> or <u>dulled</u> Lark's loneliness.

Once school started, Baz and Livvy marched defiantly through the halls, intertwined, his arm around her waist, her finger in his belt loop. They kissed at the lockers. They'd ended last year pretending to be broken up, and now they were like a big *fuck you* to everyone who'd given them grief, and indeed, the fact that they were together seemed to newly energize Miles and Roger or whoever; people were pissed, but for what exactly, it was no longer clear. Livvy heard girls at a bathroom mirror talking about her while she was in a stall. What did they say, Lark wanted to know. *Shit,* was all Livvy said. *Stupid shit.* Someone passed her a note in AP Lit and there was a cartoon of her that was big boobs and fat lips, puckered for kissing. "It doesn't even look like you," Lark said when she showed her. "Maybe it's someone else," and Livvy looked at her like there'd never been anyone as stupid. All of this happened without the loud concern of teachers and their MLK assemblies; it was basically normal now.

As for Livvy and Lark, it was as if a new skin had cooled across the top of them. Lark still hung out at the movie theater. Candace didn't work at the earrings and bangles store anymore, or at least never when Lark was there, which was okay. Livvy and Lark still wandered home together if Baz was busy.

"You got a new face," her mom said one night, reaching her sausage fingers toward Lark's cheek, and Lark remembered the worse thing than her mom ignoring her was her mom not. "Sad face," her mom said, pinching her cheek softly. Lark made them noodles with butter.

Lark mostly ate in the cafeteria with Rochelle and Dawn from geometry. They were boring and sophomores, but it was better than eating by herself, at least for a few weeks, until one day she couldn't anymore, and she stood in the hallway at the start of lunch trying to look like she was looking for something in her backpack, half-watching out for Baz and Livvy so they'd ask her along. She had a peanut butter sandwich and cheese sticks and baby carrots. When she was little, it was her mom who made her lunches, squaring her sandwiches, quartering an orange, acts that seemed like feats now. Once there was a note: *Lark—You are a* and then a five-pointed star, which set in place years of hope until she convinced herself she'd made it up (she hadn't; she'd find it yellowed and softened under her mattress at nineteen when she swapped out her bed for a futon on the floor).

"You looking for your girlfriend?" Shocky yelled, marching past with Monique. Lark thought she'd been acting like she wasn't looking. "She left with her boy," Shocky called, more loudly than he needed to. "They forget to come get you? They leave you here without parental supervision?" He laughed. She pretty much hated Shocky.

"Ease up, man," said Monique, swatting Shocky on the arm, though lightly. "Leave the girl be. Look at her."

Lark didn't know what that meant. It felt mean, except then Monique turned around and shouted, "You want to come with us?" and it was the last thing Lark expected to hear, the last person she expected to hear it from. Monique Deveraux hated Lark. And Shocky was telling Monique, "Naw, that girl don't go nowhere without her—" as Lark was shutting her locker, jogging to catch up with them, not even <u>thinking</u>, letting her feet do her <u>wishing</u> for her, doing her <u>hoping</u>.

All they did, turned out, was walk to the Safeway where Shocky got a Sprite and a bag of barbecue chips, Monique a strawberry milk. Lark hadn't seen anyone drink a strawberry milk since elementary school. "You want anything?" she asked Lark, and Lark couldn't tell if she meant did Lark want Monique to buy her something (*yes, please*) or did Lark want to buy herself something (*no money*). She shrugged. When they were back outside, they stood in front of the Safeway, Monique drinking the strawberry milk in a long guzzle, pink mustache caught in the fine fuzz atop her lip.

"This is what she's like," Shocky said to Monique. "Helen Keller quiet."

Lark had watched the old movie about Helen Keller years ago during some long, wet afternoon with Livvy. They'd laughed and laughed at the strange noises the actress had made when her hands were in the water. "Wa-wa" they aped at each other for weeks after.

"Jesus," Monique said. "Ease up."

"You ease up," Shocky said. The rancid hoppiness from the can return machines wafted toward them. Early October and the rains hadn't started yet, every day feeling like it was going to be the last before they got hammered by fall. It was almost balmy. Monique had taken off her long sleeve Nike shirt and tied it around her waist. It was both disappointing and reassuring to Lark that they didn't have anywhere to go beside Safeway.

"He's an idiot with girls," Monique said. Her arms were muscled impressively. Lark wasn't used to seeing girl arms like that.

"You play basketball," Lark said, the one thing she knew about Monique other than not liking having her hair touched.

"Yep," Monique said. "You play any sports?"

Shocky laughed. Lark shrugged. "Hang on," she said. "You're a sophomore and you're off campus."

Monique laughed into her strawberry milk bottle. "Damn, Sherlock. You caught me," and then: "No one cares. Haven't been busted yet."

Lark found this both shocking and hilarious. She wondered how many sophomores were off campus right now.

"What happened—?" Monique said, pointing to her own chin. No one ever asked that. Sometimes Lark fell into believing no one could see it anymore.

Lark told the story of the dog as if it were a memory. She left out the part about meeting Livvy for the first time.

"Jee-zus," Monique said. "That's fucked up. I hope that dog got put down."

It was the first time anyone said that, though Lark hadn't told the story in a long time. The only new friends she had had since Livvy were Baz and Shocky, and they weren't really hers.

"I don't know," Lark said, unable to picture the dog even if she'd tried. She'd seen plenty of pictures of Rottweilers since, and ones in real life. They set off nothing inside her. "I hope not."

"You *hope* not?" Monique said, in the same tone as she used with Shocky; otherwise, it might have hurt Lark's feelings. "Jesus, girl. Dog could've killed you."

"I don't think it was really his fault." Lark didn't know if it was a boy dog.

"Could put the neighbors down." Monique laughed at herself.

Lark wasn't sure what to say. *Wa-wa*. She wondered what came after standing in front of the Safeway. Her sandwich and cheese stick sat untouched in her backpack. Were they going to take out their lunches? Buy more food somewhere?

"Doesn't look that bad," Shocky said, touching his own chin. "I seen worse." He shrugged. "Can't even see it from one side."

"Awww," Monique said, loud and theatrical. "Look at Shocky talking all nice to a girl."

"Shut the fuck up," Shocky said, but he was smiling, shoving her on the shoulder. Monique shoved him back. Lark's stomach made a noise she hoped neither of them heard. It was only when they were walking back to the school that Monique said:

"You one of those little anorexic white girls?"

"No," Lark said, wanting to explain about the food in her backpack, not knowing how to say she didn't know the right time to take it out without sounding like a fool. Instead, she said: "All you had was milk." And then, in a voice that was not her own, but an imitation: "You one of those tall anorexic Black girls?" and Monique stopped right there on the sidewalk and put a hand on Lark's arm. It was fast becoming clear that Monique was the kind of girl who touched people on the arms a good deal—swatting, patting, shoving. Lark had never seen her on the basketball court, but she imagined Monique a physical player, elbow into rib, shoulder into jaw.

"Damn!" Monique said. "Ha!" she called out, as if she were performing a laugh, rather than laughing. To Shocky: "She ain't no Helen Keller. That's some ninja shit, some quiet sneaky shit." She was talking so loud, a boy several paces ahead of them on the sidewalk turned around, and Lark wasn't sure she knew any girl this unafraid to make herself big.

"I have a sandwich," Lark said. "Carrots. I didn't know when to take them out."

"What?" Monique said, performing the *What?* like the *Ha!* "You're a trip."

"Cheese stick too," Lark said to get a reaction.

"Take the cheese stick out whenever you get hungry, girl. Didn't your momma teach you anything about lunchtime?"

Later, at Livvy's, Livvy hung her head and one arm off the edge of her bed. Lark sat on the floor, playing with Livvy's knock-off Russian nesting dolls, grandpa splitting at his mid-section and opening into grandma, grandma opening into dad, dad opening into mom, mom opening into boy, boy opening into girl, girl opening into baby. Lark loved that tiny little wooden baby, always had, no bigger than a lima bean. She held it in her palm, studying the tiny swirl of features, black dots of eyes, two tiny lashes on each, red cheeks, a single black whorl of hair atop its bean head. Wall-E lolled nearby in a sunspot.

"Tickle my arm," Livvy said, and Lark did.

It'd been a while since they had an afternoon like this—no Baz, no movie theater.

"I'm bored," Livvy said, and her face was dark, blood draining to her cheeks and forehead. Her hair hung down like a big brown fan. "You should get with Shocky." Her voice sounded funny from upside down.

Lark wondered what they used to talk about. They used to talk about nothing, everything reminding them of something else, jokes repeated so often they were no longer jokes. *Wa-wa.*

"Monique Deveraux is nice," Lark said, feeling homesick but not for her house. Her house made her homesick most of all. Wall-E came over, kneading his front paws on her thighs. She tickled with one hand, petted the top of Wall-E's head with the other, reminding herself of when they used to try to pet their own heads and rub circles in their own bellies at the same time. Impossible!

"Monique Deveraux looks like a dude," Livvy said. "You seen her legs?"

Lark watched the white trails in Livvy's arm. When they were little, they would play dog attack. Livvy would pretend like she was biting Lark. Lark would pretend like she was biting Livvy. They would actually bite each other, but not hard. They would growl. "Was it like this?"

Livvy used to say, biting Lark's wrist. "Was it like this?" Lark would always say yes. She remembered how it felt, her teeth beginning to sink into the fleshy pad of Livvy's palm, into the flank of Livvy's side. She liked being the dog so much better than being the girl.

"Dog attack," she said now, because she wanted that feeling again. She would bite down this time. She would let her teeth sink in.

"Stop being stupid," Livvy said, and not even meanly. It was just the kind of thing Livvy said to Lark now.

Lark thought of the dog getting killed like Monique said. It didn't make her that sad. He was a dog; he wouldn't have known he was getting killed. Could've even died happy, laid out on a vet's table, a nurse whispering in his furry ear, the prick of a shot and memories of kibble or tree or Frisbee, or of that stretch of seconds when he dragged her around by the jaw. Could've come back to him in a flash as the poison wound through his veins, as he was taking his last doggy—

—teeth into pink flesh!

—got her!

—he got, he got, he got!

STEFANIE

She came home to Mercer, their newest PSW, doing the dishes at the sink while Nathan sat at the table by himself, Mercer always half a room away from Nathan. Naomi used to be right up on top of Nathan, often murmuring a murmur that stopped as soon as Stefanie came in the room. Stefanie had liked the idea of Nathan having confidences.

"We have a cleaning lady already," she said, more arch than she'd intended, but perhaps exactly as arch as she needed to be. It had been a while since they'd had a mediocre PSW; she'd forgotten what it was like to come home to Nathan, frayed, starting to seam apart. She saw it in his eyes, the way they didn't raise to meet her, the way he stared hard at the tabletop now, jittering his fingers at the sides of his head, slurring low *nnnn-nnnuh*s.

"Yes, ma'am," Mercer said. The best thing she could say for him is that he'd stuck around for nearly two months already.

"How are you, honey?" She leaned into Nathan's head and kissed him. He was vibrating and smelled oily and like the tang of unwashed folds of skin. "Did you shower?" she asked Nathan.

"No, ma'am, sorry," Mercer said. "We forgot that from our agenda."

She pointed to the photo calendar next to the cupboards, today's laminated photos: Mercer, toothbrush, shower. "The schedule," she said, "is important."

Bass from some identifiable music drummed through her feet. The rule was Baz couldn't close his door when Livvy was over, which usually meant his door rested against the frame, technically open, though no crack for even light to sliver through. Stefanie had stopped asking if Livvy wanted to stay for dinner once she realized the girl only ever said yes. The girl was fine, more or less, thought occasionally to clear the table, even once asked Stefanie, "What's it like to work in a hospital?"

"A guy came," Mercer said, the way he said things, picking up a mustard-yellow envelope from the counter. "And delivered this to Nathan."

"To Nathan?" Nathan didn't get mail aside from junk. Did he want to go to the Toyota dealership used car sale? New credit card, 2.5 percent introductory APR? She didn't recognize the return address, a list of three unfamiliar last names, separated by commas and an ampersand. Only later would she think that nothing good ever came from three names separated by commas and an ampersand.

"Served it, ma'am," Mercer said.

At the kitchen counter, she blinked and blinked at the words on paper, and it was the feeling of standing up too quickly from sitting, and she read and reread and reread "complaint" and "Naomi Alberson" on letterhead with the same three names, the same comma and goddamned ampersand.

There was noise up the stairs, the trundle of footsteps, the girl first and Baz behind her, both with smiles like sharks. "Hey," the girl said, but hardly, a mumble as she passed. "Hi, Ma," Baz said. The girl was into the fridge, grabbing out an Izze's without asking. Was this rude? Did Shekib ask before grabbing? Stefanie strained to think of what was it like with Shekib, when was the last time with Shekib?

The girl used the hem of her shirt to open the Izze bottle, struggling with it or pretending to in the way girls pretended. Stefanie saw a flash of pale belly before Baz took the bottle and opened it for her. She no longer wore the short shorts of summer. Now it was capri pants, her hair cut short, a recent change, blunt ends against her chin. It was a nice cut, more flattering, and yet seeing the girl through a new season and into a second hair style suggested permanence, and this is what happened when Stefanie went along, this was what happened when she rolled over, and a feeling rose in her, a feeling without words, her mind clouding with the letter, the *served* letter, her mind hurting from trying to be, especially with all these extra people in the kitchen, the kids drinking loud from their soda bottles, giggling about something no one else was privy too, Mercer not yet gone—why was he still here?—Nathan at the table, slapping the inside of his arm, soon his tender skin would be aflame, and she hadn't even taken off her coat yet, hadn't even stepped out of her shoes, still her fingers smelled like hospital, her scalp tired from the day, and was this feeling, this swirling and sinking, how Nathan mostly felt? Please, please, don't let it be how Nathan mostly felt.

By the time Derek got home, the girl was gone, Mercer gone, dinner eaten, Baz downstairs, Stefanie and Nathan on the living room couch, Stefanie with a magazine she wasn't reading, Nathan with *The Octonauts* on the iPad. (Bowhead: "We're not aiming to brag now but we bow-heads do have the strongest, toughest heads in the arctic.") Stefanie's panic had swirled into incredulity into fury and back into panic. Derek coming through the door spiked her adrenaline.

"How was seminar?" she asked, off the couch, not waiting for an answer, handing him the complaint and the summons that she'd read through so many times already, she could nearly recite it from memory. Naomi was suing Nathan—Nathan!—for $58,000 from "medical treat-ment," "pain and suffering," "income," "emotional distress," and "loss of enjoyment" as a result of her "workplace injury," of "a traumatic physical attack upon her person," resulting in "contusions," "musculo-skeletal pain," "bone bruising," "lumbar pain," and "headaches" as well as "anxiety," "depression," and "post-traumatic stress."

"I tried calling Marjorie," Stefanie said, as he was reading, unable to give him the quiet to read. "But it was after five. I left her a voicemail. I'm sure Naomi can't actually sue Nathan."

"Why? He's an adult," Derek said, with an alarming calm, even for Derek.

"Are you being serious?" Stefanie said.

"I think you can sue an adult," he said.

"What about of sound mind and body?"

"I mean," he said, "we've watched the same *Law & Order* episodes, so I don't know."

"Hello?" she said, by which she meant, *Are you in there?*

Derek looked at her, something sheepish and unreadable on his face, walking away from Stefanie and over to Nathan. There were times she thought he was no longer capable of surprising her, and then he did. "Hey, buddy," he said, kissing Nathan on the forehead.

Nathan murmured without looking up, Nathan at the end of day with the iPad the easiest Nathan of all.

"Don't worry, Boris," Derek said to the narwhal. "The bowheads will smash through the ice in a minute."

She followed Derek into the kitchen, where he scooped out chili from the pot still on the stovetop. He pulled a hank of French bread off the loaf on the counter.

"Derek!"

"I need to tell you something," he said as he sat. "Listen but don't freak out." Even after all these years, they knew exactly how to make the other crazy. "I saw her. Naomi. She called here a couple times afterward, complaining."

"Complaining?"

"Back pain. Chiropractor. Said she could barely work."

"She called and said all this, and you didn't think to tell me?"

"I didn't want to worry you."

"Jesus, Derek."

"I gave her money."

"What?"

"Will you sit? Will you please sit down?"

"Don't manage me. You worry about yourself. How much?"

"Three hundred."

"You give her three hundred dollars and you don't tell me?"

"You spend three hundred dollars on shoes," he said, his voice rising for the first time.

"Once! One time I spent three hundred dollars for a pair of shoes, and you have never let me forget. And I *told* you. I immediately *told* you. I believe I even handed you the receipt and said, 'Look what I bought—three-hundred-dollar shoes.'" She was waving a finger at Derek. He had not taken a single bite of his dinner. God help him if he had.

"And then four hundred," he said quickly. "And then I stopped. I stopped when she asked for more."

Why, twenty-three years before, had she fallen in love with a nappy-headed boy from the hick part of the state, so far south he might as well be a Missourian, who grabbed her outside the UI union ballroom after the step show to say, "I was sitting the row behind you. I watched you that whole show. Goddamn, you cute"? This boy with a chin too big and a mouth that ran and ran, who found her in a library carrel and later on the lawn outside Foellinger? Why did she fall in love with him on the patio of his apartment, third date, sky loud with crickets, air thick with the coming summer? Because he told her how much he loved playing trumpet as a kid, and how he used to keep caterpillars as pets in a shoebox except they always died, and he said it earnestly, he wasn't telling stories the way boys learned to tell stories to girls to make themselves look good, and she'd never met a boy like him, no fronting, kind to everyone, needy and funny and nervous, didn't hide his softness, wore his softness like a badge, asking, "You like me? This mean you like me now?" once they finally kissed, making a joke, but not a joke.

How was she to know then that the question would never be answered, no matter how many times it got answered, man with a wife and two children, man with a doctor in front of his name, a PhD behind, man with an associate professorship before fifty, in line for full professor by fifty-two, and still asking of anyone who might answer, including the girl on the phone who asked secretly in the summertime to take money from his family:

You like me? This mean you like me now?

WOODY

Second half of October, start of November was PSAT follow-up conferences for every junior on his roll (A-I). The sheer volume, student after student after student in ten-minute increments, normally got to him, but not this year! There was an artfulness required, every junior strong-armed into the PSATs because school participation rates were shared district-wide. Now Woody's job was to tell those who had expectedly bombed not to soldier on to the SATs; to those who had *unexpectedly* bombed, smart students who were bad at testing, push the plethora of SAT test prep courses; and finally, to those who had done well, commend them, but not too strongly, as these students needed to keep it up and perform as well, if not better, at the SAT, since aggregated scores were also shared district-wide. The district promised such aggregates would not affect individual schools, but SAT scores, like everything that measured anything, could be used as a cudgel.

Was *this* getting to Woody?

It was not. Cudgel away, district!

He would float on a plane of equanimity above all the petty politics and infighting, dick hard in his pants. His dick was hard in his pants so often now, he was like the boys who hobbled through the halls, holding notebooks at their waists. He'd never been more grateful for the antiquated arrangement of his office, which counselors like Deirdre (J-S) scoffed at, his desk facing the doorway, separating him from whoever sat in the chairs. Deirdre's desk was pushed the other way around, facing the window, so that she could twirl in her chair to meet with students knee to knee, "absent the barriers of power."

Absent the barriers of power all you want, Deirdre! Woody cared not! Woody was so happy to hide his boner in the dark cave beneath his top desk drawer, he could have kissed Deirdre for it.

Between the conferences, he checked his email. At Susan's urging he'd gotten a new email no one else knew about, Badlistener.WH@gmail.com, which gave him a real kick. He wasn't usually one for cheap irony, but he also wasn't usually one for sleeping with Susan Albrecht.

She'd also said no to texting: "Men who text always get caught." She'd also urged him to stop emailing her from beside Alison in bed.

"It's twisted," she told him. "Unless that's what you're getting off on."

He didn't think that was what he was getting off on. Her face when she said it was one of his favorite faces on her: tough but playful, a put-upon pout and a shine to her eyes. A glint. He'd never thought of *glint* in regard to anyone's eyes before. *Glint* had seemed heretofore a silly word, like *cacophony* and *semaphore*; indisputably words, but what sort of dumb mutt ever used them?

He emailed (nee.hoffman73@gmail.com, an email she'd made unnecessarily and for him, with an exhilarating nod to her maiden name) exclusively from work. He spent lunchtime at his desk, composing, a mix of witty observations—**Doug Epstein got hair plugs and it makes him look like my daughter's Ken doll**—and want—**I smell like you. Even after a shower last night and this morning, I have you under my fingernails and I can't even name it but it's you. Flour maybe, warm yeasty flour.**

She always wrote back—short quick spurts:

God, Woody, you always knew how to sweet talk a girl. Yeasty. Every woman's dream.

He laughed at his desk.

And his favorite:

When can I see you?

His life was broken up now, broken up and broken down into discrete increments: seeing Susan, having seen Susan, trying to see Susan again. One Saturday morning he said he was going to the hardware store but instead he drove to the synagogue. There was Susan in the prayer shawl and yarmulke near the front, rocking in her seat, intent on the prayerbook and the rabbi, Woody too far away to appreciate the hand embroidery, barely inside the sanctuary. He knew not to further trespass; he could run into a student easily, families, and then what would he say? *Oh, hi, I wanted to see if it would be meditative for me too,* which was a lie anyway. All he'd wanted was to catch a glimpse, which felt profane now. He hoped she wouldn't catch him like this, except for the fact that he hoped she'd turn her head and catch him exactly like this.

Home was desperate for its lack of Susan, but also startlingly sweet for its obliviousness and the way it hung in the balance without even knowing there was a balance to hang in. He had finished his wall-less pod, painted a blue gray that Alison had chosen, already christened with its first round of bird poop, and Francie showing little to no interest in it.

"Let's go have a tea party!" Woody said to her in the evenings, and she gave him her clip-on diamond earrings and one of her pink boas, the fake feathers (or maybe they were real) pricking at his neck. They sat inside the wall-less pod together, Woody's knees up to his chest in the kid chairs, Francie pouring him the invisible tea he seemed to have wanted so desperately. "What kind of tea is this?" he asked. "Tea tea," she said, sitting and looking at him like he was supposed to make the fun now. Wasn't this supposed to be fun?

Livvy's ten minutes: 2:50 on Thursday. He'd known for days, all other conferences a countdown to it. He hadn't told Susan he was seeing Livvy today. It felt a line he should not cross, if only to prove to himself that he was still a man who could draw lines and not cross them. He would tell her about Livvy if she asked, but she asked less and less, as if Livvy had been what was between them at the start, but she was no longer of them. Only they were of them. Susan was more ticklish on her feet than her stomach. He liked to pull her hair as he came, not one to have ever touched a woman like that before, asking and asking the first time, "Are you okay? Are you okay?" until she finally said, "I was until you asked the sixth time." She had a childhood scar on her lower back, a long fall from a tall tree. He found showering with her impossible without laughing for the way the soap ran down her chin, her dark hair flattened in the water like a seal, a beautiful fucking seal. She loved when he swore. He swore.

He was seeing her tonight, pretending to attend the monthly school board meeting, never so happy for the endless jabber of the board president as meetings inched into their third hour and then past, to nine-fifteen, nine-thirty, even once 10:10.

He would not have a boner beneath his desk when Livvy arrived at 2:30. Another line he was capable of drawing. He bit his cheek all through his 2:00, his 2:10, his 2:20, he pictured his mother's flabby buttocks at the poolside, the curdle of her thighs, her breasts stuffed into her flowered bathing suit. Her armpits sagged with loose skin; the crevices filled with white deodorant. That's what he was thinking when he rose from his chair at 2:30, the deodorant in his mother's flaccid armpits, as he greeted Livvy with a loud *hello,* penis proudly limp in his pants.

She didn't look herself, tired maybe, bags under her eyes, her face more sallow than normal. *Was she sick?* Woody wondered, followed immediately by: *Did she know?* and the garlic from the hummus from the lunchtime sandwich Alison had fixed for him ("We're on the Mediterranean plan," she'd cheerfully announced) rose in his throat, and stomach acid, and fuck, had Susan left a laptop open, had she laid a tablet carelessly down? Did Livvy see the one where he called her yeasty, the one where he'd referenced (adoringly) her *cunt* to see if he could? He could!

"What?" Woody said, not dispensing with the PSAT speech so much as forgetting it entirely.

"Have you seen this?" Livvy rifled her phone from her backpack, and Woody was sick with what she might show him, (badlistener.WH: "You know I go to bed thinking of your silky cunt"), for the first time sick with what he was doing, vowing not to go through with tonight, not to go through with any of it anymore.

He stared at her phone. He did not understand what he was looking at. It was a Facebook page, he knew that much, even without being a Facebooker, Alison Facebooker enough for the both of them, posting selfies of him, her and Francie, or the breakfast she and Francie cooked for Father's Day, or Woody painting the wall-less pod, coming up with all sorts of hashtags #familylife #dreamhusband #fatheroftheyear.

It was a page of kids from West, that much he understood. He saw their names and their pictures. "Olivia A. gave me a blowjob in fifth grade" from Benjamin Zucker; one of Sandy's (T-Z), a kid he barely recognized. Twenty-two likes and fourteen comments, most of them of similar ilk—"BITCH!" and "yeah" and "me too"—and here he recognized names, Bass and Cobain and Abramovitz. "i heard she showed roger her boobs in the boy's bathroom and then was upset when he rejected her and that's how everything started. is that true because if it is, that is MESSED UP"—Sadie Frost, junior, student council treasurer, having sat where Livvy was sitting right now, not two hours earlier. "baz is chill. i think it's fukked up if people r mad @ baz. he didnt do anything, he never got anyone in trouble. originol thing in the library, he just sat there (i heard)."—Jerry Andot, already graduated. Kids were coming *back* to be a part of this nonsense?

"I don't understand what I'm looking at," he said, though what he *did* understand was that he was looking at something terrible for Livvy that had absolutely nothing to do with him, and for that he was goddamned thankful, sending up a prayer of gratitude for his life, intact, and for his wife and for his child, and for Susan and her silky, silky cunt, which he was hours away from seeing, smelling, touching, three and a half hours; less, three hours and twenty-three minutes.

"Lindsay Nichols made a secret group," Livvy said. "It's called 'Olivia is such a bitch.'"

Woody tried to picture Lindsay Nichols; junior, he was pretty sure; lacrosse? He'd met with Roger Bass and Miles Cobain earlier this week, 770 and 680 respectively, neither surprised by their score, both dumbly affable. "We didn't do any of that stuff," Roger said of last spring's unpleasantness. Woody hadn't even been the one to bring it up. "You know we didn't do that, Woodman." The boy really seemed to care, so much so that Woody almost felt bad about their ban from peer tutoring services. But now, look, here Roger was, littering 🌢s in the comments, everywhere beside Roger's name, a trail of 🌢🌢🌢. Woody hated to feel like a schmo, except for right now when he was a schmo with only three hours and twenty-one minutes to go.

"They let you into a secret group about you?"

"I'm on Shocky's account. He's the one that told us."

"Facebook allows this?"

"I mean…" She pointed to the phone Woody was still holding. "I guess. Because it's there."

"Have you asked them to take it down?"

Her eyes got shiny. "I don't—" she said. "Why do I—"

He'd never seen Livvy cry before. He'd never seen her at a loss for words. "Sorry, sorry, sorry, I'm trying to wrap my brain around this. When I was in high school, people wrote on the bathroom walls." He was trying to make a joke. He handed Livvy tissues. They'd had state in-services on cyber-bullying, and at Garner across town there had been a public imbroglio when a boy had forwarded pictures of a topless classmate he'd had "cyber-sex" with. The girl's family had sued the district under Title IX, and the district had settled, after which there were state in-services on Title IX. But Woody had never been up close to it. He'd never held it in his hand.

"Okay, listen to me. These kids are in violation of the school conduct code, and if Facebook isn't going to do something about, then certainly Principal Vonn—"

"No!" Livvy said. "That's going to make it worse. If they get in trouble for it, they're going to start a new page back up somewhere and hate me more." She balled the tissue in her fist.

Woody realized he was disappointed in Livvy. He'd always believed her casual disregard for her classmates. Beyond Lark, and now Baz, she had so convincingly conveyed her attitude of indifference. It was surprising to him that she cared, and then immediately surprising that he was surprised. He was an idiot. She was a sixteen-year-old girl. Of course she did not want to be hated en masse.

God, he ached for Susan, ached on *behalf* of Susan for what she did not know.

"Okay," he said. "I'll call Facebook and see what I can do."

"You can't *call* Facebook," and it was the first time she even half-smiled.

"I'll email them or text or perform a semaphore, whatever you have to do to get their attention."

Jennifer buzzed him through the intercom. "You've got a back-up out here."

"I need a minute. They can cool their jets."

"Okay," Jennifer said in a tone that conveyed the opposite.

"Sorry," Livvy said.

"Not your fault," Woody said, starting to get his rhythm in this conversation. This was what it was like when Alison was upset too, he ranging blindly around before settling into things, taking gentle control. "Nothing to apologize for. Who do you have to talk to?"

"You know," she said. "Baz. Lark."

"Your mom?" he said, and it was the question he should have asked, the question he needed to be asking as a school guidance counselor in a crisis situation with a student. But it also gave him a deeply satisfying thrill.

"Fuck no," she said. And then: "'Scuse me."

"I've heard worse," Woody said. And: "Your mom seems like a nice lady. You know we were in high school together."

Livvy looked neither impressed nor interested. He hoped that she'd ask him to expound upon his knowledge of Susan.

"No one can compete with her pain," Livvy said. "Her husband died and everything else after that is like…the epilogue. I'm like the shitty second book in the series that everyone says wasn't as good as the first."

He saw Susan in her cleverness and her candor and her lack of pretense. They were who they were, the Albrecht ladies. He had half a mind to tell Georgina about the Facebook group. He had half a mind to tell the whole of this conversation to Susan.

"I cannot imagine," Woody said, "that anyone would find you the shitty sequel. Certainly not your mother. She loves you. She probably loves you more since your dad died."

This, the outer edge of what a guidance counselor would say to a student in crisis if that student happened to be one of his favorites, maybe his lone favorite.

"Shut up," Livvy said, but not meanly. "We'll have you over sometime for dinner and then you can see."

"Oh, will you?" and they were playing now, injecting some much-needed levity into an otherwise not-at-all-funny situation, and it all made Woody outlandishly happy, that she had come to him, that he had helped her, that he was as close to being with Susan as he could get in the absence of her, that he had run well over his allotted ten minutes with nary a word about the PSATs, which meant Livvy would have to come back, and soon. "Ignore the cacophony," he said, pointing to her phone. "I'm on it! Know that I'm on it."

Only three hours and six minutes to go. He'd sat through movies that long! Movies about the Holocaust and slain civil rights leaders! Dire, dire movies during which his ass fell asleep, and he had to leave twice to go to the restroom! "Who's that?" he had to ask Alison to get caught back up. "Who are those guys?" as they were shushed from crotchety folks in the row behind, Alison leaning in, gripping his arm on the armrest between them, her whispers hot and sweet in his ear.

Subject: Objectionable secret group
Date: November 5 3:19 p.m.
To: Facebook Help <support@fb.com>
From: Woody Hanover <woody_h@wesths>

Dear Facebook Help,
I am a guidance counselor at West High School, and it has been
brought to my attention that there is a secret page targeting one of our
students. The secret page is titled "Olivia Albrecht is a bitch," which
gives you a sense of the inappropriate content. Please take this page
down immediately. I appreciate your haste in doing so.
Sincerely,
Woody Hanover
West High School
Guidance Counselor (A-I)

Subject: re: Objectionable secret group
Date: November 6 6:17 a.m.
To: Woody Hanover <woody_h@wesths>
From: Facebook Help <support@fb.com>

Dear Woody,
I'm sorry to hear about this situation. Facebook offers several tools to
help you deal with bullying, harassment, or other abusive behavior.
• Unfriend the person. Only your Facebook friends can contact you
  through Facebook chat or post on your timeline.
• Block the person. This will prevent the person from adding you as
  a friend and viewing things you share on your timeline.
• Report the person or any abusive things they post.
If you feel you're in immediate danger, contact your local authorities.
Best,
Samantha

Subject: re: re: Objectionable secret group
Date: November 6 9:03 a.m.
To: Facebook Help <support@fb.com>
From: Woody Hanover <woody_h@wesths>

Dear Samantha,

Thank you for your early morning response. I believe I am doing bullet three, which is "Report the person or any abusive things they post," except in my case, I am reporting a secret group, which is by its nature abusive, since it exists to besmirch a student at the school. Can you please remove this group? I look forward to hearing from you before the start of the weekend.

Sincerely,

Woody Hanover

West High School

Guidance Counselor (A-I)

LARK

They walked in the rain, Baz and Livvy holding hands up front, Shocky a few paces behind them, Lark a few paces behind him, a parade, this the first time they'd all been together since the afternoon at Baz's house. Lark looked and looked around, thinking of her own eyeballs and wondering if she was high.

They'd eaten the brownies in Shocky's half-finished basement, Shocky's parents spending their Saturday visiting a college friend an hour north. Livvy had texted Lark. Did she want to come hang out? Livvy had stopped texting Lark anything like this for weeks now, more than a month, and if Lark had questions, including but not limited to *Does this mean things are back to normal? Are you going to start inviting me to other stuff too?* she knew that wasn't how it worked. How it worked was Lark texting **Yes**.

Shocky had presented a large tin-foiled square. "This," he said, "is some good shit," the brownies scored into eight narrow rectangles. "One is good, but if you want to get really fucked up, do two."

Livvy grabbed two. Baz took one.

Lark had never smoked pot. Her mom sometimes did, but it seemed like it drove her further into herself, moving like a snail, blinking, taking both Lark's hands in hers and saying things like, "Oh, sweetheart, I was thinking yesterday…" before trailing off, dropping Lark's hands and walking away, as if the pot had made Lark both more real and less to her mother. Her mom was already hard enough.

Lark ate one brownie, then a second, wishing for milk.

Shocky turned around in the rain now, looking at her funny. "You a'ight back there?" he asked.

She shrugged. "Sure," she said, thinking about her throat, her voice, the sound of her words, wondering what someone thought like when they were high.

They walked and walked, no destination in mind, past campus, till Lark's jean cuffs were wet and her feet hurt. She was cold inside her raincoat. It seemed like they would never stop, and all Lark felt like, she decided, was someone tired of walking. They made it to the pedestrian bridge that spanned the river. Livvy hopped atop the concrete half-wall of the bridge, stones set into the top. Didn't look comfortable, sitting on those wet stones, but Livvy slung her arms over the wooden railing at her chest, kicking her legs back and forth, happy as a whatever.

"Not supposed to," Lark said of the No CLIMBING sign, but half-heartedly, and Livvy said: "Come on," to everyone, Baz jumping on next to her.

Lark didn't move. It was windy up here over the river. She covered her ears with her palms.

"Come on, you big pussy," Livvy said. The bridge was low, the water craggy with big rocks beneath, the rain spattering the surface. "I love this bridge!"

It struck Lark as a dumb thing to say. Livvy didn't love this bridge. They'd ridden over it on bikes a handful of times and never even noticed it beneath them. On game days, it clogged with college students walking to the stadium. This bridge had barely anything to do with them, and Lark wanted Livvy to admit this. Lark crouched low against the inside of the wall, hoping it would shield her from some of the rain. Shocky crouched beside her. A bicyclist tinkled her bell at them as she passed, the cyclist's raincoat pressing against herself like a soggy bag. The only thing that seemed worse than walking in this rain was bicycling through it.

Was she high *now?*

"Geese," Livvy yelled. "You guys are missing out. Heron! This is like my new favorite place and you're missing it!"

Lark's back was cold against the concrete, but her thighs strong. She could crouch like this for a long time. "You ever see the chimney swifts?" Shocky said. She didn't understand the question. "They're fucking crazy," he said. She nodded or tried to. Shocky was, it struck her, astoundingly hard to listen to.

"Dare you to jump," Livvy said in a voice Lark now thought of as her *I'm being cute* or *I'm being stupid* voice, though not realizing she thought that until she thought it (Was she high *now?*).

"Shut up," Baz said.

Livvy talked about the sky as if clouds were something, and the boys said things about the sky too, until finally everyone got bored, and they started walking back, stopping at Shocky's old elementary school playground, which would've been Baz's too had he lived here for elementary school. Lark and Livvy's old elementary school was across town, and it still had the same bark chips and cat-poop sandbox, the same domed metal climber from when they were students. This playground had a zip line, a multi-level play structure with a circular slide and two-story fireman's pole, the kind of seesaw that was weighted so that a kid with no friends could ride by himself.

"Can we go?" Lark said, but Livvy scrambled up the play structure and Baz followed. She dared him to go down the fireman's pole, he dared her back; they ended up going together down the yellow circular slide, getting stuck for being too wide, Baz's legs around Livvy in front of him. Livvy screamed about how wet her ass was.

Lark went over to the swings. Her ass was wet in the seat, but she didn't scream about it, the chain-link wet and cold. She mittened her hands into her sleeves. The rain pelted her in the face, but she tried to keep her eyes open. She'd forgotten how much she used to love swinging, the best way to unwind after half a day in a classroom—math, then reading, then social studies, then speech, then worksheets, then come up to the board, then scoot your desks in a circle, then then then. On the swing at recess, she'd pump hard as she could, watching the sky get nearer, then far, nearer, then far, making the tree line and the top of the school building sway a couple feet forward then back. It was so nice to not be the still point around which everything else swirled. It was nice, for once, to swirl the world.

She hadn't heard Shocky come up behind her, so she shrieked a little (High *now?*) when she felt his hand on her waist. "Woah!" he said, then "Sorry," but there were his hands again. He was pushing her. She didn't need any pushing.

"I got it," she said.

"I know you got it," he said, his voice weird. "Helping out." Baz and Livvy nuzzled up at the top of the play structure, their feet dangling over the side in the wide gap before the fire pole. "You going to let me help?" Shocky said and there was something still weird in his voice. Lark shrugged in the swing, still kicking her legs. "You feeling it?"

"I don't know."

"Oh, you'll know," he said, sniggering, and it felt like he was slowing her down because his pushes were not quite grabs but sort of.

"Are you?" Lark said.

"Fuck yeah," he said, and when she turned her head, she saw he was smiling, his eyelids heavy. He was half-asleep, standing up, his arms out loosey-goosey as he caught her and let her go. "But I started earlier. Before you got here. Some dank swag."

She had no idea what he was saying. But who cares, right? She kept kicking her legs forward and back, kept swinging. He got better at pushing without grabbing, laughing back there, telling her a story about Satch and Satch's two fucking Chihuahua mutts and when they got into the weed and goddamn, and Lark wasn't listening nor was she not listening; she was letting it be noise like she let his hands be feeling. She didn't like Shocky, but she was getting used to him. There was a sweatshirt tied to the chain-link fence, tiny and baby blue, and its state—streaked with dirt, logged with water—filled Lark with immeasurable sadness. Who could have let that sweatshirt go unclaimed, for a day then a week then longer, and who could have let some tiny child go cold? Was no one watching out for the tiny and the cold? If she had ever seen anything as lonely as that sweatshirt, she couldn't remember it.

"Hello?" It was Shocky.

He was saying this like he said it, and his voice sounded far away, and she wanted to say something about the sweatshirt, but the words inside her felt so far from the organ of her tongue and she didn't know if her tongue was an organ, but even if it wasn't, how would she push the words of her thought to her tongue, how did people do it, so many people did it all the time, everyone better than Lark at it, Lark the worst of all, and her tongue was extra dry now, extra hairy, tiny little hairs she knew that was the ear, they'd learned about tiny ear hairs but she swore, they were on her tongue now, she could feel them, and it occurred to her that swinging made her nauseous now, except she wasn't nauseous. She was something else.

"Hello?" Shocky again.

Livvy shrieked from the play structure, and by the time Lark looked, she was already at the bottom of the pole, a fist up in the air. "Hell yeah!" and Lark tried to make sense of the situation, tried to know that Livvy was fine. "Now you go," Livvy was yelling up to Baz, still up at the top. "Come on, you chickenshit!" Livvy yelled, and Baz laughed and stepped across the air and grabbed onto the pole and fell so fast and terrible, and Lark screamed but the scream barely screamed, and she realized she'd stopped kicking and the swing was nearly still, her feet dragging in the woodchips, her face leaning against the cold, wet chain-link. She couldn't feel her ears. Baz and Livvy were laughing and kissing and shouting at the base of the fire pole and Livvy was yelling, "Come on, you guys, you have to do it too!" But Lark didn't think she could get up, fairly certain her getting up organs had failed.

"Come on, you pussies!" Livvy screamed now, and her face was red, and she was laughing, and Baz was hanging onto one of her hands and swinging it and laughing, and they looked so stupid and beautiful but also stupid.

"Come on," Shocky said, grabbing one of her hands, and pulling her from the swing. "You're not boneless, you only think you are."

She gasped a gaspless gasp and told him that he understood exactly, though without telling him. How did he know her insides now, he was kind of dumb? And he was holding her hand across the playground, and she couldn't feel her nose.

"I present you—" he announced, letting go of her hand at the play structure, and Baz and Livvy laughed and laughed. Were they laughing at her boneless?

"Come on, waste case," Livvy said, and she led Lark up the wet play structure, slippery, and now it was Livvy's hand, and her hand was colder than Shocky's hand but mostly the same as his too, not so different as she would've thought. "Do it," Livvy said. They were at the fire pole, high high up at the top of the fire pole. "No," Lark said. "No. No!" and Livvy pushed, and Lark grabbed or didn't and down rain air down ground.

It was fast and hard, and she couldn't breathe, air out of her, knocked boneless—and Lark was coughing and breathing and coughing and her lungs filled and burned and filled—and Shocky or Baz yelled, "Holy shit!" and Livvy was beside her, Livvy rocking her, holding Lark's cold and wet head against her chest holding her so tight. "Sorry, sorry, oh my god, sorry, sorry, honey, sorry, Larky, sorry," and this here now, the old Livvy and Lark, so fucking happy, so fucking happy and home.

It was Livvy and Lark holding hands on the walk back, leading the parade, Lark pointing to the metal sculpture in the front lawn of a big house. "I know," Livvy said. Same as when she pointed out the beautiful flower garden and the FREE box with flannel blankets and humming-bird feeder. "I know," Livvy kept saying, letting Lark be wordless. Lark picked up the hummingbird feeder, its handle wet and cold, but she didn't care, swinging it all the way to Shocky's.

In the basement, Lark sank deep and heavy into her chair, cast-off sectional down here, carpet remnant, TV. Lark wasn't really watching the show where the husband and wife fix up the houses. Her socks were so wet in her shoes. Her knees were so wet in her pants. She maybe had to pee. She blinked and blinked, trying to make her way out of stoned.

When the doorbell rang, Shocky jumped off the couch fast and ran up the stairs. "Nique!" he called, and Lark listened to voices overhead, and then Shocky came back with Monique behind him, Monique in head to toe running gear, black leggings, gray long-sleeve hoodie, everything skintight but not slutty; athlete.

"Hey, hoodlums!" Monique announced, steam coming off her hair (don't touch it). "Hey, girl!" she said when she saw Lark in the chair, Lark happy about this.

"Running," Lark said or asked, her tongue still with the hair, and Monique looked at Lark and said, "What did you assholes do to her?" but she was smiling, and Shocky said, "A harmless little brownie."

"Jesus," Monique said, still smiling. "Don't fuck with my girl Lark. Look at her."

It had only been that one lunch, nothing since, and Lark hadn't figured she'd be Monique's girl now; she didn't know Monique was Nique, and Nique slid onto the floor, her back against the couch, and Lark wanted to know very much what her own face looked like.

Livvy's face was like she was tasting something sour. "Hi, Monique," she said from under the crook of Baz's arm. "Hello, Olivia," Monique said, her face not sour, but she didn't even turn to look at Livvy, looking at the television and talking about "These guys crazy! They're going to sledgehammer that whole counter, aren't they?"

Shocky asked if she wanted a brownie, and she told him to fuck off. "They do tests," Monique said to Lark.

Lark was happy to have Monique here. "Tests?" she and her hairy tongue said.

"Random drug tests for basketball," Monique said, and Lark nodded or tried to, the back of her head sore, really sore. She blinked and blinked "You guys are real bitches," Monique announced. "Like getting a guppy stoned. Or a gerbil."

"You know, she's fine," said Livvy. "We got her. She's not a gerbil."

"Mmm-hmm," Monique said, staring at the TV screen. "How'd it go with her mom, Baz?"

"Stop it, Nique. You don't have to be like that," Baz said.

"She must be a real witch for you to not meet her yet," Nique said to the television. "Your girlfriend protecting you real good."

"Cut it out," Baz said quietly.

"Excuse me?" Livvy said, not quietly, Lark starting to get a headache from the spot in the back of her head. "You don't know anything about me or my family."

"Sure don't," Monique said. "Look, I told you." She pointed to the TV. "They love to sledgehammer that shit. Always knock out the whole kitchen. Wouldn't that feel good?"

"I don't really know how it's any of your business," Livvy said, and Lark touched the back of her head, and she could feel a knot there under her hair, tender, painful.

"It sure ain't," Monique said to the television. "A white girl doesn't want her Black boyfriend to meet her mom, that's not my business at all."

"Hey!" Livvy bucked forward on the couch, Baz taking her by the shoulders, trying to pull her back. Lark blinked and blinked. Livvy struggled with Baz, then stopped struggling, and he was whispering something in her ear, and Livvy looked at Lark like Lark was supposed to defend her, and then to Monique: "You don't know shit, okay?"

"Fine, fine, fine." Monique put her hands in the air. "I don't know shit."

"Everybody needs to chill," Baz said. "Okay? Everybody. Chill."

"I'm chill as a popsicle," Monique said, and Lark thought she should do something, she had to do something, but all she was doing was pressing the tender spot, until tears sprang to her eyes.

"Aspirin?" Lark said. "Aspirin."

"See! You fucked that girl up!" Monique said, and Livvy looked at Lark, and Lark didn't understand what was on her face. Lark hadn't meant anything by it except that she had a headache. Monique said, "I got you, girl. Let's go find some aspirin."

"No, no, I got it," Shocky said. "Sit your ass down," he said to Monique, "and stop stirring up trouble. You can do that for two minutes while I get this girl some pills?"

"Yes, sir, Shocky, sir," she said. "I'm just giving you a hard time," she said to Livvy, and Livvy's gaze did not waver from the television screen.

Shocky pulled Lark up from the chair by her elbow, made a whistling noise: "You gonna be sore tomorrow. You know, you can take your coat off and stay a while."

She followed Shocky up the stairs. She heard Baz saying, "She fell. At the playground," and Lark, even through the pain and the hairy tongue, thought: *Not fell. Pushed,* and something splintered in her then, something she thought had already been splintered.

In the bathroom, everything was turquoise and silver, turquoise and silver wallpaper, turquoise shower curtain, puffy silver toilet seat, turquoise soap dish. "Pretty," Lark said. Her eyes in the mirror looked a lot like Shocky's had at the swing, like she was watching herself sleeping.

"My mom," Shocky said, spilling out two pills from a white container and filling a glass. He held the pills in one hand, the water in the other.

"Nice," Lark said. At least she'd blinked her way back to words. "You're nice, thank you."

Shocky nodded and smiled, and as soon as she swallowed the pills, she realized exactly how thirsty she was. She gulped down the rest of the glassful and immediately poured another, watching the water from the faucet with such anticipatory glee, she didn't see it coming when Shocky put his hand on her chin—the good side of her chin—and turned her face to his, his mouth on hers, his lips dry, his mouth wet, his breath in her mouth, his tongue on her tongue, the water still running, the glass still in hand. There was no room in her mouth except for his tongue, and she didn't want this but didn't know how to say, but then he put his hand on the back of her head, and she yelled, "Ow!" and he stopped, and she stepped away.

"Fuck," he said, and "What the—?" like she was the one who'd done something wrong.

She didn't know what to say and where to look and she couldn't see a way back to Shocky's basement, and she surprised herself by saying, "Sorry, I have to—" and leaving the water running and walking to the front door like there was somewhere she needed to be. The back of her head throbbed hard, her lips strange, her mouth strange, her house miles away in the rain, but she didn't care, or she cared, and she would care more once she was in her own house in her own bed, but for now it was enough to surprise herself—one step, another, another—along the wet pavement.

Subject: re: re: re: Objectionable secret group
Date: November 10 5:11 a.m.
To: Woody Hanover <woody_h@wesths>
From: Facebook Help <support@fb.com>

Dear Woody,
Any type of content can be reported to Facebook. Facebook's Community Standards explain what type of content and sharing is allowed on Facebook. When something gets reported to Facebook, a global team reviews it and removes anything that violates these terms.
Best,
Samantha

Subject: re: re: re: re: Objectionable secret group
Date: November 10 8:03 a.m.
To: Facebook Help <support@fb.com>
From: Woody Hanover <woody_h@wesths>

Dear Samantha,
Your message does beg the important question—aren't I reporting it now? Isn't that what I'm doing? I'm losing hope that you are a reasonable human being who can do something. Yes or no—can you take this page down?
Sincerely,
Woody Hanover
West High School
Guidance Counselor (A-I)

STEFANIE

W ell, hello, Nathan," Marjorie said, her desk a mess of manila folders, loose forms, scattered pens. "And hello, Matthew," she said to Nathan's stuffed bear.

The bear's name was Mat, not Matthew, as in *look at all the mats in its fur from Nathan carrying it with him anywhere outside the house for nearly a decade.* The first time Stefanie and Nathan had met Marjorie, Marjorie asked Nathan, "Who's this?"

"Mat," Stefanie had offered, not correcting Marjorie when she repeated it back wrong. Four years later, Stefanie now at least appreciated that Marjorie—old enough to be her mother and always with a brooch on her blouse (today's a green-jeweled frog)—remembered that bear every time, even if incorrectly. The error was on Stefanie at this point.

Nathan sat in the chair closest to Marjorie's desk, and Stefanie passed the papers from Naomi's lawyers across him. Marjorie and a whole bunch of other HHS folks were shoehorned into a daylight basement, damp down here all winter. You never felt dried out enough as you sat.

"No," Stefanie told Nathan when he grabbed for Marjorie's stapler. Always with the stapler.

"You need a fidget?" Marjorie asked. She watched the way his body squirmed, she listened to the *ssss* from his mouth, she passed Nathan a sparkly blue stress ball, which Nathan held onto and then pressed into Mat's head, making his mostly happy *hala-hala-hala* murmur.

Marjorie nodded into the papers, issued several "uh-huh"s. A bulletin board full of photographs hung on the cubicle wall over Marjorie's desk. Stefanie could never make sense of the pictures—kids and adults of different ages, different races, a blond girl riding a horse in a bike helmet, a Hispanic man smiling at a picnic table. Were any of them Marjorie's children, grandchildren? Were they all clients? Why would clients give Marjorie snapshots? Stefanie liked Marjorie well enough by now, or maybe *appreciated* was more apt. But who in the world would think, after their child's birthday party, *You know who we should make an extra copy for? Marjorie Dennis from county?*

"Well, yes," Marjorie said now, holding the papers in her lap. "This is all technically, I mean legally, in bounds. With personal support workers, Nathan is the employer. They're working for him, and in rare cases this happens. Very rare, I'd say. They're unionized, they have lots of professional support. We've seen some liability and personal injury cases. Sadly."

She had said exactly this over the phone, but Stefanie had still wanted to come in, so Marjorie could look everything over, maybe see it differently, give a better answer. "Do they *win?*" Stefanie asked.

"Only once that I can remember." There was a girl crying one cubicle over, a man saying to her, "Remember rabbit breathing. Remember your rabbit breaths."

Nathan rolled the stress ball on his face now, his lips.

Stefanie said quietly: "Not on your mouth, honey. Not by your eyes. You don't know whose hands have been on that."

Nathan pressed the ball to his cheek, rolling it over his mouth.

"Not on your mouth, buddy. Do you want to lose your fidget?"

His eyes were closed, but he was listening. He *lahh*ed Stefanie, which was relatively new, meaning some mix of: *I'm fine, leave me be,* and *stop being an idiot.* The *lahhs* heralded either a coming calm or a coming meltdown. Stefanie was tired in her eyeballs; she felt like they had been plucked, wrung out, stuck back into the sockets.

Marjorie talked about how they could go back to the direct support professionals, who were employed through an agency, not through Nathan. They'd had a run of shitty DSPs when Nathan was still in high school special ed.

"Not sure switching at this point does us any good," Stefanie said. "Can't unring this bell."

Marjorie paged through Nathan's file, disconcertingly thick and ruffled with yellow paperwork, white notes, the intake photo of Nathan that made him look like he'd been startled by the flash, looking crazy wild. It used to make Stefanie laugh, that picture; she'd joke with Nathan that he'd put it into his modeling portfolio.

"How are you liking Mercer?" Marjorie asked.

Stefanie shrugged. "We've had better." She knew it was a dance, this thing she was doing with Marjorie, this thing she had been doing with Marjorie for years. "We were really starting to like Naomi. That's the sad part. And Carlos. We loved Carlos." She pressed her hands to her eyes. "I think I have allergies."

"Stefanie," Marjorie said. "Can we talk about something?" And: "Nathan we're going to talk about you now, okay?"

Stefanie knew plenty of stories about shitty and petulant county workers, warming their chairs until their fat pensions. She appreciated how Marjorie never forgot Nathan; there were so many ways Nathan took up too much or too little of other people's attention. So many ways to not give him his due. To get it right was not easy. It was a skill. Marjorie was skilled.

"What I'm seeing," Marjorie said, hand smoothing and smoothing the top sheet of Nathan's file, still open in her lap, the way she'd been smoothing her blouse, "is a start of a pattern. Carlos, then Naomi. I think it's an opportunity to pay attention and rethink our approach."

"Pattern? There's no pattern. They were very different caregivers."

The girl the next cubicle over had given up on her rabbit breathing. Her sobbing was full and ragged, a cry that made Stefanie grateful it was coming from someone else's kid. Marjorie pursed her lips and stared at Nathan, who was pressing the ball and Mat to his face, tapping his toe in the way that was past normal tapping.

"There was marked aggression in both cases," Marjorie said.

"There was no aggression with Carlos," Stefanie said, thinking of one stumble in the bathroom, Carlos falling into the wall. "It was an accident. Nathan's a big kid. Lost his balance." She was trying not to get loud, trying to tap her foot in time to Nathan's, his leg jumping and jumping. There were times when she could sync them up in public so that they were vibing off each other, creating their own closed circuit. He didn't like it here. Didn't like this kind of conversation, and who could blame him?

Marjorie paused, wide-eyed, peering at Stefanie over her glasses. "Let's think about that."

"Now listen—" Stefanie said, but Marjorie put her hand up. Not a lot of people were going to put their hand up to Stefanie when she took that tone, Stefanie would give her that. Marjorie was a tough old bitch.

"Carlos did not report it as an accident," Marjorie said.

Stefanie didn't know what to say, both of Nathan's legs bouncing now, he bent over into Mat and the ball, folding himself into his lap. Stefanie tried to give him some *ssss sssss* near his ear. The girl in the next cubicle screamed and screamed. "Carlos got a job at his cousin's iPhone repair shop," Stefanie said.

Marjorie looked at her for a long second before speaking slowly and evenly: "I want you to know, I want both of you to know, I am not trying to make anyone feel bad. I'm not judging. I don't see the use of hashing out different interpretations of past events when we have access to different information." She paused here to see if Stefanie was still with her. Stefanie nodded the smallest of nods. "I'm not mad at you, Nathan. I am not going to punish you or take away services. In fact, this is a great time to stop and assess if you're receiving the correct level of care."

Nathan was still folded in half. Stefanie shook her head as to mean, both "No," and "What? Tell me."

"The easiest is to get you some behavioral supports specifically around aggression," Marjorie said. "There are other PSWs or DSPs trained to help with the aggressive behaviors. They come into your home, like Mercer comes in now. It's additive. We don't take anything away. That keeps the status quo going, and we see what comes."

The way Marjorie inflected the last sentence, the pitch of *status quo* and *we see* conveyed something other than confidence in this plan. The man and girl from the next cubicle marched past Marjorie's, white man in a gray suit, his hand gripped around the little blond girl's wrist, the girl in a purple pajama top and a skirt, her face bright red. He held her wrist up high and walked fast, leading her out, the girl still wailing. He yanked her arm whenever she dug her heels into the carpet, and it seemed that he was about to beat the crap out of her as soon as they crossed through the outer doors. Nathan covered his ears with his upper arms.

"Or we think about comprehensive services," Marjorie said, as if the screaming girl had not just been dragged out of here like a bad dog.

"Comprehensive services?" Stefanie said. She knew what comprehensive services were.

"Nathan, you're already twenty-two. Stefanie, this is not unusual what we're seeing. Nathan's a young adult. He's got a lot of hormones swirling around in there. This is the age when kids' bodies are often signaling to them a need for more independence. We can see an uptick in aggression as a way for clients to signal they're ready to have a little more space from Mom and Dad."

Nathan was doubled-over, Mat pressed to one ear, the blue ball to the other. "This," Stefanie said, a hand in his direction, "is independence?" immediately ashamed for the derision in her voice.

"I'm asking you," Marjorie said, not losing one bit of patience, Stefanie wanting her to lose a bit of patience, Stefanie wanting her to yell, so she could yell back. "To take a holistic look at the situation. We've seen foster homes in particular do a lot of good in cases similar to Nathan's, caring families with lots of individual attention and supports. You'd be surprised. I would be happy to take you on tours."

"Foster homes?" Stefanie said, not trying to hide her incredulity. The idea of foster care called to mind (and she tried to call this to mind as little as possible) the dank hallways of assisted living. Whenever she called Mama now, it was loud, and her mama's voice was flat. The last time she called, the roommate was screaming.

"Mama, how you putting up with that?" Stefanie asked.

"Okay," her mama said.

"Okay? It's me, Mama. It's Stefanie."

"Okay," her mama repeated. Stefanie never thought she'd miss her mama's rancor. The screaming had the inflection of swearing, though Stefanie couldn't make out the words.

"Is she saying that to you?"

Mama didn't know.

"They took my sheets," Mama said, her words slushy like when her dentures were loose.

"Who took your sheets?"

Her mama didn't answer. The roommate continued. *Bitch,* Stefanie thought she heard. *Dumb bitch.* "Hang on, Mama, I'm going to call the nurse's station and I'll call you back." Stefanie had a whole list of Century Center numbers new in her phone: Century Center nurse's station; Century Center billing; Century Center front office. The phone rang and rang and rang at the nurse's station and no one answered. Stefanie didn't call her mama back.

Marjorie talked, and Stefanie tried to continue to listen, though not very hard. Nathan's leg bounce gave way to a low drone of noise. They had been here too long. It was time to go home, and yet once Marjorie had started, it seemed she could not stop, about how much success other clients had seen by living "near to but away from their family of origin," and Stefanie could not see her way around both the *near to* and *away from.* She was not one for knowing both of those things at once.

WOODY

Woody tried to remain still against Susan's headboard, his arms crossed exactly so, his one leg bent, the other straight. His right ass cheek was asleep; his right and left cheeks had been taking turns going numb, and he had to figure out micro-movements to get the blood flowing differently.

She'd been talking about this for weeks, wanting to draw him, all of him. "I'm terrible at figure drawing," she'd announced, "I need to practice," out of which had hatched this plan of coordinated sick days, seven hours alone in her bedroom while Livvy was in school, the largest chunk of time they'd had together to date. The lead-up had been delicious—they practiced their hoarse voices, they tried out different lies (flu, too much; cold, not enough, settling on allergic reaction: hives!), and he'd shouted the wrong lyrics to bad pop songs all the way across town to her apartment—*I got sandstones in my locket! I got cod oil on my feet!*

He came to realize, though, as he'd tried to grab and grab at her ass and her breast while she was moving and arranging his naked body, that she was serious about the painting thing. His job was to sit there, still.

"You are going to be naked too," he said.

"No!" she said. "Stop it. I don't need to be naked."

"Need is subjective."

"Stop moving." She'd taken a picture of him with an old Polaroid, flapping and flapping it until the image came through; this, so he could take pee breaks, and she could reset him exactly. He'd asked to see it and then quickly and deeply regretted it; dark, curly back hair crested over his shoulders; his gut fat not enough to be an all-out roll, but close; his penis, far too compliant, the tiny turtle.

"Approach this like they do the school photos. Airbrush liberally." He made a big show of sucking his stomach in, and she laughed, but then was serious: "Stop messing around," And: "Sit still." And: "You got nothing to worry about. You are beautiful."

No one had ever called him beautiful, nor had it ever occurred to him that anyone ever would. He laughed, despite himself, though Susan's face was set. "You are the beautiful one," he said.

"Thank you, sir," she said, though already her tone was flattened as she looked at him. Gone her perpetual half-smile, gone the way her eyes held his. She took to studying him, free of her Susan-ness and he of his Woody-ness, almost scientifically, as she put charcoal to paper.

"My back itches," he said, and she said, "Don't move," and came over, charcoal still in one hand, scratching with the other. "Down," he told her. "Down, down, over, *there*, that spot." She scratched him, gingerly, and he moved his head to kiss her, and she yelled that he was defeating the whole purpose of her coming over.

"Depends on how you define 'purpose,'" which at least got her to kiss him back, first on the forehead, then on the lips.

"You've obviously spent too much time around squirrely teenagers," she said.

"I tend to think you're the problem, more than teenagers. Look at that ass," he said as she walked back to the easel. "Chuck Kloster's wife is leaving him," he said, moving his mouth as little as possible, a bad ventriloquist.

"Who's Chuck Kloster?" She tipped her head to the left, peering at her canvas.

"Voc arts," he said.

"What in the world is voc arts?"

"Shop. He teaches wood shop. And auto repair."

"Auto repair is a high school class now?"

"Don't be a snob."

She laughed. "I'm not being a snob," she said while she rubbed her forehead with the back of her arm. "And how do we feel about Chuck Kloster's wife leaving him?" she asked, moving decidedly downward on the canvas. Part of the not-fun-ness for Woody was not being able to see what she was doing, and fearing, like the Polaroid, it would take the air out of him when she was done.

"Chuck is a loudmouth, but sure, we always feel bad for people when bad things happen to them."

"That is a very nice sentiment. You're a real mensch."

His left butt cheek tingled. He pulled his shoulders back, straightened his posture. "Am I supposed to be sitting up straight or slouching?"

She looked at him—"You're good. Whatever you're doing now is good."—and fell into a new quiet. He watched her face as she drew, the way she bit her tongue when she was shading or erasing. He had an itch under his left knee.

"Kay," he said in ventriloquist voice. "Caught up on Kloster. What you got for me? Tell me something before my whole ass falls asleep."

She laughed a little. "I'll give you a thank-you ass rub after this."

"You can give me a thank-you something else."

Again, she laughed a little. "Okay, I got something." She lifted the charcoal. "Livvy has a boyfriend." Her face broke into a smile. "She has a boyfriend and she's going to bring him over here for me to meet. He's Black, which I wasn't expecting. I mean, I'm okay with it, I am, but I guess I'm surprised. I don't have anything—I'm not like—I never thought of it. That's not how I pictured it, you know?"

"Baz is a good kid. You're going to like him. A solid, solid apple."

Her face did something. "No, I'm sure he is. That's not what I'm saying. I'm not assuming he's a bad kid." Her voice was starting to go up. "It's like you have a picture in your mind, and then you find out your kid is dating a Black kid, which is fine. Because I'm not an asshole." She stopped, took a breath, and then said, through a smile: "You knew about Livvy and this boy?"

He saw his blunder and could not figure a way back from it. "Yes, but I've been really encouraging her to tell you. I've wanted her to tell you."

Susan's smile went through the smallest gradients of change—her lips straining against her teeth, her eyes fluttering, then narrowing, her bottom teeth coming forward until it was not a smile at all, it was a grimace, or worse. "What?" she said, and something in the "What?" was a tone Woody had never heard from her, or maybe he had, but it had been when she was Susan Hoffman, when they were kids, and he was an idiot, and she knew it.

"What?" he said, goosebumps moving through his body, still trying to not move his face.

"What do you mean 'really encouraging her'? You're offering my daughter free family counseling now?"

"No, no, no," and then, "Can I?" as he tipped his head toward the blankets at the foot of the bed. "Can I move?"

"Of course you can move," Susan said, as if it was the stupidest question she'd heard. Woody pulled the sheet and top blanket over his waist.

"Listen," he said. "I am not a family counselor. I offered her nothing outside of what I would offer any student, which is general guidance and support."

"I thought you talk to kids about their GPA. About college."

"Well, sure. But I'm not a robot, and neither are they. Conversations can wander."

Color had risen into Susan's cheeks, and she was gripping the charcoal so hard, it began to crumble. "Listen, listen." He patted the mattress beside him. "Will you come sit down? I think this is a big misunderstanding. Can we talk—?"

"No, thank you," she said. "So, you knew about the boyfriend, and you didn't think to tell me?"

"I have a relationship to Livvy, I wanted to honor, I wanted to respect her confidences—"

"What confidences?" Susan was trying very hard not to yell, which had an effect more forbidding than yelling. "You said you weren't her therapist. Why did you need to keep her confidences about her boyfriend if your job is GPAs?"

"How you are talking about my job is not very nice. It's a little belittling. I'm sorry I didn't tell you about Baz. I'm sorry—"

"I know your job is very important," she said, making great effort to measure her tone, though when she set the charcoal down onto the easel, she did so with such force, the whole thing nearly toppled. She caught it, but in the process, crumpled the paper that had Woody on it. "But forgive me if it seems a little ludicrous that you are worried about respecting her and honoring her, when you are fucking her mother on the side."

"Susan, please," he said. He was going for reasonable and conciliatory, though it came out desperate. "It's me," he said. "It's Woody. Look at me. I'm not trying to hurt anyone. Look at me."

She did. He watched her chest rise and fall. The color that had come into her face was still there. She looked fierce and beautiful. He tried to say so, but she stopped him.

"How many conversations would you say you've had with Livvy that"—she held her fingers up in air quotes—"wandered?"

"I don't know." He thought of the Facebook group. If Livvy truly had told no other adult, he couldn't then tell Susan. Susan would tell Livvy, and then Livvy would trace it right back to him. If only he could explain this to Susan, though it was, of course, impossible to explain. "A few. More than average, I'd say."

She was nodding and nodding and nodding now, her eyes going wet in a way that reminded him (damn him, damn his damn self) of Livvy. Susan very carefully undid the alligator clips from the top of the easel, letting the crumpled paper slip into her hands. Woody was sure she was going to rip it in half, but instead she folded it once, and then again, and again, which was worse. He was out of bed, holding the sheet and blanket at his waist.

"No, no, no, no, no," he was saying, rushing her and the easel, in half a toga. What he would've given for his pants, which were so close—in a pile with the rest of his clothing atop the dresser behind her—but impossible. "It's nothing like you think. Whatever you're thinking, it's not that. I'm sorry I didn't tell you. I should've told you about Baz. You're right." He didn't even know if he believed himself, but he didn't care, as long as she did.

"Are you getting off on this," she said so softly, it was nearly a whisper. "Getting off on playing mom and daughter off each other? Is that the deal?"

"No, no, no, no," he said, one hand clasped behind him, holding up his half toga, the other reaching for her cheek, which she pushed away. "There is no deal except that I like you a lot a lot a lot, and you make me really happy, and you're the best thing—"

"Stop it. I'm going to get ready for work now. Salvage half a day's pay. My hives are all gone. I've recovered." By the last two words, her voice was stripped of any emotion.

She walked to her attached bath, closing the door behind her even as he called her name. He followed—he could see them still making up in the shower, letting the water bead over them, soap suds on their chests, as they had their first ever make-up sex—but the door was locked. He listened to the toilet flush and then the shower run while he got dressed, still considering staying, when he saw the Polaroid face down on the floor. Woody flipped it over with his toe, and Polaroid Woody stared up at him, the man in the picture moon-faced, naked as a penguin and trying to swallow down a grin. It came back to Woody now, the thought that lay behind that grin, before he saw the image of himself, before there was an image at all, when it was only his lover pressing a camera button across the room from him, he abuzz with newness, this outlandish adventure that was now his life: *I am everything.*

LARK

She stopped for a little while. Stopped looking out for Livvy and Baz. Stopped trying to run into anyone at lunch. Stopped calling to see where Livvy was. And it was surprising, even if it shouldn't have been, how little she saw of them once she was the one who stopped trying to get them together.

She spent lunch in the band room, where the band kids practiced and either thought Lark was part of band or did not care that she wasn't. Boys puffed their cheeks at their trombones, girls wetted their clarinet reeds, a flutist trilled, or maybe it was a piccolo. They were each practicing their own music, which made it impossible for Lark to tell if anyone was any good, not that she cared. More often than not, at some point during the hour, two kids banged out "Heart and Soul" on the piano. Lark appreciated all the noise. The noise in here was nonsensical and blanketing.

Livvy had texted: hi. Hi hi.

Lark texted back. Hi.

It wasn't that Lark was mad. She was something else, and it was not something she'd been before, so she didn't have a word for it. She was herself. She was quiet in noise. She wasn't hiding because she was right here. She was right here to herself. The closest she could come up with was that she be, and she didn't get any farther in her thinking, because it didn't really matter how to classify or explain it because the nice thing was, she didn't have to classify or explain it to anyone because she was herself here. The fall from the play structure maybe had knocked her deeper into herself. She wasn't unhappy. She wasn't happy. She be.

"Hey, girl," Monique said, catching her one day outside the band room near the end of lunch. Lark scanned quickly for Shocky, but Monique was by herself. Lark was, she realized, maybe hiding a little. The band hall ended in doors out to one of the track fields, and Monique was in running pants and a thin rain jacket, her face sheened with sweat or rain. The way she sweated seemed like the way people sweated in commercials—shiny without being drippy, her hair held back in a wide pouf in the back, a thick purple headband at her hairline. "Where you been?" Monique asked after taking a slug out of her water bottle.

Lark shrugged. "Nowhere."

"Last time I saw you, you disappeared." Monique paused, and Lark realized she was expecting Lark to say something. Lark shrugged again. "I got your bird feeder," Monique said.

Lark had forgotten about the bird feeder. "Thanks," she said, not remembering the last conversation she'd had before this one. Mr. Hammerle had called on her a couple days ago, but that hardly counted. Her mother wasn't doing great, as in her normal not doing great, their household dwindling to a series of Post-it notes. Lark on the refrigerator: *Mac and cheese in here if you're hungry.* Mom on the front door: *Pick me up my smokes?* with a five and two ones attached.

This would leave Lark twenty-one cents. Once, her mom had left a ten.

"You okay?" Monique said, slinging an arm around Lark, which surprised Lark, but not in a bad way. Monique put off heat, but she didn't stink.

"Yeah," Lark said.

"You've always got this, like, face. This face." Monique made a face where her eyes were bugging out and she sucked on her bottom lip. She looked like someone about to come around the corner of a haunted house, sure something was going to pop out at her.

"My face is just my face," she said, regretting it as soon as she did. Maybe this was why she'd stopped for a little while. It was hard—people. Monique was on her chin side and up real close. Lark peeled herself out from under Monique's arm, even though the air was cold on her bare arms as soon as she did, not even having noticed the air of the hallway until she'd been warmed from it for a few seconds.

"I'm messing with you," Monique said, looking at Lark like she was trying to get the picture to come in clearer. And then: "Don't let Shocky scare you."

Lark wondered what Shocky had told Monique. If he had told Livvy, surely Lark would have heard about it by now.

"He doesn't scare me," Lark said, which was true and not. "I don't like him. I don't like him like that."

"Story of his life!" Monique said, laughing loud enough for a boy lugging a tuba case to look over. And then: "Don't worry about it."

"I don't think I am," Lark said. "Worried. I mean, maybe." She shrugged.

"You're funny," Monique said, and Lark knew she didn't mean funny haha, or maybe she did, so Lark said: "Okay."

"You should come get your bird feeder sometime," Monique said, bouncing a little in place, like she was warming up for her next run, and Lark had the sudden worry that she was about to sprint off.

"Do you want to hear something?" Lark said, pushing open the band door, pulling Monique by her arm, Monique not resisting. There was a kid on the big bass drum, another on the tom-tom, a boy with the weird curly-cue French horn, two oboe players, one trumpeter, and a pianist, all practicing different music. It was the most separate togetherness Lark could imagine. The most together separateness. It tickled her silly was what it did.

"Jesus," Monique said into Lark's ear. "They sound horrible," and later Lark would think maybe this was why she'd brought Monique into the band room, the racket making it so they had to lean in close. If the oboists looked up, or the big guy at the bass drum, any of them, they'd see Monique and Lark and they'd think without thinking: *What are those two doing?* which kind of made them that, didn't it, if only for a couple of seconds in this hail of noise? Those two.

STEFANIE

The law office was above an art gallery, the waiting room with dark leathered couches, Derek paging through *Time*, a picture of Donald Trump behind a podium.

"I can't," Stefanie said. "Don't even."

Derek *humph*-ed in assent or dissent; it was a noncommittal *humph*.

"Hidaya says she saw a lawn sign," Stefanie said.

"I believe it," Derek said, though he'd turned the page. Picture of a brown kid, bleeding, wide-eyed in rubble. Syria, Stefanie assumed, though she needed to stop looking, *Time* magazine not helping with her state of mind. She stared into the deep recess of the law office, trying to guess at their guy, who'd been referred by one of Derek's colleagues after he was sued by a contractor. They were the sort of people who had colleagues with attorneys now.

The office was larger than it appeared from the street, its footprint ranging well beyond the gallery below. A woman in high heels and a tight bun tutted around with files clasped to her chest. A boy who looked young enough to be Baz's classmate stood over a woman's desk, scanning the tablet in his hand, poking at it with a stylus, telling her something. The woman was nodding, typing at her computer.

"Goddamn," she said, squeezing Derek's arm. "Look." She moved her head toward the boy-man and his secretary.

"What am I looking at?"

"Look at that woman." She was asking the boy-man a question now, scratching behind her ear. "That's Olivia's mother."

"You don't know that," Derek said.

"I do know that," she whispered. "I remember her from West." He'd seen her too, outside Principal Vonn's office. "Remember, she's a secretary?"

"So, we'll say hello," Derek said.

"We'll say *hello*?" she said, still hanging onto his arm.

Derek looked at her sideways. "Don't," he whispered, closing the magazine on his lap. "Don't read some tea leaves in your head. This isn't a sign. This isn't anything. This is a lady making a living." He grabbed her hand. "Relax," he said, and she knocked the side of her knee against the side of his, hard. She hated when he told her to relax.

Their guy, Stan Gable ("Everyone calls me Gable") talked from behind his desk, a wall full of fancy, hardback tomes behind him. The tomes came in matching sets—a shelf and a half black with a fat red swath bisecting the middle, others with gold leafing at the top and bottom, others still, navy with gold letters. They reminded Stefanie of the Encyclopedia Britannicas on her mantel growing up. Her mama had bought them from a salesman, paying them off in installments for god knows how long. "The Britans," she called them when faced with any question she did not know the answer to: "Go look in the Britans," or its variant "I got you kids those Britans and you hardly even look at them." Stefanie looked at them plenty, learning about submarine warfare and sand hill cranes and scuba diving and *Sesame Street* (already knew that one, reading for the thrill of recognition), and that was only *S*, *S* populous enough to be its own volume. Poor *JKL*. Poor *XYZ*.

"He is an adult," Derek explained, "but he is disabled."

"And he's the employer?"

Yes.

"And you understood that he was the employer?"

Sure.

"What kind of disability are we talking about? This is a blind kid, a deaf kid, developmental—" He didn't know how to finish. "Paint me a picture."

Derek explained the diagnoses. Stefanie let him do the diagnosis talk. All day long, she traded in diagnoses, but that was different. There was a taxonomy to Nathan as there was a taxonomy to all of them. The only difference was that Nathan's was not immediately discernable, or those who thought they were immediately discerning, were in fact getting it wrong, attaching too much meaning to the yipping and the flapping of the left arm, distracted by that which naturally distracts. Diagnosis: forest for the trees. Diagnosis: the deepest dimple on his right cheek when he is really, truly elated. Diagnosis: too much body for this world, by maybe half.

"He talks? He communicates?" Gable asked.

"You can understand him, you have to sync up," Stefanie said, explaining his special ed participation until he was sixteen, and all the

PSWs he'd really liked and who'd really liked him, and how there'd been a gaggle of kids running ragged around the house the day of the incident.

"Got it, got it," Gable said, taking out the documents they'd handed him, reading silently. When he'd led them from the waiting room, his office was a quick right turn, barely getting them closer to Olivia's mother. The woman had paid no attention, trained on her computer screen, her posture not very good; she hunched.

Derek said, "I paid her. I already gave her seven hundred dollars."

"Before or after you got this?" Gable asked.

"Before," and Derek explained to Gable.

Gable wagged a finger and said, "Tut tut," and in a tone he was trying to keep light, "Don't do that anymore. Don't have any contact with the plaintiff whatsoever. But it's not terrible; we can spin it as a settlement offer already accepted." He waved the papers through the air. "This is what I call a smorgasbord approach. These guys like to put every possible complaint out there, use depos and discovery to see what they can make stick. We're going to think about two things primarily: one, shared fault. If we can prove the girl had any responsibility for the incident, any provocation or even lack of proper training, we can reduce the settlement. Two, mediation instead of trial, our other best chance at a reasonable settlement."

"Settlement?" Stefanie said. "What about not paying her anything more?"

"Let me ask you and remember whatever you tell me stays here—" Gable talked with his hands, his left hand up in a stop sign at this proclamation. "Privileged," he said. "No one can get it out of me, even by gunpoint. Is your son violent?"

"No," Stefanie said, at the same time as Derek said, "He's a big guy."

Derek took her hand. Gable tap-tap-tapped on his lips with a pointer finger. Gable was thinking.

"One thing," he said. "One thing we need to consider in a case like this is optics. What does the girl look like?"

Stefanie breathed in. Stefanie breathed out. Derek described Naomi, as mousy, nondescript.

"She Black or white?" Gable asked, as if those were the only two options.

Derek told him white.

"Big or little?" Gable asked.

Derek told him little.

Gable tap-tap-tapped. He didn't need to explain what he was thinking. They didn't have $58,000. They barely had five thousand. All of their extra income was siphoned off to Derek's student loan debt, and Baz's college saving account, and all the Nathan-care the county didn't pay for, and now Mama's assisted living. They were the first college grads in both their families; they had no cushion of wealth. They were trying to make the cushion from nothing.

"Would the optics look better," Derek asked, "if we were looking at foster home options?"

"Excuse me?" Stefanie said, taking her hand from his.

"I'm not talking about putting him in a foster home," Derek said. "I'm talking about optics. Remember when Vaughn had the DUIs. He got probation because he went to rehab. That's all I'm talking about." Vaughn was an Alpha Phi Alpha brother of Derek's. Derek explained Marjorie's suggestions to Gable.

"I'm not going to use foster homes as leverage," Stefanie said.

Derek put both hands in the air, and it was Gable who said, "Let's all take a step back, a half step. I think it's smart to throw out all ideas and see what sticks when we're talking about optics."

"Can we stop staying 'optics'?" Stefanie said.

"Okay," Gable said, nodding at her slowly. "We'll call it…let's call it the comprehensive picture of the situation." He knocked on his desk like he was seconding his own suggestion. "So, if we look holistically, I'm not sure. This isn't my wheelhouse. I'm going to have to consult with a colleague on this one. I like the idea of you having evidence of looking at foster homes. It shows you are a family who is responsible and above-board and looking out for the best interests of not only Nathan but your whole household. The downside is we don't want to create the appearance that Nathan is too violent for his home setting."

"He's not violent," Stefanie said. "He's not." She did not like what her voice was doing, but also could not stop it.

"Let me assure you," Gable said. "I don't believe anything about Nathan. I haven't even met Nathan. I'm on his side. My job is to see this thing from every angle so I can defend him, which I plan to do forcefully and vigorously, if you choose to retain me. And listen, you are right up against the thirty days for answering the summons and we're coming up on a short holiday week. You don't want a default judgment, so you should hire me to at least answer the complaint. You hate me after that, fire me!"

Derek told him it sounded like a plan.

"Well, good," Gable said, slapping a hand on his desk. "I appreciate you putting your trust in me." He talked about answering the summons ay-sap and then beginning the deposition of witnesses, which would include Baz. He could be called to testify should the case go to trial. "It probably won't, it might not even get to that." He flapped and flapped his arms, Gable a flightless bird.

As they walked out, Derek's hand was on Stefanie's elbow, and she knew why. He was trying to steer her cleanly through the waiting room, but she veered instead to the bank of desks, and when Derek tried tightening his grip, she hissed, "What are you bringing up foster care for?" This, enough to get him to loosen up.

Livvy's mother looked up when they approached, the kind of lady with a desk out in the open, ready for interruptions with her *How can I help you?* face, smiling and alert.

"Mrs. Albrecht?" Stefanie said.

"Yes, I'm Ms. Albrecht," she said, the correction polite.

"Sorry, Ms. Albrecht," Stefanie said, reaching her hand across the desk. "Miz. I'm Stefanie Fenning." The woman took Stefanie's hand, her shake on the weak side. "And this is Derek."

"Hi there." Derek waved, a huge grin on his face.

"How can I—" Livvy's mother said, absent any recognition. "What can I—"

"We recognized you from West," Stefanie said. "That day we all had to go see the principal." That wording struck her as funny, not having been the kind of student who ever had to see the principal. "That sounds funny," Stefanie said, something unloosed in her. She felt Derek's hand on the small of her back. "We are Baz's parents." Still nothing. "Baz Fenning's parents. Olivia's—"

"Oh yes. Yes, yes." The woman stood from her seat now, the waistband of her skirt creased. "Of course. Sorry, out of context. Good to meet you. Call me Susan. I really look forward to meeting Baz."

"You haven't met him yet?" Stefanie said, turning to Derek. "Sometimes it seems like Livvy is trying to move in! Doesn't it?"

"I wouldn't, no, I wouldn't say—" Derek said.

Something faltered in Susan's face.

"Fair warning," Stefanie said. And then in a stage whisper, as she leaned over Susan's desk: "He's Black."

Susan laughed, but there was something off-kilter in it. She had the Jewish star pendant of her necklace in hand, pulling it back and forth on the chain. "I know. I knew about last year. Knew about those boys. I'm really sorry about that."

"Not your fault," Stefanie said, "unless you have something to confess!" and then she laughed, and Derek said, "People are trying to work. We should go—"

"We just met Susan," she said to her husband. "Give us a minute."

Derek looked her in the face, and she saw on his lips that he wanted to argue with her but didn't argue with her. She never knew if she loved this least or most about him, how quick he was to give up the fight.

"You know what's funny," Stefanie said. "I thought maybe Olivia had a savior complex last year."

"That's hardly fair," Susan said. To her credit, her face was set, barely giving up anything except for the small blotches of red creeping up her neck. "I taught Olivia to speak up against wrongs."

"Against *wrongs*!" Stefanie said. "That's really something." She leaned in closer. "I'm willing to admit I misjudged. Now it seems like, I don't know, like she's dug her heels in. She's never not with our son. Why do you think she's never not with him?"

"Um. I'm not really sure," Susan said. "I guess she likes him." She half-laughed and added like a joke: "Your energy is a little intense."

"My energy?" Stefanie said. *Energy* was such a white lady word, such a this corner of the country word. No one in Chicago talked about your *energy*.

"Listen, we just came out of a tough meeting," Derek said, trying to lace his fingers through Stefanie's.

"Did Livvy tell you what happened with Nathan this summer?" Stefanie said, not letting Derek grab her hand.

"Nathan?" Susan said, and Stefanie could hear it; she had no idea who Nathan was. The red had crept up the underside of Susan's chin, blossoming now in her cheeks. It was the obliviousness more than anything that got to Stefanie, how this woman could sit here at her desk and not know anything about anything.

"Ask your daughter," Stefanie said. "Or your guy, Gable." She pointed to the back offices, a fleshy, full-bodied feeling moving through her, which was maybe contempt or maybe was envy. "I bet he'll be deposing her."

WOODY

He emailed. He broke her rule and texted. He called, and when her cell phone said the voicemail still hadn't been activated, he called her work and left impeachable messages: "I'm sorry, I'm sorry, I am sorry for not telling you everything about Livvy. I'm sorry for exercising shitty judgment. I am sorry for being a dick and a bad listener and an idiot. I'm sorry I was incapable of sitting still when you were drawing me. Call me. Even if you want to call to yell at me or call me terrible names, call me."

He started biting his nails. Woody Hanover had never in his life bitten his nails. He thought of the habit as female, and when he looked down at his ragged fingertips, he felt girlish and hated himself even more. He wasn't really sleeping and deep into the night, he would try to remedy the calculus of his life—if he'd been fine before Susan, good with Alison and Francie and moving through his days happily and without a sense of missing out, shouldn't he be returned there? How was it that he was returned to barrenness? How could he be this bereft? He could barely sit with Alison and Francie at dinner, Alison relentlessly portioning out the cauliflower and the tofu steaks and quinoa, narrating the benefits of the diet that Woody kept forgetting they were on. "I've lost seven pounds!" Alison announced and Woody didn't care; worse than not caring, he hated her a little for it. "Mommy won't be fat anymore?" Francie said, and Alison cackled a laugh that was not a laugh, and Woody suspected Francie was old enough to know how hurtful such comments were but was pretending otherwise and possibly turning into a sociopath, and in normal circumstances, he would have pointed out that Alison was not fat and that Francie was rude and that eating healthy is good for everyone, especially Francie, but he could barely look at these people for the way something persistent and consuming throbbed beneath his skin. He feared they could see it pulsing at his temples, at both his wrists. He pushed his tofu steak around his plate and bit his nails, Alison thanking him when he was up to clear all the dishes as soon as Alison and Francie were finally finished (god they ate slowly), and Woody hated her for the thank you, hated her for what she did not know, thank god she did not know.

The only easing in the madness was visits with Livvy. He called her into his office the first time to follow up on the Facebook page. He showed her the emails.

"I think she's a bot," Woody said, proud of his use of *bot*.

"She's totally a bot," Livvy said. "Or an idiot."

"Or an idiot bot."

Livvy laughed, in visibly better spirits than the previous meeting, this exactly the sort of failure of the adult world she seemed to revel in.

"I'm so sorry this is happening," he said, which he meant, but also which he hoped she would carry home to Susan, the smell of it wafting off her and into their apartment. "I'm really sorry."

He emailed Susan like a dumb gopher, relentlessly: "I can't stand this. Tell me anything you need. I don't know what to do. Are we having a fight? I thought at first we were having a fight, but this is so much worse."

He didn't have a story about himself that he could tell himself. He couldn't explain it in his own mind. He felt like someone had ripped out his throat. He felt like someone had punched him in the everything.

He left more voicemails: "I swear, you put a spell on me. I have zero explanation. I went into your apartment that night and that red chair and those warblers, what were they called? Something with a *w*. They cast a spell. I'm not like this. This isn't me. I can't explain it. Please, Susan."

He called Livvy out of Danita's AP lit. They read Facebook's response together.

Dear Woody,

Thank you for reporting objectionable content to Facebook. The content does not violate Facebook's terms of service. When there are cases of harassment, we encourage social reporting. You can use the Report link to send a message to the person who posted it asking them to take it down. For example, let's say someone posts a photo of you that you find embarrassing. You can use the report link on that photo to send this person a message and let them know you how this photo makes you feel.

Sincerely,

Facebook's safety team

"I'm supposed to send a message to people who hate me telling them that it feels bad that they hate me?" Livvy said.

"Apparently." Woody sighed.

Livvy was staring past Woody now, into the student parking lot.

"Do you think Shocky would tell them to take it down?" Woody asked.

She shook her head slowly, staring past him. "I'm not, like, his favorite. I stole his boy. And Shocky likes having everyone think Shocky's cool."

"Could you at least ask him?"

She shrugged, still staring past.

"Would you like me to ask him?"

"No!" and now she looked at him. "I really don't want the school blowing this up again. Really, really, really."

"Okay," he said. "Okay. I feel compelled to tell you that we may be reaching the threshold of involving other people. I may need to reach out—"

"No!" Livvy said. "You promised me. I told you in confidence and you promised me. I wouldn't have said anything." There was such bright fury to her face, a bright familiar fury, he could hardly stand it. "Goddamn," she whispered.

There was no good answer available to him. No good option.

Livvy was leaning forward in her chair now, looking right at him, directly in his eyes, not even blinking. Christ, she had to blink at some point. He remembered her black eye. Strong as shit, these Albrecht ladies.

"Fine," he said, both hands in the air in surrender. "Okay," and then, perhaps louder than strictly necessary: "So get yourself back to class!" because he was the adult here. "Get to work, okay?"

December limped in on a Tuesday, cold and wet, wedged between the short Thanksgiving week and the fast-approaching winter break. They'd hosted Alison's parents, Hil and Sal, and her cousins, Terry and Robert, and Terry and Robert's wives, Nadine and Pepper, and all the children: Bryan, sixteen; Denise, eleven; Jennifer, nine; Dot, seven, who everyone called *Tiny* because she was the tallest of all the girls, perched high on legs that seemed fit for a mid-sized giraffe.

A holiday dinner was not altogether different from a faculty meeting, many voices competing, Woody outside the fray. When Alison insisted, as she did every year after dinner and before pie, that everyone go in a round and speak their thanks aloud, he listened to the cousin's children offer their fealty to Xbox, iPod (twice) and Wii, listened to Robert give thanks to his health after arthroscopic knee surgery, listened to Francie say, "Mommy and Daddy" and everyone else say *awwww*, listened to himself croak, "My family, of course," the *awwww*s only increasing, everyone mistaking desolation for tenderness.

"Woody Hanover," he answered his phone on December one, half past eleven.

"Hi," Susan said so softly, he wasn't sure if it *was* Susan. She cleared her throat. "Hi, Woody."

"Oh my god. Let me, hang on, let me close my door." He set the phone down, fearing she'd hang up in the few seconds it took to close the door and run back. "Happy December!" he said.

"Thanks," she said, and maybe she sounded amused. He thought back to spring when they'd begun talking, this their only mode of communication, telephone at work.

She was quiet, and he felt like he'd been the one to call her. Channukah began on Christmas Eve this year. This synchronicity felt meaningful to Woody, and he wanted to shout it out now, how their holidays were aligned. That had to mean something. Instead, he asked: "So how, how are you?"

"Will you come get me? Can you come get me during your lunch hour? I'll meet you—" She named a corner around the block from her work. "How long would it take you to get here?"

She hadn't even waited for him to say yes. Of course, yes! It would be probably ten minutes, not too long. He grabbed his coat, on the way out, asking Jennifer what his calendar looked like after lunch. Jennifer told him statewide teleconference about dual credit college courses. "Cancel," he called out. "Cancel or reschedule! Something came up!" enjoying the way he was yelling, enjoying the way Jennifer stared at him, the students in the anteroom chairs too. You're not supposed to yell in school. No yelling in school.

She stepped off the curb and into his car, trying to close her polka-dotted umbrella out the passenger door, struggling with it adorably, making frustrated sounds until finally she collapsed it and settled in, her bright red hood framing her face, also adorable.

"Little red raincoat hood," he said, and she smiled but stared straight ahead, all profile, not leaning over to kiss him, so he did not lean over to kiss her. "It's good to see you," he said, trying not to grin but grinning.

"It's good to see you too, Woody," she said. "Is it okay if we drive?"

They drove through downtown, past the library, into neighborhoods and he listened to her breathing beside him. It wasn't normal breathing, it was someone trying to regulate their breathing, and Woody wondered if Susan, too, had contended with the persistent throbbing. "How was your Thanksgiving?" he said.

She shrugged. "You know."

"I do know," he said. "Get on the freeway?"

"No," she said. "No freeway."

He turned instead toward the river, driving along the stretch of paths and parks, empty of everyone but the heartiest of joggers or sodden homeless encamped under abandoned play structures. "Can I park?" he asked of the huge, empty lot beside the playground that Francie loved in the summertime. Susan told him sure.

He turned off the engine and took his seatbelt off, turned to her, brushing her red hood off her head, touching her cold cheek with the back of his fingers. "God, I've missed you," he said when she didn't push his hand away.

"Me too," she said. "Everything is so fucked." She looked at him straight on for the first time, her left eye a startled and startling red.

"I have fucking pink eye," she said, and he laughed, and thankfully she laughed.

She told him about the Fennings showing up at Lerner Gable. She told him about going home to Olivia and asking what in the hell was going on, why were the Fennings talking to her about depositions. Olivia didn't know anything about a deposition and kept telling Susan to calm down. One of the aides was suing Nathan, Baz's disabled brother, because Nathan had attacked the aide.

"And I say, 'Baz has a disabled brother?'" Susan was acting it out for Woody now. "And she shrugs at me, and I asked what in the world any of this had to do with her, and she shrugs at me again, and I swear, I want to rip those shoulders right out of their sockets. She was a witness, apparently, a witness to the disabled brother attacking the aide, so she guesses that's why she's getting deposed, but she doesn't know."

Woody was nodding, nodding, nodding beside Susan, Susan speaking so quickly, he wasn't sure if he'd ever heard her talk this fast before. He was waiting for her to say something about him, something about him and her, though acting like he wasn't.

"And my point is," Susan continued, Woody putting a hand on her knee, "I'm hearing about all of this now? She's practically a boarder at their house, and I had to get briefed by them at Lerner Gable. I don't think she cares if I'm humiliated, and also, more to the point, what exactly have I done that's so terrible as a parent that she shuts me out completely? I don't even get the broad strokes. Thank god she'd told me about Baz, or I would've been a total fool in front of those people."

She paused for the first time. "I think," he said, "it's normal for teenagers not to tell their parents about their life. It's developmentally normal." He squeezed her knee on the last part, and she smiled a little, a closed mouth smile that was very sweet. "Channukah is Christmas Eve," he told her.

"What happened to your nails?" she said of the hand on her knee.

"Bad habit," he said. "Recently acquired."

"I'm sorry," she said. "I'm sorry for freaking out. You're married, you have some kind of relationship with my kid, I mean professional, I know it's a professional relationship, but it was too much. It was overwhelming me. And I was feeling protective of me and of her. And I don't know..." She trailed off. "I don't want to be a bad person."

"You're not a bad person. God, you're the farthest thing from. And you don't have anything to apologize for. I was an asshole, and I am not going to withhold anything from you." Even as he spoke, the Facebook page remained an asterisk in his mind. To reveal it to Susan was still too risky. He was doing it to protect him and Susan. "Livvy didn't say a word to me about this attack or a deposition. I would tell you if she had."

"It's not even the attack or the deposition, honestly. She could be out there doing literally anything, and I wouldn't know. Lea was an open book."

Woody tried his hardest to picture Lea, but nothing came to mind except Susan's bedside photo of both girls, Lea taller than Livvy, her hair a frizzy brown. Susan rested her head against the seatback, closing her eyes.

"But Lea was such a bore," he said, and her eyes flew open in surprise, and he laughed as if joking. He laughed until she laughed too.

"Fuck," she said.

"Fuck is right," he said, remembering the thrill of saying things he did not normally say.

"It's good to have someone to talk to. It's good to have *you* to talk to."

"If I kiss you," he said, "will I get pink eye?"

"Probably," she said. "It's the second most contagious disease after diarrhea."

"God," he said. "I missed your pillow talk."

"Fuck you, Woody Hanover."

"Fuck you, Susan Albrecht," he said, and he took her chin in his hand like he'd imagined doing every passing November day, and pressed his lips against hers, like he'd imagined too, wanting all the days of not kissing to collapse beneath this kiss, and the days without Susan to recede from memory, the wait no wait at all.

LARK

Monique's house was cool. As in chill, socked away at the end of a winding street, but also as in cold, Monique messing with the thermostat as soon as they came through the door. "Sorry," she said. "My dad's kind of a fascist about the heating bill. Keeps it at like forty-eight when no one's home."

They'd walked the twenty minutes here after school, instead of getting a ride from Shocky, Monique just old enough to take her driving test, which she hadn't yet. Lark kept forgetting Monique was younger than she was. Lark hadn't taken driver's ed, because it was one more class and the only car they owned sat mostly in their tiny garage, the passenger door wonky, a creepy AM radio, the indicator lights quick to flash red across the dashboard.

"It's okay," Lark said of the cold, Lark shy now inside Monique's house. It was nice in here, not crazy nice like Baz's but regular nice— hardwood floors, couches and tables, piles of stuff. Lark especially liked the piles: shoes piled on the shoe rack, books piled on end tables, mail piled on the kitchen counter, recycling piled in a box next to the kitchen garbage. It was lived-in nice here. A small, yappy dog barked from the outside of the sliding back door, the glass clouded with nose and paw prints.

"Pasta! Chill! Pasta!" Monique said as she opened the slider. The dog ran past Monique and Lark, its nails skittering loudly on the kitchen tile. It sprinted around the room in a large loop, sniffing madly, yapping, before circling back to Monique and Lark, barking, sniffing Lark's ankles, panting, Monique grabbing up the dog, holding it at her shoulder, while the dog squirmed and licked Monique's cheek and ear. "Chill! Chill!" Monique was yelling but laughing. Finally, the dog settled down enough in her arms, panting still, back legs kicking the air. "I'd like to introduce you to Mr. Rasta Pasta Theremin Benjamin Deveraux. But you can call him Pasta."

"Hi, Pasta," Lark said, waving one hand at it, and something in the way Lark said it (really, she just wasn't sure how to address a dog) made

Monique say, "Oh, shit, I forgot about you and dogs. I can put him back outside."

Lark said, "I'm okay."

"Listen, Pasta." Monique put her face up to the dog's. "I know she's new and exciting and cute, but you stand down. You don't jump on her. You behave." She put the dog down, and he yapped and yapped, running in new circles.

When Monique said stuff like that, it made Lark aware of herself and also unsure what to do—how to make her face, where to put her hands.

"You want to see my room?" Monique asked and led Lark upstairs, Pasta on their heels. Monique had posters up of women basketball players Lark didn't know, women soccer players Lark also didn't know. Pasta jumped up on Monique's bed and Monique told him to get down. He ignored her.

"I'm not good at sports," Lark confessed.

"So what?" Monique said. "I'm not good at lots of stuff."

"Like what?" Lark said, really wanting to know.

"I don't know." Monique said. "Cursive? And calligraphy. That's like some crazy cursive shit."

Lark had wanted Monique to be bad at something that Lark was good at. No one knew cursive.

"Do you want to play Battleship?" Monique said, and it was such a weird request—no one played Battleship anymore, did they?

Monique handed her the red plastic case, and when Lark snapped it open, the sight of red and white pegs, the peg boards, the little gray ships, all of which she hadn't seen in years, opened something windy and wide in her. It was the feeling from early girlhood, not knowing where things began or ended, not knowing the shape of herself, the world. It made Lark stammer: Do I put my ships up here or down here? Where do I put my pegs when I guess wrong? What are the red pegs for again?

"Girl," Monique said. "You need to relax." She did not say it meanly. She said: "I never met anyone who thinks she doesn't know stuff like you do."

Lark didn't understand what Monique meant. Did Lark know stuff or not? "I always thought you hated me," Lark blurted. She'd been wanting to say this for so long.

"What?" Monique said, squishing her face up in an expression that was becoming familiar. Lark told her about the time in eighth grade when Lark touched her hair. Monique laughed. "You are seriously crazy. If I hated every white kid who touched my hair, I'd hate about a thousand of you." Lark wasn't sure this made her feel any better.

After Battleship, they played Sorry. After Sorry, they played Chinese checkers, which Lark had never played before. She liked the feel of the cool pegs in her hands, all the colors they weren't using—red and white and black and blue. She suspected Monique was letting her win. When Pasta started barking from the bed, Monique said they should take him for a walk. Did Lark want to come on their walk? Lark liked the way the afternoon was going on and on. She didn't even know what time it was.

It was cold out, and Monique gave Lark one of her knit caps without Lark even asking. She put it on Lark, the wool itchy on her ears. "Do I look stupid?" Lark said.

"Shut up," Monique said. She grabbed a candy bar out of the pantry (Lark always envied homes with pantries and candy bars), and broke it in half, the caramel stretching between the two halves.

Pasta tried to pull Monique down the sidewalk, but he was too small to exert real force. He stopped at every tree, every mailbox post, every bush, sniffing and peeing. They weren't talking, and Lark wondered if it was okay that they weren't talking.

"Shocky won't bug you anymore," Monique said, already done with her half of the candy bar, licking her fingertips. Lark was trying to savor hers. Pasta lifted his leg at a Little Free Library. He didn't even have any pee left. "Shocky's a good guy but he's stupid," she said. "Not book stupid, girl stupid."

"I'm the one who's book stupid," Lark said.

Monique turned to her on the sidewalk. "Let's play a game," she said. "Where you can't say a shitty thing about yourself for fifteen minutes."

Lark smiled and looked at her feet. Her face was cold.

"And also, you have to walk the dog." Monique handed her the leash, showing her which button retracted the leash, which released it.

Pasta, seeming to sense the opportunity, dashed up the front lawn of the next house, Lark running, Monique yelling, "Retract! Retract!" but Lark kept pressing one button, then the other, both seeming to let out more and more leash. Pasta ran himself around and around an ornamental lamp post by the house's front porch. A large shepherd barked from behind the front window, and Lark anticipated an angry homeowner bounding out the front door. She was trying to unloop Pasta from the post when he curled his back and squatted. Monique yelled, "Pasta! Terrible timing!" and grabbed a plastic bag from her pocket, Lark handing her the leash, saying, "Sorry—"

"Nuh-uh," Monique said. And then: "You got fourteen and a half minutes," as she leaned down to scoop the Pasta poop.

Lark got the dog untangled, eventually figuring out the leash, so that she and Pasta fell into a decent rhythm, Lark letting the leash out far enough for the dog to wander to curbside shrubs, but not so far that he could run up lawns. Monique was telling a story about the two freshman girls who threw up at yesterday's practice after Coach Waller made them do a hundred burpees.

"Now you tell me something," Monique said.

Lark laughed, or half-laughed, embarrassed. "Like what?"

"Like anything."

All her stories were Livvy stories: cannonballing off side-by-side diving boards; Wall-E drooling in his sleep, leaving big wet spots on her shirt.

"There's this pear tree out my bedroom window and it smells good for like a week and then the pears rot all spring."

"Gross," Monique said, and Lark knew it was a terrible story.

"Once," Lark said. "I got lost at the mall, and the police came."

Lark told about wandering through the JC Penney women's section while her mom was shopping, and getting turned around, and ending up out the store and into the mall, trying to wander her way back, passing the pretzel store and the Orange Julius, going into a nail shop and the shoe shop. In the meantime, her mom had found mall security, and when mall security couldn't find her, they called in the cops, who eventually found her at the kid's play area, crying for all the moms, none of them hers. What she didn't say then—and didn't say now—was that she was crying for want, all these young, skinny, made-up moms, all prettier and sweeter looking than hers, in tight-fitting jeans, sipping from coffee cups, talking on their cell phones.

"Poor little Lark," Monique said, and Lark could hear Livvy saying this, though not as nicely.

Lark thought of telling about the ear piercing and Candace, but they were back to Monique's, a silver sedan in the driveway. "My dad," she said, and: "He's cool."

Mr. Deveraux was in the kitchen, unloading groceries, still in a long trench coat and suit. He was tall, with close-trimmed hair and goatee, Monique's same nose, the same wide smile when he saw them. "Baby girl," he said, and Monique went to him, her dad taking her into a side hug. She did not look embarrassed by the nickname or by the way he kissed her on the head. Monique introduced Lark, and when he reached out his hand and said, "Call me Carl," she nodded, though she knew she would not. She wouldn't call him anything, if she could help it. His grip was very strong. She couldn't remember the last time she'd shaken an adult's hand.

Monique helped him unpack the groceries from the bag—lettuce into the fridge, cans of beans into the cupboard—and Lark watched how deftly the two moved through the kitchen, he asking about her test in geometry, had she gotten to tonight's homework yet, when was she going to run? Lark had a little of the feeling she'd had at the kid's area of the mall.

"We're having tacos," he said. "Lark, you're joining us?"

"Um—?" She looked at Monique. She hadn't called home, not that she needed to. Her mom would assume she was at Livvy's. But if she wouldn't be there for dinner, she should call. She pictured her mom at the table, eating soup by herself, which was reason not to stay and reason to stay. Monique was nodding at her, smiling.

"Lark walked Pasta," Monique announced.

"That little monster," Monique's dad said, ruffling the fur on Pasta's head as the dog tried to jump up his suit pant. "Well then, we should definitely feed her," he said to the dog. "She deserves combat pay."

Back up in Monique's room, Lark said how nice her dad was. They were leaning up against the side of Monique's bed, the games from earlier still spread out on her rug.

"He's always compensating," Monique said. Monique's mom was in California. She'd fallen in love with a guy at her Krav Maga class when they were play-choking each other. Lark thought Monique was making a joke, but she wasn't. Her parents had gotten divorced when Monique was in fifth grade. She spent half her summers and every other Christmas in Santa Monica. "It's really sunny," she said, "and Marcus gets me whatever I want. A boogie board. Roller blades."

Lark had a handful of the Chinese checkers pegs in her hands, pouring them from one to another, letting them stream though her fingers and onto her lap. She hadn't called her mom, worried she'd hear something in her mom's voice that would make her go home. The smell of onions and sizzling beef rose from the kitchen.

"Do you miss her?" Lark said.

Monique shrugged. "Do you miss your dad?"

Lark shrugged. "I don't think so. I feel too used to it for it to feel like missing him. Like if I miss him, it's so normal, it feels like being regular."

"That's sad."

"I didn't mean it like that."

"I know," Monique said, turning to look at Lark, her head against the side of the mattress. "You're a sweet kid."

Lark laughed, turning her head to look at Monique, their faces so close, Monique's eyes blurred together. "You're younger than me."

"I'm a sweet kid too," Monique said, and something felt so lazy and so nice in this room. Monique inched her face even closer and whispered: "I think I like you."

"I think I like you too," Lark whispered back because that was what Lark did. She said things back, she agreed to be agreeable. But this time, she meant it. She liked Monique in the way they were talking about liking. Maybe she'd liked her like this all along, since that time in eighth grade when she'd touched her hair, Monique the girl in class who volunteered to write on the board, who raised her hand to say things like "I don't get how we're supposed to solve for speed," who unwrapped candy from her bag in the middle of class, not caring how loud the wrapper.

Monique leaned into her, her lips still sweet from the candy bar, and soft, her tongue a different species than Shocky's, Monique's gentle and tentative, both of them giggling the first time the tips of their tongues touched, laughing so that their teeth collided, making them laugh more, Monique taking Lark's hand, this too, gentle, the two of them laughing and kissing and laughing and trying not to make too much noise. Later she apologized to her mother, asking, "Have you eaten?" and taking her mother's silence to mean no, so calling out, "I'm heating you soup." As the bowl spun in the microwave, her belly danced a dance that was not hunger, and not longing, but something new, a feeling she was not used to, past all the other feelings, want scooped out into more want, bottomless and voracious, yet also and for the first time maybe, full.

STEFANIE

Ed and Bryna came from Atlanta for the holidays, disgorging presents from their suitcases, complaining about the rain, asking Baz if he still rooted for the Braves, Baz too polite to say no. "You losing weight?" Bryna asked Stefanie at least once a day. "You look too skinny," slinging an arm around her waist and pinching the skin at her hip to prove her point. "You're not feeding your wife!" she shouted to Derek in the next room. "We raised you better than this!" She took over the kitchen, frying up catfish one night, pork chops the next, while Ed decamped in the living room, Ed, bless him, spending wordless hours with Nathan, handing him—in intervals—a beaded mask from their latest trip to Mexico, a wooden recorder, a plastic set of measuring spoons. Stefanie had long given up on guessing what he would bring; always, Nathan was fascinated, though she was never sure if it was because of the strange objects or Ed's preternatural calm. Nathan, like the rest of them, reveled in the visits from Derek's parents.

Ed and Bryna so completely transformed their home, the kitchen smelling of grease, jazz playing all day from the stereo, the stairs lined with Bryna's fuzzy slippers, the table strewn with Ed's half-read *New York Times* in the first half of the day, his gin and tonic gone watery in the second. Some days, Bryna boiled orange peel and clove on the stove top "to clear the air," and Stefanie loved coming home to the smell. Ed might take the boys onto the deck with his red Audubon guide, pointing out the difference between a raven and a crow, a red-tailed hawk. He might pull up his pant legs to show off the surgery scars at both knees. "I'm bionic," he'd say, knocking on his own kneecaps, offering the boys a chance to knock too. He'd been making this same offer for years, and Baz always ended up taking him up on it; Ed was so warm-hearted and playful, he wore down usual defenses.

They even made Livvy more bearable, Livvy who had taken up residence in their home over winter break, some days leaving only to sleep, a limit that Derek and Stefanie had at least agreed on. "Come here, you," Bryna said to her in the kitchen, putting an arm around Livvy's waist as she'd Stefanie's. "You know that's our boy," she said of Baz, her tone both loving and conspiratorial. "He needs to be taken care of well. You know how to cook?"

"Not really," the girl told her.

"That will not do," Bryna said, *tsk*ing, wagging a finger at Livvy in a way that Stefanie wished she could. Soon the girl was sifting flour with Bryna, an apron around her waist, coating chicken wings, filling a pan with oil, coring apples then peeling them, Bryna telling her, "No, no, you're going to peel the skin right off your fingertips," taking the apple from her, reseating it in her open palm, angling the peeler atop it. Stefanie remembered the way Bryna schooled her when Bryna and Ed first visited their early apartment in Champaign-Urbana, lecturing Stefanie on the geranium she was over-watering and the cheap spices in their kitchen cupboard. Bryna's way of mothering—bossy, demonstrative, suffering no fools, yet with kindness—seduced Stefanie nearly as much as Derek had. She watched the way Bryna and Ed slid in and out of each other's orbit. They made it look easy, living in tandem, each taking what they needed, allowing the other the same, giving Stefanie the early impression that no effort was required in such a venture. They existed as a gentle parenthesis around Derek, bounding him, reminding him of his place within a larger whole without binding him. There was room for Stefanie too, and later, of course, the boys. Expansive was what they were, and what Stefanie hoped herself to be too, from the first time she met them all the way until now.

She went on walks with Ed in the evenings after dinner, bundled against the cold and the rain, Ed holding the umbrella overhead for the two of them, Stefanie liking the way it pulled her to him as she hooked her arm through his. He wanted to know how Eileen was doing, and Stefanie said how it was hard over the phone, how her mama had stopped answering calls, Cal the one to call Stefanie, the spend down confusing, the staff rude. He thought they should move her to a different place.

"We can't keep moving her," Stefanie said.

"Sure, sure," he said, and: "What else is bothering you?" which struck Stefanie as the nicest thing anyone had said to her in a while.

She told Ed about Naomi as they made their way down the sidewalkless hill. "Careful," she said of the loose pebbles beneath their feet, of the random divots in the road. She told him about Gable and the ninety-two-page questionnaire Naomi's lawyer had sent the previous week, its offensive and invasive questions about Nathan's social history, schooling, cognitive functioning, like they were to slice him up and pick him apart, offer him as a specimen. *Exhibit A: Big Dumb Black Boy.* She told him about the depositions scheduled for some time early next year. "A year or two," she said, of the timeline Gable had offered recently.

"How can we help?" Ed said quietly, after they'd gotten to the lowlands, out from the trees, onto sidewalk, unshielded from the canopy overhead. Just that, his question as they stepped around puddles, was enough to make her teary.

"I don't know," she said, ashamed for the croak in her throat, though Ed would never hold it against her.

"Money?" he said. "You need help with money?"

"No," she said, too quickly. Ed and Bryna had no money to spare, Derek and Stefanie the ones who paid for their trips out west. "No, we're good," and then: "Thank you."

"You made good boys," he said. "It is the world that's nasty. The world that does them no kindness." He spoke with unusual feeling. Usually, it was Bryna with the feeling.

She tried to say about Livvy, about how she was at the center of this, or at least if not the center, then in the mix in a way that was problematic bordering on treacherous, which Stefanie knew for certain and could not explain. It had been her hope that she wouldn't need to explain, that Ed and Bryna would naturally ally themselves with Stefanie. But Bryna played with the girl in the kitchen, whooping loud when Livvy spilled flour on the floor, saying, "You ever try sweeping up flour, honey?" Ed patted the girl quietly on the shoulder whenever he passed, and Stefanie remembered what it was like to get those early shoulder pats from Ed. The girl seemed hardly to notice—and wasn't that the real problem Stefanie had with Livvy, the sense the girl gave off of deserving all she got? It was no secret that Stefanie saw Ed and Bryna as parents of her own and longed for the blind loyalty accorded to children, even—or especially—in defiance of reason.

Hidaya and Abdi had them all over for cocktails the day after Christmas, Baz and Shekib quick to the basement, Shekib's older brother home with his new wife and their infant daughter, Ed with Nathan on the couch and Stefanie not remembering the last time she was free and unencumbered at a get-together with grown-ups. She hadn't realized how insular they had become. She had more than one glass of eggnog.

She and Hidaya and Bryna passed Nadia, the baby, between them. Hidaya talked about being a grandmother, and Stefanie said that tripped her the fuck out and then apologized for swearing in front of the baby. She sniffed the baby's hair, and Derek sidled up beside her and slipped a hand around her waist in a way he hadn't in recent memory.

"Don't get any ideas," he said.

"Yeah right," she told him, and "I think I'm drunk," and "Smell her head."

"Hi, drunk," Derek said, smelling the baby's head. "I'm Derek," the same corny joke he'd been making half their life.

The day before Ed and Bryna were leaving, Derek, Ed, and Nathan were out "on a drive," Bryna and Stefanie at the kitchen table, drinking tea when Baz came leaping up the steps from his room two at a time.

"Mama," he called. "Mama!" and it had been so long since she'd heard her name out of his mouth like that.

"Baby boy," she called out, a name she hadn't used in years.

Baz was holding his laptop, his face split wide open, teeth blazing white and straight. "You want to see?" he said, pointing to his laptop, and it was so funny to see him like this—playful, nearly flirtatious. "You want to see what I got here?"

"Sure do, boy!" Bryna called out. Livvy was at home in the middle of the day, a rarity that would seem to Stefanie later a gift, the universe offering her, for once, a kindness.

"What you got for us?" she said, eager to play too, though didn't she already know? Shouldn't she have? He'd been waiting for weeks to hear from Penn, and it occurred to her in those seconds before he plunked his laptop down on the table, how long she'd considered his rejection a done deal, not because she doubted her boy's brilliance, but because she knew how the world foreclosed on the dreams of kids like Baz, hemming them in and teaching them to be inconspicuous above all else, not too greedy, except here was the computer in front of them, and the email on the screen read—

Dear Brian,

Congratulations! On behalf of the entire Penn community, it gives me great pleasure to invite you to attend the University of Pennsylvania as a member of the Class of 2020...

—and goddamn it was beautiful, her son beaming in their kitchen,

Bryna whooping, that first moment—no matter all that came after—joy, pure unadulterated joy, the three of them grasping for each other and shrieking, loud in each other's ears, a jumping jumbled three-headed tangle of breath and body and mother and child, and everything blown wide open, a world without bounds, and a child who could be, would be so big in it now, wouldn't he?

They waited for Marjorie on the sidewalk, first week of the new year, reserved especially for shame and new resolve. They'd been riding the high of the Penn news since Ed and Bryna left, though something about watching the ball drop tipped them back into the reality of their life: financial aid, lawsuit, Naomi, Nathan.

"Good-sized lawn," Derek said, which it was. "Nice porch," he said, true too, the sort of porch Stefanie normally envied, covered, wrap-around, though hers would have less plastic furniture.

"Where's Nathan?" Marjorie asked as she stepped out of her car.

It hadn't occurred to them to bring Nathan. He was home with a sitter in front of the television, *SpongeBob* on when they left.

Marjorie's face was pinched, her hair still wet beneath her hood. Stefanie wasn't used to seeing Marjorie outside of her basement burrow.

"We were supposed to bring Nathan?" Derek said.

"That is kind of the point, isn't it?" Marjorie said with a smile, so that her annoyance was made to seem a joke. She was already marching up the front walk.

The point, as far as Stefanie could understand, was to mollify Gable, or Naomi, or Naomi's lawyer whose name Stefanie refused to remember. *Ampersand*, she called him, hoping herself clever.

"Ruth," Marjorie called out when a woman opened the door. She was Hispanic, as Marjorie had promised, older, fifties maybe, long black hair tied with a red scarf. She wore a T-shirt that said *SOLE SUPPORT for Parkinson's 2014*, jeans, and slippers. There was a thin dishtowel draped over her left shoulder. Stefanie liked that she wasn't dressed up, that she was plain faced. Stefanie didn't want to be sold on anything. Ruth told them to "come in, come in," asked their names, told them she wasn't going to shake, her hands were damp from dishes.

It was a house. Stefanie wasn't sure what she'd been expecting, but the front hall had a shoe rack, the living room, a couch, the bathroom a sink and toilet, notable only for being handicapped-accessible, a bench and grip-bar in the shower. In the kitchen, a boy sat in a wheelchair, gnarled and skinny. She forgot the disease was that gnarled a boy like that, though she thought of the endless telethon from childhood, when her mother would say, "How about a sickle-cell telethon? How about a poor people telethon? Who's the comedian for that?"

A man sat beside the boy, helping him with his cereal, guiding the boy's fingers around the spoon, helping the spoon up to his mouth. "Davis," Ruth said. "Michael. This is Stefanie and Darren." Derek didn't correct her. The man beside the boy gave a quick, neutral wave. The boy swung his head in their direction. It was discomfiting seeing these two at this table, fitting exactly the profile of Mercer and Nathan at theirs, as if there was an army of man-boys, armed with their soft foods and PSWs.

Ruth told them about the organic produce she buys twice a week at farmer's markets, the cupboards each labeled with their contents. *Silverware* said one drawer. *Bowls*, a cabinet door. She'd accommodated all types of diets. "Gluten free," she said. "Everyone's gluten free these days."

Derek had a hand at Stefanie's low back. The wallpaper was a repeating pattern of violet flowers.

"Nathan's not gluten-free," Stefanie said. "He eats anything," she said, trying to make her voice less defensive. "Salami," she said. "Almonds. Bread."

"Well, good," Ruth said, her voice even as could be.

The boy ate absent any self-consciousness, mouth open wide as he chewed on his bran flakes or whatever they were, his chin shiny with milk. Terrible names went through Stefanie's head, the sorts kids called Nathan when he'd spent his days in special ed. She left the kitchen.

"Do you want to see the bedrooms?" Marjorie called after, Ruth and Derek following.

The bedroom was as she'd imagined it, had she let herself imagine it—a bunk bed, unmade navy sheets, a nightstand with a digital clock and a lamp. A soccer ball sat in the corner and seemed a plant to assure them that a boy, a real live boy, lived here. The floor was linoleum, the same tired linoleum as the rest of the house.

"Nice," Derek said. It made as much sense as proclaiming *dinosaur* or *turquoise*. This room was many things; nice, not one of them.

"He has muscular dystrophy?" Stefanie said, and Ruth said—again, kindly: "We don't disclose information about household members. You can talk to Davis, though, if you'd like."

Derek wanted to know all sorts of things—how long had Davis been here, what sort of supports he was provided, what a "household member" got here that he couldn't get at home.

Marjorie and Ruth took turns talking, this and that and comprehensive care and PSW and DSP and IADL and for so long their lives had been lived inside acronyms. Stefanie was kicking her toe against the linoleum, and it made a squeaky noise until Derek took her arm in his hand. "Independence," Marjorie was saying. "That's what he gets here that he doesn't get at home."

"I know it's a lot to take in at once," Ruth said to Stefanie. She held a hand up to her forehead. "You've had it up to here, haven't you?"

How many other mothers had she spoken to in this very way? Ignoring the wallpaper and linoleum and cabinet labels, all this place was was their house minus them.

WINTER SEMESTER 2016

LARK

Shocky hit his steering wheel with his palm. "I knew it," he said. "I knew it! I knew it!"

Lark was in the backseat, Mo in the passenger seat, laughing. They were sitting in the student parking lot after school, the car warm already from Shocky's dashboard heaters. It smelled moldy in here, something long forgotten under a seat. All Mo had said was, "Guess what? Me and her," making a motion with her shoulder into the backseat.

Lark and Mo had been talking about telling Shocky for a while now. Mo had a plan. Shocky first and then Mo's dad, though her dad had probably already figured it out, a fact that stunned Lark silly. Lark had been delaying and delaying, Mo reassuring that Shocky would be cool, he wasn't a dick, he and Lark had gotten off to a weird start. But that wasn't what worried Lark; she was protective of this tender thing between them, and telling people would make it into something else, something in and of the world. But Mo had *please please please*d Lark the night before, her head in the crook of Lark's arm in a way that Lark had never imagined someone else's head in the crook of her arm, her arm falling happily asleep beneath the weight, their faces inches apart, so of course she agreed.

And now all three of them were laughing, and Lark had a good-all-over feeling like she'd been having for weeks now, long afternoons spent in Mo's room, side by side doing homework, dozing, kissing, more, Lark over and over: "Show me how to do that to you," and Mo showing her.

"I knew you were gay!" He pointed a finger at Lark. "You're such a lesbian. I told Baz. I told him!"

Lark wasn't gay. She wasn't a lesbian. She wasn't an anything except a want to be with Mo as much as she could all the time. This was part of what had worried her, what someone else would make of it, what someone else would turn it into, but now that Shocky was turning it into whatever he was turning it into, she didn't care. She only cared that Mo was laughing and happy, that they were in this car together, that Mo could reach around and put her hand on Lark's leg like she was right now. Here were the things she'd learned most recently about Mo: she still had one baby tooth, her right incisor, the adult tooth never having grown in; every year since she'd left, her mom sent her a new pair of Nike running shoes in January as a New Year present; she'd dated one boy in seventh grade, Niall Loman, who she referred to as "a limp little twig"; if she had a daughter, she'd name her Serena Joy.

"Dude," Mo said. "You need to chill," and she was both serious and joking, and Shocky finally started driving, half the cars already gone from the lot.

"I just got the other person wrong," Shocky said, almost to himself. "How long? How long this been going on?"

Mo turned around, looking at Lark, giving her a chance to answer. Lark was fine back here saying nothing, but this was what Mo was like: making space for her, wanting to hear. "Like," Lark said. "A month? Since before winter break." She was pretending she didn't know exactly forty-two days. Six weeks, enough for the secret to blossom, taking up all the space inside her. What did she used to think about? she wondered. What did she used to do? Mo had come over for New Year's Eve, and Lark's mom had even joined them on the couch. Lark's mom had never joined Lark and Livvy on the couch. Long ago, before even memory, Lark and Livvy had established themselves as separate from their parents. It had never occurred to Lark that it could—or should—be any different. Her mom was, above all else, embarrassing, though Mo acted like the three of them on the couch was normal, even trying to twiddle Lark's pinky finger in the gap between their side-by-side thighs. "My dad and I," Mo announced at 11:55 p.m., "have a thing where you have to say what you are most grateful for from the past year." (Mo: "My new friend"; Lark: "Me too"; Lark's mom: "I lost six pounds." Mo: "Good for you, Mrs. Stevenson.") If afterward, her mom had said, "I didn't know you had Black friends," Lark found herself glad it was this, and not something worse.

"God, this is so much better than Daneka," Shocky said.

Mo had dated Daneka Scott for all of her freshman year. Lark knew this now, though she hadn't at the time. Her stomach flipped a little, thinking about Mo with Daneka, also on the basketball team, plus student council and debate, tall, with perfect posture and dark, curly hair, thick-framed tortoiseshell glasses, glasses that would look silly on anyone else. Daneka seemed like the opposite of Lark, and it made Lark wavy with insecurity. The fact, though, of secret lives being lived, an undertow she—and seemingly everyone—was oblivious to somehow reassured her. To be part of that undertow—she'd never imagined *she'd* be the secret—thrilling.

"Is Livvy losing her shit?" Shocky asked Lark. She and Livvy had spent the last Sunday of winter break together, lying for hours on Livvy's bed like all the millions of times they had before, Livvy talking and talking about Baz going to Philadelphia next year, and there wasn't a good school for her there, so maybe she'd eventually meet up with him and be a barista, maybe she'd do community college, and also how Baz met her mom, and the dinner was totally stupid, her mom talking about her Black friend from work and asking if Baz's family celebrated Kwanza, which was mortifying to Livvy, and Lark realized how Livvy didn't ask her about her life anymore. Livvy used to, or maybe she hadn't; maybe it had been that they were each other's life.

It felt good to have Mo inside of her as she hung out on Livvy's bed, and she got the feeling of what it probably had been like for Livvy all these months, to have something else besides the two of them inside her and to feel its pull. It was a good feeling, a pleasure in the truest sense of the word, but also it rendered her and Livvy smaller, and she wondered if Livvy had had this feeling too, like Lark was something she needed to get through in order to make it onto the bigger and realer thing. It was ungenerous of Lark to think this way, she knew, but she kind of didn't care. All she wanted was pleasure. She felt like a pleasure monster now, having not known what she hadn't known for so long. *I'm sorry,* Lark had whispered the very first time Mo's fingers trailed over her tiny breasts, which still hadn't grown even with her period, and Mo had not heard, or if she'd heard, she'd pretended not to, her fingers round and round Lark's nipples.

"You're the first," Lark said. "The first person we're telling."

"Whaaaaaat?" Shocky yelled, slamming his palm against his steering wheel as he drove, even honking the horn two short, sharp honks. The driver in the car in front of them held up his hand like *WTF?* "That is cuckoo. I thought you told that girl *everything.*"

Mo was laughing. "Calm down, you spaz," she said. "You're going to drive us into a tree."

"I'm the first. That is some crazy-ass shit." He kept hitting the steering wheel with his palm.

"You are a child. You are such a child," Mo said. "Stop scaring my girl."

"I'm not scared," Lark said, not something she would've said before. Everything now was before or after. It wasn't technically true, not being scared; she was scared all the time that this wasn't real, that it would end, that Mo would figure her out to also be a limp little twig. She'd seen Niall Loman in the hallways plenty; he slouched, locked in an embrace with his books at his chest. Lark knew most definitely that she was more the Niall end of the spectrum than the Daneka end. But even the scare was at least, in part, kind of thrilling. She'd never imagined herself having a Mo to lose. She had a Mo to lose.

"Mrs. Stevenson," Mo said when Lark's mom padded into the kitchen as Lark and Mo were making grilled cheese on the stovetop. Lark and Mo didn't try to be quiet, and what that meant was that Lark's mom often came out to join them. It messed with Lark, how this worked now. Had being quiet all the time stopped her mom from coming out, when Lark thought being quiet was what her mom had wanted? Had Lark's mom been hiding in her room trying not to disturb Lark, as Lark was out here trying not to disturb her? It was too painful to contemplate, all the lost opportunity and tiptoeing, all the attempts at protecting each other, which maybe had been attempts at avoiding each other, stopping one sadness from colliding into another, so she tried to focus on the now, during which Lark's mom was in the room with them, halfway happy, it seemed. Maybe all she'd been waiting for was someone to talk to her like Mo talked to her, loudly, without apology: "Do you want a grilled cheese?"

Lark's mother sat heavily in one of the kitchen chairs. "Oh no, no, no." She waved a hand.

"You sure?" Mo said. "I make it with extra butter." The oven fan was on, but still the smell of the singed bread filled the air. After New Year's Eve, Mo had asked, "Is your mom okay?" and Lark felt partially exposed and wholly ashamed. "Not really," Lark had said, and Mo had shrugged and said, "I mean, she seems nice, but kind of out of it." Lark said all the words she'd known for as long as she could remember: depressive, major, episode, Lithium, Zoloft, Lexapro, Cymbalta Cymbalta Cymbalta. "That sucks," Mo said. Lark agreed, and Mo talked about how all her mom cared about was that everyone always look their best and no one screw up the annual holiday picture, including the two standard poodles she always dressed in Christmas sweaters. "Your mom's at least real," Mo said, which was maybe the nicest thing anyone had said about Lark's mom.

She watched her mom at the table now and tried not to be embarrassed by her nightgown and housecoat, her hair needing brushing. They joined her when their sandwiches were ready, cheese melting out of the sides. Sometimes, Lark's mom watched Mo so closely, Lark worried she would say something awful, or if not awful, then bad, or if not bad then semi-mortifying. They had already run through the basics ("What do your parents do?" "Do you know Livvy? Is that how you two became friends?" "Do you have classes together?") which left them mostly in quiet.

"Do you guys know MASH?" Mo said. Of course Lark knew MASH. She and Livvy used to play and play, until Lark was living in a mansion, married to Bruno Mars, driving a VW bug, and working as a taxidermist. Or shack, Charlie Puth, Porsche, and nursery school teacher. "Let's do you, Mrs. Stevenson," Mo said, and Lark's mom said, not for the first time, "Call me Shelley," and Mo did, explaining to Shelley how Shelley had to come up with four people she wanted to marry, four jobs, four kinds of cars.

"Don't," Lark said, not wanting to put her mom on the spot like this, but her mom, after sputtering and giggling and saying, "No, no," like she'd said about the grilled cheese, began: "Paul McCartney…John McCain, well, I suppose…Terence. Should I include Terence?" she asked Lark, and Lark had a sense of wanting to slap her own cheek or bite her own tongue, it was all so strange and yet not strange at all.

"Who's Terence?" Mo said. Lark had never met anyone as unafraid to talk to adults as Mo. She'd always thought Livvy was brave, but Livvy's bravery was different—mouthy, defiant. Mo talked to everyone the same. Lark found this to be remarkable, along with so much else that was remarkable about Mo—her calf muscles, the way she could hum any song on demand, how she never said *This all you got?* when she looked in Lark's fridge.

"My dad," Lark said.

"Your *dad?*" Mo said. "What was he like?" she said to Lark's mom.

Lark's mom didn't say anything for so long, Lark grew more and more certain that this was the moment it would all fall apart, but then she said, "Hokey. He was real hokey, made up rhymes like, *Roses are red, Violets are blue, the sky is jealous because your eyes took all the blue.*"

Lark had never heard this.

Mo said, "He rhymed blue with blue."

Lark's mom said, "I told you. Hokey."

Mo leaned toward Lark's mom. "Are your eyes even blue?"

Lark's mother let out a noise, a laugh. "They're brown. Light brown."

Mo hit the tabletop with her hand. "Damn, Shelley," she said. "That is some next-level hokeyness. That is no joke." And then, as if he were in the hallway, awaiting his prize: "Terence!" Mo called out. "You sly fox."

"Terence," Lark said, because they were all saying it, and it seemed like his face might come back clear, and memory would reveal a poem he made for Lark, a hokey poem about her brown eyes too. "Terence!"

WOODY

Max Murray brought a gun to school. The building went on lockdown. Police arrested Max. Girls wept openly. Max was one of Deirdre's (J-S), sophomore, loner, weak chin. Woody didn't even recognize the kid when the paper ran a story of the arrest and the plans found on Max's computer. A crisis counselor camped out in Sandy O'Hare's office (T-Z) down the hall, available to anybody, but particularly the kids on Max Murray's alleged "hit list." Doug sweat out a good amount of his body weight. Navid and Danita organized their most ambitious assembly yet: bullying, violence in schools, being an ally, and gun control.

And just like that, it was over, Livvy and Baz gone from the collective ire, held up instead as object lessons in "the petty things we did before our lives were threatened by a psycho sophomore." Lindsay Nichols took down the Facebook group and offered Livvy a tearful apology in the hallway; there was tell of hugging. Roger Bass allegedly high-fived Baz in similar fashion. "We're good," they affirmed. "We're good, man."

"Do you need any help?" he asked Deirdre once and then again later in the week. The clot of kids was back around her office door. Deirdre waved Woody off with an appreciative smile. She told him no thanks. It was good how everything had worked out for Livvy and Baz. It truly was. Only a real bastard would feel unhappy about being restored to the quiet periphery. Only a real bastard would feel a nameless ache.

He and Susan had begun an end-of-day ritual. She sat in her car in the public parking garage blocks from Lerner Gable, and he swung by on his way home. They crouched low in the back seat and sometimes talked, sometimes made out, putting hands up shirts, down pants. It was quick—ten minutes, maybe fifteen. Susan told him about Stan Lerner's torn ligament from his triathlon. Woody told her about the dream he'd had the night before, in which he'd won the Nobel Peace Prize but forgotten his pants. She laughed and nibbled on his neck like a vampire. Alison hated to hear about his dreams, without saying so. Woody for years had watched her eyes dull as he relayed the deer with one antler and their house that was not their house—no roof, a pool where the living room was supposed to be.

The parking garage made it so they were sure to see each other every weekday. This knowledge of regular contact, they both agreed, allowed for some stability in an otherwise combustible situation. And it only got Woody home twenty, thirty minutes later than usual, hardly enough to give note—"Admissions season," all he had to say to Al—his spirits so lifted, there were still days he felt that Susan was the best thing that ever happened to his marriage. He spilled over with good feeling, grabbing Al around the waist as she stood at the kitchen counter. Her face was aglow across the kitchen table. More and more, she fell asleep on the couch beside him after putting Francie to sleep, Woody shaking her gently awake, leading her to the bedroom like a man leads a child. Bleary-eyed, she'd smile from her pillow. "Why am I so tired?" she asked, and he told her: "Love," which made her grab him around the neck and kiss his face.

One time he and Susan fucked in the backseat—that's what Susan called it, pooh-poohing him when he'd said he wanted to make love to her. "I don't want you to make love to me," she'd said. "I want you to fuck me," and Woody had found this breathtaking, literally; he was so happily surprised, he choked on his own windpipe. In the back of her car, they were cramped and awkward in the five o'clock hour, so many other commuters making their way around and down the parking lot, headlights flashing through Susan's rear windshield as she and Woody tried to make themselves small and flat while he desperately bucked atop her, fearing his ass was cresting above the seat back but unable to stop.

On a recent walk to the teacher's lounge, he'd seen Livvy through the gymnasium doors during Abigail's fifth hour PE, cheeks flushed, her hair back in a ponytail, crouched low waiting for the volleyball from the other side of the net. She dove for the ball and missed, smacking heavily onto the gym floor with nary a wince; kids and their bodies, how for granted they could take their nimble limbs. Another girl casually helped Livvy up by the elbow; a teammate patted her on the shoulder. Livvy wore a near-smirk, a combination of embarrassment and pride, and it was such an Albrecht expression, the exact face Susan made when she'd handed him that napkin sketch months ago, or later, when she ejaculated all over the motel sheets or later still, when he post-coitally babbled, "I want to come live in your vagina. Or crawl up into your armpit. I'd even be happy lodged in the back of your throat," and standing there in the hallway, watching Livvy with her mother's face, he was shot through with so much—longing, guilt, joy, tension, fear, shame, happiness, desperation.

Things were going his way, which made him nervous, even though he was a guy for whom things often went his way. He'd grown so used to ordinary good fortune, he thought himself luckless.

"What if?" he said to Susan one night in the car, both of them crouched low, their knees pressed up against the backs of the front seats. "What if we went for it?" Woody said.

"Went for it?" she said.

"What if we blew this wide open?"

Susan was quiet. He listened to the sound of her breathing. It hurt his neck and shoulders to sit like this. Every night now, he was sore up his spine. "Are you serious?" Susan whispered.

"I don't know," he whispered back. "I think so."

He took her hand in his. Her fingers were freezing. They were always freezing, the car turned off. It reminded him of camping.

"Shit," she said. "You're the one with everything to lose. All I risk is a scarlet *A*." Only inches separated their faces. "I'm always up for a new accessory. Wardrobe refresher." She was whispering and laughing, and she didn't take her eyes off him, and her eyes were dead serious. "I got a kid," she said. "Whatever we do, we can't fuck with my kid. Or your kid."

"No one wants to fuck with our kids less than I do."

"I've never even met Francie," Susan said, her voice cracking a little on the name. It was possibly the first time she'd said it.

"You will love her," Woody said. "She's a riot and sweet and weird and a very good girl."

Susan was breathing again, louder now, the kind of breaths the teacher had made Woody do in Alison's yoga's class when she'd dragged him along, Woody not nearly bendy enough. There was a sudden hitch in Susan's breath so that Woody was not surprised by the tear trickling down the side of her cheek, and not alarmed either. It was the good kind of crying—he couldn't say how he knew this, but he did. He traced a finger along the wet trail, and she shifted until she was right beside

him, her head resting on his shoulder, and he kissed her hair—it smelled
of her honey shampoo—and wound his fingers through hers, and the
sound of her crying was almost no sound at all, and he did not move,
even when his neck began throbbing, and his knees needed straighten-
ing, because pain was what was required of him, this much he knew for
certain, and this pain was only the harbinger. If he couldn't take this
dull, persistent, faceless throb, he was not ready, not by half.

STEFANIE

R uth was on the porch, apron over her shapeless skirt, looking like Donna Reed if Donna Reed were brown and slightly worn-down, hair coming out her ponytail and frizzing around her face. "Nathan," she said, her voice well-modulated, neither too eager nor too dull, holding one hand out, a hand that Nathan didn't take, Nathan looking at everyone's feet. "Zameee," Nathan said, the noise he made in unfamiliar environments, not an alarm, but a reminder that all was not right. It had been a while since *zameee*, making Stefanie realize how well-choreographed their life was, ordered and orderly within the bounds of their own chaos.

This was Derek's point. Weeks and weeks of arguments had led them back here, Derek insisting that the decision ultimately was not theirs, but Nathan's, Derek arguing that they'd not given serious thought to the idea of Nathan moving out, was it not worth a moment's thought? Stefanie's argument: no. Baz was leaving in the fall, was that not enough?

"This isn't a punishment," Derek said. "No one is trying to hurt anyone."

The constancy of Derek's argument, his stubbornness in refusing to concede made Stefanie realize how rarely this was this case. For most everything, she got to say. Could they, she wondered, in her final, impotent volleys, stop for a minute and catch up with themselves? Take a breath or two? Instead of poking and poking at their sore spots? The girl didn't even bother Stefanie that much anymore; with Penn on the horizon, the girl was time limited. Was that not enough of a concession from Stefanie? Why all the sudden pushing against their own seams?

Inside, Marjorie and Davis sat in the living room, as if on a bad date, Davis on one side of the room in his chair, a book hooked up to what looked like a combination pulley-system fishing-rod that started at his seat back, made an arc over his head, and hung down in front of him. Marjorie was all the way at the other end of the couch, quick to rise when they came in.

"Nathan," she said. "Matthew." Outside of the office, Marjorie's hair looked flatter, her pants more wrinkled.

Davis was reading a book book; no pictures, a small font, Davis leaning close to the page, his nose inches away, a pencil eraser in his fist. Stefanie hadn't seen one of those fat pink erasers in years, not since Baz in Chicago, elementary school, when he furiously erased math problems he got wrong and wrong and wrong again until the paper thinned to ripping. Davis used it to turn the pages of his book; he wasn't so much holding the eraser as the eraser was wedged between two of his gnarled fingers.

Derek stood behind Nathan, all of them in the living room, Ruth too, Nathan with his eyes closed now, Davis looking up from his book, his expression either curious or just his face. Stefanie was not very fond of other people's children, never had been. Davis had a scraggly mustache, the wiry pricks of a beard recently shorn. How did it work in foster care? Would Davis be considered Nathan's brother? Fellow ward? Cellie?

"We can sit," Ruth said. "We can have a tour. We can go into the kitchen and have some tea."

"I don't drink tea," Stefanie said, sounding like Baz, a ridiculous tone of defiance. Baz didn't know they were here, absorbed in a life wholly separate from the life of his family.

"Water?" Ruth said without missing a beat, holding Stefanie's gaze plainly.

"Sure."

"I like tea," Derek said. "Do you want to join us?" he asked Davis, but Davis did not look up from his book this time.

"What will you drink?" Ruth asked Nathan. She said it as if he were a straight-backed man standing before her with eyes open, mouth thirsty. Stefanie refused to answer for him. Derek said: "Water, please."

In the kitchen, they sat on metal chairs around the table, the table-top well-scuffed. Ruth said, "This is overwhelming, I know," as she set Nathan down his water. Nathan was pressing Mat to the left side of his head, saying his *zameee*s and his *nunya*s with urgency. Mostly, Stefanie was good at letting the sound be sound, but granted new audience, she found herself awash in heartbreak; his words sounded unmistakably like terror.

"There's no rush," Ruth said as she turned back to the tea kettle. "You do what you need to do." Stefanie wasn't sure to whom this was directed.

Her phone buzzed from her purse. It was Cal. She knew it was Cal. He'd been texting all morning—Mama had a bedsore—expecting her to be able to do something about it. What did he imagine her life to be beyond his phone calls? Were she to ask him *name three things and not my family members*, he'd get her job, but what else?

Marjorie was the first to break the silence: "I think it would be helpful for you to hear about the daily routine."

"Davis," Ruth called into the living room. "Davis, do you want to join us?"

"Nawww-oooo!" This may have been the first word Stefanie had heard Davis speak. That Ruth was no better at calling her children to come, it could've made Stefanie take a liking to her under different circumstances.

"Be right back," Ruth said, her tone confiding, perhaps apologetic.

Stefanie hummed in Nathan's direction. He smelled like himself but also unpleasant, a stink that came from it being two days since a shower and also nerves. Did he know why they were here, exactly or inexactly? They had told him it was a "visit," a non-specified visit.

Davis's wheelchair wheezed loudly through the wide kitchen door. He pulled up to the table as Ruth was getting him a plastic mug with plastic straw from the fridge, parking himself next to Marjorie.

"We're talking about the daily schedule," Ruth announced.

All eyes were on Davis as he sucked water loudly up the straw, both hands around the mug. It was hard to tell his age; he was twenty-one or thirty-one, knuckles and mouth and shoulders askew.

"No schedule except meals," Davis said, an uncomfortable croak to his voice. "Morning and nighttime chores."

"What kind of chores?" Ruth asked.

"Compost. Sweeping. Dishes. Make the bed."

"S'right," said Ruth. "There are meals and chores. Aside from that, we offer whatever supports are needed and also the freedom an adult can expect."

"And Beverly," Davis said, the corner of his lip straining against his teeth. He was smiling.

Ruth chuckled. "Yes, and Beverly." She and Marjorie exchanged knowing glances.

"Who's Beverly?" Derek asked, never having met a set-up he didn't walk right into.

"Support worker," Davis said, setting down his mug and holding both hands—one arm crimped tightly at the elbow, the other slightly more free—at his chest, doing his best to clench his fingers into fists.

"I see," said Derek, merrily. "Beverly's an attractive gal," he said, holding his own hands to fondle his own mock breasts.

Davis laughed, the noise loud and wet, and Derek laughed, and Ruth chuckled, and Marjorie shook her head, though gamely. Nathan had quieted, though he was rocking himself in his seat. He was still using Mat to cover one eye, the other open. Goddamn brave was what he was for that one eye open.

The tour was slow, shuffling. This is the backyard. This is the bathroom. This is the shower. Showers twice a week, Ruth said, possibly in response to the stink. This is the bedroom. The soccer ball sat in the exact same place as the first visit. Derek followed Stefanie's gaze. "You play?" he said to Davis.

"Zameeee," Nathan muttered into Stefanie's side, and she touched his waist with her fingertips, telling him *I know, I know,* quietly. How she had loved the conspiracy of motherhood, from its very first day.

Derek was at the ball now, dancing his fancy footwork. He kicked the ball too hard against Davis's wheelchair, and it made a resounding noise, especially in this small a space. Nathan flinched and yipped. "Sorry, sorry, sorry," Derek said, but Davis was laughing. It came out like a yelp, but a joyful one. Derek liked that. "You play?" he repeated, and the joke was of course Davis did not play, Davis's body an impotent pretzel, yet somehow Davis loved the joke, and he moved the joystick on his wheelchair arm back then forward so that the momentum of the chair rolled the ball back to Derek, and Derek said, "Nate, heads up," and Nathan looked up at the sound of his father's voice, and the ball came at him. They would argue about what happened next, the way they used to argue before children, with energy to spare: either it was an accident, Nathan stepping closer to Stef, his mama, because he was scared witless, and his foot happened to be in motion, or it was an act of extraordinary will, Nathan turning his body and his foot, Nathan kicking the soccer ball.

LARK

God, it was weird. On her side of the table: Lark, her mom, Baz's brother's lawyer, Baz's mom; on the other side, the aide and the aide's lawyer, a lady typing on a steno-whatamajig two seats away. Her mom had encouraged her to wear a blouse, and she'd rummaged through the back of her closet. This one—polka dots, cap sleeves, years old—still fit.

The office was way out, on and off a highway, unfamiliar streets, and her mom had been anxious with the windshield and the rain and the address. "Look out for twenty eleven. Is that twenty eleven?" Someone honked while her mom was trying to parallel park, and Lark's mom yelled, "Damnit!" The car smelled of her mom's perfume, a perfume she never wore, which Lark had bought her for a long past Mother's Day because of a pushy woman at a mall makeup counter. She tried to remember the last time she was in a car with her mom. Lark and Mo had been spending a lot of time with Lark's mom—nearly anytime they were over at Lark's—the upside being that now existing beside her mom was more bearable, the downside being that she was gnawed with longing for Mo to be here too.

Lark had imagined a bigger conference room and a smaller number of people. The aide looked like how Lark remembered, Lark guessed, though her hair was longer, grown out and straggly at the ends, her face totally plain; she hadn't seemed like someone who wore makeup, but now it was striking how barefaced she was, the bags under her eyes looking painted on. She was wearing a sweatshirt from the state college forty-five minutes up the highway.

Baz's mom's attorney introduced himself, but Lark wasn't listening to his name—this room smelled of coffee and Lark's mom's perfume and the floors were a fake wood set in unevenly. Lark had tripped on her feet on the way to her chair. Baz's mom was very pretty and barely looked at them. The lawyer on the other side of the table went over how they were going to do this, and he talked for a very long time in the tone of a television clown—again, Lark struggled to keep hold, overwhelmed by the low ceiling and the people not looking at each other but looking at her, and the lady typing, and everyone waiting for her to say something. Her mom poked at her elbow.

"Okay?" Lark said.

The lawyer on the other side of the table smiled a big clown smile. "Great, we're going to jump right in and get started." He wanted to know Lark's full name, her date of birth, what grade she was in, if she ever wore glasses, and she was glad it was starting easy because the way the lady at the steno-thingamajig clacked and clacked lent a terrible sense to the whole thing and she better not trip up, so of course she tripped up: "Lark Denise Seven…blah, pff…Stevenson," and wondered if her *blah* and *pff*s were captured in the clack-clacking.

The lawyer asked if Lark was present at the Fenning residence on July 26, 2015. Lark shrugged. "I guess." She wasn't trying to sound like she had an attitude. She didn't know dates.

"The most helpful answers are in the affirmative or the negative."

Already Lark was getting the feeling of this swimming away from her. "The affirmative or the—?" she said, and it was her mom who said, "Yes or no," quietly, to which the attorney said, "Best to direct questions directly to me."

Direct directly, Lark thought. "Yes," Lark said, though she still didn't know the date.

The lawyer wanted to know how Lark came to be at the Fenning residence, where she was in the house at what times, when she came upstairs, what Nathan was acting like in the kitchen, what his client, Ms. Alderman, was acting like. He kept referring to her as, "My client, Ms. Alderman."

"Can you describe to me, in your own words," the lawyer said, "what you witnessed between my client, Ms. Alderman, and the defendant?"

"I mean," Lark said, "he was making noises and it seemed like something was wrong. And then he ran at her and pushed her into the window." Lark was glad to be two seats away from Mrs. Fenning. "But only for like a couple seconds."

"How were you able to assess the amount of time?" the lawyer asked.

"What?" Lark asked.

"By what means did you measure the passing of time?"

Lark did not understand the question. Her face was hot. Her face had been hot since they began in this room.

"No one did anything wrong," she said.

"Please answer the question."

"It wasn't anyone's fault," she said. "We were up there getting a snack. Something to eat."

Lark never mentioned the beer. She wasn't going to mention it to any of these grown-ups. It was strange having loyalty to more than one person, funny how Shocky was her friend now.

"Ms. Stevenson, please answer the question."

The lawyer beside her placed a hand gently on the back of Lark's wrist.

"Relax," the lawyer whispered. "You're doing great."

"What is," she whispered, "the, um…"

"Can counsel repeat the question?" the lawyer beside her asked. Both lawyers spoke at a volume that suggested an auditorium.

"By what mechanism did you, Ms. Stevenson, have to measure the amount of time the attack lasted?"

Here was what Lark regretted: her blouse. It was too old. She'd never wear cap sleeves anymore. The blouse made Lark feel like she was living in a bygone era. The blouse made her feel little, a feeling she did not want.

"Me," Lark said. "I was the mechanism." Across the table, the lawyer had his mouth around the start of his next question already. "One," Lark said, to show him. "Two, three, four…" and the lady clacked at her steno-thingamajig perfectly in time to Lark's words, a little like a song.

WOODY

He sat in the red chair. He'd taken to sitting in the red chair on Mondays, third Monday in a row now, Susan's hand in his, kissing her fingers, her fingertips, all the way up her arm, so that she would laugh when he kissed the inside of her elbow or the tender skin past her armpit.

God, he loved that laugh.

Livvy was never home before seven. Many days, she went right from Baz's to the movie theater. It took Woody fifteen minutes to get to the apartment from the high school. If he spent thirty minutes inside, and drove the fifteen minutes home, he was back by six, which was a lot like being home at five-thirty. He simply texted to Al: **Emergency meeting with Doug**; **PTO ladies are on a tear**; or simply **got stuck**. So bedrock their foundation, he could say anything, and Al would be good.

They, the they of he and Susan, had a plan. He was to tell Al first, then Susan would tell Livvy, then Susan and Woody would talk to Livvy together, then Woody would ask Doug to reassign Livvy to Deirdre or Sandy so as to keep the professional channels clear. He felt a real sense of loss at the idea of giving Livvy up to one of the other counselors.

"I'm doing it Sunday," he'd been saying for weeks now, and then coming over on each Monday. That Monday had become apartment instead of the backseat, a signal of Susan's ever-hopefulness. She did not want to begin their life in the backseat. He took Claritin for the cat.

"I will, I will, I will," he told her every Monday, today no exception.

Susan's stance was a militant refusal to push. Do it or don't do it; telling Alison had to come entirely of his own volition. She refused to carry the weight of history on her back. By each Monday, of course, she knew as soon as he opened the door, and he watched the way her eyes fluttered with disappointment or resignation or something he could not discern but equally could not bear.

He knew lots of people with second wives. Dan Sheridan had a second wife. Stuart Hammerle. Second wives were nearly as normal as first wives. Doug Epstein would have a second wife if only a second wife would have him. Woody's Monday failures had nothing to do with his desire for Susan. The present, though, Alison beside him on the couch, *CSI* on the television, was shockingly muscular. Their den was warm, the couch comfortable in all the same spots it was always comfortable, their afghan their afghan. There was a momentum required that had never been required of him in any situation before, personal or professional. He could draw no analogy. He could think of no precedent. He was creating the precedent, and, as such, he'd underestimated the amount of force he'd need to exert. To put another way: he was a coward.

"I will," he repeated, and he meant it, god he meant it, and one could have mistaken Susan's lack of response for passivity or indifference. But Woody saw the glinting resolve in her refusal to offer a simple: *I know you will* or an even simpler: *please.* She refused to allow her eyes to water, though it had occurred to Woody, and more than once, that a Monday would roll around and the knock on her door would go unanswered. One of these Mondays would be a Monday too far.

She let him kiss her face. She even leaned into him and slipped her tongue between his lips. They kissed for a long time, and when he pulled back, her lips were red from his. He loved that redness around her mouth; it looked feral. It reminded him of being a teenager.

"One week, I promise, swear to fucking god, one week," he said, hoping the blasphemy would get her to say something, anything, but she smiled a closed-lipped smile, her resoluteness as maddening as it was admirable. She'd meet up with him on the other side and gamely, but in this, he was alone.

The girls regaled him with stories of the Build-a-Bear shop in the mall. Francie sat eating dinner with a rainbow swirl bear in her lap. Its name was *Nancy*.

"That's a funny name for a bear," Woody said. He thought of the show where the American couple was Soviet spies. His life at home felt like that, if he were the only Soviet spy.

"It was Nancy or Bernice," Alison said.

"Nancy's better than Bernice," Woody said, trying to find this moment poignant, all the moments poignant, but mostly he felt clammy. His adrenaline kept going and going. Francie hugged Nancy hard, and Al told her to eat her corn. "Eat your corn," Woody echoed.

"We were at the mall after Dr. Vincent. I wanted to get my thy-

roid checked, and my iron. Make sure I don't have cancer." Alison had
continued to be exhausted, asleep on the couch each night, earlier and
earlier. For one very, very infinitesimally brief moment, Woody thought
of how much would be solved by a fatal cancer diagnosis.

"She has Strawberry Shortcake," Francie announced. Dr. Vincent
had a huge bucket of toys in her waiting room.

"And?" Woody said to Alison. This was Alison's way of telling stories, creating maximum suspense.

"No cancer!" she said.

He held up his water glass as a toast. Francie asked what cancer was.
Al clinked her water glass with Woody's, and either he or she misjudged
because they hit their glasses hard enough to spill water on the table,
an ice cube skittering along the surface, Francie screaming playfully (or
seriously), Al laughing, Woody watching the wet path across the wood,
the ice cube careening off the end of the table and landing on the floor
with barely a sound.

"Turn that off," Alison said of the television, returned from putting
Francie to bed. It was the *PBS News Hour*, Tivo'd. *PBS New Hour* made
Woody feel virtuous even if the news was salacious: a campaign manager accused of physically assaulting a female journalist at a campaign
rally. Alison never said turn off the television. "Please," she added now,
sweetly, a big smile, one Woody would think of as coquettish after the
fact. There was much he would think after the fact, tricking himself into
believing that he knew what was coming when she sat down hard beside
him and repeated, "No cancer." She smiled and grabbed both of his
hands in hers. Her smile broke into something that would have struck
him as dazzling at any other point in their marriage. In his memory, the
two-word announcement did not catch him by surprise, but came out
of her mouth at the very second that he'd figured it out for himself, so
that he hugged her back, repeated the word *miracle* that she'd just said,
clasped her tightly as she tried to clasp him, rather than rearing back like
a dumb ape, capable of only a single word, then another, over and over
again: "What?" "How?" "What?" "How?" "What?"

STEFANIE

Derek was making shredded-pork tacos with mango salsa. "Home. Made. Salsa," he said as he greeted her at the door, helping her out of her wet raincoat, telling her she looked nice. End of her day, face shiny, hair a week past needing relaxing, she didn't look nice, and she knew it. He knew it too. He kissed her on the side of her head.

"Whatchu' want?" Stefanie said in a put-on voice, though she meant it. He was in one of his aprons, an oven mitt pinched under one armpit.

"I don't want nothin', woman," he said, he with his put-on voice too. "I want my gorgeous wife home, and here she is! All a man could want right in front of him."

She *pshaw*ed him.

"No problemo," Nathan called out from the couch, cycling through *SpongeBob* in recent weeks. "Ah, shrimp."

"Hi, sweetheart," Stefanie called.

The kids were in the living room—Livvy and Baz in the middle of the couch, on their phones, Nathan at the end of the couch nearest Baz, playing with one of the cloth loops from the red plastic loom. They'd bought him that loom years ago, the kind Stefanie had wanted senselessly as a girl, an allure to pulling the loops over under over each other into a raggedy potholder. Nathan had no mind for the loom itself, though he could spend hours twisting his own cat's cradle with the loops.

"Ma," Baz said.

Livvy looked up from her phone, offered no greeting, a small nod instead, small enough for Stefanie to wonder if there was a nod at all. The girl had never gotten comfortable talking to Stefanie, which Stefanie didn't mind. She preferred this to the girl becoming too easy with her.

"How was your day?" Derek said. Dinner smelled good from the kitchen, the fatty smell of the meat, the hot pepper flakes. Derek was always heavy on the hot pepper flakes.

"My day was my day," said Stefanie. All these years, and still he tipped her so easily into his opposite, he full of gusto, so she went flat. And she tipped him right back, Derek meeting her flatness with ever more enthusiasm, taking one of her hands and holding it up high, leading her, dancing, into the kitchen, telling her to taste the fresh-made salsa, feeding it to her on a chip, the chip crumbling in her mouth, a mess of tomatoes and mango and lime down her chin, getting her to laugh, finally (three minutes through the door, maybe less) a laugh.

"So," he said at the counter. "I called Ruth."

Ruth.

Got her to laugh so he could say this.

"I called her a couple of days ago," Derek said. The pork made a noise in its pan, a low sizzle, and he said, "We went back this afternoon. Just me and Nathan, low pressure." He moved a spatula through the shredded pork, red pepper flakes, glassy onions. Derek always overcooked the onions.

"You always overcook the onions."

"Are you listening to me?" he said, but nicely, not the way she would have said it to him.

"Am I listening?" she said, her lips tingling the way they did.

The noise of footsteps came up behind her. "Hungry," Baz said. "What we having?" He opened a cabinet before either of them could answer, grabbing down a box of Triscuits.

"About to eat dinner," Derek said in Derek's normal voice, no real chide.

Baz slit open the top of the box, fighting with the bag inside till he tore it with his front teeth. "Hungry," he said, grabbing out a handful, leaning his face into his palm, looking simultaneously so much younger than he was and also newly filled out. Still a skinny kid, but he gave off a confidence now. He took up more space than he used to. It was nearly impossible to imagine this house without Baz in it.

Derek was looking at Stefanie, trying to get her to look at him, she could feel it. But she busied herself with the placemats and the plates. The girl soon followed, her nose in her phone, saying to Baz about the GED, she couldn't take it online but she could do the prep online, then go to a testing center. She put her hand in the Triscuit box without even asking.

"Only costs $120," the girl said.

"GED?" Stefanie said, and the way the girl looked at her—a little startled—filled something in Stefanie. Look, Stefanie could surprise too. She still had it in her. "Why are you talking about the GED?"

The girl didn't say anything. What did she look, scared?

"GED is for dropouts," Stefanie said into the quiet, glad her voice was strong. "I'm sure your mother's not wanting you to be a dropout."

"Ma," Baz said, but that was all he said.

"Looking at options," the girl said. Then to Baz: "You told me you told them."

"Told us?" Stefanie said. When she looked to Derek, he had that expression, cat with a bird in his mouth. Face full of caught. "Hu—" she said, more breath than word.

Baz was saying to Derek, something about something. Stefanie was listening and not, trying to catch up with herself, with her family. There was noise in her ears now, the sound of her insides beating loud.

She'd always known her family would have a season like this, assailed and imperiled, hammered from all directions. She'd known it would come, maybe since the day the moving truck had disgorged their boxes, a shattered tabletop rolled to the curbside, garbage now. No, maybe she'd known before then, long before, when the boys had only been dreams. Before they were dreams. She had known the world would catch up to her, to them, but she hadn't seen it like this in her mind, not with Derek at the stove, half a room away. He was the surprise of it, Stefanie Fenning not one for being caught by surprise.

"I was going—" Derek said, and with feeling.

Baz curled his shoulders up to his chin, rolled an ear to a shoulder, made a sound that was a man sound. A man-sized sigh. "Sorry," he said, but not to his mother. He said it to the girl, wiping a thumb across her bottom lip where she had cracker crumbs, the gesture so intimate, it felt almost obscene, his thumb across her lip all the ways Stefanie's family was no longer hers.

"Options," Baz said to the kitchen in general and no one in particular.

"I can do the GED in Philly if I didn't want to go to regular high school," the girl said, loudly. It was an announcement. Maybe the loudest she'd been all these months.

It had taken a minute, but Stefanie was caught up, save for the noise in her ears. She could handle the noise in her ears.

"Smart girl like you," she said, "without even a high school diploma?"

The girl had a look to her face, sucking on the insides of her cheeks, trying to make herself skinnier maybe, smaller, Stefanie hoped. The kitchen was very, very still. Four people in here, and all they could hear was the sizzle on the stove and Nathan, a room away, talking Mr. Krabs this, Mr. Krabs that.

"You know what we call that?" Stefanie said. "We call that a shame. Bright, attractive young woman, the whole world ahead of her, and end up, what? A waitress working for tips?" Baz snugged an arm around the girl's waist, tried to pull her close, but the girl had some stiffness to her spine now, some resistance. Tough little cookie, Stefanie saw maybe for the first time. Stefanie had been the only one who'd seen this coming, and even she had underestimated the girl. "A barmaid? Is there even such a thing as a barmaid anymore?" She was asking Derek, but he offered no answer. "That may be fine in your family," Stefanie said. "But we aim higher in this household. We expect the best and we don't get to take shortcuts. We don't have the privilege of half-assing."

Now Derek was trying to say something, but he was too late. She was going to say what she going to say. There was only so long a person, a mother, could be expected to not say. "I'll tell you something, Olivia. Livvy. I'll be straight with you since we've known each other a while now. We're familiar with each other. You can do better for yourself, even without the home training. You're a smart girl. Have some self-respect."

And then it was everyone at once, Baz, Derek, even the girl, Stefanie letting them have at it. She did not interrupt. She did not argue. She was busy setting the table. Five placemats, five plates, five water glasses, though it was for show. She knew the girl would not be staying.

Woody

They'd barely said anything. He'd told her, and she had gasped the way Woody had only seen people gasp in movies; both hands over her mouth. "I don't understand," she'd said, and then they'd sat on the strange gray cube of a couch, Susan crying into his arm, crying and crying, with a quiet vehemence that surprised Woody. Some part of him had thought she'd never really meant it, that it had been fantasy for her. He cried too, ashamed of his own tears. "You were," she finally said into his wet sleeve, "never going to leave. Never."

"Not true," Woody said, sick in his throat and his gut, desperate to lay out a plan for them to keep going. When he'd sent her a two-line email that morning: **Can I come by your place after work? I have to tell you something,** she'd misapprehended, sending back a **Yes** with three exclamation points and a heart emoji.

He should have clarified in those hours between the email and the knock on her door (six and a quarter). He should've written back. But he couldn't. He lived in those six and a quarter hours with hope in his heart about the hope in her heart.

His hands were tangled into hers now, grasping so hard it hurt the bones in his fingers, surely in hers too. "Not true," he was saying into her hair, begging really, when the noise came from the front door, a jiggling at the handle, and then the sigh of the wood against the carpeting, and they jumped, they both jumped, untangling and how, Susan wiping frantically at her face, Woody not even knowing what his body was, heart pounding in his mouth and eye sockets.

There was one blithe second of Livvy, maybe half a second, when she came through the door and was not even looking in their direction, and that second would live suspended in Woody's brain for a very, very long time. It was Susan who said, "Oh my god," and this moment too, would live on in Woody, the goddamn unfortunate choice of "oh my god," on top of so many other unfortunate choices. This one felt, though, the worst to him for how little room it gave them to navigate, to pull themselves up and out of where they were, which was scrambling apart, trying to look upright and each of a piece.

Livvy stared between Susan and Woody, her face still flat and unknowing, growing only curious.

"What? What happened?" she said, her trust in these two adults momentarily inviolable. Woody could have said something to do with test scores college entrance diversity plan, anything about the business of high school, but Susan with her "oh my god," and her wet face threw him: she made it so he had to reach for something appropriately grave. There was a final moment when the three of them existed together within the realm of reasonable explanation, if only—If only! If only!—Woody could have come up with one.

"What?" Livvy repeated, her eyes back and forth between them, and Woody could see the moment her mouth curled around a silent O, her eyes narrowing into slits. She was looking at the carpet and his feet. There, he stood in his socks, his plain black work socks, unremarkable in every way except for the fact of them here, bare of shoe at Susan Albrecht's odd cube of a couch.

"Sweetheart," Susan said, and there were a million ways to say *sweetheart,* but Susan said it as confession. "Sweetheart," she repeated, and it was even worse the second time, the two syllables utterly and unmistakably abased. Woody was kneecapped by the dual sweethearts. He was incredulous. Could she not have given him one more moment? Could she not have spared him the extra second or two to patch something together?

Well after Livvy said, "What the—? Holy fuck," and spun back out the door, running loudly down the stairs, her mother giving chase, well after he'd waited and waited and waited in the empty apartment, the door gaping, well after he'd gone home a raw and ugly ghost, well after he'd gotten the call from Susan frantic in the middle of the night, Livvy not home, not at Lark's, not at Baz's, Susan not caring about waking Woody, waking Alison, well after he'd gotten the next call in the morning, yet more frantic, Livvy still not home, not anywhere, there lay a question beneath Woody's bewilderment and his pulsing, sleepless nothingness, the same question he asked students every day, students who found themselves in a real pickle, having skipped and flunked and smoked and sassed themselves to his office, desperate for salvation: *How can I help you if you won't help yourself?*

LARK

Her phone rang. She and Mo were at Lark's house, in Lark's room, in Lark's bed, both their shirts off, pants unbuttoned, door closed. Her mother, of course, allowed them in Lark's room with the door closed. All those years with Livvy. Getting away with it, part of the thrill. It would be a couple more years before such secrets started costing her something.

Livvy was the only possible person calling. Lark tensed for the phone, but Mo drew her fingertips up Lark's side, and it wasn't that Mo stopped her—they were both lying on their sides, Lark free to roll away and fish the phone from her backpack—it was that Mo made her not want to. It was warm under the blankets, and Lark's hand ran over the soft skin of Mo's belly and her breasts, happy each time she made Mo's skin pimple with goosebumps, each time her nipples grew stiff, disbelieving the power of her own fingertips, disbelieving the fact of their days spent this way—Mr. Deveraux (she couldn't bring herself to Carl and he didn't insist) allowed the door shut too—so many days, day after day, an endless bounty. Lark wasn't used to luck like this. She wasn't used to any luck at all.

911 Transcript (Excerpt)

March 17, 2016, 7:08 a.m.

...*Dispatcher:* Is she in need of medication or experiencing any serious medical problems?

Caller: No. No. Nothing like that. She didn't come home. She was very upset. She's never not come home.

Dispatcher: Yes, ma'am. Do you suspect parental abduction?

Caller: No. I am her only living parent.

Dispatcher: Does she have mental impairment?

Caller: No. No. No.

Dispatcher: A danger to herself or others?

Caller: No, she was upset. Very upset. I want the police to come before I have to go to work. Can you send them?

Dispatcher: Yes, ma'am, I understand. These are standard questions to assess if your daughter is at risk.

Caller: That's why I'm calling. I want to file a report, a missing... whatever you do. She's never not come home.

Dispatcher: Ma'am, these are standard questions. I'm going to ask you a few more—

Caller: Will the police help me?

Dispatcher: Yes, ma'am. One of our patrol units will be on their way, as soon as I finish up...

CITY OF HORACE POLICE REPORT (EXCERPT)

MARCH 17, 2016, 9:42 A.M.

...initial report at approximately 7:30 a.m. Reporting party is minor's mother. Minor has no prior missing incidents. Current behavior reported to be unusual. Minor reported to be in emotional distress when last seen at residence at approximately 6:30 p.m. on March 16, 2016...obtained most recent school picture...current description: navy raincoat, jeans, light gray gym shoes, green school backpack, no notable scars or tattoos...positively identified by cashier, Lane Diamond, M, 43, at Dar-I-Mart (33rd Ave and Highlands, .5 miles from residence) as having been in the store "late," approximately between 10 p.m. and midnight, no reports of distress "bought a Coke, maybe cigarettes." Said she looked older than eighteen, did not ask for proof of age in the sale of nicotine...possible identification by two men, Jaime, 32, and "Fink," 38, in Arbor Park (.8 miles from residence) who "bummed a smoke" from individual matching description. Men are occupants of homeless encampment in west end of Arbor Park and came out "when rain finally stopped" at approximately 2 a.m. Did not report signs of visible distress, commented only on individual's dress: "Gets real cold at night still and she didn't have gloves or a hat. Jaime offered his gloves but she told him she was okay"... university police responded to inquiry with possible sighting of individual matching description by patrol unit 1044, Officer Greg Van Ness, on east end of campus (1.4 miles from residence) in "middle of the night" though unable to get further verification on time or positive identification...no indication that missing is involuntary... no indication of risk of injury or death...contacted all required local and national Missing Persons networks within two hours of initial report.

Body of Minor Found in Willahut River

By Don Delouth, *TheDailyRegister*. March 18, 2016

Police reported the discovery of the body of a minor female beneath the Mid-Central Bicycle and Pedestrian Bridge. The identity of the minor is known, but not yet made public out of consideration for the family.

"We were called to the scene by a morning bicyclist," Police Chief Kairns reported. "We found the body of a female minor in the river, nonresponsive, with injuries consistent with a fall from the bridge overhead."

The police declined to offer details of the injuries. The police were unable to speculate on the nature of the fall. "We are going to wait to hear on the findings of the medical examiner before we come to any conclusions." Toxicology tests are pending.

Police are diverting regular commuters from the Mid-Central…

Emergency Faculty Meeting Notes (excerpt)

3/19/2016, 6:45 a.m.

...*Principal Vonn:* There's an onsite grief counselor available all day today and tomorrow. Funnel students to the counseling offices, as needed. Let's not count absences.

Vice Principal Epstein: Your call on lesson plans. Stick to them as is useful. Be flexible when appropriate. Keep your eye out for higher need students, close friend groups of Ms. Albrecht's. Woody can speak best to this. Woody?

Deirdre Benson: Woody's not here.

Vice Principal Epstein: Not here, as in the meeting or as in the building?

Deirdre Benson: Building, I think. He wasn't in his office.

Vice Principal Epstein: Can we? Barbara, can you find out if we've heard from Woody, if he's on a planned—if it's a sick—?

Navid Langston: Are we going to talk about the elephant in the room? Is anyone else concerned that this is the same student who was harassed last spring?

Chuck Kloster: What, you think Miles Cobain pushed her off the bridge?

Navid Langston: Shut up, Chuck.

Danita Leininger: Seriously, Chuck. Shut up. Of course, I share your concern, Navid.

Chuck Kloster: Shocker.

Principal Vonn: I'm going to interrupt here so I can get through my agenda. There will be an announcement in homeroom, but we can be sure students already know. We'll ask for a moment of silence, and I encourage you...

STEFANIE

For days, he let her hold him, terrible noises into his pillow, Derek and Stefanie taking turns lying behind him for as long as Baz could bear, pressing a cheek to his shoulder blade, a forehead to the back of his neck, murmuring nothings, murmuring murmurs, the slope of his shoulder, the strong of his arms. "Baby, baby, baby," Stefanie tried to get herself around him, her legs shorter than his, trying to hook an arm beneath his neck, another across his chest, gain some purchase to rock him and rock him, and he let her, his muscles rigid and tensing, rigid and tensing, with occasional blessed release. "Shhh, shhh, shhh," she murmured. A musk came off him, stronger and stronger, spicy with sweat and what and piss. He let her stumble him to the bathroom, his face lined with pillowcase creases, his eyes nowhere, desperate for no privacy as he stood tall at the toilet, whispering, "Don't go," and he made a noise over his stream of pee, no pillow to muffle it now, Stefanie gripping his shoulder without looking, wanting for him the decency he did not want for himself.

She met Derek in the hallway outside Baz's door, day two—day three?—three—Baz finally asleep, Derek's face exhausted and ill-fit like all their faces. Nathan howled from upstairs. He'd been howling for days.

"Did I—?" she asked, the question that had expanded to take up her whole mind, the question she was as desperate as she was unable to ask. "Is this my—?"

Derek touched a hand to her cheek, same soft hand of Derek at twenty, when they were kids, when the world was not theirs but maybe, maybe, maybe someday. His eyes shone, and his face unspooled, wet eyes going wide, mouth bitten from the inside. What he looked was scared, and she wanted only for him to say. Please say.

"Baby," he said with kindness, with love.

She needed him to tell her no. She felt as if she might have to fish the word from his throat. She felt she might have to reach her hands down and get it for herself. He pulled her into his chest, his heart beating like all their hearts were beating, raggedy and desperate.

WOODY

He drove.

Alison wanted to know what was wrong, Alison with her lip shimmer and facial powder in the fine hairs of her cheeks, making herself up even on days that it was only she and Francie, Alison the eternal optimist.

"I'm fine," he told her, "sweetheart." He kissed her on the fine hairs of her cheek. He thought, *I am a man kissing my wife on the cheek.*

Alison knew a student was dead. She knew a frantic parent had called in the night. Twice in the night. How had she gotten their number? Alison was curiously concerned but not concernedly curious.

"You have allergies," she said of his eyes. "You should get some Claritin." Alison recalled a story of the camping trip when he woke with his eyes glued shut, a whole life together behind them and ahead.

I am a man placing a hand on my wife's belly.

Susan would not answer his calls. He had shown up twice, three times, and she would not open the door. Didn't matter if he banged on barely covered *Bitch*, didn't matter if he yelled, begged, cried.

He left for work in the mornings—*I am a man saying goodbye to my wife, I am a man squeezing my daughter*—but never arrived. He drove for hours, aimless, out of town and in, eating gas station food, ignoring calls from Doug Epstein, from Jennifer, from Deirdre, no appetite for anything but gas station food—Cheetos until his lips were frosted orange, burnt coffee, pretzel nubs stuffed with cheese, listening not listening to the slog from the radio, Hillary taking Florida, Trump trouncing Rubio, hand-size dick-jokes.

One time, he ended up at the coast, surprising himself with dunes and then ocean, wind chopping his ears, sand in his socks, giant piles of driftwood everywhere. *Warning Sneaker Waves* a sign told him, and it made him laugh, though the wind snatched the sound out his mouth, the sea rendered as a thick and cresting C on the sign, a blocky person set at a helpless angle in the mouth of it. It reminded him of *Sesame Street* or something, the sea a C, and Francie would like this, wouldn't she? He looked close at the figure who had not heeded, a circle for a head, one handless arm reaching up to the crest of the C, as if to protect himself from the coming wave, thinking himself a match for the ocean, or maybe just desperate, body splayed and stupid, all caught up, a handless arm his only anything and no idea how to ask forgiveness.

MINOR IDENTIFIED IN WILLAHUT RIVER DEATH

By Don Delouth, *TheDailyRegister.* March 21, 2016

…that of Olivia Albrecht, a junior from West High School. Police report that the preliminary toxicology reports came back negative for any illicit substances. "Unfortunately," Detective Martin Stanbury said, "it was one of those cold nights and best we could gather, there was frost on the bridge at the time of death. Cases like this, it's impossible to tell an accident from a suicide, unless there's a note." Detective Stanbury confirmed that there was no note.

Multiple sources from West High School, all who asked not to be identified, confirmed that Albrecht was one of the injured students in the stampede that occurred in the high school last May. Sources also reported that Albrecht played a key role in the racial harassment incidents at West this past spring. "It was her boyfriend," said one of the sources. "She was on the front lines of that hate. That's a lot for anyone, but particularly a young girl. It's a real shame."

West High School refused to respond to multiple requests for comment. Marcus Jay-Johnson, superintendent of schools, offered the following statement: "It is always a tragedy when a life is cut short. Our thoughts and prayers are with the Albrecht family and with all of the teachers and students at West High School who are directly affected by the senseless loss of Ms. Albrecht."

Funeral services will be held at Temple Bet Emet on Sunday…

MONIQUE

She went to the funeral to see Lark.

She and Shelley had tag-teamed for three days straight, holding Lark's hand, telling her to "breathe, okay breathe" when she cried so hard, she choked herself, getting her tissues, making her sandwiches, and sitting with her while she protested she couldn't eat and then took tiny bird bites, Monique even getting to sleep over, Shelley seeming relieved when she said, "Stay, of course. Stay."

It was horrible—Lark cried herself raw, two nosebleeds, one long session of vomiting her empty stomach into the toilet. And it was beautiful too. Monique had hardly known Olivia (and hadn't liked what she did know) so she wasn't grieving, and instead she could press her love into Lark all the time and without suspicion, because they were in a particular circumstance where it was okay to hug and hug, it was okay to brush Lark's hair from her eyes, it was okay to hold hands, to call her *PiePie*, such a silly private nickname that she could say all the time now, in front of Shelley at the kitchen table: "PiePie, eat your soup. It's noodle soup. Take a sip, honey," and all Shelley would do was nod and nod. "You are such a good friend," Shelley had said when Monique took Lark's hand and led her up the stairs to her bedroom.

It was on the third night, Lark crying, Monique kissing her—not horny kissing, gently on the forehead, on each temple, as chaste as kisses could be while still being kisses—that Lark said, "You need to go," and her voice was new, a deeper register, as if all the crying had eroded her usual chirrup.

"I have to what?" Monique had said, still gently, still kissing, Lark's bed having become peninsular in the last three days, connected to the rest of life but tenuously, a tiny nation-state, population: two.

"Go," Lark said.

Monique had not understood, and the not understanding had led to surprise, and the surprise had led to a fight, as unexpected as it was vicious, during which many regretful things were said, including that it was their fault that Livvy was dead Lark never should have done this and what exactly had Lark done have a life of her own without kneeling first at the feet of Olivia Albrecht and don't you talk about her don't you say her name you don't know anything about her and from what I saw she could give a shit about anything that didn't have a dick attached to it and you shut your mouth and what if I don't and it was always her and no it wasn't Lark, and yes it was, Mo, I made a mistake a terrible mistake I'm sorry but you need to go, please go.

Monique sat by herself in the back of the synagogue, beanie on her head feeling funny, though the lady had handed it to her with the prayer book. Everyone had one on, even Shocky near the front with his mom, next to Baz and Baz's dad. Shocky kept turning around, and she knew he was looking for her. When he finally saw her, he waved her up to them, but she didn't want to be near the front, and also Baz scared her a little now, how fallen apart, not even trying to put himself back together, crying with sounds, snot bubbling. Monique's dad had asked if she wanted him to come, mistaking her recent mourning as for the dead. "I didn't even know you knew her."

Shelley and Lark were in the second row, Lark's hair doing that thing at the back of her head where it spouted up out the top of the beanie. That thing with her hair gave Monique a hunger in her throat like crying. She'd texted four days of *Sorry*s, sad faces, hearts. She'd tried waiting for her outside classes, but Lark wasn't in school. She'd made Shocky drive past her house, slowly, and Shocky made her laugh by being a dick on purpose, sometimes in a bad accent—"Crazy loco white pendejo"—sometimes regular—"She's too skinny, no ass even," and "She kisses like a dead dog."

The rabbi spoke, and then Navid Langston looking like he'd gotten a special haircut for the occasion, and then Livvy's sister, Lea, who could barely talk but at least mentioned the time Livvy Sharpied their rental apartment bathtub, which made everyone laugh out of relief, and who singled out Lark as "her oldest and dearest friend," which filled Monique with pride and pain and pride, and then Olivia's uncle, who talked about Olivia's dead dad and summers in Alaska, and Olivia catching a wide-mouthed bass when she was nine, and Monique at least appreciated that Lark was right, she hadn't really known Livvy Albrecht at all. There was sitting and standing and prayers in Hebrew and the rabbi was very nice about trying to explain it all, but Monique was barely listening. Lark's beanie had fallen off the back of her head.

Afterward, people who were going to the cemetery went out to their cars, and people who weren't milled around, and Monique half-jogged to Lark and said, "Hey," grabbing her arm a little, and her face was as pink as Monique had expected, eyes too, which fucking gutted her, and Shelley had hold of Lark's other arm, Shelley looking funny outside of her nightgown and house coat, a brown dress like she showed up to a funeral dressed as a baked potato. "I didn't even know her," Monique said because it was what she could think of. "I'm sorry I didn't know her."

"No," Shelley said. "Not now, Monique. No," and it had been a long time since a mother had scolded Monique, Lark not even looking up, letting herself be led away.

Monique heard Shocky calling for her, but she didn't turn around, didn't want to talk, didn't want him to see her face, walked as fast as she could out the front doors and to her car, blocks away. She was at the end of the first street, about to cross, when a noise startled her—the sound of someone who'd been holding their breath for as long as they possibly could and then let it out all at once—and she made a noise too, feeling bare and easily startled, and she turned to the car parked at the curb, the man inside gripping the wheel hard, his glasses cockeyed, his hair a mess. It was one of the Alaska relatives, she half-thought as she stepped into the crosswalk. There'd been a giant clump of Alaska relatives, but the man looked back at her through the windshield, surprised at her surprise, looking the way people look when they know you. The sun was coming down through the glass, so he was a face for only a second before he was glare, and she was already to the other side of the crosswalk when she realized *Mr. Hanover?*

Letter to the Editor, *The Horace Weekly*

March 29, 2016

Dear Horace *Weakly*,

I usually use your paper to line my bird's cage. He loves to take a dump on your kneejerk liberal take on absolutely everything (Coal bad! GMOs bad! Business bad! Thinking badddddd!) But I know how many people read your letter section for fun (guilty as charged), so I want to use you to get a point across that us southeast neighbors have been trying to get across for years but the city council (6 out of 9 = EXTREME LIBERAL DEMOCRATS) won't listen to.

That pedestrian bridge is a menace.

Almost every year, some dummies (usually drunk college kids from TYWTTU [Tell You What To Think University]) climb up that half-wall, since it's a HALF wall, and, you know what happens once they're up on that half-wall, which happens to be topped with slippery stones? They slip! Worst bridge design known to man. Or sorry, known to women or man. Or sorry, wimmyn and brutes.

My point is thus—some kid broke a leg off that bridge a couple years ago. Another ended up in the hospital when he fell in, and his drunk friends ran away. I think he had hypothermia. Look it up!

The city council is so proud to have a pedestrian bridge, but they refuse to face reality. That girl didn't have to die. This is on YOU, city council.

With genuine concern,

Bullying a Factor in Willahut River Death?

By Don Delouth, *TheDailyRegister.com.* April 22, 2016

…a public records request revealed multiple emails between West High school counselor, Woody Hanover, and Facebook, Inc. in regard to a Facebook group targeting Olivia Albrecht, the student found dead in the Willahut River.

There is no record of West High School taking action against the authors of the posts or members of the known group. The page, according to Facebook was archived earlier this year, meaning members no longer have access to it.

Woody Hanover did not return multiple calls for comment. Marcus Jay-Johnson, superintendent of schools, added, "We have a robust system in place of reporting, accountability, and follow-up if any district employee becomes aware of harassment of a student inside or outside of school. The district will be reviewing the details of this case to be sure all system guidelines were followed. Beyond that, we have no further comment, as it is a personnel…"

To: Woody Hanover <woody_h@wesths>
From: Don Delouth <don.d@dailyreg>
Date: May 6, 2016, 2:16 p.m.
Subject: Your comment

Dear Mr. Hanover,
Don Delouth from *The Daily Register* here. I'm assuming you've received my phone calls. I wanted to give you a heads up about the story we're running tomorrow because I still would love to get you on the record. We have the emails from June and July of last year between you and Olivia Albrecht's mother. It's clear you were close to the family, the mother in particular. Be in touch to give me your side of the story. This situation is a real tragedy from what I can see, and your perspective is valuable. We go to print at **8 p.m. tonight** for tomorrow's morning edition, and the story will be live online by **midnight tonight**. Be in touch with me via phone, email, or text before eight p.m. so we can include your voice here too.
Best,
Don J. Delouth
Staff Reporter, *The Daily Register*

No new messages. One saved message:

Oh my god, Lark, call me. Jesus Christ. I need to talk to someone. Are you there? Call me. It's so fucking weird to leave a voicemail. I hate voicemail. But I want to talk talk. Are you home? I can come over. I feel like we haven't talked in forever and I know that's partially my fault too and I'm sorry. I've been walking around for hours and it's fucking cold out. I need to talk to someone. I'll tell you what's up when I see you. I'm not trying to be like mysterious, but I don't want to leave it on a voicemail, and I know you have your new friends now but. Fuck. Call me, okay? I miss you. I miss you, Lark. Like so much and I'm afraid you don't miss me back. I love Baz, but he's not you, you know? Call me? I love you even if that's gay. Call me.

SUMMER

STEFANIE

She stops by Ruth's first, Friday after work, Davis on the porch, reading a book, eraser in hand. "Mrs. F.," he says.

"Hot," she says because it is, and has been for weeks. Julys were mild their early years here, but these are Chicago Julys now, minus the humidity. Davis has a white line of sunscreen below his right eye. He needs to rub it in.

Ruth is in the kitchen, and she wipes her hands on her apron. "Stefanie," she says. "Good to see you." Stefanie has expended not a small amount of energy trying to figure Ruth out. She learned Ruth has a son and a daughter, both in their twenties, one up in Portland, one down in San Jose. She knew Ruth's husband had a heart attack and died at work, making bicycle wheels of all things, and Ruth was faced for the first time in decades with an empty house. "I was lonely," she told Stefanie. "I missed my kids. I wanted to help."

Nathan is up in his room, in the top bunk, the room dark. Stefanie had asked for him to not be in the top bunk. It could be easy for him to get disoriented up there. He was a big guy, the bed close to the ceiling. In the beginning, Ruth asked that Stefanie stop coming every day. She said it would make the transition easier.

"For whom?" Stefanie had said.

They set up a schedule, Stefanie Tuesday and Friday after work, every other Sunday in the daytime. Sometimes Derek came with her. Mostly he came by himself on other days.

"Nay," she says as she turns on the lights, opens the shades. He flops his head over the side of the bunk. "Were you sleeping, buddy? What are you doing sleeping in the middle of the day?"

"Nacho," he says.

She reaches up to kiss his upside-down face and shag his hair. He needs a cut, getting mangy. There's a bit of lint stuck in his afro.

"What you collecting in your hair?" she says, holding the lint up to him, trying to make him smile. "Come down," she says, when it seems he may not. "Come see me."

He's clumsy down the ladder, landing on the linoleum with a thud, saying "dahnahdahnahdahnah," which is new since Ruth's, there's the *dahnah*s now and also Derek gets *bipbip*s.

"You going to hug your mama?" Stefanie says, and of course he's not going to hug her, but he's close by her side, smelling like himself, musk and sweat and sweetness. "I brought you something," she says into his ear, and they move to the desk area together, and this is how it is now. Maybe they sit together downstairs, or she takes him on a Sunday to the waterfront for a picnic or she pulls out a pad of construction paper from her bag like she does today, and they sit side by side looking at the colors. Everything between them is discrete and circumscribed, even the unexpected bits, like his happiness with the brown page today instead of his usual yellow, the "dahnahdahnah," and his finger poking at the page. Even when she hands him the markers, and he scribbles with the red, even then, they are visitors, they are visiting, and maybe visitor is not the opposite of family, but Stefanie suspects maybe it is.

She goes to Hidaya's next, where Hidaya greets her at the door with a "Dear!" and a kiss on one cheek, then the other, as warm as ever. Stefanie has tried very hard not to hate Hidaya, and she thinks what mostly saves them is that Hidaya knows that she does. Hate her a little. Stefanie asks how the boys are; good, Hidaya tells her, they love their video games, but they've started getting up early and going for runs. "Runs?" Stefanie says.

Stefanie and Derek have a schedule here too, Hidaya and Abdi kind enough to open their home for dinner every Friday, so they can visit with everyone, but mostly Baz. Derek comes by himself other evenings, but they don't talk about it. She lets him slip out after dinner and return an hour or two later without comment. She understands this as a way she can be generous.

Baz moved out four days after the funeral, a funeral Stefanie didn't attend, tending to Nathan the easy excuse. Stefanie had whispered Baz fierce and earnest apologies every day, multiple times a day. She had even written Susan a letter for Derek to deliver. *I am so <u>sorry</u> for your loss. I was wrong-headed, Susan. I couldn't see the ways she was good to my son.*

They found out he was leaving when he already packed, no argument, he simply said what he was about to do. This time, at least, Derek shared her surprise. With Baz's duffel bag at his side, she tried again, tried desperately, but Baz said, "No, Ma. Don't," his tone almost gentle.

And all the frantic pleading, all the confused then angry phone calls to Hidaya, all the meetings where both households sat in the Al-Amir's living room and tried to get Baz to come home, all for naught.

Ed and Bryna came for his graduation. They all watched Baz walk across that stage, and they took him to dinner after. It was a good dinner, everyone eating special occasion food: salmon bisque, steak tartare, salad with curly strands of root vegetables. Derek let Baz drink his beer. Ed had a drawing pad out with Nathan, Baz with his bright purple cap on through the meal, all those bobby pins Hidaya must have helped him with, the waitress calling him "Penn" after hearing their toasts, first time Stefanie heard Baz laugh in months maybe, the waitress bringing him a chocolate torte for a surprise dessert with a candle and everything, and then end of the night, Baz drove himself to Shekib's, and Derek drove Nathan to Ruth's, and somehow Stefanie had tricked herself into thinking the night had changed everything back.

Bryna sat up with her while Derek and Ed slept, Stefanie's head in her lap, Stefanie listing her fuckups, fuckup after fuckup, Bryna stroking her hair, humming spirituals Stefanie wasn't brought up with, tunes she didn't know. Bryna whispered things about God's wisdom and his plan and Jesus, and the path Stefanie was on and the path her boys were on, and this wasn't normally how Bryna talked to Stefanie, and it wasn't what Stefanie would normally go for. But that night, she wanted Bryna to keep telling her, realizing this was why people went to confession, a ritual that had always struck her as self-hating because she'd only ever thought of the abasement. She hadn't realized this part, when someone handed you your life back, still full of all its ugliness, but now with a witness to it, and not too much for them to bear, so not too much for you.

The boys trundle upstairs and into the dining room together, pawing at each other's necks. Baz is tanned dark, especially on his face and arms. Stefanie tries not to ask Hidaya too much about how he spends his days; it is kindness enough, she recognizes, taking him in. "Yah, yah, yah, *Ivy League*, hey, buddy," Derek says, loud beside Stefanie, his arms wide, and Baz comes and gives him a big hug. Derek pats him hard on the back. "Looking good, son. Looking real, real good. Good to see you, buddy. Good to see a smile on that face."

"Ma," Baz says and hugs her too. This is new. Two weeks in a row with a hug. She tries to make her arms grateful, only grateful. It was a terrible relief to read in the paper all the other factors: the bullying, the guidance counselor's inappropriate relationship to the girl's mother. She wanted to talk to Baz about all the other factors, but at least had the sense to refrain. "Baby," she whispers into his ear, and he ends the hug first.

"You're running," she says. "Hidaya tells me you're running." He shrugs, looking a little embarrassed, skimming his cheek across the tip of his shoulder bone.

Abdi has made whole wheat pizzas, topped with pesto, broccoli bits, kale, kalamata olives. They are underbaked in the center and Abdi apologizes about this too much. Stefanie brought salad in a bag; Derek brought white wine. Baz is next to Shekib, across from Derek and Stefanie, with Hidaya and Abdi at opposite ends. They've sat like this from the very first Friday. Stefanie has watched in recent weeks, the way Baz and Shekib mumble their jokes back and forth, laughing into their fists, shouldering each other playfully, and she is so grateful Baz has emerged from the worst of days, when he sat across from them, slack-faced, barely lifting his fork. She watches them now and tries not to think of them as how brothers might be.

"So," Derek says. Beside her, he doesn't play his fingers on her lap. He doesn't grab her hand in his. He doesn't make the side jokes, murmuring in her ear, rough chin against her cheek. "How are you feeling these days about your defection, Shocky?"

Shekib is attending the competing state school. "Pretty good, Mr. Fenning. Got matched with my roommate this week. He's from Santa Cruz. A surfer. He seems really cool."

"Cool," Abdi says, holding up his fingers in air quotes. "Hopefully a good influence."

Shekib rolls his eyes.

"Saw Nathan," Baz says.

"You did?" Stefanie says, wishing her voice different.

"It's weird there," he says.

Derek and Stefanie talk at once, Stefanie saying well, sure, of course it is, Derek saying give it time, we all need to grow into it.

"How did he seem?" Stefanie says, again wishing her voice different, less.

Baz shrugs. "Seems like Nathan," and then: "What happened to Mat?"

"What do you mean, what happened to Mat?" she asks.

"He didn't have him with him. He wouldn't tell me. He was like *dunno dunno dunno.*"

"Dahnah," Stefanie says, scanning to think if Nathan had Mat earlier. "I was just there." Had Derek seen Mat last time he went? He isn't sure. When's the last time anyone saw Mat? Nobody can remember.

"Do you want to call Ruth?" Hidaya says into the quiet, and Derek tells her no, no.

"We're good," he tells her. "We're okay," and then when the silence has stretched thin: "You both have to list top five must-haves for your dorm rooms." He's pointing back and forth between the boys. "Take turns. You do one, then you do one, then…"

Shekib says, "Xbox."

Abdi makes a disapproving sound. Hidaya claps softly. "This is non-binding," she says. "You realize that?"

Shekib rolls his eyes again.

Derek points his fingers to Baz.

"Xbox," he says.

"No, no, no," Derek says. "No repeats, young Padawan. As unique as fingerprints, dorm rooms are."

Some of Stefanie's earliest memories of Derek, both of them still headlong and strung-out with love, were the visits home to her mama, the way he filled the silences between them, the gift he had for turning every one of her mama's barbs into a game. "You getting thick in all the wrong places," her mama might say, and Derek would place a hand chastely on Stefanie's shoulder, and say, "Ma'am, I'd like to offer my services. Those are a real nice pair of glasses, so handsome on your face, but I'm afraid the lenses might not be working proper. All due respect, I'd like to clean them if I may." It had seemed so brave then, so agile and savvy, his ability to engage even the least forgiving of people, to turn a room smoothly on its head.

"Oh my god, Dad," Baz says, but he is smiling.

WOODY

Alison drops Francie every Saturday, she and Marsha with a front-vestibule greeting ritual that has only grown more intense and intimate as Alison's belly has grown, three steadily escalating months of womanly whispers, clasped hands, confessions of the sort Woody can scarcely imagine as Francie—thank god for Francie—darts out from behind her mother's widening hips and yells simply, "Daddy!" There will come a Saturday, Woody knows, when Francie's "Daddy!" will change in pitch and tone, when novelty will turn to confusion to resentment to godknowswhat, which makes the current "Daddy!" unbearably precious and nourishing. Some weeks, he feeds off that single, glorious "Daddy!" for a full three and a half days, four.

"Francie," Woody calls, crouched low for her, catching her in his arms and lifting her. She's getting heavier, the final remnants of her toddler belly gone, long-limbed now. It is easier to notice these things when the interval is weekly. "Al," Woody says, trying to wrest Francie onto one hip the way Alison is always able to.

"Woody," Alison says, and Marsha has one hand on Alison's wrist, her lips pursed at Woody. He wants to remind Marsha that Dan Sheridan left the perfectly pleasant Gail Lindley after Marsha was their real estate agent. Did Marsha not remember the mid-century modern she'd helped Dan and Gail purchase, only for Dan to repack the unpacked boxes post-haste?

Instead, he says, "God, you're getting…" and if his arms weren't straining under the strange weight of his daughter, he would pantomime a curve over his own belly. "You look really good," he says.

"I have gas all the time," Al says. "And I'm constipated. With heartburn."

It was getting better, week by week, her willingness to speak to him in sentences. "Well, you don't look it," he says. "Really, you look beautiful."

Marsha makes a noise. He's groveling, but it's also true. Alison kisses Marsha on the cheek and leaves. She never has a comment or query for Woody. She never asks what he is doing for work or how he's faring in the Sheridan's guest room. Woody marvels at her restraint, though the possibility that she doesn't give a shit has also occurred to him.

"I have to set you down," Woody says to Francie. "You're a big girl! Such a big girl now!" Marsha comes and pinches Francie's cheek, calls her *my little booboo*, and the biggest downside to sleeping in the Sheridan's guest room is the liberties it affords Marsha vis-à-vis Francie. Dan and Marsha never had kids, and Marsha fancies herself something of a doting auntie.

"We have ice cream! Chocolate chip!" she says, and is this not Woody's time with his daughter? Marsha knows he has no leg to stand on, Marsha the sort to kick a legless man when he's down.

Woody stands at the kitchen counter while Francie eats her chocolate-chip ice cream, Dan appearing briefly from the garage, where he works ceaselessly on his hybrid-electric motorcycle. He waves a greasy hand to everyone, kissing Francie quickly on the top of her head, "Frannie Bananie," before grabbing a wad of paper towels and disappearing again. Nothing like living with a friend to realize how truly stupefying his life.

"TV?" Woody says to Francie when she is finished, because he always has to up the ante to wrest her from Marsha. Every week, he promises himself they will do something other than lie in the guest bed together and watch three hours of cartoons on the huge plasma-screen TV that hangs off a huge arm bolted to the guest room wall. The huge arm makes it so that you can position the television to suit your exact manner of slothfulness in the bed below. Woody spent his early days at the Sheridans examining all the hardware it had taken to bolt that motherfucker to the wall, halfway convinced it would come crashing down and maim him in his sleep, a thought as terrifying as it was soothing.

"TV!" Francie yells, and Marsha gets in a flurry of final volleys, because to her credit, her reach does not extend past the guest room door: "Clear your plate, pumpkin! And wash your sticky hands! Did you like that ice cream? Come and give me a kiss."

Goddamn, he loves these singing guppy children. Or whatever they are. They're hypnotic in their swimming and singing and talking and figuring out whatever needs figured out (without fail, they figure their shit out!) and it may be the closest he's ever felt to Francie, the most in sync. She is in the thrall of the singing guppy children, a shimmery sheen of ice cream dried on her chin. The commercials are shrill monstrosities, though each one does uniquely position him as the hero. "Daddy, will you get me an Egg-Hatch-Me?" "Daddy, can I have a Linkbot Racetrack with SideWinders?" "Daddy, I need those Slipper Pillows!"

Yes, Francie, yes. Of course. I know you do.

"Honey stick?" Francie asks as the singing guppy children give way to the rescue puppies, which makes Woody briefly mournful until he remembers the rescue puppies deliver nearly the same respite.

"You already had ice cream," he says, though they both know this is play acting. Of course Francie can have a honey stick. Honey sticks are foundational to Woody's new life, post-family, post-guidance counselor, post-Livvy, post-you-know-who he-knows-who Alison-knows-who all-of-the-greater-metro-area-readership-knows-who. He works in the local honeybee warehouse now. It's good, honest work: honey, honeycombs, honey and honeycomb variants, bee-keeping supplies. He stocks the shelves, fills orders, tracks inventory, all well and away from the public. He has a coworker named Leaf and another named Petra, and they are all allowed to wear headphones while they work. It is surprisingly satisfying, stocking the honey bears and honey jars and honey pails by size, packing the hive kits and the bee pollen for shipping, counting the propolis and hive mixtures and bee suits and frame parts on the inventory sheets. He has many things to do at the start of each day, and one by one, he checks them off. On the very good days, traveling through the aisles of honey-based soaps and honey oils and honey candies, none of which he'd ever considered before, something can fill him with a queer hope about the bigness of the world and its mysteries, and, on the very best of days, an even queerer hope that life can begin anew from hardly anything.

He takes out a handful of honey sticks from his nightstand drawer. Francie picks the dark purple one, blackberry. He listens to her suckling and watches the not-nearly-as-beguiling but-beguiling-enough rescue pups. He tries to stay out of Dan and Marsha's way. He mostly eats in here, back out to the kitchen to wash a day's dishes after they're to bed. He does what errands he has to—grocery shopping, pharmacy—but tries to keep himself mostly to warehouse and guest room. There are a lot of people to run into, a whole generation of students and their parents, all of his coworkers. He'd ended the arbitration meetings with his union rep, Doug Epstein across the table, after the first one; he was never going to go back. They didn't have to fight about it. He could, at least, make this part easy.

There was a night, not too long ago, that Marsha found him in the kitchen. He was eating frozen corn niblets from the bag in the open door of the freezer.

"Sorry," he said. He'd thought he was the only one awake. He liked the pleasure pain on his molars from biting into the frozen niblets. He tried normally only to eat his own food, but he couldn't sleep.

"You're fine," Marsha said, unconvincingly. "I heard you down here."

He apologized again and made to put the niblets away when Marsha asked how he was doing. It was a strange question from Marsha. "Fine," he said. "Thanks for…everything."

"It's a lot," Marsha said, and he wasn't sure what she was referring to. "You have a lot on your plate." She was in red flannel pajamas, holding a white robe closed against her chest.

"I think I'm going to—" He nodded to his bedroom.

"I wanted to—" Marsha said, and she got a look on her face then, a smile he'd seen before, knowing and conspiratorial. It was the look she got when she leaned over this very island and regaled Dan with whatever gossip she'd acquired that day at work (accounts receivable for an internet something), how Justine's son was in rehab for a *third* time, how Donald Fincher knew someone at the city who showed up for work in a dress, saying his name was Roberta now.

"So," she said now, leaning toward Woody in a way that made him worry she was going to touch him, "you know my coworker Lynda's daughter graduated top of her law class at Georgetown and came back home."

Woody did not know this. He couldn't imagine any possible way he could know this.

Marsha rushed the words out: "So she works at Lerner Gable, and Susan Albrecht moved up to Alaska." And then, more slowly: "Did you know that?"

Woody tried to betray nothing. Last time he'd tried Susan's door, nearly a month before, he'd been thrilled at the clunk of the deadbolt, the shushing of door against carpet—he'd forgotten the possibility!—only to be greeted by a bleary man and his red-veined nose.

"Her daughter came and got her," Marsha said, and now she did move to grab Woody's hand. It was, in spite of everything, nice for someone to hold his cold hand. "That poor woman," Marsha whispered.

"Can I have another honey stick?" Francie asks.

"Do you think we should do something?" Woody says.

"We *are* doing something!" Francie says, snuggled up beside him, warm and close. It is impossible for him to move. "Can I have another honey stick?"

Of course you can have another honey stick.

Alison does not come out of the car for pickup. Woody stands in the doorway, waving, while Marsha walks Francie to the curb, leaning into the backseat and clipping her into her car seat. Francie waves through her passenger window. Al turns to the backseat and says something to Francie. Francie laughs. Al rolls down her window to say something to Marsha. *Pinken* it sounds like. *Tuesday.* Woody keeps waving, even though Al won't look past Marsha. She won't wave back. He thinks of it as atonement, the start of some atonement, letting her ignore him while he waves from the doorway, and she drives away.

There is a knock on the guest room door. It's not too late, a little past eight, but the knock is still surprising. No one knocks on his door.

"Hey," Dan says when Woody opens it. Woody goes to turn off the TV, but Dan says, "No, no, you're fine." From the look on Dan's face, Woody knows. The two of them have said maybe a hundred words to each other in the past three months, though not out of hostility. Dan, it turns out, didn't have a lot to say beyond "Sorry, buddy," and "You need anything from Costco?"

"Okay," Woody says in the beat before Dan tells him: "Marsha's ready, man. You can have a few weeks to find a place. But you know."

He did know.

"Thanks, man," Woody says. "Thanks for everything," and Dan comes over to hug him, which surprises Woody, and Woody leans into it, surprised too by his force of feeling—sick with all the goodbyes, this finally one goodbye too far. He is a good friend, Dan, the way he knows to hang on, and then to let go, head down, nodding at the carpet, pretending not to notice, murmuring a slur of nothingness ("Okay, man, good, good") as he shuts the door.

LARK

They go to places they've never been. It's easier than familiar places like Shocky's basement or the whole neighborhood by the school or by Livvy's apartment. Baz drives and Lark sits in the passenger seat, and it helps to be up front—change in perspective from the backseat. She likes how Baz is quiet a lot of the time. She's quiet a lot of the time too. She likes how he doesn't ask her things. Everyone is always asking her things now, which is probably her least favorite quality in other people. He doesn't say where they're going, and she doesn't ask. She looks out the window and blurs her eyes a little, so the trees become ribbons of green.

Today, they end up at a fish hatchery outside of town.

"How do you know this place?" Lark asks as they walk along woven metal planking beside rows of dark rectangular pools. She remembers those earliest days with Baz, when he knew everything and was nice about it. His parents liked to bring them here. His brother liked the fish.

"Is he okay?" Lark says. She's never talked with Baz about his brother since that day in the kitchen. She has wanted to ask a bunch of times. She has.

Baz shrugs. He doesn't have sunglasses on, and he squints into the sun when he looks at her. "I guess," he says. The lawsuit was settled. He'd told her a while back that they'd paid the girl. Eight grand. Lark hadn't known what to say.

It's hard to make out the fish in the pools, the sun bright off the surface. Lark eventually realizes they're moving in huge schools. She'd been looking for individual fish. Once she knows what to look for, she begins to catch glimpses of movements and then makes out the textured masses of them.

They walk past the pools to bird enclosures. Lark is surprised by bird enclosures at a fish hatchery. There's an owl in one. A vulture in another. A something in a third. Falcon? The maybe falcon stares at her for a second with its round brown eyes. *Livvy?* she wonders. She wonders this a lot: feral cats in her path, a baby in its mother's papoose in the line in front of her at Safeway. One time, a piece of Otter Pop wrapper caught on the grating of her front porch. *Livvy?* It is completely stupid and not stupid at all, and it makes her feel better. She does what makes her feel better now; it is an okay way to live—take drives with Baz, look everywhere for Livvy, take dinner to her mom if her mom can't get out of bed, otherwise be sure to eat together at the kitchen table. She took her mom blueberry pancakes last week, butter melted on top, and her mom had laughed: "Pancakes for dinner." There are nights she sleeps in her mom's bed. There are days she falls asleep on the couch. She's started watching the gameshow with the pyramid and the soap opera with the hospital, and a little TV in the daytime makes her feel better but too much does not. She tries to remember this.

"Check this out," Baz says, and she follows him into the building across the parking lot and past the cinderblock restrooms. Inside, he waves his hand at a wall-sized display case. "You believe this?" he says, and he's grinning. It's a huge taxidermy scene of a jumble of animals in the wilderness. There's a cougar mid-pounce and a lone coyote and a slithering snake and two wild turkeys. More maybe falcons perch on fake tree limbs. A bunch of little birds too. Lark doesn't know any of their names. Baz never makes her feel stupid for everything she doesn't know. She is looking at the stuffed little field mice when he says, "Monique came over. To Shocky's." He is right beside her, but she does not turn to look. "She's cool, you know? She's cool."

Lark wonders how the taxidermy person could get the mice's tiny little claws right, no bigger than toothpicks.

"Real broken up," Baz says. Lark has wondered if Baz knew, and then wondered how she would feel if he did. How she feels is mixed: she doesn't want to talk about it, and she doesn't want him to keep talking about it either. But it's good for someone else to be holding it too, a relief. "She pretends like she's tough," Baz says. "But really she's a big mushball."

When she looks into the Plexiglas, she can see Baz's face right there next to hers. In real life, the snake would eat the mouse, the maybe falcon would eat the snake, and the cougar would eat them all. It doesn't make Lark feel better to think this. She puts her hand against the cool Plexiglas, her fingers spread, even with the *Do Not Touch* placard at their feet. Baz puts his hand up too, close to hers but not too close. She looks at their hands there, side by side. She thinks, *I loved him first*, but it's not true, and she knows it. She's recently started a habit of thinking things just to see if they will make her cry. Crying makes her feel better, except when it doesn't.

"It's nice they're not eating each other," she says.

Baz laughs a little next to her. "Sure is."

STEFANIE

The three of them sit out front, Davis reading, Stefanie pretending to, Nathan swinging on the porch swing between their plastic chairs. He likes to be by himself on the porch swing, which is hung low for his big body, his feet dragging on the porch. The top hinge of the swing squeaks every time Nathan pitches forward then back, but it never seems to bother him, earphones always in. Sometimes Davis and Stefanie wince at each other in time to the swing's noise.

"What are you reading?" Stefanie started asking a while back. He liked high fantasy, he told her, and she asked enough questions that he wheeled inside one time and came back out with a book in his lap.

"A classic," he said, Stefanie used to his strange face by now, more touched by the gesture than she probably should have been. The names alone—Kellanved? Genabackis?—put her off immediately, though every Friday, the book was waiting for her on the chair to the far side of the porch swing.

Mat, it turns out, was in the back of Nathan's underwear drawer. "Mat!" Stefanie called, holding up the bear and shaking it like prey. She'd been looking for days. Nathan *nacho*'d her from his top bunk, Stefanie pressing the bear against him. Next visit, Mat was put away in the shirt drawer, stuffed beside the wrinkled shirts, everything smashed in like fists.

Friday afternoons, the sun is high enough that the house shadows the porch and cuts a little into the late summer heat. She finds it almost soothing to open the book and skim her eyes over the words at the end of her week. Baz is gone for Philadelphia, already at the end of his orientation and into dorms and classes. He calls Derek's cell in the daytime when Stefanie's working. "He's good," Derek reports at dinner. "Meeting lots of other kids. Classes are hard." The blankness of the description cuts as deep as all the rest of it.

She wonders often what shape penance, the depth of it, the width, the full span. To sin on behalf of one's child, she believes now, is a different kind of sinning. Her sins come with an asterisk.

After they took Baz to the airport (*It will be a relief,* Hidaya had counseled. *You have so much built up on these goodbyes. After will be better*) she called Century Center front office. She said, "My mama isn't answering her phone. I need you to get her on the phone so I can hear how she's doing." The woman tried to make all kinds of excuses—Stefanie could pay extra to have a landline in her mother's room. It's the family's responsibility to make sure their loved one's cellphone remain charged. The cordless phone in the front office was not going to reach back to resident rooms. Stefanie said: "I am prepared to stay on this call until you get my mama on the phone." Stefanie thought, *This is what forgiveness looks like,* but it didn't feel anything like forgiveness. It felt like bad customer service.

"Danadana," Nathan says now of the passing bus. Ruth's house sits on the city bus route, and Nathan likes to watch it pass, this one of his many new habits (others: eating corn nuts loudly, building endless blue mounds from kinetic sand.) He can—and does—spend hours on the porch swing, watching the road, listening to music, the noise out his headphones no longer the bleat of Kenny G, instead watery strains of piano and strings. "He really took a liking to it," Ruth explained of the Enya she'd played once during dinner. Stefanie made a noise with her lips at this news, expecting Ruth to laugh. She hasn't figured out yet what makes Ruth laugh.

After isn't better, Stefanie wants to tell Hidaya, and maybe she will once she's square with Hidaya again, less bruised. After feels a lot like before so far, except irrevocable.

She texts Derek from the porch: **Whatchu feel like for dinner?**

She's usually the one who texts first now. The one who makes Friday dinner.

Salmon? Derek texts back. He still texts back quick, a fact for which she is grateful.

She calls her mother every day, though it is not yet habit. She has to remind herself. Staff helps Mama with the cell phone. Her mother does not know who Stefanie is. There are many days she does not speak at all. The staff is trained in getting back on the line so Stefanie can ask about her toileting and the bedsores and how much Mama is eating. She said to Derek one night in their house of empty rooms: "What if we moved her out here?" and he said, "That's a truly terrible idea," and she loved him so much for this.

She will pick up the salmon and watch the man behind the fish counter wrap the pink flanks in paper. She will watch him slip the wrapped fish in a plastic bag, almost tenderly. She will take it—also tenderly—home like an offering, calling out Derek's name when she comes through the door, they the only ones to make the noise of their house now, a fact hard to get used to. But not the hardest. She's done harder things. She has harder things still left to do. "I don't know," Derek said the next night, "maybe," and she surprised herself by loving him for this too.

"Hot," Davis says now, turning the page with his fat eraser.

"Sure is," Stefanie says, and to Nathan: "Turn that down. Gonna blow out your ears with Celtic nonsense."

If he hears her, he pays no mind, watching only the road. Does he know it'll be a half hour before the next bus? Is he hopeful with each passing car? His face betrays nothing, faint droplets on his upper lip from the heat. *Nay*, she wants to say to get him to look. *Nay*. She does not say it. She knows to leave him be.

WOODY

His roommates are friends of Petra's, Petra from the honey warehouse. They are nice, and one plays mandolin. They have a woodstove in the living room, and Max plays mandolin in front of it, and it's a lovely sight. The other, Doug, another Doug ("I once knew a Doug…") always makes extra stir-fry and leaves it in a glass bowl with a plate upside down on top of it in the fridge, a napkin with Woody's name on it. There's a question mark after the Woody every time—*Woody?*—even though the answer is always *yes, thank you, yes.*

Turns out, it's good to have roommates. He didn't want them, but he doesn't make much money and has a whole other household to support. Max and Doug are good reminders that not everyone knows him. He is not as infamous as he'd once feared. Woody Hanover is not a public figure, much to Woody Hanover's relief. He is a man who works at a honey factory with a soon-to-be ex-wife; a daughter who comes on Saturdays and now Tuesdays too; a baby boy on the way (a baby boy!)

It was a hard transition for Francie from the plasma screen to his dumpy bedroom here, no TV at all, not even anything on the walls, though the napkin portrait is tucked away in the back of the nightstand drawer. He likes to think he'll grow into a man who will forget about the napkin portrait and move without it to his next home, whenever that will be, only to remember it years later and wistfully.

"Your house is bor-ing," Francie complains, and it is, so they spend time outside, even though fall threatens rain any day now. She wants to be pushed in a stroller again, even though she's too big for it, and the family therapist they see now (orchestrated by Alison with her usual aplomb, the rotating schedule of he going, she going, sometimes Francie going with Al, sometimes with Woody, sometimes by herself, and never, ever Alison and Woody together) says it's normal, regressions during divorce, they shouldn't force Francie out of them or shame her, they should "go with it."

Turns out, Woody quite likes the regressions. It's like getting to have a do-over. And when he has to buy a stroller from the Goodwill, he springs for a fancier one than the first time, dual cupholders, a sunroof flap at the top, four compartments below for who-knows-what, and he pushes her down leafy sidewalks, reminding her not to drag her feet, she's so tall now. He passes people he thinks he may know, familiar faces, maybe a former student, maybe a long-ago parent, but he looks away quickly, and no one ever stops to talk. There is even one Sunday when he is pushing her along the waterfront past the playground with a few stubborn holdouts, a child on the molded swings, another down the slide, the parking lot where he and Susan sat in that rainy car with her pink eye and his desperation, hers too, and he hates himself plenty, he surely does, no way around that, he figures that will be lifelong, but he does manage to find some not pleasure, but pleasure's painful cousin in remembering, and he thinks about what if he'd listened to Susan Hoffman in that long-ago closet, the course of their lives then. But of course, it is foolishness, because the course of their lives brought him Francie and soon a baby boy (a baby boy!), and brought Susan Lea and, of course, Livvy, and he hopes that the loss of Livvy hasn't killed Susan, has to think that she is out there looking for her whimbrels. If there was one thing he could tell her, it wouldn't be that he still loves her (he does), it would be that he knows the loss of Livvy is not his. He thought so at the start but knows better now. He does not share it with her inside himself. It is not, he knows, his to share.

"Daddy!" Francie calls. "Let's do the playground!"

He is about to say yes. He always says yes to Francie. The therapist has told him he must work on this. But he sees Lark Stevenson on the grassy hillside past the swings, and while he can handle a vague face or two these days, he is not ready for a Lark Stevenson, there with another girl, what was her name, he can't believe he is already forgetting the names of students on his roll—is that a good sign or bad?—the Black girl from the track team, the one who walked past his car as he sat outside the funeral.

"No," he tells Francie. "Not today."

LARK

The grass is cold beneath them. The bed of leaves. Cold enough to feel wet but each time Lark feels her butt, it's dry.

"What you doing, feeling yourself up?" Mo says. She says it in her joke voice. She does the joke voice a lot now. Lark knows Mo's being careful. Neither of them is themselves again yet. They are halfway themselves maybe.

They are on their backs looking into the tree above them, half its leaves gone, half still there and yellowing. "Isn't it weird to think this all used to be an oak savanna?" Mo says.

Lark didn't even know this was an oak tree. She is okay not knowing the names of things.

"Okay," Mo says. "Lie under where you think the next leaf is going to fall. See if you can get a leaf to fall on you." Mo is still on her back, knees up, scooching herself with her feet.

"You're so weird," Lark says.

"*You're* so weird," Mo says.

They are both smiling. Sometimes she feels a lot younger when she's with Mo, like they are kids together, little kids. Sometimes she feels the exact opposite. She hopes she will always feel this way with Mo. She cannot imagine there being anyone after Mo, even though Mo is already after someone she couldn't imagine there being anyone after. Her mind does not think of it that way, though. Her mind thinks about it all jumbled up. A leaf flitters down the tree between them, and Lark thinks *Livvy?* She scooches in the grass like Mo scooched, but she's not playing Mo's game. She doesn't care if a leaf falls on her. She just wants to be closer.

ACKNOWLEDGEMENTS

Thank you to Jason Bates, Claudia Center, Sam Crane, Clarissa Kripke, Rachel Kripke-Ludwig, Alexis Reed, and Cheryl Theis for sharing your insights, experiences, and expertise to help me get this story right. Thank you to the Turner family for serving as inspiration for the Fenning brothers; your story is not their story, but you planted the seed. Thank you to Jaynie Royal and Regal House for your belief in this book.

I began some of the earliest pages of *Closer* in a writing circle hosted by Lara Bovilsky and CoDaC at the University of Oregon and finished draft after draft in residencies at Playa, Kimmel Harding Nelson, Hypatia-in-the-Woods, and Wildacres. Generous readers offered essential feedback and encouragement, including David Bradley, Marty Brown, Ingrid Cabrera, Susanna Daniel, and the late, great Cai Emmons. This book would not exist without Debra Gwartney, who read it in its earliest draft and championed it for years after.

I can only write—often in far-flung and remote places—when steeped in home. You are my home, Jordan and Eli; Rebecca and Tim; Nora and Eliza; Cole and Lizzie Lou. Sometimes I forget I am the luckiest. I'm writing it here to remember.